I0661010

Maurice Fluegel

The Zend-Avesta and Eastern Religions

comparative legislations, doctrines, and rites of Parseeism, Brahmanism, and

Buddhism - bearing upon Bible, Talmud, Gospel, Koran, their Messiah-ideals and

social problems

Maurice Fluegel

The Zend-Avesta and Eastern Religions
*comparative legislations, doctrines, and rites of Parseeism, Brahmanism, and Buddhism -
bearing upon Bible, Talmud, Gospel, Koran, their Messiah-ideals and social problems*

ISBN/EAN: 9783337247072

Printed in Europe, USA, Canada, Australia, Japan

Cover: Foto ©Andreas Hilbeck / pixelio.de

More available books at **www.hansebooks.com**

THE ZEND-AVESTA
AND
EASTERN RELIGIONS

Comparative Legislations, Doctrines and Rites
of Parseeism, Brahmanism and Buddhism ;
bearing upon Bible, Talmud, Gospel,
Koran, their Messiah=Ideals
and Social Problems.

BY ·MAURICE FLUEGEL,

BALTIMORE,

Author of "Religious Rites and Views ;" "Spirit of Biblical Legislation;" "Messiah-Ideal, Jesus' Ethics ;" "Paul and New
Testament ;" "Mohammed and Koran," etc.

H. FLUEGEL & CO., PUBLISHERS,
BALTIMORE, U. S. A.

1898.

CONTENTS.

PART I

THE ZEND-AVESTA.

INTRODUCTION.

Having treated in the preceding volumes of this series of the doctrines and legislations of the three great Western religions, Judaism, Christianity and Islam, we have now arrived at the discussion of the Eastern Religions, those of Iran, India, Ceylon, China, Japan, etc. These are Parseeism, Brahmanism and Buddhism. We shall treat here especially of Parseeism. The important doctrines, the social scheme and legislation of Eran or Iran, the bible of Zoroaster, the *Zend-Avesta* is the leading theme of this volume. Brahmanism and Buddhism, the religions of the Hindoos, Chinese, Birmans, etc., will be discussed as important corollaries. The bearing and influence of these Eastern systems upon the Western ones is the object of this study. To find out their relation towards one another, what affinities and what discrepancies, what analogies and what contrasts, what gain or loss, advance or retrogression, these two leading religious sets exhibit towards each other, to find out the different phases of each of these groups and of every member of the group, how they represent but one continued chain of development, one ethical and social growth of the " Tree of life and of knowledge," termed religion, connecting all the races, creeds and systems into one unit of civilization and humanization—that is the final scope of this volume ; devoted principally to the study of the Zend-Avesta with its relation to and bearing upon the Western biblical religions.

- *Parseeism.* In far-away Hindustan, in the capital of British India, the magnificent and powerful commercial emporium of Bombay and its vicinity, there live among the native Hindoo and Mohammedan populations, the remnants of an ancient people, apparently of a bodily and mental type different from its neighbors. Though colonized there for many centuries, they nevertheless are not absorbed by, nor even amalgamated with the genuine natives, by whom they are outnumbered as ten thousand to one. They pertinaciously cling to their own creed, nationality and ancient tongue ; to their own sacred books, laws, manners and customs. They form a distinct race and a sect. Debris of that same nationality, creed and race are, rarely enough, to be found also in old Iran and modern Persia. They are all chips and atoms of an ancient powerful nation, the once world-domineering Persians, the conquerors under their historical *king of kings*, the masters of Asia, Africa and Europe.

In the middle of the seventh century, P. C., that once mighty people was subjugated and absorbed by the Islamic Arabians. Small remnants only have escaped the catastrophe and survived in some clefts, nooks and mountain-fastnesses of their own conquered and alienated country. Their comrades, after long disaster, reduced to a small remnant, have wandered away to Hindustan and settled there in and around Bombay, one of the great emporia of the Asiatic world. There they have joined the English masters, have learned their civilization and speech, their crafts and industries, and thus have become by far superior to the native Hindoos, bodily, mentally, and economically.

These highly interesting last debris of an ancient, vanquished race and creed have, besides, many more titles to our interest, our curiosity and our sympathy, viz: *their sacred books.* These have, apparently, nothing in common with the Hindoo popular mythology. They inculcate to abhor idolatry and to believe in the One only God, eternal and incorporeal. Their ethical laws teach justice and virtue, work and charity. Studying these laws we find there so much akin to our own Western religions, our own morality and idealities, that we sometimes rub our eyes and ask whether we have not unearthed there the silent tombs of our own fathers, whether these Parsees have not once been a branch of our own race, creed and civilization, flesh and bone of our own faith and culture! No less kinship do we find with their mysticism and supernaturalism, their superstitions and notions, their hopes and fears, sayings and teachings; as if a fraction of the Western races in by-gone ages had been torn away by some social upheaval, exiled into some other regions, and was now rediscovered and exhumed; we feel as if we see the relics of Roman civilization found in the resurrected cities of Pompeii and Herculaneum.

Now these remnants of an old race, with their fractions of a literature, their creed, manners and notions are the last debris of the world-renowned ancient Medo-Persian people, now called Parsees; and their remains of doctrines. laws and customs form the book, *Zend-Avesta.* Both, people and laws, have much that is strikingly akin to our Western races and Western biblical laws. That code, civilization, creed and people are the themes of our consideration in this present volume. Indeed, studying that theme, we shall not be a little surprised to see how much of Parsee doctrines and views we can retrace now among those of Christian, Jew and Moslem, for good and for bad. We shall discover there a deal of our own beliefs, hopes and aspirations ; of our own notions, cravings, fears and superstitions. We shall meet there, in rudiment, our metaphysics, our dogmas, our mysticism, our angels and demons, heaven and hell ; much of our dietary laws, much of our marriage, birth, death and funeral ceremonies. We shall find them there in their first stages, rudimentary, and shall recognize with surprise that we, in 1898, in Europe and America are but the continuators and successors of those once in Babylon and Persepolis, that we are their spiritual descendants, that they are our historical ancestors and that we are but developing a civilization which they have inaugurated ; that Arian or Semite, Asiatic, European or American, Jew, Christian or Mohammedan, men and women, we are simply flourishing upon the graves of them, our predecessors ; so it is in geology and so in ethics.

There is cause for glory in, not for shame of such a genealogy. To say that our Bible has many contrasts and many parallels with the Zend-Avesta ; that the Talmudic *Pharisees* were influencing and influenced by the Avestean Parsees and identified perhaps by that name ; that the new Testament was cradled by the lullaby of Persian-Essenian enthusiasm and hopefulness ; that the Koran has found there many of its views, its paradise with the black-eyed houris chanting in perfumed groves on elevated brocade *divans*, as also its hell with Eblis and his black fiends—to hint at that, would now not offend any rational being ; since Darwin has accustomed the thoughtful to the possibility that, at a much earlier period, man may have had the simian genus as his progenitor and hence, that the Parisian belle and the London fashionable may have descended even from the wolf and the monkey. It is not origin and descent, but degeneration which is disparaging. To improve upon our original status is our destiny, our glorious birthright. As long as development is improvement, man has done his duty and can glory in its performance.

The Method. In our copious selections and renditions from the Zend-Avesta, particularly the Vendidad, we have carefully collated the great masters of the Zend-science and chosen the best, Especially have we followed Darmesteter, Spiegel and Haug. We

have often given, besides them, the translations of other leading
Orientalists, so as to offer the reader an opportunity to judge for
himself. But we have been independent in the interpretation of the
texts. The prominent and distinctive feature of this volume and its
predecessors is to adduce parallels and analogies at nearly every
opportunity lent by the themes, taken from the other creeds, codes
and doctrines. By this we believe to have substantially assisted the
reader in elucidating the often enigmatical Zend-passages, in helping
to penetrate deeper into their real meaning and scope. This may
constitute perhaps the chief claim to usefulness and merit of this
modest contribution to the literature on the Zend-Avesta. I do not
pretend to rival any of my predecessors in that field of learning. I
simply selected what I deemed the best among the translations already extant. Nor do I claim to have here brought forward anything better in the simple translations of the texts. There I follow
scrupulously my predecessors and masters, after selecting the apparently best among them. But this treatise has one leading feature,
new and useful, which I hope will render it a valuable contribution
to the Zend-science, and this feature is constantly pervading the
volume and giving it its real place and import, viz :

The Parallels. It is its method; it is its salient mode of producing the doctrines, it is not simply a translation of the Zend-ßible;
it is comparative religious and social legislation. The Zend-doctrine
is first produced, and next, many analogies from kindred domains.
The reader has thus the opportunity to study each, by comparing
them all. Adducing constantly numerous and striking parallels
and analogies from other literatures, codes, bibles, sacred and lay
books, mystic and rational, etc., above all by the hundreds of quota-
tions adduced from the Talmud, the Bible and Aggadists, passages
which are so strikingly analogous, yea often identical, that they
evidently point to lasting mutual relations and influences of the two
doctrines,—by such collations and juxtapositions of parallels and
contrasts, I believe to have substantially contributed to the better
understanding of the Avesta doctrine and literature, as also to that
of the Talmud. When these pages suggest that the well-known
Hebrew Credo (V. M. 6.4) was the protest of Mosaism against the
dual principle of Zoroasterism; that its reiterated insistance upon
and emphasis of man's freedom of action and hence, his responsibility, was the protest against the Zend-Avestic Ahriman doctrine ; that
Isaiah (41–46) polemized against such views and their fatal conse-

quences; when I confront the Greek, Assyrian and Egyptian mythologies with the nobler views of the Avesta and the yet higher ones of the Biblical religions, etc., when I bring in parallel the doctrines of Zoroaster, of Abraham, of Sinai, of Brahma, Plato, Karmel, Nazareth, Tarsus and Mecca,—this confrontation will help the thoughtful reader a great deal to find out for himself the real meaning and standpoint of the Zend-teachers. Such collations I believe will, besides, take away all the dryness and ambiguity of the abstruse theme and give it all the freshness and actuality of living and contemporaneous studies and subjects. In thus connecting the past with the present, gray theory with green practice, Persian, Avestean paragraphs and legislations with those of our own codes, our own century, creeds and homes, we feel that we do not simply study dry, abstract matter of by-gone times, but concrete and live ideas, feelings, customs and practices, inaugurated long ago by our predecessors, but alive and potent among us and our contemporary neighbors. In thus combining the past with the present Brahmanic, Parsee and Buddhistic doctrines and legislations with those of Teutons, Latins and Slavs, the study is no longer dry and theoretical, but green and actual, present and close by; and this, my method of parallelism may have contributed to bring about.

Brahmanism and Buddhism. This volume is devoted to Parseeism especially, to the analysis of the Zend-Avesta, its relation to, and its bearing upon, the present living religions. But besides the sacred books of the Magi, we have devoted considerable space and attention to the doctrines of the Brahmans and the Buddhists also, we have given here a comprehensive outline of these two great Eastern denominations. For a full understanding of Zoroaster, that of Brahma and of Buddha is absolutely necessary. The subject of this volume is, therefore, the bearing of the systems of the East upon those of the West. It is a close comparison of the spirit of the religious legislations of the Orient with the spirit of the Biblical legislations of the Occident; and the result of this examination is surprising and cheering to the extreme. As we have seen in the preceding volumes of this series, in the treatises on Bible, Gospel and Koran, so we shall find here too, in Zarathustra, Brahma and Buddha, the spirit of toleration and good-will to all, breathing in their doctrines. They, too, teach, as the quintessence of the law, the golden rule: "Thou shalt love thy God with all thy heart and all thy might;" and as its sequel: "Thou shalt love thy neighbor as thyself."—Apparently the Brahma religion starts from many gods and many castes; Buddha began with skepticism and the doctrine of despair; Parseeism with the admission and enthronement of the principle of evil. Yet all three at last coincide in Monotheism and altruism as the noblest faith and the best social base. All three declare in different words, but to the same point, that doing good to our fellowmen is the only way to self-improvement and universal happiness. We emphasize this as the result of this study, and this volume, viz : Brahmanism, Parseeism and Buddhism, just as Mosaism, Christianity and Islam stand upon the Biblical Monotheism and altruism. They all teach that doing good to our next is the highest homage to God and the nearest road to human salvation. That is their common platform, their messianic ideal, the last object of all sociology, the goal of man's destiny. This result is, no doubt, interesting and cheering, a worthy subject of meditation.

The Growth of Religion. In the course of our studies on the great religious legislations of the world, we have now arrived at that of Zoroaster and Parseeism, the Zend-Avesta. That system stands nearest to the Western religions. It influenced them greatly. Zoroasterism in its turn was influenced by the doctrines of Brahmanism, etc. It is here critically shown by analogy that the several Eastern creeds as the Western ones are, each and everyone, no isolated phenomena. They did not rise suddenly as Minerva from the head of Jupiter. No, there are ever constant developments of ethical thought going on in the different divisions of the human species, each evolved from its predecessor, the outcome higher than the origin. Each succeeding religious phase is a growth from the root of the preceding one and necessarily presupposes it, as the offspring evidences its progenitor. Religion is thus not miraculous and inspired in the popular sense, but in the highest and noblest sense of the term. The divine spirit of human improvement termed religion, works from within, not without. As the steam is constantly propelling the locomative, etc., even so is that divine spirit ever impelling the human mind to nobler creations of religious, ethical and social models. This is religion, working in the mysterious channels of man's ethical intelligence. The impulse is divine, the agent human. It is a wonderful process, yet a rational one.

Having treated of the relation of the three religions of the West towards one another, we now have to consider the tenor of those of the East, the spirit pervading them, their doctrines, the

laws, their ethics and their scheme of human destiny, termed the
"Messianic-Ideal." We have to examine their bearing upon the
Western religious codes and teachings. The reader will find here
a full discussion of the Zoroastrian legislation and a succinct outline
of the doctrines and the tenets of the two other great Eastern denominations. The Parsees are now but a bare remnant of a people;
while the Buddhists number a third part of mankind in their ranks,
and the Brahmans some thirteen hundredths of the entire human
race. Nevertheless we have devoted the largest space of this
volume to Parseeism; because it stands nearest to the Western
races, religions and civilizations. It influenced them more power-
fully and more directly than India, China, Ceylon, etc.

The ancient Iranians and Medo-Persians were actually absorbed
by the Western denominations, hence, must they have influenced
the latter greatly, in their blood, their thoughts, feelings and faith.
Having absorbed such a vast contingent of Iranian blood and
thought, Christianism and Islamism must be strongly colored and
modulated by that amalgamation. This must be admitted *a priori*,
on theoretical grounds; and really we shall verify it practically in
these pages, *a posteriori*. This will be shown in the numerous
analogies of this volume, between the religions of the East and those
of the West. We shall find it out when examining and comparing
the tenor of their respective sacred books, etc.

Encouragement. Our preceding treatises having met with kind
approbation from the Press, leading scholars and earnest readers, we
feel encouraged to come forth with this fifth volume of the series,
requesting the same indulgence in its behalf as for its predecessors.

Let me now tender my sincere and warm thanks to the press
and the scholars, to my readers and my subscribers for their kind,
continued encouragement in my labors, no doubt, necessary to sustain the perseverance of the writer. Especially grateful do I feel
towards the great and revered Oxford Professor, Max Mueller, who,
repeatedly honored me with his cheering letters; Dr. Ad. Neubauer,
of the same University, our friend and reviewer in the London
Quarterly Review, who, correctly presumed and advised my treatment of the Zend-Avesta; and the late, hoary savant, Ernest Curtis,
Rector of the Berlin University, who sent me his kind word with
his dying breath. Blessed be his memory.

Last, not least, I feel happy to mention my dear and honored
friend, Eduard Cohen, Esq., artist, of Frankfurt A. M. and his un-

remitting, unflinching, warm interest in behalf of my publications. He is one of those rare, unselfish men who do good for its own sake, solely for the advancement of knowledge and useful literature. To him and to all my friends, close by and far away, may this volume bring my hearty greetings.

MAURICE FLUEGEL.

Baltimore, January, 1898.

CHAPTER I

Zoroaster and his Doctrines.

PARSÈEISM.

In the preceding volumes, I have treated of the several bibles and their diverse contents, of the ethical, religious and social Legislations of the Old Testament, the New Testament and the Koran. There we were yet comparatively standing on firm, well known ground. Those venerable documents are within comparatively historical times; preserved in languages which are yet fairly accessible to the present scholar. Their aspects and ideas, though not all of our times, are nevertheless not too far removed from our modern feelings and thoughts, We can yet grasp them, we can think and translate them into our own modes; we feel yet to be standing upon solid ground when speaking of them. Now we are about to approach a bible with a system which is far removed from us, far away in space and time, especially so mentally. Nevertheless, since in A. 1700, Hyde of Oxford, published his attempt of a history of Parseeism, the modern mind feels irresistably attracted towards that study. From the moment we became aware of the existence of that hoary phase of ethics, we felt as if we had met with the spirit of our long departed parents, as if we had discovered the genius of the past and the ancestor of the present; as if we had found out the long searched for head of the religious Nile, the source of our own civilization. We feel charmed, surprised and delighted, as when the explorers of this American continent for the first time met here with *terra firma*, as when they first beheld the Gulf of Mexico, or that of Panama, the Magellan Route; or on seeing the Pacific Ocean from the top of the Rocky Mountains. No less surprised and delighted feels the modern scholar on contemplating that vast *ethical ocean, Parseeism.* Groping in the dark at the imminent risk of error and delusion, we nevertheless feel irrisistibly attracted towards that *Fata Morgana.* We feel as if there murmured the sacred well whence flow the world's ethical inspirations; that there we contemplate the great religious Albert and Victoria-Nianza Lakes, from which came the first impulse by a circuitous, mysterious route, to the leading doctrines of Israel, of Christendom, of Islam and of the Reformation; that from that fountain sprang

forth those vast ideas, those humanitarian aspirations, those grand
hopes and fears, and those efforts which are the essence of old Judaean prophetism, of later Essenian and now dominant Christianity, of
ethical Mohammedanism, of the Protestant movement and of modern humanitarianism. It is not without hesitation and misgiving
that I approach this theme so grand and obscure, so irrisistibly
attractive and so frowning and forbidding. As the Egyptian sphinx
with a virginal, smiling face and cruel lion's paws, beckoning us to
approach, yet remaining unriddled, even so is the impression of
Zoroasterism upon the modern fancy. We are fully aware that we
know so little of that oriental sphinx and that its masters hardly
know more. The sacred books of that hoary system are written
in idioms long ago mute and dumb, in letters hardly decipherable,
in pictures, images and figures of speech entirely lost to us, written
probably, expressly and on purpose, not to be understood by the
laity, and to which but an exclusive priesthood held the key. Now
that priesthood is extinct and that key is lost! I shall therefore
frankly premise to my kind reader that most of what is now affirmed
of Parseeism is rather guesswork than real science and knowledge,
and that the masters of that oriental discipline are far from being at
one as to the result of their laborious researches. Each of them
tries to study and unriddle the grim sphinx, all toiling in the sweat
of their brow and bringing up to light a few pearls from the bottomless deep, pearls which may turn out to be mere glittering pebbles·
Nevertheless the little we know or guess is worth while studying and
pondering over, because we correctly presume that from among
these pebbles some genuine pearls may be sifted out, that from sur-
mising we shall proceed slowly to positive knowledge and to accur-
ate science.

THE PARSEES.

In the far away Asian East, in the South Eastern inaccessible
Persian mountains, there are a few rare settlements of aborigines,
remnants of an ancient, great people and a great creed, an oasis in
the surrounding Mohammedan population, counting but a few thousands, all told, of poor souls in wretched bodies, ostracised by the
present masters of the country. They go by the name of *Parsees*,
Guebers, fire-worshippers. Further East, in N. W. India, in Guzer-
ate, Surate, Baroach, but especially in Bombay, the principle debris
of that interesting people have for centuries taken up their abode,
driven thereto by conquest, long persecution and untold wanderings,

exiled by the intolerant masters of present Persia and Afghanistan. In and around Bombay, their chief nucleus, the number of the Parsees may count now from one to two hundred thousand persons at the utmost. Since the occupation by the English of those vast Eastern regions, the Parsees have been following the settlements, the ascendency and the fortunes of civilizing Albion. They have thriven by that alliance. Slowly they have acquired good repute, wealth, Western civilization with European industries, views, and habits. They are now occupying with commence and crafts. They are generally more cultivated than the native Hindoos. They are the preferred and trusted friends and allies of the Europeans. A few of them have established great industries at the side of the English, following them from Hindustan to China and to London. With all that, they cling to their own ancient faith which they understand and interpret so as to square with and assimilate to Western European monotheistic modes of religious thought. This is the small remnant of the once great people, creed and world-empire of Persia ; Persia that once under her illustrious princes, the *Achaemenides*, 550–332 B. C., was the mistress of the then known world. The Persians, after their subjugation by Alexander the Great, lived for centuries under the Greek Seleucides and the Parthian Arsacides, until in 226 P. C., they regained their old dominion and ascendency, and for over four centuries longer were the rivals of Rome and Byzantium. So it was until the time of the fierce invaders from Mohammedan Arabia, who in 632 P. C.., routed, subjugated and annihilated the Persians and compelled the rest of them to accept their own faith, Islamism, or to be exiled from the country. From that great race, dominion and creed, all that has remained is a few oases in the Persian mountains and the flourishing colony in and about Bombay.

Studying the history, fate and status of the modern Parsees, the reader will recognize with wonderment that in the East they are, as described by numerous contemporaries, another edition of the people of Israel in the West. A proud past, centuries of long and bitter persecutions, exile and emigration ; the acquisition of great elasticity of body and of mind, wonderful adaptation to circumstances combined with indomitable will power, tenacity and perseverance ; all is the outcome of the principle of " survival of the fittest and natural selection." But we shall see and be even more surprised to learn that that affinity is not new. It has been such from times immemorial ; it is going on and may originally have been derived from a kinship of mind and a similar national psychology and history. We shall see that from hoary times onward, there was a parallel line between Persians and Israelites, between the followers of Zoroaster and those of Moses, and that Monotheism and an exalted morality is the essence of both the systems. So it was in Biblical times and so it is now. The Bombay Parsees tenaciously cling to their religion of old, which, nevertheless they rationally expound as pure Monotheism. Though parallel to Hindooism, and living for centuries in Hindoo climes and surroundings, they yet feel akin rather to the Western English, because they assume Monotheism to be the essence and kernel of the religion of both, the English and the Parsees. So are their ethics derived from the same source, identical in both the creeds, their best result and their noblest aspiration. These Parsees or *Guebers* are the last debris of that ancient people, the Persians and of that great creed, Mazdaism or Zoroasterism. Their doctrines, sacred books and teachings are the objects of our study.

ZOROASTER, THE LAWGIVER.

The founder of that antique religion of the Persians is universally accepted to have been Zoroaster, called in the sacred books of that creed, *Zarathustra*, in their later modern literature, *Zerdusht*, and by the Greeks *Zwroastys*. The meaning of the word is doubtful and differently interpreted ; by some, prosaically, as meaning "possessor of old camels." I should venture to suggest it means "brilliant star," bright luminary. He is named and repeatedly designated in those sacred books as the prophet and the author of the old Iranian religion and bible. He was celebrated throughout antiquity by the leading classic writers as " The founder of the wisdom of the Magi." He was much better known to the Greeks and Romans of classical times than were Moses and David. Since the Persians were not so fiercely prominent in their antagonism to Polytheism, since they later admitted even some sort of idol-worship, Zoroasterism was more favorably appreciated than Mosaism by Greece and Rome.

THE CLASSICS ON ZOROASTER.

Already at the time of Socrates, Persia was well-known to follow the doctrines of that sage. He was claimed by some writers to hail from Media, by others from Bactria, from the West, from the East, etc. He is respectfully mentioned by the leading masters of Classical literature ([1]). Plutarch compares him to Lycurgus and Numa,

---

()Xantus, Plato, Hermedatus, Hermippus, Trojus Pompejus, Diodorus, Pliny, Ctesias, Plutarch and others ; not by Herodotus.

etc. As the place of his birth, so is the time of his existence most undetermined. Some suppose him as contemporaneous with Darius Hystasp, (500 B. C.) Hermippus thinks that 5000 or even 6000 years before the Achaemenidean dynasty would not be too much. Others affirm him as having existed in the period between Moses and Abraham. Some call him even Ibrahim Zoroaster, a name suggestive of wonderful possibilities. Thomas Hyde almost identifies him with Abraham, believing at least that the Persians learned his doctrines from the Jewish exiles in Babylon. Others again take him for a mythical person, a personified force of nature, as the storm-god purifying the atmosphere by thunder. So do especially Darmesteter and E. Myer. No doubt in later Persian literature, he is claimed as having accepted the mission declined by fabulous Yima of the Golden Age of Iran and that he was a son to Purushaspa and born at Airyana-Vaego. He is depicted under mythic colors and with supernatural attributes. As of Jesus of Nazareth, so it is told of him that he smiled at his birth; that in his youth he was dreaded and tempted by the evil spirit; that at his advent, the devil and his hosts fled in dismay to hell. It is further believed that he familiarly talked with the Deity and brought down the law from Heaven, etc. Soberer passages in the sacred books allude to Rhaga in Media, as his birth place. Others claim this as the later residence of the priestly chief, and that a place of Atropatene, in Media, or Balkh, was Zoroaster's residence. All seem to agree that whether he came from the West or the East, his main activity was in Bactria, East of Media, Iran and Persia. His protector, friend and partisan was Vistaspa, a half legendary king of Bactria. He died at a ripe old age, murdered at the hands of a horde of invading Turanians, at Balkh, after having firmly established his religion and his polity!

ZOROASTERISM OUTLINED.

As his epoch, his birthplace and his writings, so is his doctrine not perfectly agreed upon by all the modern Zend scholars. I shall begin by giving here an outline of those features nearly acceded to on all sides. Zoroaster appears to have been the reformator of the former Eranian, or Iranian, pupular religion. Instead of the preceding, material pantheism, nature worship and ancestor worship, he arrived at the new conception of mind, of spirituality, of God, Asura, Ahura, and he enthroned that principle in place of nature. The phenomenon of the bodily universe, suggested to him the existence of a spiritual Deity. The diversity of forces behind the bodies united in harmony, suggested the Supreme power, Divine Intelligence. He spiritualized and personified the universe; its supreme Rule is mind, not body. Thus he made a strong approach toward pure Monotheism to unify and enliven nature and its forces. The one God idea loomed up before him, slowly and dimly, instead of the infinity of bodies and agents. He taught Ahura Mazdao, the Divine Wisdom, as the Supreme Deity.

ZOROASTER'S DOCTRINE.

He taught morality as the great object of religion and of state, of the church and of society. The highest religion to him is: "Purity of thought, word and deed." He thus was the forerunner of Judaean prophetism, of Gospel and Koran ethics. But finding also in the world, apparent, clashing disharmony, stupidity, wrong, vice, misfortune and ill, he concluded that there must needs be two Powers in existence, the principles of Good and of Evil, each working with autonomy. These he symbolized as the genii of Light and of Darkness. Thus he taught instead of god-nature or gods-forces, dualism, the God-Holy-Spirit and the god-Unholy-Spirit. Here is the genesis of the Jewish and Christian holy-spirit and of the devil. His definition of the evil spirit is: Negation, destruction, lies, ignorance and ill.—Veracity, honesty, purity in body and in mind; agriculture husbandry, breeding of domestic cattle, irrigation, all usefel activity and productive work,—not empty creed and cere-mony—were his ideals of humane life, virtue, happiness. His dual-ism was cosmic and ethical. Two Powers are in existence, not only in the universe, but also in history, in the human sphere. These two are ever in contention; they are symbolized by Light and Darkness. Light is the power of goodness, happiness, truthfulness, etc. Dark-ness is the power of negation, lies, destruction, sin. These two have been from the beginning, ever in contention. A virtuous, humane life is ever in the service of the light-principle, helping to subdue and extirpate the evil principle by the annihilation of its creation and its worshippers. A vicious, beastly, selfish life is in the service of the daevas, and harms the good creation by meanness and fraud.

Yasna XXX., 3, etc., is claimed by the Zend scholars to purport this dualistic-theory: "At the beginning of things there existed two spirits, Ahura, Mazda and Angro Mainyu; they represent good and evil." According to Spiegel's translation, it reads literally: "These two heavenly beings, the *twins*, announced at first both, the good and the ill, in thoughts, words and deeds. These two divine beings met to create life and mortality and all that the world was to be. The Evil One created for the wicked; for the pure ones, the Good One created (Ahura Mazda). The wicked chose the Evil One. The pure ones preferred the Good Spirit. "Yasna XXX., continues to say that man is free in his choice; he can select the good or the bad; hence is he responsible for his actions;" a line of reasoning exactly as throughout the Pentateuch. (Deut. XXX. 19 and in many other passages).—"Reward and punishment for good or evil deeds are beyond the grave, in paradise and in hell. After death, the dead are interrogated, their conduct is strictly examined and sentence infallibly passed upon. If they have a surplus of merit, they easily pass the awful *bridge of judgment* and enter Garonmana, (paradise). If the exact scales show an overweight of guilt, they tumble down into the pit of burning hell beneath. There is no grace nor pardon; sacrifice and offerings are of no avail." The Deity is therefore strict justice and intelligence, not love and grace, Jewish moralists are divided on this head. Paulinian Christianity, building upon faith without work, had to accentuate divine love, not justice.

HIS KINGDOM OF HEAVEN AND LATER MYSTICISM.

Zoroaster, as Jesus, expected the "Kingdom of God." This was his great message. Now is Ahura in bitter contention with Angro Mainyu. So it must be according to a decree of fate, such was the solemn agreement. Both are twins, sons of fate, infinity, Zrvana Akarana. For 12000 years, according to some and for 9000, according to others (1), that rivalship will continue. At the "End of Days," this world will be annihilated and the Kingdom of God—Ahura-Mazda's—will alone be established. This will take place 3000 years after Zoroaster. Angro Mainyu and all the daevas will be vanquished; the resurrection will take place, all by *Soshiosh*, the saviour, a descendant of Zoroaster. Here we see the exact meaning of the "Kingdom of God, Messiah, Saviour," later taught by the Essenians, etc. The Kingdom of God meant the triumph of the rule of light over the rule of darkness, to be brought about by the *Soshiosh* or Messiah, who would vanquish Angro Mainyu, establish the government of Light and resurrect the dead. The dead were the triumph of the Evil principle, and its destruction must be followed by resurrection. Parseeism thus claimed: Evil is inherent in this world. To eradicate evil, the world must be destroyed and a new one built up. The two opposing principles logically had two

(1)Viz: Zoroaster was born 9000 A. M.

full creations, one of good and one of evil, necessarily battling
against each other. But this double world was of limited duration.
Evil was destined to be destroyed and the creation of good alone
eternally to be established. There is a hereafter following this life,
and there is besides, the Messianic age at "the end of days" when
the dead will be resurrected by the Messiah or Soshiosh. These are
the dogmas of Parsee creed and the reader will easily see how far
they influenced the dogmatics of the later creeds.

The Pentateuch teaches: The world was good, but man's deed
spoiled it and obedience to the revealed law is its remedy. Paul
combined both the doctrines: The world was originally good, but
Adam brought the curse, and the higher Adam, Christ, will restore
it to its pristine condition. Jewish mysticism taught that of the
Messiah, son of David. In Magism, it is the Soshiosh, son of Zoroaster. Some Zend scholars believe to discover in the *Ghathas*—
the most ancient part of the Yasna, containing the doctrines nearest
to the original views of Zoroaster—that he, Zoroaster, taught absolutely one God, Ahura, to whom Ahriman was subordinated, just as
Satan is to *Ihvh* in the Bible ; that all the other gods, Amshaspands,
Yazatas and Genii are but divine attributes, or personified ideas, or
natural forces ; that later priests gave to his doctrine the present
expansion of dualism, and that still later arose the sect of *Zervanists*.
These believed that originally *Zrvana-Akarana*—Eternal time and
space—was supreme and that the two powers of Good and of Evil
developed from the split of the first. This mysterious divinity, the
very abstract of Pantheism, corresponds to the Greek fate or blind
necessity, before which Zeus and the entire Olympos were trembling.

One may be much inclined to assume that the doctrine of
Zrvana-Akarana is of old Iranian stock, at first pushed into the background and later resuscitated. It fits the oriental mode of reasoning.
Pantheism and fate are inexorable. Hence was at first Zrvana, then
ensued the split by which Good and Evil came out. In the future
shall evil be vanquished and Mazda and Zrvana again be one.

Even so Christology ; God is unknowable. His emanation, the
Messiah and Satan rule the world. Christ is finally to vanquish
Satan. Then Son and Father will be one again. This corresponds
to Zrvana, Ahura Mazda and Angro Mainyu. This last one vanquished, Ahura alone will be omnipotent through the *Soshiosh*. In
mysticism, Jesus has such a double role, Messiah and God. The
Parsee doctrine of the "last things" and "Kingdom of God" ex·

plain the real meaning of Christology. The *Verb* too, is to be found in the Avesta, it is called *Honover*, by which Ahura created the world.   It is to be distinguished from the Manthra-Spenta, the " holy word," the Avesta Scriptures. Whether pure monotheist or dualist, at any rate and with all the fervor of his soul, did Zoroaster believe in the final triumph of Light over Darkness, of the principle of Good over that of Evil, of God over Devil. The ultimate triumph of God is the ethical postulate, the essence of his teachings. He placed that victory, not as heathendom, at the cradle of mankind, but as prophetism, at the " *end of days*," (¹) in the far future, as the result of all human experiences, struggles and efforts achieved by the Messiah ; the same Jewish and Christian Messiah-Ideal, the aspiration of moral and of social science.

ZOROASTER'S WRITINGS.

It is generally assumed that the writings of Zoroaster were very numerous, that he has left behind, some two millions of verses at least, in hymns and meditations ; Darmesteter thinks that, latest, at the time of the Achaemenides they were all and fully written. Parsee tradition affirms that the sacred, old, Persian literature was written in golden letters upon twelve hundred cowhides, some claim even upon 100,000 cowhides, left in the palace library at Persepolis, the first capital of the Persian Great-kings, and destroyed by fire at the express order of Alexander, or at least connived at by him in the conflagration of that capital. At any rate, upon the conquest of Persia by the Greeks, these writings were either destroyed by fire, or neglected and scattered, and soon definitely lost. Later in the second epoch of the Persian Empire under the Sasanidean princes,(²) they were re-written in 21 nosks or books. Then with *the last catastrophe* of that empire brought about in 632 P. C., by the Mohammedans, that second edition of the sacred books was lost again and later gradually re-written by fugitive Magian priests, from memory and only in fragments, most imperfectly, just what was necessary for worship and for practical religious life. These fragments make up the present sacred books, debris of the once Zend-Avesta, the bible of the present Parsees. Most of the parts now extant of the collection are of later date, but they generally bear the stamp and leading features of Zoroasterism, though strongly altered, containing later adulterations, borrowings from surrounding nations and

---

1 Isaiah II. and Micha IV.   באחרית הימים
2 Ardeshir Babegan and his son Shahpur I.

creeds, with but rare passages coming down, genuine from their hoary originator. The *Ghathas* alone, a notable portion of the *Yasna*, one of the books of that bible, are excepted. These are claimed and actually may be more or less the identical ideas and sentences of that Eastern prophet, since they appear to be prior to the later Persian mythology and better to reflect the beginning of a national religious period. The Vendidad, too, is claimed by some to be one of the original books of the 21 works restored under the reign of the *Sasanides*. It is the priestly book, corresponding to Leviticus of the Pentateuch and has been preserved better than the rest, because it is the code of Parsee practical religion.   Having given a short and succinct outline of the system of Zoroaster as far as pretty generally known and accepted on all sides, we can now enter upon a closer analysis of the system, the sacred books and the several doctrines of that hoary oriental prophet and his legislation.

MODERN WRITERS ON THE AVESTA.

Here we must not expect unanimity among the many writers on that comparatively new branch of science and Persian philology. Nearly every prominent writer has his own opinions about that. I shall follow here the train of ideas and views of leading masters, especially of Fr. Spiegel, M. Haug, James Darmesteter, etc., corroborated, interspersed and revised by, the opinions of others, as Windishman, Klauker, Roth, Bopp, Geiger, Oppert, E. Meyer, etc.; everywhere carefully accompanied by my own independent, frequent remarks, elucidations and analogies, setting forth the scope of this book, the biblical legislations, their parallelism and original universality in their leading features, all pointing to the same humanitarian goal, termed the "Messianic Ideal," viz : the last issues and aspirations of human history and social improvement.

THE ZEND-AVESTA. ITS SEVERAL REDACTIONS.(1)

Zend-Avesta is a collection of the sacred writings of different contents and epochs, persons and countries, containing religious hymns, invocations, psalms, prayers, confessions, supplications, laws, moral precepts, sacred reminiscences and myths, compiled and classified, pretty much unsystematically, hurriedly, almost confusedly, in great variety and mixture ; composed during a long period of time, according to some, many thousand years, and according

---

[1] In many passages of these pages, I followed Dr. Martin Haug's Zend-Studies in Zeitschrift d. Deutsch-morgenl-Gesellschaft, IX., Vol. Leipzig, 1855.

to Haug, Spiegel, etc., during at least one thousand years B.
C. In the shape these writings are now before us, they contain some very old parts and some of less ancient date. They
are the debris of antique sacred writings now lost twice, probably,
since the times of Alexander the Great, after the conquest of Persia
and the burning of Persepolis, as mentioned, when these Zoroastrian books too, according to Parsee tradition, were burnt along with
the rest of the great library, 331 B. C. Historians justly doubt that a
conqueror so jealous of his fame and so kind that he wept at Darius'
death and tenderly took care of his family, should have committed
such a brutal incendiarism. Nevertheless he may have done it.
He may have ordered or at least tolerated that brutal incendiarism
of the capital and the sacred writings of the Achaemenidean Great-
Kings, either from exuberance of triumph and wanton pride, or
perhaps from political reasons, viz: to show and convince the world
that the great Persian house, nation and creed were no more, and
that his own, Greek family, people and ascendency were to take their
place; as Belshazzar of Khaldea, he was little dreaming what misfortunes were in store for himself and his own nearest and dearest.

HAUG ON THE AVESTA. ZOROASTER, REFORMATOR.

Haug says substantially the following: "The author of the
Zend-Avesta and the founder of that religion, the Parsees claim to
be *Zoroaster*. Looking closely at the many and various fragments
of the book and its doctrines, we are not disposed to adhere to that
opinion. There are besides, wide discrepancies in the language of
the several parts of the book which witness to the diversity of hands,
ages and countries of its composition. The doctrines taught there,
too, show evident signs of slow development and of diverse stages,
requiring centuries for their successive formations. Thus, the book
cannot be the work of one person. To all appearance, Zoroaster is
not the originator of that Iranic religion, but he has developed,
shaped it and brought it to a higher degree of perfection and spirituality." These propositions are generally assented to. He continues:
"That spirituality is the leading trait of Zoroaster's creed, though he is
not its originator, as little as he is of the Zend-Avesta in general; but
undoubtedly his hand and mind are predominant everywhere."
This last part of Haug's opinion, finds its adherents and its opponents. James Darmesteter "is in doubt whether Zoroaster is a man
apotheosized to a god, or a god later converted into a man." To
him, he is rather the latter. He says: "Haug erroneously con-

verted Mazdaism into a religious revolution against Vedic polytheism. (Vend p. XXIX). According to Darmesteter, Zoroaster
dwindles into a myth, the purifying storm-god; and Mazdaism is
not a revolution, but an independent development of Hindooism,
the dualistic and the monotheistic ideas being at the bottom of both
the systems, seemingly polytheistic. Agreed to that Zoroaster is
not the founder of the Avesta religion, he is no doubt its reformator
and a historical person. The preceding Hindoo nature-force-and
ancestor-worship he spiritualized and refined. He gave it a soul, he
breathed life into it. He added a higher God-conviction: the
spiritual God-idea and with it a higher man-idea. He thus made a
great approach to spiritual Monotheism; as an important, necessary
result and logical sequence, he taught a purer morality, the One
Ahura-Mazda could not teach the many Hindoo castes, but ' one
law and one right.' Since this is generally attributed to Zoroaster,
I see no reason to question his person and his influence in Mazdaism. I cannot see why certain writers, otherwise great and illustrious
scholars, are so quick in declaring every extraordinary historical
personage to be a myth and fiction. As if only the vulgar are real
and existent! To some, are Nimrod and Semiramis, Abraham,
Moses and Macabeus but myths. I believe if even many attributes
of such persons are exaggerated and legendary, yet in each there is
a solid nucleus, a kernel of historical fact, hence they existed and
were the forces of their times. I am inclined to believe that even
myth was originally history, reality apotheosized. I recognize that
in the domain of critical history, what is not proven is not to be
posited and affirmed. But I think what is assumed by universal
consent and is not positively contradicted by reason and fact, is entitled to credence. Here we find in hoary times a great religion
rising, impregnated with new, startling and truthful elements, having their reverberations, to this day in the leading religious systems
of the world. By common consent, they are attributed to Zoroaster,
why doubt it? Cui bono? Must not somebody be their author?
Why not Zoroaster? By one method of unreasonable doubt the
existence of Moses, of Homer and of Jesus is doubted; and by another way of arguing I conclude that they are real historical persons.
Whether they have written all that is attributed to them, criticism
could not affirm. But that they existed, acted and gave the impulse
and start to the creations and literatures bearing their names, that is
fairly acceptable; even so Zoroaster.

MOSES AND ZOROASTER.

In many respects, indeed, is Zoroaster comparable to the Hebrew Lawgiver. Whether Moses wrote every word and scroll of that Pentateuch, criticism may differ. But his genius and his impulse are visible everywhere there. Even so, is that of Zoroaster, in the Avesta system. His mind, person and hand are visible in its best parts. He is surrounded by a halo of sanctity. His epithet is ([1]) "Spitama." all holy, sanctissimus. As in the ancient, cosmic philosophies, each species of creation had its prototype and ideal, representing that genus in its superlative perfection, even so was Zoroaster the supreme type of the human kind; he was later half and half divinized; he was the mediator and prophet between God and man, bearer of divine revelations, head and patron of this sublunar world. He occupied among the Parsee masses of the East a position much akin if not superior to that of Moses with the Jews. "There never arose a man like Moses who spoke with God *face to face.* ([2]) But the Parsees claim more of Zoroaster, the *Yazata.* With the Jews Moses was never divinized. His grave is not known. But he died and was buried. Later legend says "*Moses died not.*" ([3]) Zoroaster is in later Persian myth fully apotheosized with all the paraphernalia. His role is therefore even more comparable to that of the Essenian Messiah, or even with Jesus in Christology. Indeed the supernatural Messiah Ideal, as we find it in the Apochryphae, the Talmud, Targums and later in the Qabbala, is Zoroastrian; that type especially which was elaborated as a State religion by the Gentile Christians in the Christ-idea, as a hypostasis and a person of the Triune Deity. The type of that idea and the pattern of that ideal appears to have been taken from Zoroaster, the mediator between Ormazd and man, between heaven and earth, the opponent of Ahriman. At any rate, Moses, Homer and Jesus are historical persons and no myths. They are the heads and authors of the systems bearing their names. Even so is Zoroaster the leading author of the Mazda religion.

GATHAS AND ZEND UNCERTAINTIES.

A striking example of the uncertainty in the Zend-studies are the various explanations of the very name Zoroaster. According to Haug, the meaning of Zoroaster or Zarathustra is: "*Praise·Singer,*" a chanter of divine hymns   Others say it means " Possessor of old

---

1 Some think Spitama or Cpitama was his family name.

משה לא מת 8 פנים אל פנים 8

camels." (1) I suggested that it may be a metaphor, meaning : Brilliant star, starry luminary. (²) It strikes me that when Moses de
Leon of the Thirteenth Century, P. C., the presumptive author of
the *Zohar*, the Bible of the Jewish mystics, called his book *Zohar*,
light, lustre, he may in his mind have alluded to Zoroaster and to
his doctrines, there being great affinity between his theories and
Zoroasterism, as shown by Professor Frank (³) of the Paris Sor-
bonne and as I shall corroborate later. It is pretty nearly agreed to
by all Zend scholars that the Avesta contains many parts, chapters
and passages which may well be derived directly from the Bactrian
ethical Teacher. One notable portion of the *Yasna*, denominated
the *Gathas*, meditations, may well be so verbatim, or at least in ideas
and expressions. They bear the stamp of genuineness and reality,
without that pomp of myth and exaggeration which is usually the
sign of later ages, when the hero has passed into a state of legend
and myth, surrounded by the halo of smoke and of incense, of admiration and adulation, as we see among other races, as Hercules
and Theseus among the Greeks, Romulus and Bacchus among the
Latins, etc. In the more ancient parts of the Avesta, Zoroaster
figures as the author of religious song, the greatest poet of hymns ;
poet and prophet and religious teacher being yet synonymous in
those infantine times. These old *poems* claim that " he has shaped
the words into song, has advanced godliness and purity by his
hymns ; upon whom Ahura-Mazda has bestowed the gift of oratory ;
who took the tongue into the service of the intelligence ; who was
the only one who listened to the teachings of the highest God and
was able to hand them down to men." His powerful friend, co-
worker, and zealous adherent was Kava Vistaspa, King of Bactria.
Many more friends of his religious initiative are mentioned in the
Avesta. It is immaterial whether Vistaspa, etc., are history or myth.
No doubt his movement must have been supported, or it would have
collapsed.

ZOROASTER'S EPOCH.

As to the age when he flourished, as hinted at above, the opinions of historians greatly vary. Some believed that he lived 400 or

---

See Spiegel Comment, Avesta, Vol. II., VIII. 6.

² From Zohar, light, lustre, זחר and *astýp*, stella, sterna, sitara, Scr. :
stri, stara ; Zoroaster is later described almost mythically, and his
name, too, bears probably such a character of myth.

³ La Cabale.

500 years, and some 5,000 or 6,000 before the present era. Dr. Haug, whom I often follow in these pages, presumes that he flourished 1,500 to 2,000 years before the Christian era. " Since in 400, B. C., the very latest doctrine of Parseeism is already developed, viz : that of the resurrection of the dead ; that is mentioned for the first time in one of the youngest fragments of the Avesta and is fully described in the late *Bundehesh*. Theopomp, a contemporary of Alexander the Great, mentions that doctrine as belonging to the Magi. It would therefore not be too much, says Haug, to assume that at least 1,000 years had elapsed since the dawn of that religion, as described in the oldest poems and hymns of the Avesta, to the resurrection doctrine, its latest development." Some objections have been raised to that, from the fact that in many passages in Herodotus and other early Greek writers, we see that *burying of the dead* was the general practice of the Persians under the Achaemenian kings ; a practice which is most rigorously denunciated in the Avesta as now before us. Some claim therefore that this is an evident proof that the Avesta is posterior to that dynasty. But Darmesteter and others have justly shown that those passages in Herodotus prove only that in the Achaemenian times the practice of destroying the dead bodies by beasts of prey, on the *Dakhma's*, was not yet accepted by the people, but it was law and practice with the Magian priests. It was the law, but later, under the Sasanides, with the full ascendency of the Magi, the people, too, conformed to it. It takes a long while until certain theories become practice, and this was the case with substituting the Magian mode of disposing of the dead to that of burying them, as universally practiced.

TIME OF COMPOSITION OF AVESTA.

The idea of the immortality of the soul that sweetened the death of Socrates and the life of Plato, is but the rational kernel and contents of that other, more popular conception of the resurrection of the body. Neither of them is yet to be found in the earlier parts of the Hebrew canon. They are faintly alluded to as a problem, by Ezekiel and the sacred writers after the Babylonian Exile. That double idea of the immortality of the body and the soul must be derived from later developments of Zoroaster's doctrines, but hardly did it originate with that Teacher himself. The Pentateuch and I. Isaiah, 38.18 has it not, though Egypt taught it. But the post-exile canonical books, some later psalms, Daniel, the Maccabees, Apochraphae, Mishna, Aggadah and Halacha set it forth promin-

ently. The New Testament and the Koran are brimful of that doctrine.   Now since the Pentateuch has it not, and Isaiah I. expressly
declines it, that proves it is a later idea and hence must the dawn of
Zoroasterism be placed earlier, much earlier than 1,000 years B. C.
We shall elucidate that.   The immortality or resurrection idea is not
taught in the five books of Moses, but is in the later parts of the
Hebrew canon, viz: of the post-Babylonian epoch; hence it must
have been a growth upon Parsee soil and accepted later by the
Sacred Writers.   But since the Pentateuch itself is contemporaneous
with Zoroasterism, as we shall clearly show in a large number of its
regulations, positive and negative, running in parallel lines with, or
in express opposition to, Avesta doctrines, therefore are we bound to
admit many and long phases in the development of the Zend-books.
We have to allow them a commensurate space of time for development.
They must have existed, not only contemporaneously with, but even
prior to the Pentateuch, and their unfoldings must have continued
during post-Pentateuchal times.   Zoroasterism seems therefore to
be older, in part at least, than Mosaism, and that proves the Avesta
to date back further than a thousand years prior to the Achaemenides.   The claim that Zoroaster has lived during the century of
the Persian Darius Hystaspes, about 550 B. C., is decidedly errone-
ous, justly agree all the writers on our subject.   That opinion rested on
the false identification of that name with the Bactrian legendary king,
Kava Vistaspa.   Now "it is against all probability that from 550 to
400 B. C. the Zend religion received all those vast developments in-
tervening between its venerable origin, the hoary hymns and songs,
down to its latest and full dogmatic completion as found later in the
Bundehesh," says Haug ; that is conclusive.   It is by some ([1]) assumed that the whole religious system of Iran has been elaborated
in its antagonism against Hindooism.   The *Vedas*, India's sacred
books, represent simply a system of poetic personifications of the
forces of the cosmos; they are a poetic divinization of nature.   Yet
in rudiment, the leading theories of the Iranian religion are to be
found in the Vedic ones.   Haug continues: " There we find the ru-
diments of later Parseeism, *Dualism*, the *good gods*, gods of light,
as half-way spiritual beings, and in opposition to them are the wicked
demons who try to hinder the efforts of the good spirits and to harm
man.   But as yet these gods are mere natural forces personified,

1 By Haug and others, but contradicted by Darmesteter, who denies
any such revolution, but admits a slow evolution (Vend. p. 38.)

good and bad ones. They are as yet really no free agents. In place
of that nature-cult, the sages of Iran, and more so of Bactria, labored
to refine and spiritualize the divine conception. These sages were
called: fire-priests, holy men who lighted the sacred fires, " Saosky-
anto." The later Parsee dogmatics made of their chief sacred func-
tioner the *Messiah, Soshiosh.* They worshipped the good spirits with
kindling pure fires. But since they conceived them as moral, spiritual powers, greatly repugnant to the ideas of the old Hindoo
sages, that was considered as heresy, apostasy. A fearful religious
war was kindled between Iranians and Hindoos, the religious split became permanent. Zoroasterism and his new sect arose from that
momentous difference."

CHAPTER II

AVESTA DOCTRINES AND PARALLELS.

Haug closes : " Now came the far-reaching reform of the great Zoroaster. He was one of the fire-priests. His merit consisted in having reduced *the many good spirits into one*, and the many bad spirits, also, he reduced into unity. He spiritualized both these sets of agents. Naturally, he denominated the Good principle of the universe : the *Holy Spirit*, Spento-mainyu ; Supreme Wisdom, Ahura-Mazda ; light was his first-born Son or great attribute. Whilst the evil principle he called Angro-Mainyu, the wicked spirit of darkness, Drukh, lie, fraud, etc." Here we see the original meaning of *Holy Spirit*, so prominent in Hebrew Aggada as "Ruah haqodesh" and in Christology as a divine person of the trinity. It is perfectly plain in Parseeism : The entire creation was pervaded by two spirits, the holy one and the unholy one, and the holy one was the highest God. There was a real perfect identity, the Holy Spirit was Ahura-Mazda. The Holy Spirit-idea in Judaism may have come from there, but it had another meaning. There *Elohim* or *Ihvh* was the reality, essence, creator of the universe, and his Holy Spirit was but an attribute designating prophesy, the divine in communion with the human. In Christology it had both the meanings, it was an attribute and a substance, hence independent, yet one with God. Zoroaster introduced Monotheism in the far East. Curious, his name was Ibrahim !—Especially did he understand that opposition of the good and the evil principles rather to be such morally than physically, inwardly than outwardly ; more in the human consciousness, in the heart, than in the objective world, in the brute forces contending in nature. Even so do we find, throughout the Aggada, among all the Hebrew moralists, after the Babylonian Exile, prevalent the doctrine of a good and an evil spirit (yezer hara and yezer hatob) inducing men to do good and evil. " The 30th chapter of *Yasna*, probably derived from Zoroaster, embodies that doctrine. It teaches : " Two original spirits exist in the universe, a good and a bad one, in thoughts, words and deeds.. Both these spirits have joined ; the one created existence, the other caused the annihilation of existence. Wickedness is of the godless ; goodness is of the pious. Choose one of these two spirits ; the lying, mischievous one, or the pure and holy one. Either choose the worst lot or worship Ahura-Mazda with good and truthful deeds."([1]) Both these spirits have revealed their doctrines and laws. The one is a speaker of truth, the other an orator of lies. The name of the good one is Spenta-Mainyu, i. e., the Holy Ghost, *Ahura*, living, and *Mazdao*, dispenser of wisdom, both together gradually form God's proper name. They are really but attributes of the Supreme, Holy Spirit. Both these words go together in the Avesta literature and form the name of the Supreme Being. At first, the epithet of *Mazdao* belonged to *many* good spirits. It is the merit of Zoroaster that at last it became the special designation of the only One Supreme Being. Thus, in Parseeism, the *Holy Spirit* was declared the Supreme God. In Christology, the Supreme God was given the attribute of *Holy Ghost*, but which attribute is at the same time an independent, divine Being. This double meaning is the result of its double derivation, Parsee and prophetic.

According to the "*Sacred poems*" this is Ahura Mazda, the Supreme Intelligence, the Omniscient, the Creator of Good, the truthful, the omnipotent, under whose dominion stands the universe. Sun, moon and stars have their orbits prescribed by Him, and all the forces of nature are under his control. So also is the earth created and ruled by him, and surrendered to man as his dominion and inheritance. The earth is termed his daughter. Everything good he created. He is the author of life. He is wisdom and intelligence, author of good conscience, purity and truth. He rewards the good ones with happiness, and the wicked with evil. He is gracious and merciful and allows existence even to the wicked, awaiting their repentance. Opposed to Ahura is the Evil Spirit, Ako-mano, ([2]) or Drugh, *Drukh*, the lie, fraud, "*Angro-Mainyu*," the wicked, harmful, angry Spirit, commonly abbreviated into Ahriman, a later appellation of the Evil principle. He is the creator of the daevas, devils or bad spirits, he murders life. The safest means to annihilate his creation is wisdom and knowledge. His essence is lying. Doubt too, is his work. Both of these, the lie and the doubt, produce all human perverseness. He taught his wicked doctrines to oppose the pure creation. Do not trust him. He renders the fields barren and harms the pure ones.

1 This is the approximate sense of the verses.
2 The Talmud designates by עכו״ם all idol worshippers, it alludes to the Parsee principle of Evil, ako-Mano.

DUALISM. ORIGIN OF EVIL. AMESHA'S SPENTA'S.

Some Zend expounders claim that there is also another version concerning the origin of Evil. According to a passage in Yasna 48, 1, Ahura Mazda created the good and the Evil Spirits. Hence is the Evil one subordinated to the Supreme Ahura Mazda. He alone is the Supreme Ruler. ([1]) This is the Jewish view, as in Bible, Talmud and Moralists. Again, another version is: The Evil comes from wickedness and lust; wicked men create the daevas by their evil deeds. Hence are impure spirits the result of bad men's deeds. Such too, we find in Hebrew Aggadas, " Every sin committed, creates an evil spirit."

The court of Ahura Mazda is supported and graced by a Council of grandees or peers; the Amesha's *Spenta's*, Amshaspands, viz: the sanctified immortals. They are six in number. The older poems do not mention them. They are of later development. At first they appear to have been mere attributes of the Supreme Deity, his benefactions and emanations. Gradually they assumed personality and self-existence as leading genii, angels, assistant companions of Ahura Mazda. They are at the same time personifications of virtues and types of special creations. *Vohu-Mano* is the good intention; Ashem-Vohu is purity and holiness; *Khashatrem* is possession, property, earthly power, good luck and material blessing; Armaiti or Spendarmat is the earth and its spirit, the home, the hearth, also the genius of devotion. So are all the Ameshas Spentas and the rest of their colleagues, peers of Ahura, his attributes and agents, symbols of moral virtues, patrons and lords of special parts of the bodily or moral world. They are in reality but personified forces, raised by the vulgar into independent, divine entities. The Church transferred that patronage to the Saints. Thus also the Hebrew Aggadah gave a Court of six or seven grandees to the Deity, called the *"Pamalia-shel-male"*([2]) heavenly Council. In the later Parsee mythology, they assume more personality, more body and become more independent, peers of Ahura. The six Ameshas Spentas are the following with their full names: Vohu-mano, Asha-Vahista; Khshathra-Vairya; Spenta-Armaiti; Haurvatat, Ameritat. Sometimes Ahura Mazda figures as one among them, they make thus together seven *Ameshas.* This may give the clue to the question: Why in the entire Orient the number seven is considered holy; why the simple utter-

---

1 Haug, p. 689, Zend studies.   2 פמליא של מעלה

ance of that number was an oath. The semitic *Sheba* (¹) means *seven*
and *oath*. It was commonly explained because they believed that
the heavenly bodies were seven. More probably, it is on acccunt of
the seven Amesha's Spenta's. Of course the Persian Great-King had
a Council of seven grandees. Whether the court was the model for,
or the imitation of, heaven, cannot be decided. Of course Ahriman,
too, had his court of six wicked peers and his long retinue of impure spirits.

AHURA MAZDA.

Fr. Spiegel thinks *Ahura* means master, lord,—as in German
Herr. *Maz* is great and *das* is knowledge. The whole meaning,
the omniscient Master. The same writer in his "Commentary on
the Avesta, p. 2, says: Ahura Mazda, written in one word or in two,
according to Burnouf and the unanimous tradition of the Parsees,
means: The very wise Lord. . . Ahura may also designate other
masters. It is nearly akin to *ahu*, meaning both, world and master,
sometimes also soul. In Sanskrit *Asura*, *asu* corresponds to it; the
root is undoubtedly *Ah, as, to be ; Ahu, Ahura* is thus: the really
existing one, as the Hebrew *Ihvh*. (²) Of the word Mazdao, Burnouf has uncontrovertably proven that it consists of maz, great and
dao knowledge. . . He is depicted as the highest Spirit, the most
holy light. Ahura may mean light, akin to *Orah*. (³) He is spiritual, yet in later Avesta writers he is corporeal, too. He is also
called Spenta Mainyu, the Holy Ghost, opposing the Unholy one.
Before Jews and Christians the Parsees had their "Holy Ghost," the
opponent of the Wicked one. He is the highest, not the only one.
He is corporeal, too; he has wives and children. In later myth he is the
protector of men, Creator of the light-universe, Lord of the hosts, of
creation, corresponding to *Ihvh Zebaoth*, Author of the Ameshas, of
earth, water and good genii. His residence is in Gara-nmana or
heaven. Angro Mainyu, the wicked spirit, is the counterpart of the
above, and he too, has his own full creation. *Amesha's Spenta's* means
the holy immortals, the perfect and increasing ones ; Ahura, their
creator in one of them, the first. He is the central sun, they are his
rays, really his attributes. Philo's Emanations too, were one with
the Creator. The Mishna Aboth and Talm. Babli. Hagiga (12. a)
substituted ten instead of seven, because it was assumed that the first

אורח 3   יהוה 2   שבעה 1

chapter of Genesis contains ten times: " God spake," hence was creation effected with ten fiats. ([1])

·The Qabbala borrowed from both : God Supreme created the ten Sephiroth. The ten were all contained in the first Sephirah, and this first one is *one* with God Supreme. Christology built further out the same idea. The first Emanation is *Adam Qadmon*, and he was one with God and the holy spirit, hence tri-unity. So the ten are equal to three and the three contained in one. ([2])   Fr. Spiegel ([3]) gives the following attributes to the Ameshas Spentas, the holy Immortals, the Emanations and peers of the Supreme: I. Vohu-mano ; Good spirit, Intelligence, Prince of peace, Sar Shalom, the attributes of the Messiah in Prophetism and Christology. He is the patron of men, hence Anglo-Saxon, "*woman*," probably, the genius of man. Plutarch calls that genius *Oeos eunoios*. II. Asha Vahista, Patron of fire, purity, holiness, light, opponent of Angro Mainyu and daevas. He is *Oeos Alydeias*. III. Khashathra-Vairya, Shahrivar, genius of empire, dominion, Oeos eunomios, charity, The Hebrew "*Rah-man*," also of metal and of many more attributes. IV. Spenta Armaiti, holy mother, earth, wisdom, good and useful things, *Oeos sophias*. V. Haurvatat, genius of water, plenty, blessing, Oeos Ploutou. VI. Ameretat, genius of vegetation—epi kalois ydewn.—Both preside over earthly enjoyments. Inclusive of these six or seven Ameshas, the Persian Pantheon has some thirty to thirty-three greater and smaller deities, as many as days in the month ; further, a larger number of minor grandees and princes, called Yazatas, holy and pure ones, dwellers of both, heaven and earth, companions and creatures of Ahura, who is the supreme Yazata. The patron-saints for every day of the Roman calendar have their model there.

DAILY GODS AND SHIROZAS.

But the parallels go even farther. The thirty days of the Persian month are each presided over by a god, beginning with Ormazd and the six Ameshas Spentas, each presiding over one of the first seven days of the month and followed by other genii. For each of the thirty days, a god is detailed as the special patron. Now when we ponder over the names of our present seven week days, we justly surmise that this was the case too, in the diverse mythologies of the Greek and the Saxon pantheon. Sunday was devoted to the Sun-

---

[1] בעשרה דברים נברא העולם, בחכמה, בתבונה, בדעת, בכוח, בגערה   Hagiga 12. a.
[2] See Qabbalah, by M. Fluegel.
[3] Spiegel, III. vol., page 8, etc., Avesta.

god, Monday to the moon-god, etc. Each day of the week or the
month had its special protecting genius or god. Scanning the ritual
of the present cults, we find the same holds good to this day, as far
as the present theologies admit of it. The Parsee *Yasna*, contains
thirty *Shirozas* or hymns and devotions for each day of the month,
addressed to its respective patron genius, superscribed by that name,
Ormazd, Vohu-Mano, Mithra, etc. Scanning the Hebrew common-
prayerbook, we find its analogy in past and in present times. First
we find the hymns (Shir Mismor) used by the Levites in the ancient
Moriah Temple. Each day of the week had its special psalm. For
the first day came the Ps. 24; for the second day Ps. 45, etc. The
Sabbath had Ps. 92, bearing yet the name of *Shir of the Sabbath day*.[1]
That group of hymns has the superscription : " The disciples of
Ari—the known Qabbalist Luria—have recommended such psalms
to be said daily, ([2]) Qabbala being in part a derivation from Parseeism. The Synagogue has besides extra hymns for each day, called
Shir-hajichud, hymus of unification ; viz : While the Persian *Shirozas* addressed each day another deity, the Hebrew sang day by
day, but to the only one God. These pieces are among the finest of
Hebrew philosphic hymns, combining depth of metaphysics with
beauty of poetry. The church, too, has such special songs appro-
priated to each day, besides its particular saint, patron of the day.
Thus the *Shirozas* praise the Persian Pantheon, the Church chants
trinity ; and the synagogue, unity. Here are the parallels and contrasts.

YAZATAS.

The dignity of Yazata pervading the Avesta corresponds, I presume to the sober Semitic epithet of the "just and righteous, the
humble, the poor, the pious, the friend of God, the servant of
God."[3] By that the Hebrew designated a human being who by
his piety stood nearer to God than the common mortal given to
worldliness. While the Parsee Yazata implied something divine, of
the superior nature of the gods ; Ahura was the highest of Yazatas.
As everywhere in ancient mythology the boundary-line between
God and man was indefinite, as the shades of colors in the rainbow,
even such was the undetermined nature of the Yazata, human and
divine. II. Isaiah in chapters 41, 42, 44, 45, may allude to that,

1 Ps. 92.   מזמור שיר ליום השבת

2 Derech Hahai Vienna, 1862.   בתבו תלמידי האר״י שבכל יום יאמר אחד ממזמורים

8   צדיק ענו עני חסיד אוהב עבד

speaking of Cyrus, Abraham, Israel, etc.([1]) In later Psalms and Es-
senism, the "righteous, poor, indigent and pious" take that place;
so in the Mount Sermon and in Christology, the " poor in spirit"
and in purse, are the preferred ones of God, alone worthy of the
kingdom of Heaven. Such a person, human and divine is the messiah in the later Qabbala. Even in the present Jewish Hasidaism
there is the *Zaddiq*, the pure and holy one; he is as in former Parseeism, the trusted friend and *confident* of the Deity, participating in
omnipotence! So became Zoroaster himself in later myth, such a
Yazata, the highest on earth, friend of Ahura, the highest in Heaven;
the vehicle of the revelations of Mazda and author of the Mazdayasnian religion and Law, God's *Spenta Manthra* or holy Word.

FRAVASHIS—THEIR PARALLELS.

Remnants of the hoary ancestor worship have left their traces
in the Avesta. The souls of the distinguished departed were imagined to continue their existence in heaven. These souls were
termed *Fravashi*. They were the genii of the past protecting the
present generations by their vigilance, their occasional warnings,
principally by the surplus and superabundance of merit which they
carried away from earth and kept in store ever available for their
living posterity. That idea and term, the over-merit of the ancestors,
available for the *short-comings* of the descendants, came from the
Parsees into the Synagogue and to the Church. It was not wanting in Greek and Roman conceptions, and is yet potent in our to-
day's notions of birth-aristocracy and blue blood. To such a feeling of pride and duty, of ancestral worth imposing severer tasks
upon the descendant, alludes Æneas, the Trojan prince, when he
pleads his imperious duty to abandon Dido, the Queen of Carthage,
and go in search of new dangers and of Italy. ([2]) The idea there is,
that Anchises had such a surplus of goodness that it came down to
his weak son who was now on the point of forgetting his glory for
the sake of love *for a woman.* This was the Fravashi of Anchises.

There is nevertheless this difference there: The Classic meritorious ancestor imposed upon the descendant superior duties, be-

---

1 See below on Abraham and Zoroaster.
2 Et nos fas extera querere regna,
Me patris Anchisæ, quoties humentibus umbris,
Nox operit terras, quoties astra ignea surgunt,
Admonet in somnis et turbida terret imago.
    (Virgil Aneis, liber IV., v. 530.)

cause "nobility obliges." The Parsee and Semitic one condoned with
the weakness of the offspring, since the ancestral over-merit came
good to him. Such Fravashis were always at hand to help a poor
sinner found wanting in the scales of the severe judge and on the
point to go to hell. This idea is often to be found in Jewish legendary and as Sekhuth Aboth, (¹) the surplus merits of the ancestors,
particularly of Abraham, Isaac and Jacob, the patriarchs, invoked in
daily prayer and on days of special import. Such a specially meritorious soul is called in Zoroasterism : *Fravashi.* The soul of Zoroaster was continually invoked in prayer by the pious Mazdayasnian
to come to his rescue and protect him against the wicked attempts
of the daevas. This great Fravashi-Soul of Zoroaster seems to me
to be the pattern of the legendary and mystic messiah-soul in
heaven, sheltered beneath the divine throne, ever ready to come
forth and deliver mankind from the clutches of Gog and Magog and
of the Anti-Christ. This latter one again is no other personage
than our Parsee genius of Evil, Angro Mainyu. Fire, too, was such
a protecting genius, we shall later see, against the Evil one, used on
critical occasions. In holy places, it was eternally kept up. It was
the chief cult of Parseeism. It was so with the Vestals in Rome
and the Druids in Gaul, etc. So in the Moriah Temple, ordained
Levit. 6. 6 : "An eternal fire shall burn there, never to be quenched."
The Parsee festivals, in parallel with the Sabbath of Genesis II. 2,
were instituted to remember the creation of the world, etc., by
Ahura, against Angro Mainyu, ever inculcating to be a Mazda-Yas-
nian, an opponent of the daevas, etc., and ever reminding that the
good creation is by Ahura. Ahriman's wicked creation had its full
corps of spirits and genii. They were called daevas, drukhs or
drughs, pairikas, led on by Angro Mainyu the angry spirit, the
wicked unholy one, or Gano-Mainyu, the smiting, destructive and
denying one. Their habitation was in hell, *Duzhaka* or *Acesta Ahu,*
the evil place. Darkness was there such that one could grasp it
with the hand. The death-angel, *Ahsto-Vidotus,* is one of them,
so is *Aeshma,* a specially wicked devil. The Hebrew *Azazel*(²),
the "satyr" of Greek mythology, is not mentioned by that name,
except perhaps the *Arezura,* which will be spoken of later.

BIRTH, DEATH, MENSES, AHRIMAN.

Women in their periodical sickness, the menstruation, are
under the influence and in imminent danger of the evil spirits.
Altogether that clumsy mode of human propagation is a device of

עְזָאזֵל 2 זכות אבות 1

Ahriman. Women in their menses must be separated from man's society (Vendidad XVI). Nor must they look to the sun, nor approach the fire ; that would be defilement to the holy light. That period lasts nine nights. A woman in child-bed is 41 days unclean. Her purification is with cow-urine and water. She is in special danger of the wicked daevas, and a lighted candle is the proper remedy recommended to her. In the same danger are the dead of the wicked drukhs. *Nasu* is the spirit of uncleanness, of dead persons. At once when death occurs he jumps upon his prey. There is an "*evil eye*" much to be dreaded.(¹) Light, or a chapter of the Avesta, renders it harmless. Later on when treating of the Vendidad, we shall show the above in their proper significance. According to the Avesta did Ahura create the pure universe in the course of 365 days, a Parsee year. He did his work successively. He selected a time when Angro Mainyu was careless or dissipated, and did not interfere with the good creation. Each kind of creation had its prototype or model in heaven. The first man and woman are called *Meshia* and *Meshiana*, in Genesis,(²) Ish, Isha.

SYMBOLIC VESTMENTS.

The Mazdayasnian or Mazda-believer must be distinguished by his dress. He continually wears a cap on his head, a *Sadder* or short wrap over the upper body with a pocket in it, the *Penum* over his face and the *Kosti* or girdle with four mystic knots. This is a parallel to the attire prescribed to the Jewish ritualist. He, too, wears the infallible skull-cap, the dress with the mystic fringes and the girdle around the waist.(³) The mystic pocket of the Parsee dress reminds of the breast-ornate(⁴) of the high-priest on Moriah. Little sleep is recommended; to watch the night or rise at least with the crow of the cock is meritorious. So do rise the Jewish and Christian pietists. Many times daily are prayers prescribed, and benedictions at any enjoyment. Before falling asleep, the pious shall recount his actions and say his prayers. Such, too, are for any and each human action. Especially are good deeds recommended. To wrong an animal is sin. Dogs were particularly recommended to man and holy to God. Most of these laws on purity, prayers, manners, etc., are in the *Vendidad*, the sole remnant of the 21 nosks or books of the ancient Avesta, of which later more. Then come the Vispered and the Yasna-ritual, meditations

---

1 עין הרע 2 איש אישה

3 See M. Fluegel's 'Religious Rites,' p. 39. 4 חושן המשפט

and hymns. Later were added the Bundehesh, systematizing and expounding the doctrines of the Avesta.

MAGIAN PRIESTS. FUTURE LIFE. PARADISE. HELL.

The priests belonged to a caste and claimed to be of one origin and family, as in the Pentateuch were the *Kohanim, Ahronids.* That caste was called the Magi, well known already to the classics. The Avesta knows not that name yet. Commonly, a priest is designated there as *hathara*, later as *mobed, herbad* and *destour* May be Magus meant originally : great, akin to magnus, grandee, noblenran, just as in Hebrew, Kohen meant nobleman, and but later became synonymous with priest. According to stray Aggadas, the tribe of Levi, of the twelve Israelitish clans, was distinguished from the brother tribes by superior freedom and education even in Egppt. The Ahronids, its noble family were later designated as Kohanim, noblemen, freemen ; and "*Kohen*" became the synonym of priest, religious teacher. Something akin to that were the Magi. First but a clan, later a priestly denomination. Chardin III. 130 Ed. Amsterdam, says : "Later *mobeds* interpret their name, Magus, as meaning : men without ears, claiming that their teacher, Zoroaster, learned all in heaven, not from men." Herodotus and Marcellinus say that the Magi were one of the six or seven tribes, originally inhabiting Media. They were a clan devoted to religion, as the tribe of Levi. Later they emigrated to other countries and gained those populations over to their own creed. Darmesteter believes even that *Magus* may originally have implied their foreign origin, hence something inimical. Later when naturalized, it may have become a title of honor and akin to priest, which originally it was not. Herodotus and Marcellinus claiming the Magians as one of the several Median tribes, make them a striking parallel to the clans of Levi and Ahron. The Avesta mentions three estates ; the first is called Hathara ; Warriors and Tillers come as II. and III. estates. Magus was simply a title, as in Hebrew Sar, Asura, Herr, Ahura and Magus corresponded thus to the contemporaneous Aramaic title : Rabbi, Rab. In Jerem. 39 : 3, we find both combined, *Rub-Mug.* Later on both came to designate priests exclusively.

The belief in a future life beyond the grave is old, yet it received but later its fuller developments. There is the life terrestrial and the life in the far future. This latter is not the life beyond the grave, after death, but a future period of bodily re-awakening and

existence on earth. In Yasna (34 : 8) is mentioned : " Those not
pure in thought, etc., are far from the good heavens. To Garo-
demana or nmana, the happy, holy heaven, Ahura Mazdao brings
those that are pious and wise. The place of the wicked is *Drukhs
demana,* "lieng house," in the later Zend-books. Hitherto come
and stay forever all the impure ones in thought, word and deed,
and those of a bad creed."—Such we find in Daniel([1]) alluded to
the resurrection, life hereafter and eternal hell." At that time
Michael will rise, the great lord, the genius of thy people. It will
be a time of anxiety and trouble. . . . Thy people will escape .
. . many of those sleeping in the dust will awaken ; some to
eternal life, and some to horror and eternal *darwon,* (hell). The
same is in Revelation XII. 7, etc.: *Michael fighting the dragon.*

KINVAD BRIDGE.

The bridge leading to paradise or heaven, and passing over
hell, is called Kinvad. Later Persian legend mentions it. It is the
bridge of judgment. The pure, the just and those of good faith
will pass it safely and enter heaven. The godless will fall, deep
below, into the precipice of hell, the abode of torment. There
stand Mithra and his colleagues and pass summary judgment over
the dead. If preponderantly good, they pass on to heaven ; if sin
has the surplus, they at once tumble down to hell. *"To fall into
hell," "Nophel le-Gehenim,"* is also the expression in Jewish and in
Christian legendary, no doubt borrowed from the same notion of
the bridge over it. As to the method of Mithra, that was prompt
and exact. According to later legendary, expounded further, this
expeditious judgment was rendered easy and close by the money-
scales used there ; viz.: Each sin and each merit had their exact
valuation in money. The debit and credit of the defendant were
thus exactly reckoned out to the cent and farthing, and the balance
struck. If it is in his favor, at once he goes to heaven; if not, he
drops into hell. But what of our *"Silver Question ?"* Poor Mithra
would be puzzled had it existed at his time. The souls of the pious
departed, the spoken of Fravashis, are protecting genii ; they, too,
make their appearance in later Persian literature. Earlier they are
termed *urvano,* souls, with the genetive, *ashaonam,* of the pure. As
in life, they continue fighting against the wicked, in untired array
against the prince of evil. They are the remnant of ancestor and
hero-worship, practiced at an earlier date. The four elements are
holy. Fire and earth are especially revered. Fire is the noblest

---

[1] XII. 1-3, דראון. So, too, Isaiah 66:24.

emblem of *Ahura Mczdco*. He is worshipped by kindling and keeping up eternal fires. One of the old hymns mentions: "In thy honor, we pray near the great fire," etc.

HOLY FIRES. THEIR PARALLELS.

The sole external cult of the Parsees consists in holy fires. Parsee or Persian has the original meaning of fire-worshipper. They did not worship fire, indeed, for its own sake, but as the most worthy symbol of the Supreme Deity. Possibly, etymologically, the word Ahura may, too, mean, *Light*, corresponding to the He-brew words: Or and Orah. We must remember that the worship of Light, in Magism, was no new invention there. It was derived from Brahmanism, or rather from their common religious source. Ahura may thus be akin to the Semitic word *Orah*, dating back to times when Arian and Semitic were yet one speech. Ahura may thus *mean especially*, God of Light. Zoroaster divided all existence into good and bad, pure and impure. That dualism he metaphorically and symbolically designated as light and darkness. Entire creation, bodies and minds, he thus subdivided in two halves, one of liight and one of darkness, effected respectively by the Holy Spirit and the unholy one. The cult consisted therefore in keeping up holy fires, to remember this leading distinction. Such fires were burning in the temples, on heights and in dwellings. Prayers were offered in presence of these fires. They were invoked as protecting genii, as the "son of Ahura." Priests were devoted to eternally and carefully entertain such with pure, best wood, several times daily, as the leading feature of the entire Parsee cult. I clip from the daily Press the following:

"*Temple of Zoroaster, Mecca of the Guebres, or Fire-Worship-pers of Asia.* For 2,500 years the Guebres, or fire worshippers of Asia, were in the habit of making pilgrimages to the celebrated temple of Zoroaster, their prophet. This holy shrine, although deserted by the Parsees, is still in existence. Formerly a flourishing monastery, it has come into the hands of the Russian Government, which preserves it as an interesting relic. It is situated in the mineral oil district of Baku, on the Caspian, and the religion to which it is dedicated seems to have taken its rise from the mystery of the hydro-carbon gas which impregnates the soil of the region and readily ignites. The temple as it is to-day, consists of a large, square courtyard, surrounded by small chambers, formerly the cells of the monks. The square tower in the centre, from the four corners of which flames ascended, was a crematorium, where the

remains of the faithful devotees were consumed, and a larger tower
was the residence of the chief priest, and inclosed a chapel cell,
where the eternal fires burned on rude stone altars."

That was by no means the crematorium for Parsee dead, for
the plain reason that Magians forbade cremation as the most heinous of crimes. But those fires may well have served as a fire-altar
for their worship, and later, by the ignorant, believed a crematory.
Nor would a Parsee priest take up his residence in such a proximity,
that was an abomination to him.

HOLY FIRES ON SABBATH AND MAGISM.

Thus originally, fire was the symbol of the Deity, and this is
idolatry! All idols never were more than symbols, at least to the
initiated, of course not to the masses. The reader will now remember and feel the import of the pregnant verse, Exodus 35: 3, "Ye
shall not kindle a fire in all your dwellings on the Sabbath day."
This verse the Talmud literally and cunningly interprets as prohibiting the kindling of fire on penalty of death or of stripes.(¹)
Now it may be the verse has a greater import: *it refers not to
kindling, but to entertaining* a fire on the Sabbath; viz.: Many
are the speculations about the real meaning and object of that
interesting verse. As the most plausible one, it is affirmed: That
in ancient times fire was the chief tool and means of work; hence
its emblem; and since the Mosaic Lawgiver rigidly prohibited all
such menial work, even preparing food on the Sabbath, he peremp-
torily forbade all kindling of fire. Now let me here suggest that, most
probably, there may be a deeper meaning hidden in the verse: It
was a practical protest, a public demonstration against the surrounding Parsees as fire worshippers. They used to kindle on their
Sabbaths for devotion specially bright fires at home, in temples and
on sacred hills, as the most becoming worship of the Deity and
pray not to, but in the very presence of such fires, the only divine
symbol allowed, all other forms of idols being prohibited.

NO SABBATH FIRES IN MOSAISM.

The Pentateuch, by such verses, took good care rigorously to
prohibit that idolatrous practice, to discredit the belief in the special
sanctity of fire, and practically to oppose the doctrine of Dualism,
of one God of light and another God of darkness. Mosaism
rigorously insisted on Monotheism and on harmonious creation;
the only One God created both light and darkness, the apparently
good and evil, the life and death, etc. Hence, there are no two

---

1 Iebamoth 6 b. and Sanhedrin.   הבערה ללוא יצתה דברי ר יסי ר נתן אימר לחלק.

creations, no special God of Light and God of Darkness; hence, no fire-temple, no fire-kindling and no praying in presence of holy flames; hence, the rigid prohibition: " Thou shalt not kindle a fire in all your dwellings on the Sabbath day," a day celebrated by the Parsees, too, especially by the renovation of their " eternal fires." How did Mosaism account for evil in the creation of a God, good and omnipotent ? God's creation has no evil. But man's freedom and the abuse of his freedom create it. Disobedience to the laws of nature and God, presumptuous curiosity, frivolity, reckless desires, ambition, crime, folly, ignorance. etc., create evil. Let us acknowledge that view is known to the Avesta, too, but it was not acted upon, it was an isolated view.—Practically, Zoroaster estab-lished his system upon the idea that originally there were two opposing principles, Good and Evil. According to Ovid—Meta-morphosae liber XV. v. 237–269, Pythagoras has correctly realized that in nature there is nothing bad and low. There is no life and no death, no birth and no decay, but all is constant change, each wave of existence is followed by another wave.([1])

PENTATEUCH AND AVESTA CONTRASTS.

The Pentateuch had especial cause to guard against exag-gerated idolatrous Parsee doctrines. For there run often strong parallel lines between both. The serpent in Paradise (Gen. III.), his seduction of Eve and Adam, the consequent entailment of death, loss of Eden and innocent happiness, the curse of the earth to produce " thistles and thorns ;" trouble, labor and disgrace for Adam ; menstruation and pregnancy, child-labors and subjection for Eve ; eternal war of both against the offspring of the Snake, Angro Mainyu, the principle of Evil—that is a Parsee parallel. A large section of the dietary and the ceremonious laws, the sending away of the *" kid of the leper "* in *Numbers*, of the scape-goat to *Azazel* (Levit. 16), the Red-heifer rite paralleled in the Persian " barashnum." certain " unclean " animals—of Ahriman's creation—and especially the innumerable enactments concerning menstrua-tion, birth, death and Levitical impurity, sprinkling with water and ashes, etc., all that is partly sanitary, but partly, too, in striking parallel with Parseeism. As often in history, the cause was removed, the effect remained. Dualism gave way to Monotneism,

1 " Nec species sua cuique manet, rerumque novatrix ex aliis alias reparat natura figuras, nec perit in tanto quidquam mundo . . . nascique vocatur, incipere esse aliud quamquod fuit ante, morique, desinere illud idem. . . .

but dualistic feelings and views remained. They are partly reflexes
of current Eastern popular opinions, remnants of polytheistic times,
accommodations and adaptations to surroundings. But as often,
such prescriptions are solid, sanitary, wise measures of public
hygiene, pervading both the Parsee and the Biblical Legislations.
To declare that all so-called, ceremonious, levitical, dietary, etc.,
Mosaic Laws, are mere remnants of ancient, vanquished, childish
views, is rash and unscientific. That is often but the mask for the
ignorance of the presumptuous critic. I conscientiously believe
that a good deal of such enactments have a solid basis in fact, and
are wise measures of purity, cleanliness, hygiene and chastity;
preventive of crime, sickness, irregularity and dissipation; measures grown out of the circumstances and surroundings; in part
superseded by, and in part in full consonance with, our times and with
human nature in general. In studying the ancient legislations and
meeting with such enactments, apparently "ludicrous and superstitious," let us not be hasty and fall in with that vulgar cry of " superstition !" but carefully weigh and ponder whether the lawgiver had
not weighty, cogent reasons for his statement, hidden behind a
customary, popular screen, but in reality aiming at some great
boon, physical or ethical, of society. In one word, I am not much
inclined to assume a great lawgiver to be either a fool or a knave.
So we shall later see the Vendidad prohibiting the throwing
about of pared nails and cut-off hair, as " creating devils and
harmful to the crops." In reality, it was a wise measure of
cleanliness and orderliness. So the Magian lawgiver recommended
as meritorious, intermarriage between near relations. The Mosaic
Legislator forbids it as an abomination. Was either motive superstition? No! Zoroaster, legislating for poor, rare, scattered clans,
declared it a great virtue to take care of a relation. Mosaism,
legislating for a comparatively dense population, wished to break
family egoism and clanishness, so it bade intermarriage of tribes and
deprecated "*incest.*" Hygienic and ethical causes besides are at the
bottom thereof, too. In one word, we must discriminate and try
to get at the hidden sense and the Spirit of Legislative commandments or prohibitions, not frivolously and hastily shout at superstition or priestly knavery.

TALMUD OPPOSING MAGISM.

The Pentateuch, as also the Prophets, contain many passages
that are intently aiming at contrasting Monotheism with Persian
Dualism. So is the Talmud, too. Indeed, the parallels and the

contrasts there to Magism are legion. We shall later treat of that
largely. Here we shall offer but one example of rabbinical, intentional opposition to Parsee doctrine, practice and views. At the
first glance the critical reader will recognize that that is a piece of
legislation intending to oppose Parseeism. Here is such a Mishna
and Gemara: "Whosoever prays: 'To a bird's nest, O God,
Thou extendest Thy mercy;' for the good Thy name shall be
thanked. 'We thank Thee, thank Thee! he shall be bid to hold
his tongue." The teachers now discuss this Mishna: "Who repeats:
'We thank Thee, thank Thee,' shall be interrupted because that
appears to acknowledge two divine powers (Ormazd and Ahriman).
The same who prays: "For the good Thy name shall be thanked,"
that sounds as if one God were the author of good and another
God (Ahriman) is the author of bad, whilst indeed we have learned:
"We must thank God for good and for bad, all being derived from
One God;" but when one prays: "Thy mercy reaches out to the
bird's nest," why should he be stopped? The rational answer is:
Because he intimates that the attribute of God is love, while that is
really justice, fitness. In Mazdaism, Jewish Mysticism, Gnosticism
and the Trinitarian Church, the claim is that there is a God of justice and another God of mercy. Our Mishna holds there is but
One God, embracing both and many more attributes. Many
examples that same passage quotes, where the official reader used
such phrases and others, reminding of Mazdayasnian tautology,
perhaps also of Gnostic one, and he ever was silenced by his
monotheistic superiors. The discussion concludes: "By no means
to allow any such phrase in the ritual which might imply a divine
plurality."([1]) So we read in Babli Sanhedrin, 38 a: "Let no one
say there are many powers in heaven." We read again there, page
46, b: "King Shapur asked R. Hama: Where does the Law
ordain burial in the earth? R. Hama remained silent. R. Aha
indignantly exclaimed: The world is delivered over unto fools!
He, R. Hama, should have quoted: "Thou shalt indeed bury
him" (v. M. XXI. 23) ([2]). King Shapur was the known restorer
of the Persian empire, in 226 P. C. Then the Parsee custom was in
full force, not to bury the dead but to have them devoured by
wild birds, in order not to defile the earth by a corpse. The
Jews had the custom of burial. Hence the controversy between
both; the question of the king: "Where does your law ordain

1 Berakhoth 33 b. חכרותא כלפי שמיא מי איכא

קבורה מן התורה מנין אשתיק. אימסר עלמא בידא דמסשאי 2

burial ?" the prudent silence of R. Hama and the indignant reply
of R. Aha; the Jews later had to endure bitter persecutions on
account of burial. Hence also the discussions among the Rabbis·
That passage quotes many more instances of burial in Sacred Writ.
But it concludes that it is but a *custom, minhag,* not a positive Law,
thus holding open the door for reconciliation with the Persian
masters.

FIRE-WORSHIP EVERYWHERE.

Remnants of fire-veneration, if not of worship, are to be found
among nearly all nations and sects, in all climes and regions, as
previously alluded to. That fire-worship, impersonated in god
Agni, is older than Magism. It pervaded its kindred religion,
Brahmanism. To all appearance have both inherited it from their
common religious parent, be it in their later seats, Iran and India, or
in their original ones, beyond the Hymalaian mountains from whence
they had emigrated. Fire-worship is of most hoary antiquity.
Agi, Ignis, was one of the supreme gods; and the kindling of holy
fires during worship was one of the leading rites of Brahmanism.
Hence, we find it in Zoroasterism, and gradually in nearly all the
other cults. At last it lost its character as a deity and assumed
that of a sacred symbol, emblematic of some spiritual idea, known
and utilized even in our own times and cults. So we read in the
first hymn of the Rig-Veda: "Agni, thou art worthy of the praises
of ancient and living poets." (Rig-Veda III. 120). Again: "I
have proclaimed, O Agni, these thy ancient songs. These great
libations have been made to him who showers benefits upon us: *the
sacred fire has been kept from generation to generation.*" So (Max
Mueller Sanscrit Literat. 492). " Then the sacred fire was kindled
by friction. It was lighted at the full moon and the new moon,
and likewise at each of the great natural divisions of the year." So
in R. V. III. 29, 10: " Sit, thou Agni, and make our prayers prosper.
This wood is thy mother every season." In the first hymn of the
II. (1, 9) Mandala, Agni receives the epithets of the very supreme
deity; he is called: " Ruler of the universe, lord of men, wise
king, father, brother and friend of men;" all the powers and names
of other gods are attributed to the god of fire. In other hymns he
is described more humanly: as the priest administering to the
sacrifices and rites. So in Reg-Veda VIII. II.: " Thou Agni art
the guardian of sacred rites; thou art to be praised at the sacrifices
and the festivals. Like a charioteer, thou carriest the offerings to
the gods. Fight and drive away the fiends, the ungodly enemies."

Thus we find that the kindling of fires was a leading ceremony on New-Moons and holy seasons. The offering of wood was considered as a sacred sacrifice. So it was in the Talmud, offered to the ever-burning fire on the Altar of the Moriah Temple. The prescriptions there are very minute. The Hindoo priests considered it as propitious to prayer. It was called forth by friction, and was originally the only fire kept up in the community for the benefit of every household. Hence, its importance and its sanctity, for in primeval times men worshipped everything that was beneficial to them. Fire is no doubt the greatest benefactor of men, hence it was considered a great deity, and the kindling of fire a sacred ceremony. That kindling done by friction of dry wood or flint is also expressly mentioned by Virgil in the Aneid, etc. The vestals in the Roman and Greek world kept up such eternal, holy fires. The leading temples of antiquity had an altar with eternal fire. Such had the Druids in Gaul and Britain. Such burned in the holy groves of Germany. Such a fire flamed on the altar of the Tabernacle and the Moriah-Temple. "An eternal fire shall burn on the altar, never to be extinguished." (Levit. VI. 6). God appeared in *Burning bush*, and on the *flaming* Sinai. He is a *consuming fire*, (II. M. iii. 2– xix. 18–V. M. 4:24–18:3–Is. xxix. 6–xxx. 30–xxxiii, 14, etc. Such was the fire-censor carried by Aaron in the wilderness to drive away the raging pestilence from the camp, that " stood between the dead and the living and stopped the plague." (4 M. XVII. 11). Such was the fire-censor swung daily in that ancient Moriah-Temple. Such burnt on the golden chandelier before the holy screen, *Parocheth.* (¹). Such was the fire-vase brought into the Holy of Holies on the atonement day by the officiating high-priest. It was the very central act performed on that solemn occasion, with his most solemn supplication, to bring down from the Deity forgiveness and reconciliation. That fire is continued now in the *Eternal Lamp*(²), *Ner Tamid*, in the Synagogue of to-day, in the church and the mosque of to-day, just as in the Parsee temples at Bombay and Guszerate. The many other holy usages of fire and light to-day, the tapers in day-time in Church and Synagogue ; the use of a lighted candle in the house of mourning, at child-birth, at wedding ceremonies, at festivals, public, judiciary oaths and many other solemn occasions among all sects and creeds, proves the tenacity of the instinctive belief that light is beneficent and holy. We must not forget primi-

מנורה פרכת 2   נר תמיד 1

tive times. Fire was indeed the greatest benefactor of man. Without fire, man would be yet a brute, at the mercy of the elements
and the beasts of prey. To keep up fire, ready for use, was in
hoary times no doubt the first care of society. It was kept up as
the dearest treasure of the community. They had no matches nor
electric wires to strike fire at will. It was therefore kept up in one
public place, in the temple, ready for all; guarded by the magis-
trate, the priest, on the altar. Thus utility and veneration were
linked together in the mind of the people, light and holiness as
identical, remained a kind of category, a standard idea of primitive
man. Therefore, was Light accepted as the noblest emblem of the
Deity, calling forth holy thoughts, earnestness and solemnity;
striking terror and inspiring awe, discarding frivolity, bringing cheer
to the despondent, calling forth to human mind the thought of
divine presence, of deity on earth, its earthly image, the mystic
Schechinah. From Zoroaster to Moses, from Ezekiel to the humblest worshipper of to-day, wishing to picture to himself the Divine
Presence, the pious will realize it under the emblem of a "bush in
flames—ever burning and never consumed." (Exod. III. 4). One
may say that is idolatrous, heathen, foolish, sacriligious; vain sen-
timentalism! It is human, it is effective, solemn and worshipful.
The fancy, the heart, the animal man needs such crutches to uplift
himself to the presence of the Delty. Hence, all churches and
lawgivers have used emblems of the divine and will continue so.
It is a *category* of the human mind. True,(¹) Herodotus claims the
Persians had no temples; true, fanes were not so important there as
in other creeds; but they had, at any rate, places of worship where
the holy fires were ever flaming.

PARSEE TEMPLES AND WORSHIP.

Such temples are mentioned by the Arabian Scharastani, and
affirmed to be older than Zoroaster. Firdosi mentions such shrines
as a matter of course. The most celebrated temple of that kind,
often mentioned in *Shah-name*, is *Azar Gushasp*, not far from Balkh.
The name of such houses of worship *Jzesne Khane*, *Yasne*-house,
house of celebrating prayers, the *Yasne*. None are allowed to enter
there except the priests and their assistants; there burns the holy
fire. It is the sole emblem of the deity in their Holy of Holies.
Two Mobeds, ministers, are ever guarding that sacred flame, bringing wood to it five times daily, never allowing it to be quenched,
having their mouth and face carefully covered with the *Penom*, a

---

¹ See Fr. Spiegel, II. Vol. p. 64.

kind of veil or mask and their hands muffled up in sacks to guard against all defilement. They pray ever with their faces turned towards that fire and the sun, and no shoes on their feet. So the Jewish priest had his head covered; no shoes on; his face turned towards the holy of holies, veiled face and bare feet being the sign of solemnity. ([1])

VESSELS OF FIRE-CULT. ANALOGIES.

The leading sacred objects and pharaphernalia of the cult, are the holy fire-flame, symbol of the Light of Ahura, the only visible cult-object and the *Baresma*, bundle or branch of green twigs, emblem of opposition to Evil, Light and Darkness being the two principles of Parseeism. There are further some more utensils for the performançe of the cult of that worship, viz: The *Atashdan*, fire-vase. It is in the form of our pottery or marble flower-holders in parks and gardens, a large pot of brass, broad above, slowly narrowing down below with a foot as in a goblet. It is filled with ashes, the burning coals on the top and incense lit in the flames. That vessel stands upon a stone pedestal called: *Adosht.* The cleansing of that stone is one of the most holy ministrations reserved for the priests. A great deal of legend clusters around that stone. It is believed to be the foundation and rock of the world. So used the high priest of the II. Jewish Temple, bringing the fire-pan, on the Atonement, into the Holy of Holies, to place it upon the stone in its midst, pour the incense thereon and pronounce his prayer; that stone was called "Eben Shethia,"([2]) and "considered the center of the earth" by priests and laity. So in the principal mosque now, at Jerusalem, such a rock forms its center and is revered as the one of Isaac's sacrifice and the "*center of the world.*" That hyperbolical figure of speech is easily explained. In the Parsee cult as in the Mosaic one, that was the center and leading feature of worship, and worship was the great business of Jew and Parsee, hence its import. Whether the words *Adosht* and *Shethia* have not a kindred sense, philology may determine. *Shethia* in Hebrew means undoubtedly foundation; and both, Parsee and Hebrew legendary, claim those stones as the corner-stones of the universe. An apparently kindred and similar word: Ashdoth, ([3]) is often mentioned in Sacred Writ and may everywhere mean a hill, ridge, rock, where such Heathen fire-cults were kept up, for we have seen, that such forms of worship

1 See my 'Religious Rites,' p. 12, 27, 35, etc.

2 אבן שתיה as חבור הארץ

3 אשרות הפסגה Deut. III. 17, IV. 49, Joshua XII. 3, XIII. 2, etc.

have been universal and not confined to the Parsees. With them it was the unique mode of cult; with others it stood side by side with more idolatrous practices; that may have been all the difference. The Baresma or Barsemon, was a green twig chiefly from palm or date trees. It was cut with great ceremony by the priests. Such was the "mistletoe" cut down by the Druid priests on Yule festival. In the synagogue, the palm-tree-branch occupies that place. But the Pentateuch took care that it never obtained any idolatrous import akin to the Persian baresma which, there, was almost divinized. This Baresmon symbolized the battle of the Mazdayasnian against wicked Ahriman. I believe that the striking of the "*hoshanoth*" or branch of twigs on the last day of Booth at the Synagogue, and perhaps the shaking of the palm-tree-branch, (lulab,) during the entire Booth festival, may have some kinship with the use of the Baresmon in the Parsee-cult, viz: "to drive away the evil spirits." Such hints are thrown out by some Aggadas; whilst oftener it is claimed to symbolize the divine omnipresence.(¹) Besides there were several vessels for administering the Haomo-rite; the *Lavan*, a mortar to grind that plant; the *Tali*, a plate for the flowers and fruit of the offering; the *tasta*, a cup of gold with nine holes for pressing out the juice of the *haomo*; a bottle for the milk of the *offering and many minor utensils and ingredients for that* fire and haoma Cult.

HAOMA AND DRAONA. MAZZA EUCHARIST. PYTHAGORES

We have seen that the fire-cult symbolized the worship of the God of Light, principle of Good, Ahura Mazda. Now the leading sacrifices offered are the *Draona's* and *Haomo*. The first were small, round, flat, white flour-cakes, of the size of a dollar. These cakes are called. *Draona, darun.* Such are offered on frequent occasions, eaten by the priests with the solemn benediction: "I am ready to eat this at the command of Ahura." Some are in the shape of the sun; and some of the moon. On some special occasions, a slice of meat is added to the cake. As a rule, Parseeism does not allow any bloody sacrifices. Later on when men were generally eating meat, an animal was slaughtered with a benediction, by a special man and a slice was offered to the deity. Originally flesh-meat was forbidden. So Pythagoras deprecated on Parsee principles, the use of flesh for human food. He rediculed the idea that the gods relished bloody sacrifices. So Ovid *Metamorphoses liber. XV.* v.

---

1 See my ' Thoughts on Religious Rites," p. 36.

110: ([1]) With these draonas was offered a sacrificial beverage. It is the Haoma. It is identical with the Hindoo *Soma*. The white haoma is a fabulous herb, growing in the fabulous lake Vurukasha, conferring immortality, as mythological *nectar* does. The real Parsee Haoma is yellow, growing on the summit of mountains, known already to Plutarch and well-described by *Anquetil Duperron*, as found near Yezd in Kirman. A certain kind of it is searched for and culled under solemn ceremonies. From that plant, the juice is pressed out, called *Para-haoma*, and drunk by the priest with certain ceremonies. That juice is semi-intoxicating. Closely looking at that Draona and Haoma-offering, we are strongly tempted to take it as the Parsee version of the Hebrew Passover cake, the " Show-bread," the " Aphikoman," and the sacred " wine-cups." It is the version of the Christian " mass," hostia and eucharist.([2]) Both haoma and draona are imagined to be things and offerings, as also divinities, deities hidden in bread and drink, much akin to the mystical *"Real Presence "* in the church!—Thus have we seen that a large number of religious forms and ideas are common to Parsee and Biblical systems, Jewish, Christian and Mohammedan branches. A greater number yet might be added. The Pentateuch, therefore, had to be on its guard concerning forms and ideas that are downright idolatrous. It therefore, entrenched itself behind many *bulwarks*, against Parsee doctrines of which we shall speak soon. So, too, it stated emphatically: " Ye shall not kindle a fire on the Sabbath-day in all your dwellings," private or public. The lawgiver knowing that many forms of cult in Bible and Mazdaism are common to both, he, the more rigorously set his face against its many remnants of rank idolatry; hence, his prohibition of Sabbath-fires. Showing in these pages such striking similarities between ideas and forms of the modern religious systems, the intention is not to desecrate them, but on the contrary to render them more venerable by showing their universality and therefore our duty of broad toleration.

---

1 Nec satis est quod tale uefas committetur, ipsos, Inscripsere deos sceleri, numenque supernum. Caede laboriferi credunt gaudere juvenci. Victima labe carens et præstantissima forma (Nam placcuisse nocet) vittis insignis et auro, Sistitur aute aras, auditque ignara precantem, Imponiqui suæ videt inter cornua fronti. Quas coluit, fruges, percussaque sanguine cultros. Inficit in liquida prævisos forsitan unda. Protinus ereptas viventi pectore fibras Inspiciunt, mentesque deum scrutantur in illis.

2 See my ' Messiah Ideal,' vol. 1, p. 55, etc.

CHAPTER III.

ISAIAH ON MONOTHEISM AND PARSEEISM.

Isaiah (the second) frequently alludes to Parsee views and doctrines, sometimes approvingly and sometimes disapprovingly. Is.
45–46 is especially of that nature. The prophet of the exile an-
nounces the advent of Cyrus of Persia, with great rejoicing and
hopefulness. No doubt that the leading features of Zoroasterism
were established long before the dynasty of the Achaemenides.
Because in that chapter, the prophet alludes, as long established
things, to both, the great affinities and the discrepancies of Zoroasterism and Mosaism, of pure monotheism and qualified dualism of
the Parsees. There were great and striking affinities between the
two systems, yet no identity. The Persians conquoring Media,
Babel and Assyria, Bactria, Syria, Egypt, etc., may have yielded in
some points, yet on the whole, they have brought about for the conquered a purification of worship, less idolatry and more exalted
ideas about Deity, One God, Ahura, Spiritual, Eternal and Sole
Creator, no images, few temples or none, no human sacrifices, one
human race, little of castes, one duty and one right for all. With a
higher God-idea, the Persians brought no doubt a purer morality.
On the whole they were nearest to Mosaism among the nations then
extant; hence their salient sympathy towards Israel, their lack of
jealousy, their assistance towards a reconstruction of the Hebrew
nationality, as a strong bulwark against the idolatrous Assyrians,
Egyptians, etc. This alone explains the reason, why broken Judaea
found such powerful patrons among the Persians; why it clung to
them to the very last of their fortunes. With all that was the Persian dualism strongly clashing with monotheistic, prophetic Moasism.
At first it taught two supreme principles with two creations; that of
Good and that of Evil, instead of one God and one creation. It is
not impossible that the II. Isaiah, so often inveighing against dualism, alludes distinctly to the Persian Ahriman. He says (Chapt.
42: 6–8): "I, *Ihvh*, have called thee and made thee, O Israel, a
light to the nations, . . . to open the eyes of the blind and release
the imprisoned ones from the dungeon, those dwelling in darkness.
Ihvh is my name, and to '*Aher*' I shall not yield my honor, nor
my glory to the idols," (Persian and Babylonian). The usual
translation is: "and to another" (Aher). But it may well be a
verbal equivocation, a hit upon *Ahriman*, whose by-names were

Ughra, Aghra, Aghar, *Aher*, etc., as will be seen below. To the
Persian belief in the principle of darkness, the prophet may sarcastically allude by : " To release those imprisoned, from their dungeon," " the dwellers of darkness."(¹) Alluding to this *Aher* in
Isaiah, the Talmudists call Elisha ben Abuja "*Aher*," since he held
to dualism.(²) Next, the Persian dualism embodied a long crowd
of subordinate deities, perhaps not seriously meant, but popularly
idolatrous, genii associated with the Supreme Deity. Apparently
it boasted of allowing no idols ; only few sacrifices, no human, and
hardly any animal bloody, offerings. Yet really it had the fire-cult,
Mithra, the "*Sun chariot with horses*," and a whole mythology of
gods and idols. The Parsee morality, no doubt, was infinitely
purer than elsewhere, indeed purity and cleanliness in body and
soul, or as the Avesta expresses it : " Purity in thought, word and
deed," was the essence of their ethics. The system represented
the highest evolution of ancient Polytheism. It was a strong reform
and a decided gain over Greek and Hindoo Asian sensualism and
worship of beauty. Yet it was not entirely beyond it. It was but
a refined, vast, mythic allegory. The coarser mythological element
was eliminated, not so its more hidden errors and sores. They
were the nearest to, still not identical with Mosaism. Indeed, soon
idol-worship crept in again. This position towards prophetic
Mosaism is expressed in Is. 45, etc., " Thus speaks Ihvh to Cyrus,
whom I have taken hold of by his right hand, and before whom I
have weakened the loins of kings, submitted nations to him and burst
open their bolts and gates . . . I shall walk before thee. I shall
demolish and nivelate to the ground their fortresses, break down
their gates and yield to thee their hidden treasures . . . That thou
shalt learn that I, Ihvh, have called thee by name . . . for the sake
of my servant Jacob and on behalf of Israel, my chosen one. I
have called thee by name, I have established thee,(³) though thou
knowest me not : I am the Supreme Being (Ihvh). There are no
other gods besides me. I have armed thee, and thou dost not
know me . . . That they shall all know, from the rise of the sun
to his setting that there is none besides me. I am Ihvh, there is no
other Power, (Evil, Angro Mainyu). I have *formed the light and
created the darkness. I make for peace and create the (apparently)*

לחוצא ממסגיר אסיר, מבית כלא יושבי חושך 1

(Isaiah 42;6 8.)   אני ח' וכבודי לאחר לא אתן

(Bab. Hagiga 14 a, etc.)   אחר קיצץ בנטיות. שתי רשיות הן

  ₃ Or I denominated thee אכנך

evil. I, Ihvh, have made all. The dew from heaven, the fruit of the earth, justice and salvation, I, Ihvh, have created them all, (not the Ameshas Spentas, etc., etc., the assistants and peers of Ahura Mazda). Woe to the clay opposing its maker. Woe to the creature rebelling against its creator, (alluding to the antagonism of Ahriman in the Parsee dualism). Thus spake Ihvh, the holy One of Israel. You question my creation? I have made the earth and man upon it I have called forth; I have created the heavens and all their hosts. I have bidden all. (Not the myriads of genii or creative types and patrons pervading the Parsee Olympus, where each kind of being, from the fly to the mounts, suns and stars, each concrete thing or abstract idea claimed to have its celestial type, its protecting genius or god in heaven). Even so, I have awakened him, Cyrus—I shall make even his path. He will build my city and free my captives, without ransom or price. Thus spake Ihvh, Lord of the universe." . . . The chapter goes on setting forth the coarse myths and follies of the idolators of Egypt and Ethiopia, of Assyria, Babel, etc., just as the more refined idolatry of Persia. It closes with the superiority of Israel's Monotheism (45: 20): "Gather around and let us be confronted, ye remnants of nations. You, carrying your wooden idols, invoking gods that cannot help. . . . Who has announced that from time immemorial, who but I, Ihvh, the only One; besides me there is no saviour. Behold Baal and Nebo, they are wandering into exile."

THE SEVERAL CREDOES.

The credo of Israel, that word to which the faithful are bound from the cradle to the grave, appears, also, to be intended emphatically to confess Monotheism and to protest against the [dualistic Mazdaism. Zoroaster (Gathas) affirms that from the beginning of existence there were Two Principles in the universe. The Avesta teaches that from the dawn of Creation the universe split into two dominions, two opposing principles, one supreme in the creation of Light and the other supreme in the creation of Darkness. It thus breaks the all of existence into two halves, in eternal deadly antagonism to each other. It posits that all human goodness is resumed in man's honest struggle against the principle of Evil. The Pentateuch, therefore, as the prophets, teach with all solemnity and emphasis, and with a great display of circumstantiality, the unity of Deity and the harmony of creation. This is the great Credo: "Hear, O Israel; Ihvh is our God, Ihvh is one." (Deut. 6: 4). This Credo is expressly instituted as the motto of Mosaism. It is

the Credo and the dividing line of Mosaism, in contradistinction
from Polytheism and Mazdaism; in place of the many gods, the
ancestor and hero-worship, the star-worship, the sun-worship, the
physical nature-worship, the Assyrian, Babylonian and Egyptian
triads and the *dualistic Parseeism* in special. The first were simply
force and body-cult. Parseeism was an approach to spirit-worship,
yet splitting the universe in two, from an imperfect understanding
of the natural phenomena. Prophetism, better grasping the perfect
harmony of the universe, correctly postulated the unity of the
divine plan and the object of existence. It, therefore, formulated
its Credo: " God is the Eternal Being, and Being is one." From
the Monotheistic Credo Christianism derived its own leading
formula. It adopted the *God-One* Symbol with its own mystic
development, viz: the One God under three aspects, as were all the
triads of those times, inclusive of the Philonian : The Unknowable
God-father, the Logos-Son and the Holy Spirit, viz: the spirit
of prophecy or communion with men; the Persian Holy Ghost
epithet of Ahura ; the Greek Theos Demiurgos, and the emanated
universe, the created world. Even so Mohammedanism. It adopted
the Hebrew Credo, God-One, with its own variation : " There is
but one God (not trinity or plurality) and Mohammed is his last
Prophet, (Jesus and Moses being abrogated); He is Messiah.
Those different views on existence and its cause, pantheism, polytheism, dualism and Monotheism were not accidental and arbitrary.
Nothing is accidental in the universe of matter or mind. Pantheism and polytheism were the rudimentary views of the poetic youth
of man. As many forces and bodies as there are, so many free
agents or gods. Riper manhood grouped and reduced the number
of free forces. It reduced them from pantheism to a few supreme
powers. Mazdaism made then the great step of reducing polytheism to dualism : Two supreme powers explain all existence with its
conflicts. Mosaism and prophetism made the further advance in
showing that the two powers are inadequate, and that one Supreme
Intelligence answers best the phenomenon of the universe and of
history. Thus there is a logical sequence in these diverse views
of the world's religions.

ZRVANA AKARANA AND DUALISM.

There is in Parseeism, no doubt, a great monotheistic phase.
Professor Max Mueller, in his recent researches on Hindoo thought,
showed there the dawn of monotheism. This is expressed in two
different ways. One is : **Ahura Mazda is the One and only God,**

but, from the begin, he created two subordinate deities, of Good
and of Evil. The other mode is: From all eternity there existed one
Supreme *Zrvana Akarana*, Eternal Time and endless Space; in his
attributes he is akin to the Greek *Fate*—before whom even *Zeus*
and Olympos tremble. At the rise of the universe out of Chaos, a
differentiation took place. The neutral Chaos split into two distinct
worlds. One was created by Ahura Mazda the God of Light, the
other by Angro Mainyu, God of Darkness. When twelve thousand
or nine thousand years of their simultaneous rule will close, the
latter will be vanquished and thrown into hell, and Ahura alone
will rule supreme. Jewish and Christian mystics borrowed, consciously or not, from such views. It is usually assumed that the
Zrvana-system is of later date, when the Zoroastrians tried to
simplify their dualism and bring it nearer to Monotheism, as the
present Hindoo-Parsees do. It is not entirely impossible that the
Zrvana-doctrine is older, akin to the Ihvhistic one (Gen. 4 : 26),
but limited to a few priests. It may have long been the lucid kernel
of hoary mythology and nature-worship, which, ostensibly pantheistic, have Monotheism as their nucleus. It supplies a necessary
link in the development of original religious thought. Dualism
must have sprung from pantheistic unity, *Zrvana*, as Greek Polytheism did from ancient grim *fate* and absolute, inexorable necessity.

PARSEE IDEAL OF VIRTUE.

The earth is especially holy; her patron and her name is Armaiti. She must be kept in purity, without any defilement. There
was not to be allowed on her bosom any graves, scattered dead
limbs, morasses, stagnant water, useless debris, increase of obnoxious animals, insects, vermin, etc. To kill such *"Kharafstras"* is
virtue, a sacred duty of the pious; it atones for sins: the *baresma*
or bundle of rods in the hand of the Magian priests symbolized that
duty. Another of man's most sacred duties is tilling, cultivating and
increasing the arable land, hedging it in and rendering it useful to his
species, by irrigation, culture of trees, etc. Between the Good
Spirit and the Evil One there is ever waged a war of life and death.
Such a war, too, is going on between the worshippers of the two
great Opponents. The duty of the servants of Ormazd is to keep
pure in thought, word and deed and to fight Evil in any shape. To
kill the worshippers of Ahriman, obnoxious beasts, snakes and insects, to dig wells, render rivers navigable, drain swamps and morasses, fill up pits, build bridges, clear woods, etc., that is virtue.

To tell lies, practice fraud, commit murder, adultery, theft, etc.,
that is worship of the Evil Spirit. The Avesta Laws and Ethics are
couched in metaphorical and mythic language, peculiar to those
times and surroundings. But their hidden kernel proves a high degree of rationality and goodness. Here are a few specimens:

PATET QOD—CONFESSION.

(From Khorda Avesta after Spiegel and Bleek:) "I praise the
good thoughts, words and works. I curse the wicked thoughts,
words and works. I praise the best purity, I chase away the Devs.
I confess myself a Mazdayasnian, a follower of Zertusht, an opponent of the Devs; devoted to the faith in Ormazd. Of all manners
of wrong whereby men become sinners and go to hell, I repent with
thoughts, words and works. Pardon!" . . . Such short specimens
of devotion seem to have been in the daily use of the Parsee. They
combined both profession of faith, deprecation and confession of sin
and promise of improvement. They are couched in mythic, sectarian language. But their sense is plain and sound. The confessor
deprecates the bad and devotes to good. A standing phrase in
Avestian religious terminology is: *"In thoughts, words and deeds."*
It is very remarkable that this phrase is expressly used in the Hebrew confessions on similar occasions. The Atonement Confessions
contain literally that sentence and in the same place: Pardon all
sins, transgressions and rebellions committed in "thought, word
and deed." [1]

CONFESSION OF THE PARSEE.

"My sins which I have committed against father, mother, sister,
brother, wife, child, relation, friend . . if I have broken the whis-
pered prayer, or eaten without prayer ; if I have gone without *Kosti*,
or defiled my feet, or practiced deceit, contempt, idol-worship, told
lies, etc.—I repent with *patet*. Pardon!"

JEWISH CONFESSION.

"Thou God knowest all secrets ; Thou searchest the mysteries
of the heart, nothing is hidden from Thee. May it please Thee to
pardon my sins, transgressions and rebellions. . . . Sins committed
with or without freedom of will ; sins of hard-heartedness, ignorance,
inchastity, fraud, deceit, over-reaching, disrespect of parents and
teachers, sin of violence, blasphemy, impure speech, lying, bribery,
dishonest dealings, immoderate drinking and eating ; sins of usury
and illicit gain, pride, idle talk, hood-winking, impudence, shirking
of duty, simulated love, envy, frivolousness, obstinacy, tale-bearing,

---

1 בין במחשבת, בין בדיבור, בין במעשה   .

perjury, dishonesty . . . and all other sins, pardon, forgive and wipe
off, O God of forgiveness." (from the Atonement "*Al het*" Prayer.)
The prayer-books of all other modern creeds will furnish like specimens. Jewish fervent and tender prayers of confession, etc., are
those destined for the Ten days of repentance before the Atonement
day,(1) and those for Mondays and Thursdays.(2) But most thrilling is the daily confession of sin and the prayer for political and
social redemption : (3) " Pity and mercy ! I have sinned, God miser-
icordious ! Have pity upon me and receive my devotions. Do not
punish me in thine anger, grant me mercy, for I am weak, do for
thy mercy's sake.(4) . . . . Lord, God of Israel, forego thine ire and
consider the evil fate of thy people. Look down from on high
and see : We have become the laughter and scoffing of nations ;
doomed, like sheep to the slaughter, the object of derision, maltreat-
ment, ruin and death. The barbarians say : There is no hope for
them. Be Thou gracious to the nation hoping in thy name. Pure
One, hasten our redemption. Protect us in thy mercy. God deliver us not into the hands of those tyrants. They scoff : " Where
is their God !"—Withal we have not forgotten Thy name. God remember us ! Listen to our plaints. Forsake us not to the power
of our enemies blotting out our name. We are but few now,
nevertheless we remember thy name ; O God forget us not !"—Thus
prayed Israel of yore and recently, too, in the East ; thrilling to the
utmost !

PARSEE CONFESSION OF FAITH.

"I believe in the purity of the good Mazdayasnian faith, in the Creator Ormazd, in the Amshaspands, in the furthering of righteousness,
in the resurrection of the new body . . . As Ormazd has imparted it to
Zertusht, his successors and the Desturs have brought it down to us."
Here we have a model of the Credo. Mark also : " Written Law "
and "traditional Law " as among the Rabbis of the Talmud. It is
not easy to determine when the above passage of the Khorda-Avesta has been composed. It was surely, at any rate, long before the
Gemara ; perhaps even before the Mishna—hence then already the
Zoroasterians distinguished between written and traditional laws.
That no doubt, is interesting in the extreme. It runs in line with
the Talmudical Halachath of Moses from Sinai.(5) Let us quote
here a parallel to that Persian profession of faith, vaguely ascribed to
Maimonides and commonly called " *The 13 principles,*"(6) to be re-

1 אבנו מלכנו 2 והוא רחום 3 רחום וחנין 4 Ps. 6, and prayer-book.
5 הלכה למשה מסיני 6 שלשה עשרה עקרים and אני מאמין

cited daily after the prayers: " I believe with perfect faith that the Creator, His name be blessed, creates and rules all creatures, He alone is the Maker in the past, present and future. I believe in perfect faith that the Creator is One, the Only One without any comparison. He alone is God in the past, present and future; He is incorporeal, incomprehensible by any bodily being and without any comparison; He is the first and the last; He, alone is to be worshipped and none besides Him." Follows next the faith in the prophets and in Moses as teacher and the greatest prophet; in the Thorah as coming from him; never to be changed nor substituted; the omniscience of God; reward and punishment for good and evil; the coming of the messiah and the resurrection." Closely examining this Credo or declaration of faith of the Talmudic Israelite, we find that it originated as a protest against Mazdaism. But more, we at once see it contains elements and verses of olden date and of more recent date. Part of its verses are ostensibly directed against ancient polytheism and against Mazdean dualism; part is against trinitarian and Mohammedan claims; and part even against modern infidelity of " The higher criticism." It states: " I believe with perfect faith that the Pentateuch as now in our hands, is identical with the one given to Moses, our teacher." It rejects both, Christology and Mohammed's supreme prophecy, but declares its firm belief that the messiah will come. It emphasizes the Unity and uncorporeality of God, and confirms the belief in resurrection, as in Mazdaism, Christianity and Mohammedanism. It might well be said of it that it represents rather a religious mosaic than the Mosaic religion. Some elements of that Credo must be very old as in opposition to hoary Parseeism, and some very young, deprecating, modern infidelity and rash conclusions.

KHORDA AVESTA CONTINUED.

"I have this *patet* as an atonement for sins. I have a share in the reward for good deeds, joy for the soul, to close for me the way to hell and open for me the road to paradise." The mentioned, well known, Hebrew profession of faith and the confession of sins on the Atonement day, "Ani mamin" and "Al-het," may well have taken their models from such instances, conception and expression are strikingly alike, but differently executed, according to the theologies and morals of the respective creeds and nations. There was here no plagiarism, no servile imitation. The parties borrowed and rejected consciously, with eyes wide awake. The Credo was a need of the times; each party formulated it according to its own genius and conform to its doctrines. Each Credo represented its partial adhesion and partial opposition to its neighbor-Creed, corroborating what it accepted and contrasting what it repudiated.

SPECIALLY AND TYPICALLY PARSEE.

"If I have sinned against any kind of cattle, if I have beaten it, slain it wrongfully, given it no fodder, no water, or castrated it, not protected it from robber and wolf, I repent . . . of all kinds of sins, theft, lies, false witness, pride, thanklessness, revenge, envy, wilfulness, spiteful hostility to Yazatas (disrespect to the priests), inchastity, intercourse with menstruous women, adultery, walking with one shoe, going without the Kosti (girdle), neglect of prayer, enjoyment without the proper benediction . . . if I have made water standing upright . . . if I have honored the Devs. etc. I repent." It is not allowed to have any sort of enjoyment, bodily or mental, even satisfying the natural necessities, without giving a benediction to Ahura. Just the same is the case with Hebrew moralists and casuists. Their standing maxim is: "A man owes a hundred benedictions daily to his maker." Such benedictions in the customary three to five daily standing devotions, with grace at meals, minor enjoyments, religious duties, natural needs, etc., made up the full hundred. Magian and Rabbi could truly say: " Ye shall be unto me a kingdom of priests and a holy nation." As to the Devs or Daevas they were, according to Haug, the old gods of the Eranians and Hindoos, and after Zoroaster's reformation they were declared devils and degraded to hell. Just so were the Greek gods after the rise of Christianity. The people continuing to believe in them, the priests had to declare them Evil spirits; history repeats itself.

PRACTICAL VIRTUE.

Vendidad farg. III. 76. "Who rejoiceth the earth with the greatest of joy? He who fills up holes, cultivates the fruit of trees and grass on the fields, provideth for water, tills the ground, etc.—He promotes the Mazdayasnian Law . . . When there are thick ears of corn, then the Daevas fly." This remarkable paragraph shows the lawgiver as by no means befogged with the notions of spirits and drughs, but simply using the popular language better to impress his hearers. Virtue is simply to do good, to be useful to his fellow-men, to create things for their comforts. Such a man is pleasing to God. " Where there is plenty the devil flies." Viz: temptation loses its opportunity. It is excellent, common sense popularly expressed: or, as the Talmud has it: " The law speaks in human language."

DEFILEMENT.

"Creator! If one buries in the earth dead dogs or dead men and does not dig them up and remove them . . . what is his punishment? Five hundred blows!" (Ibidem.) After man, is the dog the holiest creature and his dead body defiles the holy earth. A grave contaminates the soil. The Magian custom was that the dead were exposed to be devoured by carnivorous beasts and birds. The dog, the companion of the Persian shepherd and farmer, plays an important part in the Avesta. He is a good omen for man in life and in death. A four-eyed dog (?) or a two eyed one with yellow ears, or at least with two spots above the eyes, was brought into the room where the dead was. The dog looked into his face. The ceremony was called "*Sag-did,*" and by this look the evil spirit *Nasu,* who was about taking hold of the corpse, was frightened away to hell. Apparently this was a remnant from aboriginal times when the faithful dog was man's keeper and screened him even in death from the devil, his enemy. So we read in Virgil (Aenis liber. VII. 150), "Alas! thou knowest it not, one of thy faithful companions lies inanimate on the shore, and defiles thy entire fleet by the presence of his corpse, while thou art here . . . "[1] The belief that a dead body defiles the living was universal. It intended probably to inculcate the sacred duty of decently burying the dead; the more respectable the man, the greater was that duty. This will also explain another strange-appearing idea in Parseeism and in Rabbinism. According to both only a co-religionist defiles; a stranger does not! Why so? The foregoing makes it plain: The pious wish of burying a dead fellow-man contrived the notion that his unburied corpse defiles the surroundings. Such a duty was the burying of a *fellow-religionist;* for a stranger such a duty did not exist; hence, did not the claim either, that his corpse defiles. The above Virgil passage concludes therefore with an injunction to Aeneas to "bring his dead companion to an honorable grave and offer him black sheep as an expiatory sacrifice." These ideas were thus universal, with Greek, Persian and Hebrew. So the Prophet Jeremiah threatens the Judaean princes, etc., with obtaining no burial,[2] but to rot on the ground. Even more pathetic, yea, harrowing is that feeling expressed by Ezekiel 24: 16: "Behold, O man, in a pestilence I shall take away the delight of thine eyes (thy wife).

---

1 "Jacet exanimum tibi corpus amici, heu! nescis, totamque incestat funere classim."

2 Jeremiah XVI. 4; XXV. 33.

Yet shalt thou suppress all tears and sighs nor wear any mourning
. . . . Even so Israel shall I desecrate thy sanctuary your eyes'
delight, and your tender sons and daughters will perish by the
sword, and you shall not mourn, nor weep, nor wear any mourning
apparel." To die and not obtain the customary funeral honors was
the height of ignominy. In other regions and environments the
motive of that same custom may have been a hygienic one, viz:
the desire of the Lawgiver to moderate the excessive filial piety
which induced the relatives of a beloved person to keep the corpse
too long for the health and the cleanliness of the surviving. In
some countries they kept it so long until it passed into decay.
Hence, the legislator stated that dead bodies, unburied, are under
the sway of the Evil principle, impure and defiling, and declared
that true piety is not to keep the body, but to give it an honorable
burial. Thus diametrically opposite reasons may underlie one and
the same legislative enactment and religious funeral rite. The
above quoted chapter of the Aeneis gives us the narrative of a
model burial of hoary, mythological times, which in some respects
contrasts, but mostly coincides with what we have seen concerning
funeral ceremonies, (Virgil Aeneis liber VI. 213 to 229.(1) "In the
meantime the Troyans mourn over Misenus lying dead on the
shore, and render to his insensible remains their last duty. They
raise an enormous pyramid of oak and resinous woods, rising to
the clouds. The edges are garnered with lugubrious, dark leaves,
and cypress trees stand in front. Brilliant arms decorate the top
of the pyramid. The body is carefully bathed and washed in warm
water and embalmed. Shouts of regret and loud lamentations are
widely echoed and tears abundantly shed. The corpse is placed
upon the funeral bed and costly purple garments thrown over it.
Torches are then applied to the pile, the faces turned away. Oil is
poured thereon, sacrificial meats and costly spices added. When
the whole has burned to ashes, the bones are picked out, washed
in wine and piously placed into a metal urn. An olive-branch in
hand, the priest walks around; he dips it into holy water; he
sprinkles with it the entire funeral cortege and assembly, throwing
over them a thin spray of pure water and pronounces the last

1 "Nec minus interea Misenum in littore Teucri flebant, et cineri
ingrato suprema. ferebant. Principo . . . Ingentem struxere pyram.
Idem ter socios pura circumtulitunda Spargens rore levi et ramo felicis
olivae, Lustravitque viros, dixitque novistima verba," . . . That was
no doubt a solemn closing prayer, as the modern requiem and Kaddish,
etc.

funeral prayer. This is termed the *expiation* or purification.
Aeneas then raises a lofty monument to his friend, affixing thereto
his arms and insignia."—Jeremiah 8: 2 undoubtedly alludes to the
same funeral rites in Judaea. They were also Roman and Greek,
but later the Magians changed them greatly, forbidding both,
cremation and burial. They also forbade the waste of costly garments upon the funeral occasion. Virgil, too, reminds of the
sprinkling with pure water and an olive-branch, corresponding to
the Baresma and the water purification of Parseeism, and the
hyssop of the Biblical " Red-heifer-rite." (IV M. 19, 6). Thus
we see the belief in defilement, the duty or burial, purification,
raising a monument, mourning and tears, lustrations of the funeral
cortege, even the Baresma or green twig, etc., are to be found
among Parsees, Judaeans, Roman and Greek mythologists. And
the same ideas are yet at the bottom of our own funeral rites to-day.
Mosque, Church and Synagogue have preserved them under different names and claims. So are the notions that the dead defile ; the
public burial, sprinkling water, lustrations, incense, eulogies and
closing rites corresponding to our *requiem, mass* and *Kaddish.*
The above Aeneis passage concludes as follows, illustrating our
theme: "Aeneas, wondering, asks the Sibyl : "Tell me what means
the crowd at the stream (to the nether world)? What do these
souls desire, some being allowed to pass the river Styx and some
being discarded ? She replies : This crowd are the unfortunates
who had no burial . . . Only those are allowed to pass who were
buried. Without that honor they must flutter about a hundred
years before they are permitted to cross the boundary-river."[1]

MAGIAN BURIAL.

As said, the dead could not be cremated by fire, nor buried in
the earth, nor deposited in the sea. All the elements were holy ;
they were defiled by the contact of the dead, who belonged to
Ahriman. This was Magian doctrine, and since the *Sasanidean*
domination it had become the custom of the people. According
to Herodotus, during the Archaemenidian period, the Persians
buried yet their dead in the earth. Only later the people conformed to the Magian custom of having them devoured by beasts

---

1 Aeneas miratus . . " dic quod vult concursus ad amnem ? Quidve
petunt ? . . . Haec omnio quam cernis inops inhumataque turba est . .
. Nec ripus datur horrendas et raura fluenta transportare, prius quam
sedibus ossa quierunt . . . Centum errant annos . . . Tum demum
admissi stagna exoptata revisunt . ." (Virgil Aeneis liber VI 216-330).

and birds of prey. This took place in the following way : Far away from the city, a desolate, isolated, barren height was selected. A tower twenty feet high was built, called the tower of silence, *Dakhma ;* beneath it was a deep pit ; on the top of the tower iron cross-bars were laid. The corpses were placed thereon, formerly naked, now in plain, clean clothes, the face turned to the sky, the body tied to the bars, thus exposed to the birds of prey to be devoured. Their clean bones then fell down, washed and purified by the rain, to await resurrection. Certain mystic, golden wires or threads were used in that construction to ideally or symbolically represent the isolation of the tower from the earth as if it hung in the air and thus did not contaminate the holy earth on which the tower really stood.(1)   That ritualistic or symbolical fiction of ideally representing the contrary of the really existing, is well known to the Talmudist. By such a wire he surrounds the whole street and town and imagines them as private property.(2)   We shall later come back to this theme.

PURITY AND CHILD-BIRTH. REMARKS.

Vendidad farg XVI. (After Spiegel, by Bleek). " Creator! when a woman is affected with blood marks, how to act? She must be removed from trees made for fire-wood (that being holy) to some dry hill, isolated, away from fire, water, baresma and pure man—" (not to defile them). The law prescribes the manner of feeding her to be isolated, very plainly and sparingly. The theory is that woman during her menses is under the authority of Ahriman, and that in the Messianic age the mode of human propagation will be otherwise than by conception, birth, etc. Gen. III. 16, may contain a reflex of this ancient, oriental view concerning woman having yielded to the temptation of the Principle of Evil, the snake, etc.   In Gen. III., too, the allegory represents Eve as being doomed to increased pain, pregnancy and child-bearing, to yearn for her husband and be subject to him. This may well be an echo of the hoary idea that man was born for immortality, and by sin and obedience to Ahriman he became subject to death and to propagate by conception and pain.

We have thus far given a general outline of Zoroaster, the lawgiver and prophet of the Magi and the Mazdian religion, of his doctrines and ethics, etc. We shall later give copious specimens from the *Vendidad,* the leading book of his bible. There he will

1 See Spiegel page 91 and D. Framjee, Modern Parsees.
2 רשות היחיד

speak for himself, and the reader, fully prepared by our remarks, will easily follow him. It is not easy to determine which of these mentioned doctrines belong to *Zoroaster* and which to his predecessors and his successors. But undoubtedly it was he who spiritualized, moralized and purified the original cult of nature of the Iranians. He broke the power of idolatry and superstition and introduced nobler ideas about divinity, humanity, duty, human dignity and worthy aspirations. As to the superstitions of his times he had to reckon with them. Many he no doubt abrogated. Many others, stronger than his civilizing influence, he had to spare and let alone. As the ancient Rabbis on similar occasions he said : The Thora uses human language. He taught virtue in the name of God, holding up the serpent Ahriman as a stimulant for virtue and wisdom, just as the coachman holds up his whip for the lazy horses ; or as the nurse frightens the child into obedience by the story of the goblins. Dualism was his cosmic philosophy. But the Daevas and drughs were but the whip of the schoolmaster, an educational means, a fiction.

ZEND-AVESTA SURVEYED, ITS BOOKS, ITS NAME.

Anquetil Duperron, the Frenchman who first attempted a translation of that collection of books, renders *Zend-Avesta* by "*Living Word.*" Burnouf, the first scientific translator of it, claims its meaning to be "city-speech, *the language of cities.*" I. Mueller, Fr. Spiegel and others explain it as denoting: knowledge, wisdom, gnosis. Haug takes it as expressing "intuitive knowledge," science reached by direct tradition, from mysterious sources, by a higher revelation ; "Zend" meaning conscious or intuitive, and "Avesta" being, knowledge; hence, Avesta is: direct higher science, *divine revelation :* Zend denoting expounding and knowledge, Zend-Avesta means thus the explanation of the divine revelation. The philologist Oppert has his own opinion and definition. So have other philologists. The language, the grammar and mode of writing of the debris of the Avesta now extant, are far from being accurately known and definitely settled. That writing, language and meaning are rather guessed than really known. The learned expounders of those themes are therefore not at one in their opinions. Indeed, the key to the handwriting, the alphabet of the Avesta collection is far from being found. Next the idioms in which its several parts are composed have been forgotten ; their etymology and grammar are rather guessed than known. But the greatest difficulty is the meaning of the technical words and of the figures of speech. It is all expressed in sectarian formulae, in religious poetry, in hyperboles, in metaphors, probably with the express intention to be unintelligible to the uninitiated. It is full of religio-technical terms which the stranger can not easily master. Thus it is a sealed book. Read any of the renditions of the Avesta, and you feel the translator gave you the words, not its soul, not its inner meaning. The inner sanctuary was not accessible to him. Indeed, let a Mohammedan attend a Roman Catholic service, it will be a riddle to him. A university professor reading the Talmud, though ever so good a Semitic philologist, knows the words, never does he grasp its inner sense. It will remain to him a "sealed book." A born Parsee with a cosmopolitan education and modern speech, could alone, perhaps, unlock the full sense of the Avesta.

ZEND, PAZEND, BY HAUG. LATER LITERATURE.

A well known Persian dictionary, the Burhan-i-gate, says on our subject: "The Avesta, Abesta or Asta is the exegesis of the book *Zend.* This is a book of the Magi which Zertusht has composed on the fire-worship;" and further: "Zend is the name of a book which Ibrahim Zertusht has claimed to have come down to him from heaven. *Pazend* is the expounding of the *Zend.* Again, others believe Zend and Pazend are two works composed by Ibrahim Zertusht on fire-worship. Mohammedan writers contradict the opinion that the Zend is the original text of the revelation and Avesta is its expounding. They claim the very contrary, viz: that the Zend is the expounding and Avesta the text."[1] Professor Haug concludes essentially as follows: Avesta, Zend and Pazend are the names of sacred books which legend refers to Zoroaster; viz: Avesta is the most hoary one originated by Ormazd. Zend is its exegesis and Pazend is a further expounding of that doctrine. According to the Pahaleve translation, *Avesta* is the denomination principally of older sacred songs, verses, prayers, laws, and statutes now mostly lost. They contained among others also dietary laws. The Bundahesh is a later treatise containing an outline of the *Zend* doctrines. *Pazend* is a further commentary on the *Zend.* The books of the Avesta proper are: the Vendidad, Yasna and Vispered. The Khorda-Avesta may also be counted to it.

In the Third Century P. C., the Persians reconquered their independence and soon, too, their old religious ascendency under the dynasty of the Sasanids. Their king Ardeshir and his son Shah-

---

[1] See Haug Zend Studien, ' Deutsche-Morgenlaendische Gesellshaft,' p. 702.

poor raised the monarchy and the Zoroastrian religion to their pristine lustre. Two great religious teachers collected and re-wrote the ancient books. They added a commentary and a translation in the *Huzvaresh* language, an idiom standing between the Avesta, the New-Persian dialects and the surrounding Semitic tongues. At that time the Avesta seems already to have been in part unintelligible. Later on, a new literature arose on the Parsee religion. The most important work is the mentioned Bundehesh, a theological work, a compendium on the Avesta. The *Ardai- Viraf-name* brings mystic doctrines ; further, the *Minokhired* is a book of polemics against other religions ; the *Bahmen Yesht* is of the seventh century P. C. Then came the *Sadder, Zertusht-name* and some modern works. (Spiegel Vend. 18–23.)

MUTUAL INFLUENCE OF PARSEE, JEW AND CHRISTIAN.

In that Sasanidean Period the Talmud was compiled in the several Babylonian Academies, those of Nahardea, Sora, Pumbadita and Machusa, while the Romano-Judaean schools were decaying. Babylon became Israel's center. Jews cultivated Persian jurisprudence and learned the Persian language. There was naturally a frequent intercourse and mutual influence between the several sects living all at peace. The Talmud brings a great many narratives witnessing to that intercourse. Forms and ideas in state, science and worship were interchanged between them. Leading Jews were received at court. Many had high military posts. It is not quite easy to determine who was the borrower. Apparently that was mutual. The same was the case between the Christian sects and the Persians. There, too, was no doubt an adaptation of religious forms and ideas going on. On the whole, Jews were well treated by the adherents of the dominant creed. The Christians of Roman faith were less so, from jealousy. For dissident Christian sects found hospitality in Persia and thrived there till the advent of the Mohammedan conquerors in the seventh century. From the Sasanian period on, the third to the seventh century P. C., date the mutual influence and the numerous parallels between the three denominations, the Persian, Christian and Jewish. There was a constant, though silent process of adaptation, assimilation and accommodation going on. When several sects live together under a wise and just government, which allows no mutual oppression or coercion, such a process will be the inevitable result. The several sects having an opportunity to collate, compare and choose, there will result a constant improvement, a purifying and chastening of ideas and forms in the entire ethical and social domain, "the law of natural selection and survival of the fittest" will prevail and a certain similarity, if not identity, will be the outcome. This was the case in Persia under the Sasanids. Hence, came the striking similarities in the views, doctrines and customs of these three leading denominations. The Talmud is full of such parallel ideas and usages in the domain of religion, worship, jurisprudence and social ways. Sometimes one is puzzled to guess which party was original and which copied. The best answer probably would be that in each instant the most rational party was prevalent, without any regard to whether that was the dominant creed or not, the fittest survived.

SHORR AND KOHUT.

The late distinguished scholar and keen-eyed critic, *O. H. Shorr*, published in a Hebrew Periodical called, *He-Haluz*, in the years 1865-1869, Frankfurt A. M., a monograph on parallels between the Mosaic Bible, Targums, Talmud and the Avesta-books. He showed there striking identities and contrasts in many doctrines, views and customs, in religion, worship, marriage, mourning, jurisprudence, etc. He pointed out surprising likenesses between their views concerning paradise and hell, creation, deluge, angels, ghosts, good and evil spirits, resurrection, immortality, social hopes and issues; the Messiah, last end of things and other views of the Talmudists, which he assumed as borrowed from the Parsees. Casuistical Principles of Law, jurisprudence and religious customs were coming from the same source. These parallels in juxtaposition are exceedingly interesting and pointed, sometimes striking and offering much food for reflection. Shorr's range of reading and thought was immense and his critical acumen sharp and bold, deep and vast. It is an intellectual delight to read him. Withal that I think that he was onesided and exaggerated in his criticism. I believe it is far from safe to assume that in all his quoted instances there, the Talmudists were ever the borrowers and the Parsees ever the lenders. There was a mutual borrowing and lending rather, I think. The late Rev. Dr. A. Kohut, of New York, took up the theme after Shorr, evidently having utilized preceding works on that subject. In 1871, he published a tract on "Angelology and Demonology in the Talmud dependent upon Parseeism." I could not get hold of that pamphlet and cannot judge of its merits. Shorr felt aggrieved that *Kohut* did not mention him, (Shorr) and others as his authorities on that subject and was occasionally very sarcastic on that score. No doubt *he published first* his monography, and that with an unparalleled wealth of thoroughness, wit and learning. But as he published it in Hebrew, it was passed over unnoticed. On the contrary the treatise of his younger and later competitor, being a thesis on a public occasion, at a German University and written in German, received all due attention, publicity and applause, the previous Hebraic Shorr being passed in silence in spite of his just and loud protest. Both the wiiters and compeers are now in paradise I am sure, and have cordially settled their difficulty about priority to fame. In the halls of eternity they have heartily shaken hands and in the best of colleagueal humor, remembered a Mishna, amicably settling their controversy.([1]) Peace be to their ashes and a wreath to their blessed memory! Let the controversy be closed. As to the result of their tracts practically, I think the question whether the Jews were ever the recipients and the Persians the constant lenders is not yet settled. The Talmudists hailing from prophetic, monotheistic Mosaism were fully equipped to evolve new forms and ideas and to pay their full share towards the progress of their time. Proof thereof is Hillel, that humble Babylonian, yet keen Judaean reformer; he knew how to make the most important innovations and ingraft them pleasantly upon the old Thora-parchments, simply by methods of pliable hermaneutics. Nay, those ancient rabbis were abreast with the Persian doctors, and if they ever borrowed, they fully repaid their donors. We shall in the course of these pages bring more parallels illustrating the above.

PARSEE AND JEWISH MYSTICISM.

But I coincide with Shorr and Kohut, that mysticism has its primary source in Parseeism,([2]) spreading its white wings and its ghostly shadows to all parts of the world, to all creeds, peoples, ages and regions; to Christian, Jew and Mohammedan.([3]) There is no doubt that Parseeism has been teaching, as long as Mosaism, that God is pure Spirit, a bright spirit of light and intelligence. This is a great acquisition to mankind: the idea of spirituality. That was a new religious departure. Whether this idea came simultaneously into the human brain, in Hindustan by one man, in Media-Bactria by another and in Chaldea-Haran by a third; or whether this was but one intellectual movement, starting from one impulse and as the sunlight, spreading its rays from East to West, is hard to

---

שניס אוחזין בטלית זה אומר אני מצאתיה וזה אומר אני מצאתיה יחלוקו 1
(Babli Baba Meziah 1, a.)   [2] Conjointly with Brahmanism.
[3] See my ' Gedanken ueber relig. Braeuche, p. 62.

determine.   At any rate, Parseeism has the great merit of being
among the first to. have started the One-God-Spirit idea, which is
now pervading the intellectual world.   On the other hand did Parseeism teach a second principle, that of Darkness, and this became
a source of darkness indeed to the intellectual world at large.   Possibly Zoroaster meant by the Evil Spirit just the same as the Hebrew moralist, viz : the inborn evil passions against which man has to
contend.   Unfortunately that figure of speech created the idea of an
· external personal Evil one, which notion increased the evil, in place
of diminishing it.   Instead of subduing our own passions, we tried
to exorcise and ban the imaginary devil, thus wasting our force in
fighting not the ill, but merely its shadow.   Mazdaism announcing
side by side with the One God of Light, another sovereign Principle of Darkness, has created an inexhaustible source of superstition
not closed to this day ; a real intellectual darkness not yet overcome
in the face of the closing nineteenth century.   A thousand observances perpetuate to this day the bright and dark sides of Magism.
Christian, Jew and Modammedan light, to this day, candles, perpetual lamps; chandeliers, torches and funeral piles in death, mourning,
child-birth, etc., to cheer the patient, to invoke the protection of God
and chase away the Evil one.   Parseeism has created hell and devil,
angels and carnal paradise.   Parseeism teaches, the dead are
conquered by Ahriman who springs upon them in the shape of a fly
" *Nasu.*"   This explains our modern fears, superstitions and practices in cases of death and mourning, to guard against the devil.
When the Pentateuch enjoins to use water with the ashes from the
Red-heifer for purification against contact with defilement and death,
Parseeism gives the cue to that : cow-urine was used there for lustrations.   When the Vendidad warns against the throwing about of
hair and nails cut off from the human body, as defiling,(¹) this explains similar usages in present times and creeds, well known to the ac-
ute observer.   When Parseeism taught : God of Light, Ahura, and another God of light, Mithra, his son, or Supreme Intelligence, Logos,
emanation—that doctrine is not extinct even now.   When the
most powerful sect among the Judaeans, sticklers to exaggerated
rules of purity and godliness, authors of hair-splitting casuistry
about artificial cleanliness and uncleanliness, allowed and not allowed,
are termed *Parashim*, Pharisees, we see whence they hail.   When the
Pentateuch forbids the kindling of fires on the Sabbath I see that
was a protest against fire-worship.   When Isaiah insists upon "God

---

1 Spiegel Vendidad p. 27.   Brahmans used cow-dirt for sinners.

Creator of good and evil, of light and darkness," I see it was in opposition to dual Zoroasterism. When we read of that system advancing seven gods, seven Ameshas Spentas, we know why seven is
a holy number and an oath. When I read :(¹) " The righteous are
met in Paradise by their own goodness, in the shape of a beautiful
madien," I find out whence hail Mohammed's *houris*. Again there
I ˙read :(²) " To it offered Haoshyano with Baresma bound together with overflowing fulness. . . Grant me that I may smite the
daevas, sorcerers and pairikas and subdue Agro Mainyu . . " I recognize in that rite and water-prayer of Parseeism its kinship to the
known synagogal rite and service on the seventh day of Booth
"*hoshyano-Rabba*" with shaking of the palm-branch and smiting
the green rods called, (³) *Hoshyanoth* and invoking *Hoshyano.*
K'horda-Avesta ordains prayers with washed hands and uplifted
Haoma at the shining fire.(⁴)   Here is "hand washing" and "hostia,"
its formula was: " I am about to prepare to do as ordained by Mazda." Exactly the same is the Hebrew formula :(⁵)   The Avesta had
a benediction for each enjoyment ; especially so after meals ; so the
Hebrew ritual, so the Roman Catholic and Mohammedan ones.
Khorda-Avesta teaches a judgment-day at the bridge *Kinvad* and
hell beneath ; three judges there administering prompt justice.(₆)
The same legends are current to-day about awful doomsday, hell-
fires, judge and saviour, etc.; and Parseeism gives the best cue.
The Parsee used to write in the legal marriage contract "according to
the laws and customs of the good Mazdayasnian Law."(⁷)   Just such
a phrase is in rabbinical notary acts.(⁸)   The same source mentions
the seventy-two letters of God's name; or even seventy-two divine
names.(⁹)   The numbers one, three and seven were sacred to Magism. So it is in modern mysticism. " Charity is the noblest virtue " is a Hebrew-Persian maxim. The Hebrew had Tqiath Kaph.
The right hand pledged the faith ot Parsees, Greeks and Romans.
Truth was an epithet of Mazda " so Aggada : " The seal of God is
truth." The Destur or Magian high-priest was dressed in white.
So was the Hebrew one. So is the bride now. So was the Essenian puritan, so the Hassidean *Zaddik* now. So are the dead
among modern Parsees and orthodox Jews now. The Khorda-

1 Spiegel Bleek Khorda-Avesta, 137.
2 Khorda-Avesta p. 111, Spiegel Bleek.
3 חושענא   4 Ibidem p. 144, Spiegel Bleek.   5 חנני מכין ומזומן
6 Spiegel Khorda-Avesta, 171.
7 Ibidem, 173.   8 הכל שריר וקוים כדת משה וישראל   9 Ibidem, 199.

Avesta brings specimens of Mazdean confessions of sins,([1]) a veritable *Al-het.*([2]) They resemble similar confessional prayers in the common Hebrew prayer-book, as two eggs do each other. They especially mention the sin of " walking with one shoe," or " without a skull cap," or " without the *kosti,*" or neglecting the priestly purity-rules, or omitting saying grace after meals, evacuation, etc." Confession of wrong done to animals([3]) is unique in Magism. There is one thoughtful remark there which should be supplemented in our modern prayer-books. It reads (Ib. 136): " Which is the best prayer, worth all that is between heaven and earth ? That when one renounces all evil thoughts, words and deeds." We shall later adduce more parallels and illustrations. A religion with such a high God-ideal, truth and virtue-ideal, man-woman-and-work-ideal, devoted to purity, usefulness, diminishing of evil with vice, and practicing charity, etc., such a religion is a glory to humanity, worthy to be remembered and studied as one of the great inspirations of mankind. But we must not overdo. We must not flatter and extol. We must not be slow in frankly adding, that it contained a great deal of superstition and extravagance which it would be desirable to see eliminated from human thought and practice. by meting out impartial justice to its bright and its dark sides, we shall render justice to the past and to the future. We are the heirs of the past for good, we should discard harm from the future by eliminating effete usages of the past.

---

1 Spiegel Khorda-Avesta, 154–156.   2 על חטא

3 Spiegel Khorda-Avesta, 164–167.

CHAPTER IV

BRAHMANISM IN INDIA.

For a full understanding of Parseeism, the doctrines of Zoroaster, the religion and legislation of Eran or Iran, it is absolutely necessary that the reader's attention should be called to the group of its sister-religions of Asia, the cults which preceded it, which had their simultaneous developments with it, which even outstripped and survived it. Such are the Arian denominations, and Brahmanism in its earlier and later forms especially. Brahmanism had the same origin as Magism; it departed from identical premises, from the same geographical, historical, ethnical, etc., surroundings, it necessarily had, in part at least, the identical evolutions. The march and unfoldings of both these great creeds and legislations are at first analogous; until later and gradually with the change of circumstances, geographical, physiological, political and social, their ethical differentiation became more and more marked; until at last they stand as diverse religions, systems and sociological schemes. From that high, heaven-towering mountain-chain, stretching about 350 miles in length and 40 to 50 in breadth, called the Himalaya, the *Snow-Palaces* of southeastern Asia, flow down its two mightiest streams, the Indus and the Ganges, amidst vast, highly fertile plains, forming the great peninsula of Hindustan or East India, the "country of the seven rivers," of the Indus and the Ganges with their five tributaries, the Pentjab and Hepta-Sinth. These great rivers give it its special and salient character, climatic and geographic, its flora, its fauna, its wealth, its advantages and its drawbacks, its races, castes, political, social and religious, peculiar traits and physiognomy. This is the scene and patrimony of Brahmanism, the great rival and sister-religion of Zoroasterism. Its dawn is gray with age, lost in past ages of prehistoric times. At the begin of the sixth century, B. C., it had to contend against a great secession, Buddhism, the Protestantism of the East. But it vanquished it and remained victorious on that congenial soil, until in modern times it has to divide its dominion with Islam, recently with the Gospel, and at last with rationalism (Brahma Somaj, etc).

THE ARIAN INVASION.

In prehistoric epochs, a great impulse started from among the Arian tribes, roaming on the numerous habitable hills, in the vast valleys and oases of the mighty Himalayan mountain ridges. One

of the most powerful races of history, the Arians, began to emigrate
in search of new homes, as did later the Teutonic tribes invading
Europe. On one side that emigration wended its way to the countries southeast of Asia, intersected by the Indus and its five auxiliaries, the Pentajab. After long centuries of invasion, having
conquered that most fertile country, the same tribes of Arias, or
Arians, spread further and further eastwards, and invaded the even
more luxuriant shores of the Ganges and its 'subsidiaries. That
entire, vast region was conquered after long, bloody and hard
fighting against the aborigines, who were compelled to recognize
the Arians as their masters and submit to their rule. And while
one branch of that mighty Arian stock descended from the Himalayan Mounts and subjugated the vast and wealthy regions of the
Indus and the Ganges, another tribe of the same family emigrated
in the opposite direction, the less sunny and less fertile highlands,
geographically denominated as Iran, Eran, a name derived from
the same root, Aria, Arian. Fighting and advancing, this tribe
of Arias gradually occupied the vast and varied western regions.
Some parts were then already peopled, some were so rarely, and some
had no aborigines at all. These Eranians, or Western Arians, gradually gained the many, varied countries stretching west of Hindustan
and occupying the whole of central Asia, from Bactria, Arachosia
and Mount Paropamisos to Armenia and Colchid, having the Scythes
or Massagets, the Caspian and the Black Seas as their Northern
frontier; the kingdom of Lydia and Cappadocia as their western
limits ; Arabia, the Persian Gulf with the Erythrean and Indian
Ocean as their southern boundaries. Now these vast countries
of Iran became for long centuries the patrimony of the Magi and
the Zoroastrian doctrine. Whilst east of that vast region in the
southeast of Asia, all the countries situated between and beyond
the powerful rivers of the Indus and the Ganges, covering now the
possessions of English Hindustan, with the empires of Birman,
Siam, etc., remained to this day the inheritance of Brahmanism,
its daughter religion. As hinted at, for some time the religion of
Buddhism had created a vast secession in India. But, soon it was
overpowered, driven beyond the frontiers and compelled to take
refuge in Birman, Ceylon, Thibet, China, etc., and Brahmanism
remained sole mistress of the seven rivers' country. Until in comparatively modern times as mentioned, Mohammedanism conquered
and religiously encroached upon it ; and at last the Dutch and now

the English have mostly subdued and made it tributary to the
nations of the Cross. Nevertheless is Brahmanism as yet the dominant religion of India.

THE VEDAS.

Long before the Christian Era, began those mighty migrations
and invasions of the *Arias* from the Himalayan Mountains down
to the Indus and the Ganges on one side and towards the West,
from Bactria to Parthia, etc., on the other side. Not only that
history cannot designate the exact epoch of that powerful movement, but hardly can the century when it began be determined.
Nor has history unraveled the extent of time during which that
impulse continued, how long it lasted before the Arias invading
those vast plains, those "regions of the seven rivers" conquered
and subdued them. It took many long centuries of strenuous,
bloody fighting to accomplish that work. That is the heroic epoch
of the East-Indian Arias. The Vedas, the holy writings of Brahmanism seem to have been the records inspired by those heroic
deeds of the prehistoric Arias of Hindustan. The Vedas are the
epic and religious poems of the Hindoo Arians. As the Greeks
have their Homeric, etc., songs, as the heroic poetries of Ossian,
Edda, Niebelungen, etc., of the Teutons ; as the Hebrews had their
epics of the wars of Ihvh,[1] even so are the Vedas the heroic
legends of the Arians of the East. They narrate under a mythological guise those supernaturally colored deeds of heroism which
gave to the valorous Arias dominion over the rich valleys of India
and Bengal. The stories of the gods, the spirits, the heroes, the
mythology, the fabulous achievements and the gigantic battles, the
triumphs, the disasters, etc., are narrated, sublimized and apotheosized
there with all the naivity, the faith, the fervor, the sincerity and the
admiration of proud and pious descendants, recounting the great deeds
and the valor of the ancestors who gave them a country, a home, a
hearth, wealth and dominion. The original Vedic mythology of
both, India and Iran, is akin to the Greek and Roman mythologies
of even later times ; the same views and ideas. naive notions about
gods, men, world and virtue, as the Greeks and Romans hailing
from the same Arian stock. Such mythologies are nature, hero
and ancestor worship. Such gods are forces of nature personified ;
or heroes, leaders, patriarchs, chieftains of dynastic families and
tribes, later apotheosized. Such gods are half-men and such heroes
are demi-gods. The earth is the center of the universe and heaven

1 ספר הישר מלחמות יהוה

is but the residence of the brave, the great, the good ones. These Vedas seem to have been composed by Arian sages, holy men, *Rishis*, later claimed to have been supernaturally inspired. They chanted the gods, taught the religion, presided over the worship, the sacrifices and, sometimes also, the councils of their tribes, clans and hamlets. There were several such groups and nuclei of sages, families of priests, poets and leaders in worship. Each tribe had its stock of priests and singers. When the Indian conquest was achieved and fully established, the several cults, inspired poems and sacred rituals were sifted and revised, settled and harmonized all alike. Those writings became the Vedas, the knowledge, the Scriptures, and those families of priests became the Brahmans, the legitimate leaders in worship and sacred lore.

BRAHMAN AND CASTES.

The etymological meaning of the word *Brahman*, is not definitely cleared up. Having nothing positive on it, I shall venture a mere suggestion which criticism may adopt or reject. Brahm, Brahma, Brahman, the Supreme godhead of the Hindoo-Arian mythology and the only One of reformed Brahmanism, may be akin to the Greek word *obrimos*, powerful, its root is: *brim bri*, heavy, weighty. *Obrimos* is an epithet of the leading gods of Hellas, the great divine powers. Even so in the Shemitic tongues, in Bible, Koran, etc., God is termed, Elohim, *El* Eloah, viz: Power.[1] Among primitive peoples, the deities were conceived as the personified forces of nature, and the leading Deity was the *Power*. Hence, Obrimos, El, Eloah; power being the highest spiritualization of nature, in the primitive, human mind. It may be even that the name of the Semitic patriarch, Abraham, originally Abrahm, is connected with the same root, *bri*, *brim*, power. As that patriarch was the first to conceive an All-power, the highest power, "*El* Elyon, owner of heaven and earth," so he, too, was called by that name, just as the Hindoo priest, teaching God-Brahman, was himself called Brahman. Gen. 17: 4, 5: deduces that name from the Shemitic *Ab-ram*, " High-father," enlarged to "father of many nations." But even *Ab-ram* is rather an epithet of God than of a man, and a synonym of *El Elyon*, the highest God, the greatest Power. Thus *Ab-ram* also comes near to the Greek *Obrimos*, the mighty One, and to the Hindoo, *Brahm* and *Brahman*, the name of the highest god and of the priest teaching that god.

Brahman, the creator of all, of course, is the origin of the castes. From his mouth came the Brahman-priests ; from his arms

1 אל אלוח

the military; from his body the laboring class; and from his feet the Soudras and all the subjugated masses. To all appearance, Brahman meant in the Vedas a worshipper—one who leads in prayer, a priest. For a long time Brahman was identical with a priest who offers prayers. The leading tribes of the Aria had each their own Brahman family. These united later and became a caste, the first caste of the Arian society, the spiritual class. The conquering Arias were subdivided into three classes, which settled down as castes. The first and highest was that of the Brahmans, priests. devoting their lives to religion, worship, study, teaching and educating. The second caste was the *Kshatrya*, the militia, the soldiers. Their head was the king; they alone wielded the sword as the military aristocracy, defending and ruling the people. The third caste was the *Vaisya*, the tillers of the soil, the traders, mechanics, dealers, etc. Thereupon followed 'a fourth recognized caste, the *Soudras*. That class embraced originally the remnants of the conquered tribes and races which had made peace with and submitted to the Arian masters. They were the '' Gibeonites '' of the Indian society, " its hewers of wood and drawers of water." But beneath them soon sprang up a host of conquered peoples, forming separate castes, that were rightless and considered as far below even the humblest Soudras. These corresponded to the European Gypsies. They outnumbered by far the above four recognized castes. It is claimed that India counted over thirty such subdivisions, and that the Parias were as ten to one to the said four categories recognized by law. Their names were many. Each variety of conjugal alliance of two castes or of two sub-castes, constituted a new denomination, with its own position, treatment and craft in society. All mixed marriages were either forbidden or at least constituted a *mesalliance*, a degradation of caste, a descent in social rank. Whilst any matrimonial alliance of the first four classes with those beneath them was considered a defilement and constituted the offspring as outcasts, out of the law, and forming a new variety of sub-caste. The law of *Manu* alludes to them as outcasts, Tchandala, Paria, etc. There were in all, some forty castes remaining hereditary, from parent to offspring. So were their diverse rights and duties, social standing and occupations. After the ecclesiastical despotism of the Brahmans, and after the political despotism of the military class, came that social despotism of the forty castes. It was the most crushing and baleful, the greatest obstacle to improvement. That accumulated tyranny, accounts for

the enfeeblement of that numerous Indian people, their yielding to
the Mongols, the Mohammedans, the Dutch, the English, etc.

BRAHMAN REFORMATION.

Many long centuries have passed since the invasion of India
by the Arias. More centuries have elapsed since their conquest
and firm establishment in those regions. Many more have closed
since the definite settlement of the upper strata, the classes over
the masses, since the surrender and submission of the Soudras, the
Tchandalas, etc., to be the "hewers of wood and drawers of water"
of the three reigning castes. All that may have taken thousands
of years. At last the Aria-Hindoo State and Society were firmly
settled. The Brahmans, the top of the social scale, took the lead.
They presided at the temple, school, justice, worship, the palace, and
at public festivals. As a class, they were not too glaringly ambitious, not too eager for wealth, dominion and sensual enjoyments.
They really devoted themselves to the study of religion, the Vedas,
the cult, to teaching, meditation, sciences and public improvement,
as far as understood then and there. As a body, the Hindoo priesthood were indeed a spiritual and ethical aristocracy. Study and
meditation, thinking and improving others was considered the most
worthy occupation for them; it was so even above the cult and
above deeds. Earnestly meditating over their myths, their gods
and their worship, ceremonies and purifications, their heaven and
hell, etc., they began to rise above these and soar up to the purer
realms of religion and philosophy, to a nobler conception of nature,
deity, man and cosmogony. Gradually they elaborated a great
reform, the new Brahman religion. That is a great epoch in Eastern history, just in our times being recognized in the West. It was
no less important than the advent of Abraham, Moses, Elijah,
Isaiah, etc., is for the Shemitic races of Western Asia. It appears
a new wave of thought and ethics swept over the world, revolu-
tionizing mankind, renovating church and state, called by different
names and with different leaders, but the movement is identical.
It was the advent of a higher religious and social phase, the advent
of monotheism; monotheism of course with a certain popular
allowance, with formal, external concessions to the customary,
hereditary polytheism of the Arians.

BRAHMAN AND THE WORLD.

That doctrine was: There is really but one God, Source of all
existence, of the spiritual and the material worlds. He is pure
spirit and immaterial, infinite, everlasting and unchangeable, His

own cause and Supreme cause of all that is. He is perfect and all-holy. He is the Vedic Brahman. He is without will, desire or external object, impassible, immovable, unaffected by any prayer or sacrifice. He is self-existent and self-sufficient. He is the essence of all the souls and bodies, of mind and matter ; He pervades all space and time. He is the *Athman*, the breath and life of the universe, hovering over and pervading the chaotic elements of existence.([1]) He is impersonal, *Tat*, the universe lies undifferentiated in His bosom. Behind the sensual earth, sky, ocean, stars, etc., behind all that is visible to our eyes, there is the reality of being ; behind the screen of nature, there is its essence, the principle, the veritable being, the mysterious source of existence. That source is immaterial, purely spiritual, beyond the senses. It can be grasped or rather guessed as through a veil, by the human mind alone. Nature is but the shroud of deity. The Deity is veiled in the magnificent robe of the universe.

ATHMAN, TAT, SOUL, NEW DOCTRINE.

Let us follow a while Max Dunkar.([2]) As in man, so in entire nature, there is a visible, sensual body, and an immaterial soul. Even so behind this perishable, external, visible universe, there flows the internal source of being, there lives the divine soul, pervading all individual existences. Behind all these changeable appearances, there is but one breath, one life, one soul, *Athman, Param-athman*, the universal soul. This must be the creative, the conserving, the divine power, the principle and the bearer of all phenomena of life, nature's life, soon rising and flowing, soon ebbing and sinking. This soul of the universe was identified with Brahman. Brahman is its name in the Vedas. As the priests had found behind the prayers and the holy ceremonies an invisible spirit which really and alone gave to these their energy and effectiveness ; as it was that holy spirit who swayed the national deities and compelled them to listen to the prayers of man; as behind and above those gods was the saint, the power behind the throne, that being the most divine, the highest divinity,—hence that self-same spirit should be looked for, too, behind the great and various phenomena of nature's activity. It must be the same spirit who reigned here as there ; who is, in heaven and on earth ; who gives efficacy to the prayers of the Brahmans, who called into life the manyfold creations of nature and causes them to move in their prescribed orbits ; He who

1 So Gen. I. 3. The Spirit of God hovered over the waters.
2 Max Dunear, 'Geschichte des Alterthums,' II., 94.

is at the same time the highest God and the Master of the gods. Thus the Holy Spirit reigning over the gods, grew and expanded into the world-soul, pervading all the phenomena of nature, breathing life into them and maintaining them. From prayer and devotion, mightier than the might of the gods, from that inner fervor and concentration which, according to Hindoo belief, reaches over to heaven, the priests had thus arrived at the conception of one God, not represented any longer by any phenomenon of nature, and he was accepted as the Holy One. And this Supremely Holy One was also the world-soul, the emanator of the universe, or rather its principle, its efficient cause, its spring. The universe emanated from Him as the stream does from its source. Brahman, the *Tat*,(1) the impersonal being, say the expounders of the Vedas, is no antithesis, no contrast to the essence and the specific nature of the world. No, it unfolded itself as the universe. Brahman is the undeveloped world; the world is the Brahman revealed. " It was neither being, nor non-being "—so it reads in one of the latest hymns of one of the youngest books of the Rigveda—it was not the world, not air, nor anything above it, nor the differentiation of day and night. This universe was shrouded in darkness, it was neutral, undifferentiated fog or water. But Tat—the impersonal Being(2)—breathed without breath, alone, positing his own Self, the Self-Existence, being and essence. Desire (to unfold and create the world), *kama*, arose first in his mind. This desire, *kama*, became the original creative seed. One sees how side by side with the pure, spiritual potency, Brahman, the original matter, too, is postulated: At the side of non-being, the undifferentiated Brahman, the fructifying water from heaven is presupposed to have existed, and this claim is maintained altogether illogically." Thus far, Dunkar.

BRAHMANISM AND QABBALA.

In our later studies(3) on Neo-Platonism and Qabbala, we shall see that the mystics teach God, the Unknowable and Infinite, *Ain-Soph*, exactly as the *Vedante* does its impersonal Brahman, viz: that the Infinite emanated first the spiritual world containing the material one, Adam Qadmon and Sephiroth. So here, Adam Qadmon is the personal Brahman of the Vedante; the Self-Existent, the undifferentiated Brahman unfolded the world under the guise of the personal Brahman, who created the material world. The

---

1 Tat in Sanscrit is identical with the English that.
2 Akin to the Biblical Ihvh, being in the abstract.
3 See Fluegel's Philosophy and Qabbala, following this volume.

Qabbala designates God also as *Ain*. So, too, the Vedante calls him *non-being*. The analogies are in other respects also most striking. In the Qabbala, the Unknowable God, *Ain-Soph*, creates Adam Qadmon. In the Vedante and Veda, the impersonal Brahman, Tat, the Self-Existent, creates Brahman the personal one. According to either, is God the infinite substance, not the immediate Creator of the universe. The incongruities of Brahmanic metaphysics adhere to their latest offspring, the Qabbala and also in some sense to Neo-Platonism. Let us explain :

EMANATION, TRANSMIGRATION AND NIRVANA.

How does the Vedante, the philosophic commentator of the Vedas explain the existence of this sensual world ? By emanation. The pure and holy spiritual Brahman, emanated Brahman the second, the personal God who created bodies and souls, mind and matter, the gods, the spirits, man and the world. For these emanations are the more deteriorating, the further they are from their divine Creator, the personal Biahman and his sire, the impersonal one, the original, incomprehensible, Self-Existent. Matter is thus nothing else but spirit condensed and darkened. The material world is the dim and obscured opposite pole of the spiritual world, the immediate development of the personal Brahman, who thus contains in potency, both mind and matter. This doctrine, too, Brahmanism entailed upon all the mystics and the Qabbalists also. The human soul is a spark from the divine mind. As the fiery forge gives forth light-chips, so the divine world-soul radiates souls which are its own parts and elements. They are destined once to return to their source, Brahman, after their earthly pilgrimage. The human soul, contaminated by its shell, the earthly evil, is purged by hell-fire and then by innumerable transmigrations and wanderings. It assumes temporarily many new shapes and bodies, of the several castes, the animals, from the elephant to the vermin, the plants and the minerals, according to its merits and demerits. After long and painful metamorphoses, it is purified, restored to its pristine effulgence, ascends to and is absorbed in Brahman, its original source. It becomes one with him. It is lost and assimilated in his divine being. This is termed *Nirvana* in the Brahmanic sense, meaning absorption in the deity. Buddhism, too, teaches this *Nirvana* doctrine. But, being atheistic, it means there simply annihilation, ceasing to exist. Brahmanic Nirvana means ascension to and absorption in the divine Essence. These latter doctrines, divine absorption and transmigration of the soul are also entailed upon modern mystics. Indeed, Brahmanism as the Qabbala conceives, is a most rigorous monism, which leads to pantheism : There is but one substance. That substance is undifferentiated: it is self-existent; it is its own Cause and Cause of all. As the sun-light, it splits into several rays, into mind and matter, into the spiritual and material worlds. Gods, angels, spirits, bodies, men, animals, plants, minerals, good and bad, are all its emanations. The further and later the emanations are, the less spiritual, the less pure and lightful they are; until at the other extreme end they are matter, dark, bad, devilish. As the aether becomes air, says the Brahman, as air condenses into water, into snow, into hail and ice; then again, the same process is reversed ; ice becomes water, air, aether, etc., even so do from Brahman emanate the gods, spirits, souls and bodies. They amalgamate with bodies and are brutalized. Then again, they are purified, spiritualized and returned to the bosom of Brahman, their source.

BRAHMANISM AND VIRGIL'S ANEIS.

We have seen how the leading reformed Brahman doctrines of grey antiquity are identical with the Qabbalistic ones, especially with those of the Zohar, of comparatively modern date, the thirteenth century. But we shall find them squaring also with Romano-Greek philosophy, as expounded by Virgil in his *Aneis*, book VI. The very same views are reflected there about the universe being one body, animated by one divine mind; that world-soul permeates the universe in all its single parts and governs it from within, as the human soul does the body; the human soul is a divine spark, wandering in this darkened world of matter, attached to some of its individual bodies for a special time ; it becomes badly contaminated by this forced contact and is cleansed and chastened by fire, sufferings and new transmigrations into other bodies; until at last it is purified from all its stains and earthly dross and enters its highest condition of apotheosis. When the Roman courtiers imagined the dying emperor becoming a god, this was later but a flattery; in earlier naive times it was a doctrine, a religious assumption, a philosophy in full earnest. The emperor was the highest and last transmigration of the wandering soul. In that imperial shape it had attained at all its pristine purity and lustre; thus freed by death from its body, it re-assumed its original condition, it became again a part of the god-head in *elysium* or in heaven. This doctrine which is first Brahmanic, which we find again in later Jewish mysticism, we meet also in Virgil as a philosophem and creed of the

Romano-Greek mythology. Here are Virgil's words (Aneis VI., v. 724) which Anchises addresses to his son Aeneis in Hades: "Learn, my son, that from begin, the heavens, the earth, the liquid planes, the lustrous globe of night and the brilliant luminary of day are vivified and nurtured by one soul common to them all. Penetrating and permeating the limbs of the world, the soul imparts the movement to the universe and infuses itself into that entire mass. It forms thus the diverse species and kinds of individual beings. The flame animating these is never dying and ever proving its celestial origin as long as it is not burdened with the admixture of the gross clay, as long as it languishes hot, imprisoned in the earthly senses subject to death. From this gross association are derived all the imperfections and passions of men. The spirit entangled in that dark prison of the senses, cannot pierce their obscurity and look up to heaven. Even then when death has freed the soul from its earthly bonds, it cannot free itself entirely of the stains necessarily contracted during its union with the body. The inveterated spots of vice ever leave their profound impressions. These are purged only by punishment and sufferings, by blasts and fire. We have all to undergo such expiations. At last we arrive at elysium, but only for a short time mostly, and after long purgations, freed from all earthly admixture and having recovered all our original purity. After a thousand years have elapsed, these souls are led to the river Lethe, in order that drinking oblivion in its waves, they begin to wish again to re-enter a body and return to the earth, without any remembrance of the past." Anchises now shows his son their own posterity, souls about to return to earth and vivify human bodies, successively to be kings of Latium. Thus we find here the hoary, Bramanic ideas about God and world-soul creation, government, Hades, human soul, its struggles, destination, sin, transmigration and redemption—all that we meet among the Greeco-Roman mythologists and the modern Jewish mystics. This is another proof of the essential identity of leading popular views and doctrines.([1])   Also Bab. Sanhedrin mentions the millenium.([2])

PANTHEISM. ASCETISM. EVIL.

Brahmanism thus conceives all existences as an infinite scale or chain of beings, from the impersonal, supreme, Self-Existent, Brahman, down to the mineral bodies; and from the stone upward to the highest and holiest, the world-soul. First emanated the personal Brahman; from him emanated all the national gods of the Arias.

1 Virgil, Ænis VI., verses 724-751.   2 שית אלפי שני חוו עלמא וחר חרב   97 a.

They are the appointed governors and patrons of the several parts
of creation. There were eight such gods in the first line, superintending the eight regions of the world—according to the notion of
the Hindoos. They had to protect them from the evil spirits, etc.
Such were Indra, Yama, Varuna, Surjah, etc. Of course gods Agni
and Soma (fire and Ahoma) were not missing. Soon their number
rose to twelve, as the months in the year; to thirty-three as the
monthly days; as found also among the Parsees; soon rising to
3,339; to 33,000 and even to 330,000,000 of gods. Of course that
divine host needed their food and praises, and the ancient sacrificial
cult was continued in their behalf. After the gods, Brahman
created the spirits, the several castes of men, the animals, the plants,
lifeless, dumb matter came last, the disspirited and lightless, final and
farthest emanations, the darkest condensations of spiritual Brahman.
The entire material world, spiritless, lightless, impure, imperfect and
unholy, was thus of evil. It was so already with the Hindoo Brahmans, not only with the Magi. It was even worse. The Magi discriminated in the material world between a creation of good and one
of evil, that of Ahura Mazda and that of Angro Mainyu. Nature,
the bodily universe was originally created by Mazda for good, as is
the biblical view. Ahriman spoiled it by counter-creations. Hence,
there was according to Mazdaism, a holy and an unholy nature.
Worse in Brahmanism; all nature, the sensual world, is Brahman
dimmed, imperfect, perishable, ephemeral and transient, as the bub-
bles on the water appearing and disappearing. It is impure and
sinful. It is essentially evil, has no right to exist and is to be annihilated. The soul is therefore to get rid of the body by all the
means at its disposal, even by fire, sword, exposure, starvation, actual suicide. Hindoos are to spare their neighbors and the animals,
even the flies, flesh-meat was forbidden on that score. All was to be
spared except one's own body. Ascetism invented the most ex-
cruciating torments to shorten one's life, to get rid of existence, for
then only could the soul return to Brahman. Of course the Hindoo
philosophers were not ever consistent in that view. It was yet a
partially accepted duty to build a house, raise a family, defend
society, etc. But this was done but half-heartedly. The best of
mankind, the Brahmans, at a ripe age, were to leave the world, go
into the forest to become *dvidsha's*, hermits in the forest, live on roots,
on alms, exposed to the inclement weather, to cold, rain and heat,
to wild beasts and starvation, and devote to meditation and prayer,

to the severest forms of ascetism and self-torment and die in [the contemplation of deity. Having seen children and grandchildren, they retired from the world, renounced country, family, home, friends and all comforts and wilfully sacrificed health and life. Nay, they renounced at last even prayer, and thinking, and all mental occupation, spontaneously interrupting their brains in any and all instinctive activity, mechanically muttering but *Om*, a symbolical recognition of Brahman, and a few other corresponding holy words— Bhur, Bhuvus, Svar ;([1]) till they at last perished from inanition, alone in the forest, or drowned in the sacred waves of the Ganges, in order to get rid of their own hateful life, of this sinful world, of impure nature ; martyrizing thus the flesh to free the soul from its prison and to return after long and wearisome regenerations to Brahman, the only place of refuge from odious, sinful, degrading and brutalizing existence. The absorbtion into Brahman was the only paradise, *Nirvana*, the unification with God. That was the final Hindoo ideal of a saint, a dvidsha, a hermit, a sage.

BRAHMANIC CASUISTRY.

Transgressions of morality, of purity, of the dietary laws, of the religious duties and observances are punished in this world and hereafter. Transmigration, repeated births in different bodies, is the great resource of priestly rewards and punishments. A good life in one body will be rewarded by regeneration in a nobler body, a higher caste, or a finer animal. A mean life will have to pass into a lower body, even myriads of times ; into that of a wolf, a rabbit, a mouse, a frog, a plant, a thorn. All individual bodies are but the shells and temporary habiliments of souls. Yonder cow, ass or snake may be the residence of the soul of some one's parent, brother or friend. Hence, comes the prohibition of killing animals for food, from fear it may be one's own father one slaughters. Ovid, the Roman poet, puts that plea into the mouth of the philosopher Pythagoras himself.([2]) Some of such ideas are characteristic : The slanderer is punished with stinking breath([d]) in this life, besides hell

---

[1] Manu. II., 76–78.   [3] Manu. IX., 47–54.

[2] Ovid Metamorphos, XV., 75. Parcite, mortales, dapibus temerare nefandis Corpora ! sunt fruges, sunt deducentia ramos Pondere poma sua, tumidæque in vitibus uvæ ; Prodiga divitias alimentaque mitia tellus Suggerit, atque epulas sine cæde et sanguine præbet, Carne feræ sedant jejunia.

Take care mortals, not to soil your bodies with abominable food. You have grain and fruit weighing down their branches. Liberal earth furnishes sweet nourishment in abundance, offering food without murder or blood. Wild beasts appease their hunger with flesh. . . .

and innumerable mean transmigrations after death. Prayers, fasting, self-castigation and suicide may mitigate misdeeds committed. To chant one thousand times certain prayers can atone for crime. Who uproots uselessly a plant, should in atonement follow and tend for a day a cow, the favorite animal in India. He who ate something forbidden shall for a month eat but rice, beginning the first day with fifteen mouthfuls, going down to one, and after fifteen days take each day one mouthful more up to fifteen mouthfuls.([1]) Such crimes are also atoned by eating cow-dirt, mixed with cow-urine, drinking water boiled in Kussa-grass and alternating that with fasting. When we wonder at the minute prescriptions of Christian or of Talmudical casuists, in medieval times, their endless litanies, benedictions, prostrations, self-castigations, fastings, hair-splitting crimes and atonements, we may find here in this curious repulsive casuistry and petty ritualistic prescriptions of the Brahmans, the models of such rigorism and futility. Partaking of intoxicating drinks is punished with especial severity. Whosoever contravenes intentionally, shall so long drink boiling rice-water or cow-urine, until his bowels are burned. Murder was punished most severely, but differently, depending upon the caste of the murderer and of the murdered one.

BRAHMAN CEREMONIAL.

The Braman is to rise before dawn; he shall bathe and sing a hymn to the sun-god; he prays long at morning and evening; he offers sacrifices five times daily to the gods, the spirits and the ancestors, invoking Brahman with repeated exclamations of *Om !*([2]) His garments must be ever clean and white, never worn by any other person; his hair, nails and beard must be clipped. He wears golden ear-rings and a wreath on his head; he holds in one hand the Bamboo-staff, in the other the kussa-grass, (corresponding to the Magian Baresmon) and a water-pitcher, emblem of poverty and purification. He shall not play dice. He must never sing or dance, except as a part of the ritual. He should not gnash his teeth, nor

---

1 Manu. IX., 212-216.

2 This *Om* exclamation is a solemn affirmation, true l sure ! It is to all appearance akin to the Hebrew אמן, the Greek *amyn*; latin and all modern languages, amen ; hence *omnomi, omniw, omosw*, I swear, the root of which is the nearest to the Brahmanic *Om*. It must be of hoary antiquity, identical in Arian, Eastern and Western languages, as well as in Semitic ones. I am inclined to think *omen* to be a derivative from the same root, not from *osmen* as believed by others.

scratch and cut his head nor any other limb. He must not step upon ashes, hair, bones, nor on growing corn-stalks. He shall not in any way damage the soil, nor the plants, nor hurt man or animal, especially a cow, the favorite animal there, Morning, midday and evening, he shall not look into the sun. When at the altar, or reading the sacred writ, or when eating his meal, he is to bare his right arm. This corresponds to the covering and uncovering of the head during prayer, in the church, mosque and synagague. Fire must ever be sacred to him. Kindling the fire is the beginning of worship. He shall not stir it up with his breath ; nor otherwise treat it as a mere tool ; nor throw into it anything rotten, offals, etc. Nothing impure must be thrown into the water either, as blood, unclean water, spittal, etc. (¹) The dietary laws are very severe and elaborate, especially minute for the Brahman. The Catholic church distinguishes, too, between layman and priest concerning the diet. The Pentateuchal dietary laws were also intended mostly for the priests. It was not so exacting concerning the common Israelite. This we can especially recognize in the suggestions of the prophet Ezekiel on that head. The later Pharisees nivelated that point, extending these privileged priestly observances to all the Israelites ; all are realizing the ideal of a "kingdom of priests and holy nation," expressed already in II. Moses 19. 6.

BRAHMANISM AND ZOROASTERISM.

We have thus attempted to offer a short and succinct outline of Brahmanism, no doubt a very imperfect one, a mere sketch, to the end of enabling the inquisitive student to gain a correct view of Zoroaster's doctrines as found in the Zend-Avesta. The intelligent reader will see at once that between the two doctrines there are strong parallel features and a community of physiognomy. He will easily recognize that both are daughters of the same mother. The ancient ancestral religion or mythology had been entailed from the pristine Arian stock ; it spread from the regions of the Himalaya, on one side, East to the plains of the Indus and Ganges, and on the other, West, to the Iranian countries from Bactria to Media and Parthia ; after centuries of battling against the aborigines of both these great divisions of the land, the Arian mythology at last had to yield and mould itself to the new circumstances and surroundings, to the new populations and times, to its new and vaster home, to the new social features and arrangements ; above all to its own new genera-

1 Parallel to Parseeism, its sister religion.

tion of Arian children. From rustic, humble, marauding, poverty-stricken nomads, these had become proud conquerors, owners of vast territories and great wealth, masters of a population far advanced in the arts of refinement and of luxury. That original, gray, naive, Himalayan religion, of primitive nature, interfused with hero and ancestor-worship, had now to submit to great reforms, to startling innovations, nay, to radical changes, especially in its philosophical, metaphysical aspects. The Brahmans in India as the Atarvans or Magi in Iran, spared as much as they could, the popular myths, conceptions and observances. But the inner sanctum, the kernel of the system and cult had to give way. West and East, the new Arian generation adopted new views and ideas about world, man, worship, God, objects of life, etc., and these created here Brahmanism and there Zoroasterism.

ARIAN REFORMATION.

In India these new views and ideas arrived essentially, though not formally, at a real, spiritual monotheism. Brahman, the Athman, the life and breath of the universe, the Supreme Intelligence, the world-soul was the unique substance of all existence. He was the Supreme God. All the popular gods were but his subordinates, agents, messengers, or perhaps simply his attributes, his phases, divine aspects from a human standpoint. While among the West-Arian races, in the Iranian countries, Zoroaster or the Magi brought about their own reformation of the same Arian mother creed. They, too, postulated a qualified monotheism, the religion of Ahura Mazda, who came even nearer the Shemitic Elohim, Ihvh. He was the only one, supreme, spiritual God, Providence and Creator.—But at his side the Magi gave somewhat more prominence to the principle of evil than the Brahmans did. They admitted thus a formal dualism. Opposite to the one, supreme God of Light, of goodness and truth, sat Angro Mainyu, the dark, wicked spirit, the author of lies, evil and sin. The Magi were decidedly monotheists. But recognizing the stern fact of evil in the world, they did not slip over it, they emphasized it boldly. They put their finger upon that clashing hiatus in the universe. They declared that there must be a pretty independent principle of Evil, too. Hence, human virtue means not so much as to pray, meditate and offer sacrifices, but a deal more, viz : fighting evil, making efforts for good, and assisting actively Ahura Mazda in his good creation, co-operate with him and help forwarding good and resisting evil. This they termed virtue, worship, wisdom, serving Mazda and battling against Ahriman. Theirs was a religion of deeds, less of creed and prayer. This view of active religion, assisting the deity in doing good, we find also among Jewish moralists: "by such deeds, man becomes a partner of God."[1] This Persian doctrine is termed dualism, in contradistinction with monotheism. Yet this distinction is really without a difference. The Zoroastrians or Magi, did not worship two gods. They were really monotheists. They described Ahura Mazda nearly as the Bible does Ihvh. They worshipped not Angro Mainyu, they feared him, abhorred him and fought him. The very emblem of a Magi was the *Baresmon,* a bundle of rods to destroy the creations of Ahriman. Just as the Brahman bore in his hands a bamboo-staff and a bundle of kussa-grass. Thus we see that both the branches of the Arias; East and West of the Indus, reformed their former naive polytheism to a qualified but essential monotheism. Both revered but one God, though they allowed the ancient mythology a place, for popular purposes.

EVIL IN INDIA AND IRAN.

Why was the principle of Evil more prominent with the Magi than with the Brahmans? This question is best answered, I think, by interrogating the surroundings of either, by examining the climatic, political, social, economical, etc., circumstances of India and of Iran. In India, the climate is generally very mild and often unbearably hot; hence, it is effeminating, weakening, predisposing men to inactivity, despondency, submission, contemplative habits, averse to all exercise, inclined to religion, given to dreaming, supernaturalism, looking up to superior, all-dominating forces, political or spiritual. Nature is there mostly spontaneous, rich and luxuriant, producing men's food and clothing in abundance, with very little effort on the part of the cultivator. On the other hand the heat is so all-conquering and so enervating, that usually man is passive, listless, little ambitious, little capable of continued effort, and soon tired of existence. Add now to these climatic, physiological, economic and psychic factors, the political, social and ethical ones. A foreign race had conquered the children of the soil and placed upon them an eternal, crushing yoke, coupled with ignominy. The Arias declared themselves an everlasting aristocracy, sanctioned by the Supreme God himself. The vast majority of the inhabitants was declared to be born to serve and tremble, contaminating even by their looks. The higher classes,

1 נעשה שותף להקב״ה במעשה בראשית

the Brahmans and Kshatryas, the priests and the soldiers of these
Arian conquerors, have subordinated their own kinsmen, the
Vaisyas, subjugated the native aboriginal races and forever dis-
franchised them. The Brahmans were to be considered as the
expounders and oracles of the Supreme God. Every Brahmanic
priest was himself a living embodiment, an incarnation of the god-
head. He was himself a deity. The Kshatrias were the next born
lords. They were the custodians of the national force, the born
rulers, a military aristocracy, divine blue blood, living for dominion
and bloodshed. The native was forbidden to touch them, to look
at them, to draw his breath in their presence. In their presence he
had to fall on his knees, fold his hands, drop his eyes. Calculate
now the psychical effect of all these features and factors together ;
enervating, weakening, inert climate; slight inclination for work
and for enterprise ; crushing, racial, foreign dominion ; abject pros-
tration of the vast majority of natives; more crushing and overbearing despotism of castes and crafts; the State coercing every
social member to follow in the limits of his guild ; at last the most
abominable religious despotism ever recorded in the annals of mankind; pretending almost a divine homage and prescribing a
worship, a ceremonial, a ritual, etc., most exacting, cruel, minute,
interminable, extending over the entire life and hereafter ; sacrifices,
endless litanies, genuflexions, cruel fastings, self-castigation and
self-murder ; prescribing on all occasions and at each moment, a
host of petty observances and rites, as means to escape the wicked
spirits, devils, a future of terror, etc., and to come nearer to Brahman
and the good gods. Such interminable observances and forms
made it impossible for even the most conscientious stickler not to
sin. And the threatened punishments were cruel and lasting, extending to myriads of new births under the most repulsive shapes.
Combining now this multiple despotism of climate, soldier, priest,
caste, etc., we shall find the solution to the Brahmanic religion, state
and society to this day. We shall learn why the Hindoo loathed
life and declared all existence to be of evil; why virtue is not work,
effort, building up houses, families, farms, riches, ambitions. For
nature and society had crushed out all such sense of enterprise, had
robbed man of all force and energy, and handed him over, hand
and foot bound, to the blasting clime, to weakness, to despotism
and to superstition He therefore despaired of nature and of earthly
happiness ; he declared existence a curse, a cruel dream, an illusion ;

there is nothing real but Brahman; man's soul is a spark of God
driven into exile; rid yourself of life, of the body, then the soul
returns to the Supreme, is again united to its source, and enjoys
rest; rest in God is the only beatitude, the only paradise, only
heaven. That is Brahmanic faith, philosophy, sociology. The
unfortunate Brahmanic society created the pessimism of the Brahmanic religion.

SPINOZA. BRAHMA-SOMAY.

That reminds of Spinoza's fate, of his philosophy, and their
inter-connection. Hated by the priests for his independent, sharp
thinking; disliked by the rich for his proud, honest poverty; generally neglected by the masses for his ethical and intellectual
superiority, he was ostracized as Aristides in old Athens. He had
to live out of their reach, in his ethereal atmosphere of mentality,
virtue and dignified modesty. The silken mob and the cotton mob
could not follow him there to that sublime, isolated height of
thought and goodness. Reduced to himself, standing in the world
as a lighthouse amidst the raging sea waves, he lost sight of that
world and saw everywhere nothing but deity. Everything else was
but accident, ephemeral, a bubble, a wavelet on the raging ocean.
Everything was passing, yet necessary, inexorably prescribed by
inexorable law. He, himself, was but a paragraph there, once to be
united to the Code. That was his *Nirvana* in his Brahman and
world-Substance. Had he lived in more congenial environments, in
a kind and respectful community, with loving persons surrounding
him, with sweet family ties entwining round his heart, with thinking
compeers rising to his intellectual level, with social leaders aiming
at the public good and revering mentality and virtue as great social
factors, Spinoza might have otherwise perfected his philosophy.
He would have recognized that as the epithets of deity are infinite,
so are the manifold sides of sweet, humane existence, and that
besides mentality, there are also many other beatitudes than hard
logic, cold thinking. Even so the Hindoo society. Should England
succeed in really bettering that country, improving the climate,
mitigating fanaticism, enlightening superstition, softening military
egotism and moderating the race and caste pride, then the Brahmanic religion would lose its austerity, its pessimism. Life would
become worth living; existence no longer be a curse; the sage
would no longer suicide; the widow not ascend the funeral pile,
and *Nirvana* not be the sole hope. That is the task of the present
rising reform in India, the Brahma-Somay. Rajah Rammohun

Roy, its first founder, and Keshub Chunder Sen, its continuator, have correctly guessed the intrinsic monotheism and essential rationality of Brahmanism of 2000 years B. C. They coming nearly 2000 P. C., justly reconnect their social and religious movement with that hoary date. Their predecessors of 4000 years ago, may have had their reasons for retaining, at the side of their monotheism, the castes and parias, the myriads of observances, with polytheism and ascetism. The leaders of the present Brahmanic reformation can safely afford to drop the old Arian gods, castes, sacrifices and the pessimistic Nirvana. They can securely teach the biblical One God in spirit, one human race, equality of sexes, one right and one homogeneous society with "pure thoughts, words and deeds as cult," and the hope for education, happiness and freedom for all peoples and individuals, as the goal of human history.

ZOROASTER'S REFORMATION.

Though starting from the same, original creed and the same premises as the Indian Arias, Zoroaster's reformation arrived at other theological aspects and other sociological, etc., conclusions. That vast conglomeration of countries and peoples of Iran, from Bactria to Parthia, from the Caspian Sea and the Oxus river to the Erythrean and Persian Gulfs, exhibited the most varied, yea, opposite climates, soils, vegetations, political formations and societies imaginable; the extremes of cold and heat; of blooming, rich, luxuriant oases, and of arid steppes and sand-deserts; howling winds and blizzards coming from the northern seas, lakes and mountain-ridges, alternating with the vast, intermediate transitions and extremes, with sunny valleys and earthly paradises, as in Persia, Susa, Media, etc., contrasting so abruptly with the dreary steppes, the snow and sand deserts often close by. These startling contrasts of soil, clime, vegetation and living growth; the formations of mounts and adjacent valleys, of peaks over 20,000 feet high and of bottomless precipices, of gardens and steppes, paradises and deserts— that gives the first clue to the religion, the philosophy, the polity and the sociology of the Magian religion. Dualism was here imprinted on the face of nature and man. The icy winds, the scorching sun-rays, the avalanches of sand and of snow, the miasma of swamps, and the chills of vast pools and dark forests, clashed horribly with the frequent oases of green, lovely, cultivated lands, busy, flourishing cities, industrious and thriving husbandmen and craftsmen. Here were paradise and hell side by side, staring the beholder in the face. Here the helpful hand of man was all important; laziness was the greatest crime. Activity, draining swamps, cultivating orchards and vines, raising crops, extirpating the wolf, the bear and the tiger from the entangling woods, were great virtues. It helped the good creation of Ormazd. It annihilated the mischief of the wicked drughs. Labor, effort, solid work, building cities, draining, clearing, irrigating, opening wells, planting fields, raising breeds of dogs, horses, cattle, sheep, storing up provisions, developing crafts and tools, paving streets, opening roads and canals, restraining lawlessness, theft and murder, protecting life and property, erecting homesteads, rearing families, establishing government and order—that was virtue, that had sterling meaning, a scope fully worthy of man. Here that was possible and desirable; it required strenuous efforts and continuous labor, but it was meritorious and useful. Hence, the leading doctrines, the principles of *good* and *evil* were more salient in Iran and less so in India. Man could cope with nature in Iran; he was powerless in India. The blasts of cold and heat, storm and steppe could be overcome there; heat and pestilence and tyranny could less be vanquished here. India induced despair and asceticism, Iran effort and perseverance. Hence, virtue and religion in India meant resignation, self-mortification, passiveness, renunciation of happiness and of life, desiring nothing but Nirvana, absorption in God. Hence, the Hindoo philosophy: The world is but an illusion, existence and life are a curse and a punishment; body and nature are lies, sin and impurity; really there exists nothing but Brahman; from Brahman man's soul was derived and to him it is destined to return; that was religion, virtue, social science, the messiah-ideal. While in Eran, man could subsist only by will-power, work and effort; therefore, religion was not resignation, contemplation, a hermitage in the forest, and starvation. No, in Eran, Zoroaster taught: There are two contending powers in the world, life and death, light and darkness, truth and falsehood, creation and destruction. These he personified as Ahura Mazda and Angro Mainyu. He called upon his adherents to follow the one and to abhor the other; to do this not by prayers, meditations and observances solely. No, he emphasized deeds, works, and efforts daily and continuous, as the most efficacious divine service, as the most acceptable to Ahura Mazda. He associated man in the work of creation. He made him the companion of God. By useful work, by creating arable

Zend-Avesta by Maurice Fluegel.

lands, gardens, houses, bridges, wells, by drying marshes, draining swamps, extirpating wild beasts, he fulfilled his duty, he prolonged life, he built up paradise on earth and earned heaven here and hereafter. That was practical holiness; for God was practical good. That was Zoroaster's version of (Levit. 19): "Holy shall ye be, for holy am I your God." The Mosaic lawgiver had a ready-made country in view, and holiness meant to him morality and charity. Brahmanism had an unhappy clime with castes, and holiness meant resignation, submission and ascetism. Zoroaster legislated for wild territories; so religion to him was to conquer savage nature, brutal man, the fierce tiger, and build up a civilization. Thus the one and same original Arian mythology, called forth monotheism in substance in both, India and Eran. While physical and political causes brought out in India the ethics of resignation and ascetism with contemplation and pessimism. In Iran, monotheism was accompanied and explained by dualism, a recognition of the existence of evil and the duty of man to fight it. Religion and morality there, meant help thyself, work for good, be active, resist manfully the evil, evil physical, ethical, social and intellectual. Ormazd and Ahriman were the personifications of the two poles of human existence, of happiness and its reverse, of the battle for existence, of the bright and the dark sides of nature, from a human standpoint. Essentially, religion meant for Zoroaster the active contribution of moral and rational man to the triumph of good and the defeat of evil. Thus is Brahmanism a metaphysical monotheism, based upon monism, one only substance in the world, and ascetism is its ethical ideal. Zoroasterism is a practical monotheism, based upon a dualistic, cosmic view, and its ideal is practical virtue, useful activity. This dualistic view of Parseeism is not original with the Magi and Zoroaster. It is to be found even as a fundamental aspect among the Hindoo Brahmans. It may hail from the ancestral mythology of both. Yet they differentiated; vanquished by physical and social difficulties, the Hindoos despaired, lost heart, gave up the fight against evil and took refuge in resignation and *Nirvana*, declaring life a curse and nature an ugly dream. While the Eranians did not despair of nor resign life. They acknowledged the principle of Evil, and declared it to be man's great duty to fight it. It became there the leading feature in the worship of Ahura, the author of good, to resist actively Ahriman, the author of evil. As the ostrich hides its head from its pursuers when in danger; while rational animals face the enemy and fight him; even so the Brahmans denied the world and took refuge in ascetism and *Nirvana*. The Magi faced Ahriman and grappled with him, making an effort to assist Mazda and convert the earth into paradise.

HINDOO MONOTHEISM AND POLYTHEISM.

Hindoo Brahmanism and Eranian Zoroasterism are monotheism essentially and really; while formally and ostensibly they are both polytheistic; both have a substratum of their respective mythologies, their popular myths. Nay, when we closely examine, we find the mythologies of India and Eran to be identical; a proof that both started from the same religious stock. The undifferentiated Self-Existent of the Vedas is the Persian Zrvana-Akarana. The personal Brahman, creating the world, is the Avestean Ahura Mazda. The nature-illusion of the first is the Ahriman-lie of the latter. The " despair " of India is softened in Persia into " fighting evil and finally vanquishing it." The Hindoo closes with *Nirvana*, " absorption in God ;" the Parsee with the victory of the messiah and the defeat of evil. The former despaired of happiness and took refuge in heaven. The latter hoped for happiness at the " end of time," as Isaiah ([1]) The dualistic conception of good and evil, of bright and dark spirits is identical in both. In both was Soma-Haoma the high form of worship; in both it became itself one of the highest gods. In both was Agni among the chief deities, and fire-worship among the chief features. Brahmanism counted eight leading gods ; Parseeism had seven. Thirty-three deities, as the monthly days, were counted in both. Most of the names of the gods were in both creeds identical or nearly so. A few names were controverted. So Ahura identical with Asura, was the god of good in Eran ; Asura was the god of evil in India. Daevas were here the bright ones, the good spirits ; there they were devils, the evil spirits. Haug believes to find here intentional opposition; other scholars doubt that. In both cults these several gods were retained as subordinated to the purer God-idea, of Brahman there and of Ahura Mazda here; because the people would not let them go; because the unthinking learn but slowly. It is at great intervals only that they rise to higher, purer and more rational conceptions; because in popular religion, names and forms count for much; hence it was deemed prudent to continue the mythology of the national pantheon. So were retained in both the creeds the prescriptions on diet and cleanliness ; the three yearly harvest festivals ; the leading three castes of priests, warriors and agriculturers ; the

---

[1] באחרית הימים Isa. II. 2. Micha IV. 1.

entire formalism of the ancient cults, with sacrifices, purifications, litanies, incantations and charms, observances and ceremonies ; with the Soma-Haoma and fire-worship on top. The mythology of the Himalayan Arias was thus purified and chastened in both India and Eran, and enriched with a nobler theology and purer ethics as its real essence and kernel. Yet the popular myths were retained to please the people and to substantiate the claims of priest, soldier and wealthy ; for all goes by compromise and concession in the practical world.

MONOTHEISM EAST AND WEST.

It thus appears that more than fifteen centuries B. C., Arian peoples in India and Eran had dimly guessed God behind existence; that behind the forces and bodies of nature, there resides the great Soul of nature ; that the popular gods were but rays, forces, messengers, agents or perhaps mere attributes of the Universal Spirit. Thus both, Brahmanism and Zoroasterism, with all their apparent polytheism, are really monotheistic; and this no doubt is very interesting to ponder over. Now while this was going on in Eastern Asia, a similar movement took place in the West, in Ur of the Chaldees in Haran, in Hebron, perhaps in Egypt and Arabia, too ; surely so in Israelitish Canaan fused in Judaea. Were these rays accidental and scattered, coming from different suns and different motors ? This is not probable indeed. At any rate the impulse must have started from one great center, from the Sun of suns, the mysterious Central Intelligence behind and above the screen of nature. It would be stupidity to accept here a mere accident and hazard. No, these several movements were directed by one Supreme Intelligence, monotheism. Israel's monotheism, the Shemitic reformation began with Abraham. The Western mythology paled and yielded to the " *Highest Power*, owner of heaven and earth." Gradually that Abrahamic, timid, qualified monotheism proceeded ever bolder under the guidance of the phophetic school, to expunge the remnants of the mythologic gods and worships, notions and practices, which outside of Israel kept their ground yet for 2000 years, to the advent of the Nazareth and Mecca initiators. While in Israel, monotheism became fully victorious with Esra and the return from the Babylonian exile. With Abraham, commenced the aggressive policy of monetheism. It grew with Moses, Joshua, the prophets, the psalmists, the scribes, the Pharisees and the Maccabees. These defied and vanquished mythology and enthroned pure and unalloyed monotheism. Having gained a firm hold in

Israel, it resumed its conquest over the Greek, Assyrian and Arian myths. It achieved there its victory fully one thousand years after the Babylonian exile, under the forms of Christianity and Islamism. Modern sects, especially the Brahma-Somay, are establishing it in India and Japan.(1)

KAPILA'S PHILOSOPHY.

The Hindoo Reformation had, in theory, dethroned the gods in favor of Brahman, the one God in spirit. It had disestablished the universe and postulated God as the only reality. It had declared nature, matter, bodily existence but a dream and illusion. Hence, was the human body so, too; the human soul is to return to its source, to Brahman. Kapila in his philosophy, called "*Sankkya*," viz: considerations, meditations, doubted all that. The existence of Brahman was to him as doubtful as that of the mythic gods. But the reality of the bodies, of nature appeared to him beyond any doubt. The bodies, the individual, sensual beings do exist. Next exists the human soul, the intelligence. It cannot be derived from the body, since light cannot come from darkness. Hence, must intelligence, too, be self-existent, uncreated and eternal. There are thus two self-existent things, nature or bodies, and intelligence or souls. Every effect has its cause; so all created things are the effect of nature. Nature creates blindly, unconsciously, mechanically, eternally and endlessly, in time and in space. At the side of nature, there is the other great factor which is undeniable, viz: intelligence; and its cause can be but the soul of beings. Nature, matter is designated as *Prakrite*, and soul or intelligence as *Purusha*. The soul has an ethereal shell which ever accompanies it and is immortal as itself, termed *linga*, original body, elementary, *Ahankara*. This arch-body accompanies the soul on all its wanderings and transmigrations, while its material body changes at each birth. The Qabbala (2) and generally mystics speak also of the several elements or the composite nature of the soul. There is a multiplicity of souls, they are the reflective parts of beings, ever in connection with these beings. The material body belongs to nature, is perishable and changes with each new birth of the soul. The soul is eternal, uncreated; it is uncreative but reflective and perceptive; it is the mirror of nature. The misfortune of the soul is its fancied identity with the body, derived from its connection with,

---

1 See on that the Classical historians, Colebrook, Wilson, Muir, Spiegel, Dunker, Lassen, Benfay, Roth, etc.

2 See Fluegel's Philosophy and Qabbala on it.

and its intimate adherence to, that body. The liberation of the soul and its happiness require it to free itself of this intimate companionship. Unfortunately after the decay of the body termed death, the soul assumes another body by the law of transmigration. What should the wise man do? He should but find out that he is deceived, that he himself is the soul, the soul alone and not the body; that his real being, his *ego* is spirit not matter; he should realize that his body is hardly his; still less is it his real self; it is simply an involuntary, external connection, a clumsy, brute parasite, his temporary dark shadow, or his dismal prison.([1]) By that mental divorce, by dint of such stern reasoning, by thus repudiating the body, man will accustom himself to the fact that he has no concern in his material shell, that his body is simply a stranger and a burden to his real self. Hence, true wisdom and virtue consist in solving mentally that imagined union, in disrupting the intimacy of the soul with its coil even during life-time, not actually sever it by suicide, but by indifference, by the logical process of absolute differentiation of soul from nature or body, not mortify, starve or kill the body, but let it go and vegetate instinctively, hold it on sufferance, until it is decayed; in the mean time fully realizing that our true self is unconcerned in our material garb. That is liberation, beatitude, the highest at which the sage can attain. Such knowledge is redemption; its ignorance is enslavement and hell.([2])—Thus Kapila denied the popular gods, the priestly, only one Brahman, the supernatural authority of the Vedas, the entire cult, heaven and the ascension of the soul to Brahman. He acknowledged the fact of nature and sensual existence, yet he declared them a burden to man who is condemned to transmigration, which can be overcome only by repudiating that clumsy comrade, and realizing existence as purely intellectual.

---

[1] The body as a prison is assumed by all mystics, Hindoo, Jewish and Greek.

[2] See Weber, Roor, Kepper, Burnouf, Max Dunkar, St. Hillaire and others on this.

CHAPTER V.

In the North of India, near present Napaul, in Kapilavas-
tu—City of Kipila—Buddha, a great ethical initiator arose in the
latter part of the seventh century, B. C. He started apparently
from the doctrines just outlined. At least his theory, his abstract
doctrines were in the wake of the just delineated, sceptical philosophy of Kapila. The Brahman priests had declared life and existence to be of evil; natue with all its bodies but an illusion; human
life a torture; best to end by any means; to escape from it and
from transmigration, there is but one way, *Nirvana*, extinction of
self and absorption in Brahman, the world-soul, the divine Substance. Kapila started from that same theology after a strong and
essential modification. He denied not only the gods, but even the
existence of Brahman. He accepted the many, individual, rational
souls instead of the World-Soul. On the other hand he fully admitted the sad reality of nature with its individual bodies. But he
advocated the separation of the soul from nature as the only way of
escape from tribulation and disappointment. He recommended to
men the mental divorcement of the soul from the body, and thus escape regeneration, that widespread scare and bug-bear of the Hindoos
and other races, curious indeed, of entire ancient mysticism. It
meant perpetual torments in different bodies. Now, Buddha, started
from that philosophy after a considerable modification for the worse,
viz: Sakya-Muni, the Buddha, the knower of truth, the Enlightened,
was, with all the Brahmans, thoroughly convinced of the vanity, the
futility and the misfortune of existence. He rerecognized and be-
wailed the fact of the renewed births, of the continued existences of man
by transmigration. He denied with Kapila, the existence of Brahman,
of Providence, of the inspired Vedas, of the utility of religious observances and of all the popular worship. He acknowledged with
both that.human life is but a string of disappointments. But more
distinctly he affirmed that birth, the desire to live and love, to enjoy
and propagate the race is the root of misfortune ; that existence is pure
evil, and that the only escape from it is total extinction of body and
soul, annihilation. To annihilate the body and the soul, to
cease existing in nature and in spirit, that is the only rest, the only

---

1 We follow Burnouf, Dunkar, Koppen, etc., on this subject.

mode of happiness. Nirvana to him meant thus : total annihilation, blowing out the flame of life, putting an end to our being in any and every sense. There is neither world-soul nor Brahman, neither God nor gods. But unfortunately there is nature and the individual souls, and both are the source of disappointment and tribulations. Different from Kapila, he placed the gravity center of existence, not in nature, but rather in mind, in the soul with its perceptions and desires. Hence come its longings for life, or union with the body. Hence the curse of transmigration, the fact of its assuming a new body again and again. This continuity of regeneration, this interminable existence is a misfortune. "All that is should be destroyed." This is the only remedy for the prevailing world-evil, *to be*. Indeed all is vanity and disappointment under the sun. (1) Birth is followed by weakness, helplessness, dependence, want and sickness. With youth and manhood come error, vice, ambition, struggle, rivalry, evanescent triumph, alternating with real defeat, disappointment and heart-chilling uncertainty. Then steal upon us age, dotage, death—to be born and live again and pass through the same cycle of pain and tribulations, with all the sharp edges of constant change, cutting deeply into our flesh, ever hoping for the better and finding the worse. So is birth ever accompanied by helplessness, childhood by dependence, youth by desires and wants, manhood by struggle, age by decrepitude, and death is followed by myriads of regenerations. And this career is not an exception; it is the rule; it is for all; kings and saints are not exempted. Men and animals are subject to the same fatality, because life and all existence is the evil. Existence and evil are controvertible terms. Who lives must suffer and bear. Suffering ceases only with annihilation. The only possible way to happiness, viz: rest, is non-being, Nirvana.—The orthodox priests arguing on the same line, closed with the hope of *Nirvana*, meaning life and absorption in God. Buddha, the skeptic, in the wake of Kapila, denied the existence of Brahman. He acknowledged the sad reality of nature, he emphasized the superior import of the soul. The soul is the mind-power, faculty of thinking, perceiving, desiring. There is the evil. The soul's hankering after the world is the cause of the continued heartthrobbing, of the ever recurring disappointments. Here Sakya-Muni transcended Kapila. That skeptic advised the sage to disengage himself from nature, to dissolve all the ties with matter, to alienate his soul from his body, and by this estrangement, he may

---

1 Buddha's Philosophy found its translation in Ecclesiastes.

hope to escape any and all new births and continue to exist as pure mind, as an individual soul. Hence, Brahman priests, as Kapila, held out some hope for a happy existence, the first in Brahman, the other, independently, as mind-power. Not so did Buddha. He offered nothing. He said, not nature, but the soul is preponderant. The root of the evil is in the soul, in its perceptions, its longing for the world, its covetousness. As long as these exist, the new births, the desire after the body will continue; and even so will the misfortune of existence. Hence, the wise man must tear up the evil by the root. All existence is evil. The soul, too, must cease to be. Only then will the misfortune, life, stop. The sage should do both, divorce his body and kill his soul. He must give up all contact with the world. He must not perceive, not think, not see, not desire; he must become indifferent to his matter and to his mind; he must mortify all and everything, his body and his soul. This is the only beatifying Nirvana, annihilation, total extinction, the lamp dies from want of oil, its flame then is fully and forever extinguished. Then follow rest, quiet, the beatitude of no more to be, the only one possible and true. Here was a radical cure for all the tribulations of existence. The priests left yet the existence of the soul in Brahman, with Brahman as a reality; Kapila denied Brahman and repudiated the body, but left the soul to depend upon itself and exist intellectually, divorced from its body. Buddha declared war against all, God and nature, mind and matter, being in any shape. All existence, body and soul, is evil. The soul is constantly striving and longing for the world and for the body. This is her inborn instinct, her native law is to unite with a body. As soon as one coil is worn out and decayed, she immediately assumes and clothes herself in another shell, and this fatal longing is the cause of the eternal regenerations. All existence being an evil, its only and radical remedy is extirpating all existence. The evil is in both, in the soul and in the body. Destroy then the soul with the body; stop all thinking, refuse all perceptions, shut out the world, kill all desire, eject all food for reflection, then you will annihilate the soul, the thinking power. Then you shall have rest. Rest is alone in annihilation, that is the only Nirvana, the only heaven.

INDIAN AND JUDAEAN SCEPTICISM.

This bold and unmitigated war declaration to all and every existence, God and nature, body and soul, here and hereafter, is the more interesting when we remember the romantic career of that atheistic and radical philosopher. His soldier blood is visible

even in his friar philosophy. Gautama Siddhartha Sakya-Muni
was a Kshatrya of the princely military caste. He was the heir-
apparent to a Hindoo monarch. His father loved him, was
proud of him and conceived great hopes of that gifted young man.
Being thoughtful and of a serious turn of mind, he was surrounded
by a doting father, with all the pleasures and luxuries of an Asiatic
court to cheer and beguile his time. " Palaces and paradises,([1]) a
host of servants and courtiers, charming wives and other beauties,
singers, dancers, and sooth-sayers were attending his orders—all
in vain! 'Vanity of vanities, all is vanity!' All his eyes could
see, all his heart could desire was at his disposal, ready at a nod to
do his bidding. But he found that all is vanity and cheating his
while. Play is foolish, joy is fleeting, wisdom and folly meet with
the same fate.—He hated life, work and all effort. For that brings
no advantage nor improvement. Whatfore all work to leave its
fruit to an idle successor! All men's days are woe, tribulations
and disappointments. Buddha finished with desponding of life and
despairing of happiness. His heart bled at the sight of the sufferings of the common people ; at the ravages of nature, castes and con-
quests ; at the misery of the surrounding majority, the nine-tenths
of his human fellow beings, the Tchandalas, the Parias, etc., grov-
eling in mire and dirt, victims of the arrogance of the priest, of
the insolence of the soldier and of the over-reaching of the trad-
ing class. The inequality, the poverty, the ignorance, the superstition, the weakness and the wretchedness of the degraded outcasts filled him with pity and dismay. The surreptitious claims,
the hypocrisy, the brutality and the mean cunning of the upper
classes disgusted him and aroused his indignation. Then the
young, luxurious royal prince determined to cast away all his social
advantages, to give up crown and palace, beauties and flatterers
and devote himself to the regeneration of his country and his fellow-men ; to break with the priestly, the military and the plutocratic
associations and devote himself to alleviate the wrongs and the
wretchedness of the victims of social and of natural arrangements.
His reformation embraced Church and State. It was an emancipation at once religious, political, economic and social. With a

---

[1] That is a translation from Ecclesiastes, in matter and spirit corresponding to prince Gautama's scepticism. It is a reflection from
Buddhism, not Egypt. A later hand tried to mitigate it and confused
it.

self-sacrifice rare in human history, he devoted his energies to the improvement of his fellow-men. No pedestal is too great for his grandeur and no crown too lustrous for his brow.

BUDDHA'S ETHICS.

This proposition of acquiring rest through self-mortification, of giving up thinking, perceiving, desiring, and thus to gain the panacea of self-annihilation, is philosophy, mysticism; it appealed only to the few, the select ones. For the masses, Buddha taught a system of morality which had a practical, real, value, which contributed indeed toward making life more bearable, less irksome. His ethics made life more humane and suave. The divinity which was missing in his theology, we find again in his ethics. The fact that he taught such goodness and purity proves him worthy of his mission. He taught to moderate passion and egoism, to live humbly, modestly and peaceably; to do right and be altruistic; to live and let live, and feel with one's fellow-men; to be compassionate and sympathetic; not to be ambitious, to shun ostentation and pride, to avoid the world as much as possible, worldliness being the door to sin; to curb one's own passions, moderate one's desires, for they really are our worst enemies; to be chaste, unostentatious, and simple in one's apparel; not to be too greedy for acquisition, nor too eager for enjoyment, nor for outward distinctions. Those evils that are unavoidable in life should be patiently borne; then they will be least molesting. We must bear equanimously even injustice and wrong; not be revengeful, not hate our enemies. Even assaults depriving us of life and limb are hardly worth avenging, since life and limb are perishable and all existence is but an evil. Since all that happens to us is a reward or a punishment for our deeds, good or bad, done by us in this or in a preceding existence. It is hardly worth while to pine over and regret our own misfortunes; but we should regret those of our fellow-men. Thus he taught, no doubt, a noble morality. It contributed greatly to soften the character of his adherents and improved them individually and collectively, by mitigating the sting of egoism, avarice and ambition, and inculcating duty, altruism and love of next. Of his disciples and fellow-workers, he asked but a comparatively mild asceticism, viz: to renounce the world and its vanities, to live in chastity and in poverty as he himself had lived, humbly dressed, begging their bread, studying, thinking and preaching modesty and purity to the people.

HUMAN FRATERNIZATION.

He did not expressly abolish the castes. But with his new theology and his new ethics, they lost their base, their reason to continue. For with him the castes originated not in Brahman's head and feet, nature linked them all alike to one fate and destiny, whether priest, warrior or pariah. All men were an unhappy brotherhood, suffering from the tribulations of existence. Their duty is to alleviate and mitigate these by mutual sympathy and helpfulness. Hence, the equality, the fraternity of all races and their equal claims to the love of each other. Justice, sympathy and charity are to render life less intolerable ; hence, universal justice, forbearance and altruism. What good we can do for others, we should do as if for ourselves. We must be liberal to our relatives, charitable to the poor, the sick, the weak, the lonely, and hospitable to strangers. We must be kind to animals also. No animal should be killed and no flesh-meat used as food ; we shall give them no pain, and nurse them when sick. Nor shall we be ostentatious with good deeds. But we must openly acknowledge any wrong committed by us ; sincere repentance and confession will mitigate them. Buddha's ethics are resumed in chastity, patience and charity. To moderate one's passions ; calmly to bear the ills inseparable from earthly existence ; to be sympathetic, and actively assist in relieving the wants and pains of our next; not to commit wrong, to do good and curb our passions, such are the truly noble ethics of Buddhism.[1] In Buddha's spirit his successors added :[2] " No fire is so consuming as hate and passion, and no stream rapid as cupidity. Desire yields little joy and much pain. He who conquers his own self is truly happy. Contentment is the best of treasures." So we read, too, in the Rabbinical morality :[3] " Who is a hero? He who curbs his passions. Who is rich ? He who is satisfied with his lot." Further proverbs of Buddhist Bhikshu (monks) are of the same caliber: " He who broods forever over wrongs sustained, will never come to rest. The avaricious will not go to heaven. Even the humble-fortuned should be charitable. The liars go to hell. The duties are best dictated by the heart. It is useless to kindle the sacred fires even for a century, or to offer sacrifices even for a millennium. A month of expiations and an entire year of sacrificial offerings will not change the nature of one wicked

---

1 In most of that we have followed Burnouf especially.

2 Dhama padam v. 251.

3 Abboth.   .איזהו גבור הכובש את יצרו, איזהו עשיר השומח בחלקו

deed. Crime ever follows the perpetrator; there is no place in the universe to escape from its pursuit. Only good deeds may atone for it. Good is that deed which is followed by no remorse." The Buddhists were extremely tolerant towards other sectarians; peaceful and chaste; tender and respectful to parents. The privilege of caste and birth yielded to personal merit and behavior. The high-born were more humane, and the low-born were lifted up in the social scale. Ceremonies yielded to convictions and deeds; moral self-restraint and personal responsibility were considered paramount.

BUDDHA'S CHURCH.

Thus Buddha may have created a system of philosophy of doubtful value. But he sketched and practiced a doctrine of morality highly meritorious. He lived a life of the grandest import and became thus one of the great teachers of mankind. No doubt he followed in the steps of Brahmanic, perhaps, too, of Zoroastrian moralists. Many of his sayings are common to him, to them, and to the Hebrew Aggadic ethics. He denied Brahman, the gods, the authority of the Vedas and the saving power of Hindoo worship and observances. He slighted the state-religion and created no substitute. Soon his successors found out that the people need more than metaphysics and negation. His was an ethical system, not a positive religion. The Brahmans raised the cry of atheism and nihilism; a social war ensued and his followers were expelled from Hindustan. They took refuge in Birman, Siam, Ceylon, etc. They fled and gained to their doctrine Thibet, Mongolia, China and Japan. But they had to yield to the demands of the people for a God, a religion, a worship, a church. They created that. They established a church, a positive cult and creed, wrote a bible, *Sutras*, etc., a ritual, introduced ceremonies, created saints and angels; above all, they found their God-ideal, to whom the people should turn in their devotions and their longings for heaven. The life of Buddha was so great, it had made such a deep impression upon the Asiatic world, that it became the base and the material for one of the greatest religions of mankind. His followers raised the ascetic and begging monk into a semi-deity. Gautama Siddhartha Sakya-Muni became the ideal of divinity. With thinking Buddhists he was and remained but a holy man, a great and noble mortal. But in the eyes of the masses, he assumed a mystic role, the part of the highest ideal of manhood; the divine principle of holiness and goodness was incarnated in him. He is looked up to and revered by the East-Asian peoples as the highest object of human contemplation and imitation. He became the *Buddha*, the enlightened, the inspired, the divine. He corresponds there in some sense to the Messiah-ideal of the Western nations.

MESSIAH IN BUDDHISM AND BRAHMANISM.

Brahmanism already taught that the holy men, the great Rishis and Manu especially, were above the gods; nay, that the glow of devotion, the force of penance and goodness is superior to, and more potent than, the gods; that fervent prayer and holiness compel the gods to do the will of the saint, an idea often met with in the Qabbala, too. Here I find the elements of the messianic focus, the rays which later developed into the messianic ideal. The Brahmanic first Manu and the Rishis were primordeal, they were instrumental in creating the world, the gods and the spirits. They were the first emanations of the Supreme Self-existent. These are the powers, the position and the grave import, later vindicated to the messiah. That is Manu in Bramanism and Sakya-Muni in Buddhism. That mystic, supernatural force of devotion and holiness was personified in India by the Brahman-idea. Brahman was the impersonal force of holiness. It was further embodied there in Manu, and with the Buddhists in Gautama-Sakya. He became the Buddha, the concrete emblem of the divine, of the holy element in the universe. With him, as the messiah and lawgiver of the new sect and religion, was inaugurated a church, a cult, a hierarchv, ceremonies, holidays, and all the paraphernalia of a great sect, just as Brahmanism had; less the castes, the sacred despotism of priest and soldier; less the burning of widows; less the Tshandalas, and parias, and all the social usurpations yet now dominant in Hindostan. This revolution was accomplished under the impulse of the great life of Gautama, of the apotheosized Buddha. Undoubtedly it was a clear gain for human advance, a historical era. We thus find the Messiah-ideal not only in Judaism, Christendom and Islamism, we find it also in the Eastern religions, in Zoroasterism, Brahmanism and Buddhism; everywhere it means the same, the ideal made real, the divine incarnated in the human, the "kingdom of heaven" on earth, the deity engrafted upon man. This it means for the philosopher, at least for the thinking mystic. But the people have no room for such abstruse idealism. The people everywhere have translated it into plain, concrete terms. To the mass of votaries, Buddha is God incarnate. At every great historical turn-point, at every millennium such a miraculous divine incarnation is to appear upon the earth, to redeem mankind and lead it upon the path of virtue and holiness. Practically Buddha is the top of his own Church. Buddha had left his principality at the age of thirty years. He lived to the age of eighty as an ascetic, a student, a mendicant, a teacher of humility and goodness.—He died([1]) revered as a sage and a saint. Parts of his body are claimed to have been conveyed to different East and South-Asiatic countries, where they are receiving now almost divine adoration, in golden shrines and magnificeut temples. Nearly a third part of the human race belong to that denomination. They care little for his philosophy. But they are attracted and subdued by his morality, by his noble life, his goodness and self-sacrifice. They look up to him as the highest pattern of human wisdom and purity. He is their messiah-ideal, the Christ of the Eastern world. His noble code of morality is their "Sermon on the Mount." With the Christian founder, with the Hebrew prophets, with the Pentateuch, he practiced and taught, "Thou shalt love thy neighbor as thyself!" What is asked of thee, man? but to be just, kind and modest! King Asoka([2]) of India appears to have been the Constantine of that sect. He made Buddhism the state-religion. In the spirit of Buddha—of broad religious toleration, one of Asoka's inscriptions reads: "The ascetics (teachers) of all creeds teach the essential rules of conduct. A man should honor his own faith. But he ought never to abuse that of others." So the Pentateuch: "Do not insult the (foreign) gods." So Mohammed: "All my prophets have taught the same religion."—Having given an outline of Brahmanism and of Buddh-ism, let us now return to Zoroaster's doctrines and study the analogies of the Eastern and of the Western religions.

AVESTA AND VEDIC ANALOGIES, CEREMONIES AND INSCRIPTIONS.

According to Max Dunker, Windishmann, Fr. Spiegel and others, is the Avesta but an evolution of the Vedas, as everywhere the succeeding is a development of the preceding. While, according to James Darmesteter, both Avesta and Vedas are parallel developments of their common parent, the creed of the Arians, the predecessors of Hindoos and Iranians. Many of its leading ideas and forms are common to both the systems. The Haoma of the Parsees, as the Soma of the Brahmans, is a leading conception and rite of both the systems. It is alike assumed in both that a god holds therein his "*real presence.*" We have in former pages alluded to the Aphikomen-rite of the Hebrew Passover-banquet,

1 Probably in 543 B. C.   2 Died in 226 B. C.

and to the Eucharistia, the hostia, the wafers and the wine of the
Christian Church, claiming the real presence, or at least the symbolical one, of the remembered messiah. But such parallels are
legion between the religions of the East and those of the West.
The reception of the novice into the religious Community takes
place among Parsees and Brahmans at the age of 8 to 13, even to
24 years on some occasions.   Then the novice is solemnly invested
in both creeds with the sacred cord or girdle, which is never to be
removed, for it is a vestment, *as the Soudra*, of ominous import,
provided with mystical knots.

At that age the youth has to learn, respectively, the Vedas
or the Avesta. Till that time he is properly irresponsible of sin ;
his faults and transgressions are imputed to his father. Something
analogous we find in the rites of the church and the synagogue.
The Church has its *confirmation*, initiation, white robes, penance,
religious instructions with numerous customs and preparations connected therewith. The Synagogue has its *Bar-mizevah* ceremony
at twelve or thirteen years, when the boys become accountable for
their own behavior, when the father thanks God "for no longer
being responsible for his son," when the latter attains at his religious majority. He then gets his *philacteries* and *talith*, or sacred
scarf, even his *girdle* with the "small *talith*"([1]) its four knots and
fringes—just as Parsee and Hindoo.—We have spoken of the
diverse interpretations of *Ahura*, the highest God of Mazdaism.
According to Spiegel, is Ahura indentical with Asura in the
Vedas, Herr, Sar, Sire, Sir. It is akin to Ahu, viz: world, existence, being ; in Sanskrit Asura, asu as, ah, viz: being; Ahu and
Ahura mean the existing, the Hebrew יחוה יח. (Spiegel Com-
mentar Avesta I., page 3). Now it has been justly remarked that
Ahura, identical with the Hindoo Asura, is the highest God of the
Parsees, and the Devil with the Hindoos. As an offset, the daevas
are the Bright ones of the Hindoos and the creatures of Darkness
of the Persians. Even so is Indra the highest God of the Arians
of the Indus and Ganges, known among the Parsees as Andra,
dwelling in hell. The same it is with Sarva or Civa—there an
honored Deity and here a follower of Ahriman: what was sacred
there is unholy here. This fairly goes to show that in hoary antiquity, a religious secession had taken place, so argues Haug, between the
two kindred peoples and creeds, the Iranians and the Hindoos.
Both are of the original stock of the great Hindu-Germanic race

[1] ברוך שפטורין ‬ בר מצוה טלית קטן

that has been since prehistoric times to this day, gradually migrating from Hindostan and Bactria to West Asia, North Africa, Europe and America North and South, and Australia. The Arians or Iranians wandered away from Eastern Asia further and further towards the West, and gradually evolved their new religion, Mazdaism. Just as in modern times English dissenters, etc., emigrated to America. The oldest monuments of the Persian people are the cuneiform inscriptions of the Achaemenian Great kings Darius, Xerxes and Artaxerxes. There the Parsee religion in its outlines,' appears to be identical with that one we find in the Avesta as now extant. Ahura Mazda is the highest God, Creator of heaven and earth. Mithra, too, is mentioned there.([1]) Fr. Spiegel thinks the dialects of the Avesta and of the cuneiform inscriptions are decidedly identical and much akin to the idiom of the Vedas. From this similarity of language, as also of mythology and religious customs, Spiegel argues that the Avesta must have been composed at an early, prehistoric epoch, its failings, difficult and unintelligible passages belonging to later redactions. He opines that "in historic times the Persians have undoubtedly borrowed from their more cultivated Semitic neighbors. Much is to be expected from the deciphering of the Assyrian inscriptions. But even now the architectural monuments of Nimroud, Khorsabad and Persepolis show the art-connection between these diverse peoples."

PARSEES AND SEMITES.

To all appearance have the Persians learned from the Semites. The delineations and traits of Ahura Mazda on the Behistun monuments and those of the Supreme God of the Assyrian sculptures seem to point to a kinship in their theologies. Another proof of Semitic influence upon Eranian religious thought, Fr. Spiegel finds in the old Persian mode of writing. All the alphabets of the Persians, the cuneiform inscriptions inclusive, have a Semitic shape. The Avesta is as old as, if not older than, the epoch which goes back to our information about Persia ; and Zoroaster seems to have been considered by the classics as its author. A hoary age is attributed to him ; so ancient as almost to make of him a mythical person.([2]) He thus argues that Zoroaster is the author, not of the Avesta, but of the religious system embodied there; that that collection of religious teachings, etc., can in no wise be later than 600 B. C., or the age of the Achaemenides, but probably it is of much earlier date. Haug thinks at least by a 1000 years, Zoroaster must be earlier than

1 Fr. Spiegel Vendidad, p. 11.   2 Spiegel, Vendidad, p. 12.

that dynasty. This he deems to be the least space of time necessary for the natural development of that system from its origin to the shape as now extant; and a thousand years is rather too short. That would bring up the time of Zoroaster to at least 1500 to 2000 years B. C.

PROFESSOR MAX MUELLER ON MONOTHEISM AND CREATION IN THE VEDAS.

Now Professor Max Mueller of Oxford, in his "*History of Ancient Sanscrit Literature*," shows that, in the Vedic hymns, the poets dimly guessed the one supreme, ruling Power behind the forces of nature, and that the fabled gods of Hindoo mythology were nothing but the several attributes of that one supreme, invisible Deity. Groping in the darkness of hoary polytheism, they sometimes expressed that yearning for One divine Father, faint-heartedly and ambiguously, and sometimes with all the clearness and boldness desirable. He says (p. 559 and 567): " There is a monotheism that precedes the polytheism of the Veda, and even in the invocations of their innumerable gods, the remembrance of a God, one and infinite, breaks through the mist of an idolatrous phraseology, like the blue sky that is hidden by passing clouds. . . In Rig Veda, I. 164, 30, the poet chants: Breathing lies the *quick moving life*, heaving, yet firm in the midst of its abodes. The *living One* walks through the powers of the dead. The *immortal* is the brother of the mortal. (Then in Ibid, verse 37): " I know not what this is that I am like. Turned inwardly I walk, chained in my mind. When the *first-born of time* comes near me, then I obtain the portion of this speech." . . . At last boldly the poet declares that there exists but one Divine Being, though invoked under different names. (Ibid. v. 46): " They call Him Indra, Mitra, Varana, Agni; then he is the well-winged heavenly Garutmat, *that which is One, the wise call it many ways.*" The Rishi (Vedic poet) designates here the Supreme Ruler of the universe as the: " Quick moving life breathing " through nature. Another passage adds even: "breathing, breathless," viz: the Deity breathes without the need of air. It is itself the breath of life permeating all existence. He depicts it as the " living one walking through the realms of the dead," as the life-principle of inert matter, the "immortal allied to. the mortal." He feels dimly his own double nature of soul and body, and staggers at the riddle. Until at last dawns upon him the natural revelation of one God spiritual under the many attributes and names of the popular creed !

The "*first-born of time*" may be identical with the "*Ancient of Days*" of the prophet Daniel and of mediaeval Qabbala.

Zoroasterism being either a development of Brahmanism or its younger sister doctine, both evolved from the same mother religion, it will be interesting to learn something more on the above subject, viz: The dawn of the pure God-idea in India and the Veda, on the Infinite, Substance, existence, mind, creation, etc., there. We shall see how at the very hearth of polytheism, India, monotheism was evolved. Gradually the one-God in spirit dawned there. He loomed up clearer and brighter with the sister branch of the Arian race, among the Persians, as Ahura Mazda, to find its highest and noblest expression as *Ihvh One* in the Abrahamic family. To watch the beginning of that great religio-philosophical movement in India, let us follow Prof. Max Mueller on this theme in that same thoughtful and learned work on Sanscrit Literature, p. 559: "There is a hymn of peculiar interest in the 10th Mandala, full of ideas which to many would seem to necessitate the admission of a long antecedent period of philosophical thought. There we find the conception of a beginning of all things, and of a state previous even to all existence. "Nothing that is was then," the poet says; and he adds with a boldness matched only by the Eleatic thinkers of Greece or by Hegel's philosophy, "even what is not (*to my on*) did not exist then." He then proceeds to deny the original existence of the sky and of the firmament, and yet, unable to bear the idea of an unlimited nothing, he exclaims: "What was it that hid or covered the existing?" Thus hurried on, and asking two questions at once with a rapidity of thought which the Greek and the Sanscrit languages only can follow, he says, "What was the refuge of what?" After this metaphysical flight, the poet returns to the more substantive realities of thought, and throwing out a doubt, he continues, "Was water the deep abyss, the chaos, which swallowed everything?" Then his mind turning away from nature, dwells upon man and the problem of human life. "There was no death," he says, and with a logic which perhaps has never been equalled, he subjoins, "therefore was there nothing immortal." Death, to his mind, becomes the proof of immortality. One more negation, and he has done. "There was no space, no life, and lastly there was no time, no difference between day and night, no solar torch by which morning might have been told from evening." Now follows his first assertion: "*The One*," he says, and he uses no

other epithet or qualification—" The One breathed, breathless, by
itself: other than it, nothing since has been."[1]   This expression,
" It breathed breathless," seems to me one of the happiest attempts
at making language reflect the colorless abstractions of the mind
" That one," the poet says, " breathed and lived ; it enjoyed more
than mere existence ; yet its life was not dependent on anything
else, as our life depends on the air which we breathe.   It breathed
breathless."   Language blushes at such expressions, but her blush
is a blush of triumph.   After this the poet plunges into imagery.
" Darkness there was, and all at first was veiled in gloom profound,
as ocean without light."   No one has ever found a truer expression
of the Infinite, breathing and heaving within itself, than the ocean
in a dark night without a star, without a torch.   It would have been
easy to fill out the picture, and a modern writer would have filled
it out.   The true poet, however, says but a single word, and at his
spell, pictures arise within our own mind, full of a reality beyond
the reach of any art.   But now this One had to be represented as
growing—as entering into reality—and here again nature must
supply a similitude to the poet.   As yet the real world existed only
as a germ, hidden in a husky shell; now the poet represents the
one substance as born into life by its own innate heat.   The beginning of the world was conceived like the spring of nature, one
miracle was explained by another.   But even then this being or
this nature, as conceived by the poet, was only an unconscious
substance without will and without change.   The question how
there was generation in nature, was still unanswered.   Another
miracle had to be appealed to in order to explain the conscious act
of creation : This miracle was Love, as perceived in the hearts of
men.   "Then first came love upon it," the poet continues, and he
defines love, not only as a natural, but as a mental impulse.   Though
he cannot say what love is, yet he knows that all will recognize
what he means by love—a power which arises from the unsearch-
able depths of our nature—making us feel our own incompleteness
and drawing us, half conscious, half unconscious, towards that far-
off and desired something, through which alone our life seems to
become a reality.   This is the analogy which was wanted to explain
the life of nature, which he knew was more than mere existence.
The One Being which the poet had postulated was neither self-

1 God, the One, is the only Substance," thus anticipating Spinoza's
Ethics.

sufficient nor dead; a desire fell upon it—a spring of life, manifested in growth of every kind. After the manifestation of this desire or will, all previous existence seemed to be unreal, a mere nothing as compared with the fulness of genuine life. A substance without this life, without that infinite desire of production and reproduction, could hardly be said to exist. It was a bare, abstract conception. Here then the poet imagines he has discovered the secret of creation—the transition of the nothing into something—the change of the abstract into the concrete. Love was to him the beginning of true reality, and he appeals to the wise of old who discovered in love, "the bond between created things and uncreated." What follows is more difficult to understand. We hardly know into what new sphere of thought the poet enters. The growth of nature has commenced, but where was it? Did the piercing ray of light come from below, or from above? This is the question which the poet asks, but to which he returns no answer, for he proceeds at once to describe the presence of male and female powers, nor is it likely that what follows is meant as an answer to the preceding inquiry. The figure which represents the creation as a ray entering the realm of darkness from the realm of light, occurs again at a much later time in the system of Manichaeism, but like all attempts at clothing transcendental ideas in the imagery of human thought, it fails to convey any tangible or intelligible impression. This our poet also seems to have felt, for he exclaims: "Who indeed knows? Who proclaimed it here, whence, whence this creation was produced? The gods were later than its production, therefore who knows whence it came?" And now a new thought dawns in the mind of the Rishi, a thought for which we were not prepared, and which apparently contradicts the whole train of argument or meditation that preceded. Whereas hitherto the problem of existence was conceived as a mere evolution of one substance, postulated by human reasoning, the poet now speaks of an *Adhyaksha*, an overseer, a contemplator, who resides in the highest heavens. He, he says, knows it. And why? Because this creation came from him, whether he made it or not. The poet asserts the fact that this overseer is the source of creation, though he shrinks from determining the exact process, whether he created from himself or from nothing, or from matter existing by itself." Prof. Max Mueller concludes (Ibid 569): "I add only one more hymn, in which the idea of One God is expressed with such power and decision that it will make us hesitate before we deny to the Arian nations an instinctive Monotheism : (R. V. X. 121), " In the beginning there arose the Source of Golden light. He was the only born Lord of all that is. He established the earth and the sky. Who is the God to whom we shall offer our sacrifices ? He who gives, life and strength; whose blessings all the bright gods desire; whose shadow is immortality; He is the King of the world, who governs all; whose power mountain and sea proclaim; who established heaven and earth, air and light; He to whom heaven and earth look up, trembling inwardly ; He, the God above all gods, to Him we offer our sacrifices !" This is a most happy discovery in philosophical history. It is no small claim to glory for that venerable scholar and sage to have shown that monotheism was dimly guessed by the Arians, just as by the Semites, and most probably at about the same time. He is now writing on Hindoo philosophy, and most assuredly will bring out many more pearls in proof of the parallel thoughts between Arian and Semite, and thus show the identity of the human mind and its categories. Thus we see that the Vedic hymns contain often enough, a faint glimpse of the idea of One God, Cause of all existence.

PROFESSOR MAX MUELLER ON VEDANTE.

So again Max Mueller, in his recent work, *"Origin of the Vedante,"* p. 25, states that about 1500 to 2000 years B. C., in Hindostan, a great movement toward Monotheism took place. He says: " We see in the Vedic Hymns the first revelation of Deity, the first discovery that behind this visible, perishable world, there must be something invisible, imperishable, eternal and divine. . . . We see how the individual, dramatic deities, ceased to satisfy their early worshippers, and we find the incipient reasoners postulating One God behind all the deities of the earlier pantheon. . . . We see in the ancient hymns already, say 1500, B. C., incipient traces of this yearning after One God. . . . The gods, though yet several individualities, become really but phases of the same being . . . the Great Divinity. . . . These steps we can watch clearly in the Vedas, from the simple invocations of the unknown agents behind the cosmic bodies, to the discovery of One God, the maker of heaven and earth, the Lord and Father, the One Divine Essence, Brahman."—Curious ! The Aggadas about Abraham, his doubts about the native gods and his discovery of the highest God, sound exactly like Prof. Max Mueller's striking reasonings about the Hindoo theosophers. Did the Oxford Professor give here a sketch from Hindoo Vedas or from Palestinian Midrashim ? Is it not possible that the One-God meditations were going on simultaneously in Chaldea and Haran, Hindostan and Bactria? These reflections of the Oxford Professor throw some other important side-lights on interesting subjects. He says: " The gods, though yet several individualities, become really but phases of the same great divinity. Now this accounts for the otherwise wonderful biblical expression, Elohim, as identical with Ihvh. The plural *Elohim*, no doubt, is a polytheistic term meaning the '*Gods*;' we see that slowly it merged into *Ihvh*, the Supreme Being. He further defines the Hindoo *Brahman* as 'One God,' maker of heaven and earth, the Lord and Father, the One Divine Essence.' Now this is the very definition of *Ihvh*. (1) We saw before, too, Spiegel showing that Ahura, Ahu, means the existing One, corresponding, too, to Ihvh. Thus the same Supreme Being Israel denominates Ihvh, the Parsee called Ahura and the Hindoo Brahman! This may point to a simultaneous monotheistic movement in the East and in the West.

ZOROASTER'S IMPULSE. ABRAHAM.

At any rate, there is a strong possibility, that the monotheistic or spiritualistic phase in the far off East India and Bactria, as that in Chaldea and in Canaan, was identical with that of Zoroaster. There was a religious commotion in the Arian world, starting from wheresoever, Media or Bactria, etc., which lasted long enough, so as to make its incipient trials. Its first rays are hazy and obscure, except the salient and chief fact, viz: that Arian thinkers began to come out of the choas of mythology and to vindicate all the phenomena of nature to one single Cause, an immaterial omnipotence, mind, spirit, intelligence, located in one single living Supreme Center; hence came monotheism with Ahura Mazda; and the name of the man who gave that new impulse to Media or Bactria was *Zoroaster*, the " bright era," the " brilliant star."

We have seen that Zoroaster is claimed by the Avesta to have come from the West, Persia, Media, Ragae, Airyana, (Haran ?). He was the head of the priestly tribe, called the *Magi*, who are affirmed to have spread to Persia and Bactria from Media, Ragae, Balkh. . .On the contrary the classics speak of that Lawgiver as hailing from the East, Bactria and Iran. What does that prove ? It evidently proves that he had lived very long before the Classics and very long before the Avesta, as now extant, was written; hence the uncertainty of his place and his time. Now from unimpeachable Semitic sources, it is known that 2000 or 2200 years B. C., a similar

1 יהוה root היה

monotheistic movement took place in the West of Asia. Abraham is affirmed to have lived in Ur of the Chaldees, that he left his country and his people and wandered in different directions, (¹) haranguing and disputing and everywhere battling against the idols, discussing theology with princes and peoples and proclaiming the "highest Power, El-Eljon, owner of heaven and earth." He was teaching and practicing rational and pure morality, moving to and fro, to Haran, Canaan, Philistia, Egypt, etc. There are numerous legends and midrashim claiming him to have publicly taught in Egyptian Academies. Other legends, Hebrew and Arabian (²) have him wander to Arabia and to Eastern Asia, ever preaching the "highest God, Owner of heaven and earth." Abraham is affirmed by the Sacred Scriptures to have founded a monotheistic people, and that one of his descendants, Moses, centuries after him, elaborated that idea of the highest God; he formulated and brought it up to the Ihvh conception, the Supreme and Eternal Being, the only One God. On the other hand, some of the most trustworthy authorities claim Zoroaster's name to have been Ibrahim Zoroaster. Arabian tradition too, knows the Biblical Abraham as Ibrahim. His first emigration to Haran may be identified too, with Airyana Vaega, the mysterious City where some Avesta passages place the Bactrian prophet.

MOVEMENT OF ZOROASTER AND OF ABRAHAM.

Would not all this tend to show that the Biblical movement toward pure monotheism united to morality, justice and equity, going on among the Semites and led by Abraham and Moses—is identical with that of Zoroaster, of the Avesta in Media, Persia, Irania and Bactria? May not, furthermore, that be identical with the one spoken of by Prof. Max Mueller, as going on among the Hindoos about 1500 to 2000 years B. C. (³) I am far from pushing this mere hint to a hypothesis of the personal identity of Abraham of Chaldean Ur and Haran, with Ibrahim Zoroaster of the Avesta and the classics. The data are not enough for a personal identification of them. Such data are too few, too vague and too discrepant to war-

---

¹ Gen. 12 and Midrashim thereat.
² Midrash Yalkut, Abraham and Nimrod to Lech Lecha, etc. See the Koran on that.
³ Dr. Fr. Spiegel's 'Eran . . Beitraege zur Geschichte,' 1863, brings forward not an identical but a parallel line of considerations on Zoroaster, Abraham, Haran, etc. It is discussed by Prof. Max Mueller, in his 'Chips from a German Workshop,' p. 143. Genesis and Avesta.

rant any certainty about the personal identity of the Biblical Abraham with the Avesta Zoroaster. But I think that the co-incidence of facts and persons, that the outline, the *silhouette* of times and ideas is great enough to call the attention of scholars to it, viz: that there may well be a connection between the several religious movements that took place some 1500 to 2000 years B. C., (¹) simultaneously in Hindostan, Bactria and Media; in Chaldea, Haran and Hebron, etc., all going to the same assumption, that behind nature there are not only forces, but also one concious, Central Intelligence guiding all, called Ahura Mazda in Bactria, and Brahman in Hindostan, while in the West that same Central Intelligence was termed, El-Eljon, the highest Power Divine, Creator of heaven and earth, and at last Ihvh, Supreme Essence. All these doctrines have the same social morality, as the result of the same view of the Cosmos (Weltanschauung). Is that startling coincidence not of great interest, worth while to be carefully examined into? Thus we have seen that in far off Eastern Asia, as in Western Chaldea, Persia and Palestine, about 2000 B. C., the reigning nature and Star worship began to pale among thinkers, and that Zoroaster in the East and Abraham in the West, began to spiritualize their cosmic ideas and worship.

PARALLELS. ABRAHAM AND ZOROASTER.

Let us compare the data about these two men, stars of the East and of the West of Asia. Both taught that behind nature there is mind, behind force there is intelligence and behind automatic activity there is spontaneous direction. The same ethical phase and movement appeared in Hindostan, the bold assumption, "that behind the visible, perishable bodies, there is something eternal and divine." This spiritualization was carried on by Zoroaster in the East and by Abraham in the West. There the Supreme Deity was called, Ahura Mazda, Supreme Intelligence, Omniscient Master; and here, Highest Divine Force, Creator of all. Afterwards, some 2 to 4 centuries (²) later, deity was elucidated as: Ihvh, Supreme, Eternal Being. Much later a similar movement went on among the Persians, in the times of the Sasanides, when Ardai-Viraf rejuvinated Mazdaism, bringing it nearer to Mosaic monotheism. Pondering over both these ethical initiators, Abraham and Zoroaster we shall find many more parallels between them.—Fr. Spiegel says:

---

1 Max Mueller, 'Origin of Vedanta,' p. 28.

2 The Pentateuch speaks of 430 years. The Talmud reduces it to some 200 years.

" Unanimously it is accepted that the founder of the Persian religion is Zoroaster. He announced to King Vistaspa his Law which
he accepted. From him it came down to three successors who announced it to the world. It was then propagated in the family of
Aderbat Maresfand who purified it and taught it."(1) Here too, is an
interesting parallel with the three biblical patriarchs continuing the
doctrine of Abrahm, viz: Isaac, Jacob and Joseph; and finally a
Moses and his Levites who restored the Abrahamic tradition and
taught it to regenerated Israel. Another striking analogy is: that Zoroaster taught but qualified monotheism. Ahura Mazda was really not
the *Only* God, but the highest one; that he had his peers and assistants,
the Ameshas Spentas, Yazatas and other genii. Even so did Abraham
not teach: Ihvh is one, but he is "the highest God, owner of heaven
and earth,"(2) just as Ahura Mazda was. At the side of the "Highest
God" there were yet numerous subordinate genii and assistants, angels and messengers the highest. It is but centuries afterwards that,
in place of the "highest," the "only One," the Supreme, Eternal
and Only Being, was taught.(3) Even so did Aderbat Maresfand
purify and finally formulate Mazdaism. As that same doctrine was
further expounded in the III. century P. C., was purified by Ardai-
Viraf, and the *Husvaresh* Commentary added to it, even so came
after Abraham and Moses, later, Ezra, the Mishna and the Gue-
mara, or Talmudical tradition, which expounded, elaborated and
elucidated the Thora. These teachers are also called *Parashim*,
Commentators, with the additional meaning of Puritans, Separatists
and perhaps, too, Parsees, because there may have been a certain
parallel in their purity doctrines and their logical methods derived
from there, Persia, etc.

ANTHROPOMORPHISM. ANGELS, DEMONS, YAZATAS.

The chapters in Genesis narrating the intercourse of the deity
with men, as Adam, Kain, Henoch, Noah, Abraham, Loth, etc.,
have yet much of polytheistic coloring. There is there a certain
familiarity between the divine and man, an exchange of opinions,
a persuading and disuading, an offering and accepting of food and
drink, entering into a covenant or agreement, on one hand to worship
God, only, on the other to be the God of Abraham, Isaac, Jacob, etc.
God promises and repents, acts and regrets, is pleased and pleases
others, is indignant and thunders, or is gracious and pardons for the

---

1 Vendid., p. 41, by Spiegel; also in Yasna, Patet.

2 Genesis 14, 19. אל עליון   3 Exodus vi. 2, (and Deuteronomy vi. 4)
Moses taught: יהוח אחר. ושמי יהוח לא נורעתי להם

sake of the fathers, or for the consideration of a sweet smell and
sacrifice. Quite another phase looms up in later parts of Exodus,
Leviticus and Deuteronomy. There God is the Only One, incom-
parable, above all creatures. The Anthropomorphic and anthropo-
pathic elements are mostly, if not totally, obliterated. This process
goes on in Deuteronomy, later in Psalms, Targums and Talmud.
Now these same phases are striking in Zoroasterism. Ahura Mazda, in the Avesta, is the highest in the creation of Good. But there
is another creation, that of Evil, and its chief is Angro Mainyu,
almost the peer of Ahura. There are the Ameshas Spentas, *Yazatas*, and innumerable other genii, all holding a certain independence
in their respective spheres. So Zoroaster confers with Ahura on
almost familiar terms. Ahura treats him with the utmost kindness
and respect, almost on terms of parity, as one of the gods in the
hierarchy. This hierarchy and Dualism of Parseeism reacted upon,
or, at least, was re-echoed in Judaism. There, too, we find soon
Satan, angels, spirits, etc., good and evil, the heavenly Council.[1]
Comparing the later developments of Judaism and Zoroasterism,
we find between both systems, a constant interchange of ideas and
customs, attraction and repulsion, befriending and antagonizing. So
Is. 45 terms Cyrus "Ihvh's anointed." He describes a man as
(41 : 1–8) "friend of Ihvh." He designates him (41: 2) as *Zedek*
or *Zaddik* which may very well be identical with the Avesta *Yaz-.
atas*, both meaning, at any rate, venerable and pure beings, chiefs
in the hierarchy, types and genii of their respective classes. Thus
we see clearly the systems reciprocally influencing each other.

---

[1] פמליא של מעלה

CHAPTER VI

THE MESSIAH IDEAL.   ESCHATOLOGY.

Even so are the last issues of history and the messiah-ideas alike, yea, almost identical in both the systems. Ahura Mazda has to contend against Angro Mainyu during the existence of this world. But at last the kingdom of heaven will come, and Angro Mainyu will be vanquished and annihilated. A prophet will arise at the end of time, Saoshyance, by name. sprung from the loins of Zoroaster, who will fight and subjugate the spirit of Darkness and his hosts.([1]) The Avesta describes the messiah enthusiastically, as the great, the victorious, etc., almost identical with Is. IX. 8: " The wonderful, councillor, divine hero, eternal father, prince of peace." Compare the following with present Christology, and you will wonder, indeed, at the, almost, identity of the idea and the ideal environments, persons and ornamentation in the several creeds. Concerning the Parseean Messiah,([2]) Fr. Spiegel says: " From Vendid. Farg. XIX. 18, etc., we see that the Parsees expect at the end of days a prophet, Saoshyance, and according to others, even two more such prophets, by other names. Each of these prophets will reign 1000 years, *hazare*, millennium. Towards the end of the world, great calamities and wars will befall mankind. Human gore will flow so abundantly as to drive the mills. Some respite will follow. But evil will be uppermost again. Man and beast will emulate to render life wretched. The dew from heaven will be blood. Plagues and pestilence will ensue and all will be defiled. A prophet, Oshedar-Bami, will appear. He will add a book to the Avesta and restore pure faith. He will do wonders. Then will a horrible winter come on, and all creatures will perish. The garden of Jemshid will be thrown open to re-people anew the world. Another prophet, Oshedar-mati, will appear and all wicked creatures will vanish. Again comes irreligion, and Saoshiosh will appear. The right faith will be accepted and wickedness disappear. Then follows resurrection and mankind will be like angels. A new book will be added to the Avesta." Here is the epitome of all the messiah-dreams of Parsee, Christian, Jew and all mysticism, the messianic wars and calamities, regenerated men and rebuilt cities, resurrection with *spiritual* bodies, renovated laws, triumphs and untold hallelujahs with peace and happiness for all the pious.

[1] Fr. Spiegel Vendid. 16.   [2] Fr. Spiegel Vendid. 32.

Since the Jews re-echoed the doctrine of the Evil principle, they most naturally reflected this view, too, that Satan, the Semitic Ahriman, will be vanquished by the messiah at the end of days. So have Daniel, the Apochryphae, the Talmud, Qaballa, etc. Christianity, that even more emphasized the power of Satan, had to give even greater import to the messiah theory. All this shows the mutual influence of the several religious doctrines. Parsee, Jew and Christian postulate the Messiah-idea to square the anomaly of evil in the creation of the God of Goodness; the several periods or millenniums in that process of salvation; the great commotions to bring it about; the renovation of the world, of law and faith; the annihilation of wickedness, of death and tears; the resurrection of the dead, and the establishment of the kingdom of God—that means the undivided dominion of the Principle of goodness, peace and wisdom.

ABRAHAM AND ZOROASTER IN ISAIAH.

We have tried to interpret some chapters of Isaiah the II., the interesting chapters 45 and 46 in his harangues and discussions concerning the religions of Cyrus and Zoroasterism, of Bable and polytheism, of Judaea and monotheism. Close by, there is by the same prophet, another passage throwing further interesting light upon our subject. It is in chapter 41, 1, etc., which reads thus : " Be silent, ye maritime lands, and ye nations step nearer by and let us reason: Who has from the East awakened "Zedek" (justice, equity), who called on him to follow and to wander? ([1]) He prostrated nations before him and kings he subdued to him; his sword renders them like dust and his bow does as chased stubble. He pursued them and passed in safety a road he never came by. Who has caused that? He who called forth the generations from begin, I, Ihvh, the first and the last, the omnipresent."—He goes on discussing the merits of monotheism, of Israel "the seed of Abraham, my friend," their struggles and their hopes in the battle against *paganism*. Now is the question, to whom does the inspired poet-patriot allude by: " Who aroused from the East *Zedek*, the Righteous one ?—Some Commentators think it is Cyrus, the Great-king of Persia, a worshipper of Ahura Mazda, half a monotheist, a friend, a protector of Israel, just on account of that religious affinity. But I believe talmudical tradition hits better the mark than that. The Commentators, Rashi, Kimchi, Abarbanel, etc., follow that better inspiration. They refer those verses with *Zedek* not to Cyrus, but to Abraham. Indeed discussing the merits of the doctrine and

---

[1] להגלו alluding perhaps to לך לך מארצך, Genesis. 12.

the ethical fitness of monotheism and of polytheism respectively,
Abraham appears justly to him a greater hero than even Cyrus.
Especially so is verse 8 of that chapter, enthusiastically exclaiming :
"And thou Israel, my servant, Jacob whom I have chosen, seed of
Abraham, my friend . . . . fear not, I am with thee !"—That shows
to all appearance that the prophet was alluding throughout that
chapter, not to Cyrus, but to Abraham, who first of all taught the
doctrine of mind and intelligence as the Supreme Power, owning
heaven and earth. Abraham, he assumes " to have been aroused
from the East." He gives him the epithet of *Zedek*, justice and
equity, to him he subjects dominions and kings, whom his sword
and bow have reduced like chased stubble, and who passed in safety
the road of bloody war. Verses 2 and 3 show the entire chapter 41
as alluding to Abraham's victory over the five kings as in Genesis
14. He calls him the " friend of Ihvh," as often leading teachers
and initiators are termed by the Hebrew prophets, alternating with
"servant of Ihvh." Now does not this description of Abraham also
describe Zoroaster, "awakened in the East" of Judaea, Media or
farther Bactria, whom Western Greek classics too assume as having come from the East ? Are there not current about Zoroaster
similar legends as those about Abraham ? Zoroaster too was the
friend of Gustasp, King of Bactria and his active ally in war, no
doubt, since he at last perished at the hands of Turanian invaders.
There can be no doubt that in hoary times, eastern Asia entertained about Zoroaster similar reminiscences and traditions as western Asia did about Abraham, viz : that he had subdued nations and
vanquished kings, with worldly and with spiritual arms ; that he was
called up by the Supreme, whose friend and prophet he was ; that
God revealed to him his Law and made him emigrate to Airyana,
etc. Closely looked at those Isaic verses, it seems they vaguely
describe a half legendary and half historical person, revered by posterity as the patriarch, the pride and strength of the Judaean nation,
appealing to, and relying upon his merits, (1) as their Sire and
inaugurator of a new socio-ethical order, teaching the Supreme God
as the object of worship ; peace, justice and morality, as the rule of
conduct. This prophetic picture is as vague as the nucleus of a halo,
as a hazy transparent, as a historical kernel surrounded by the neb-
ulae of legend. Isaiah calls him : "*Zedek*—righteousness" and
"friend of God." Such fits well to both, to Abraham in the West
and to Zoroaster in the East. These two antique traditions, he may

---

1 זכות

have identified as one and the same, the first movement in the direction of monotheism and morality, hence: " God's friend, servant and Zedek."(¹) The Avesta gives such titles to Zoroaster, the Hebrew Bible to Abraham, Moses, Job, etc. Both those initiators were no full historical persons, both were looked upon through the haze of legend and veneration. May not Isaiah, in chapter 41, have identified both, as one and the same nucleus of a similar phase of religious thought, and without naming either, have alluded to both, as one great illustrious era in the past influencing the present? . . . I do not wish to be understood as advancing here the positive theory of the identity of both these intellectual phases, but simply as hinting at the mere possibility that the nucleus of the Semitic tradition about Abraham and that of the Arian legend about Zoroaster may be but one center of the same constellation; a possible hypothesis awaiting more substantiation from future studies on these weighty themes. Another remark concerning Isaiah's *Zedek* is the following: Besides the long list of supreme, assistant and subordinate gods, Mazdaism taught a longer hierarchy of transcendently holy beings: *Yazatas.* Ahura was the highest Yazata in heaven, and Zoroaster the highest Yazata upon earth, patron and type of the human kind. Yazata in the Avesta means the venerable, pure and holy spirit or person. To the soberer Semitic, monotheistic Judaean, the Parsee Yazata may have been the *Zaddik*, the later Chassid. Isaiah applies this epithet to the initiator of monotheism and morality, called Abraham in the West and Zoroaster in the East. It may be the same conception apotheosized in the East, humanized in the West, myth in the Avesta; tradition in the Bible; there a demi-god, here a social and ethical reformator, a sage.

THE ETHICAL MOVEMENT OF ABRAHAM AND ZOROASTER.

We have seen above that the Greek classics assume unanimously Zoroaster to have come from the East. So has Abraham, Genesis XI. 31, etc. So Isaiah 41: 2, "Who aroused from the East *Zedek, Yazata.*" This verse Jewish tradition justly refers to Abraham. The Pentateuch calls him *Ebri*, from beyond, East, coming from Ur of the Chaldees. The Avesta, on the other hand, assumes Zoroaster as hailing from the West, alluding to Airyana-Vaega, which may well be the Biblical Haran (Genesis XI. 31). So as we have seen above, Dr. Spiegel, Prof. Max Mueller, Shorr, and many others, hold Airyana to be identical with Haran. The Abbe

---

עבר איהב צדק 1

Bannier, a century ago, hinted at the latter place whereto Abraham emigrated, "as the capital of Sabism, whilst Magism was followed in Ur of the Chaldees." (Mythology and History I. 3, 3). Here may have been the point of contact between the two leaders of monotheistic thought. The best date presumed of Abraham and Zoroaster is over 2000 B. C. The description of Abraham by Isaiah 41 suits perfectly well to that of Zoroaster by the Avesta and the classics. According to both, he was a man of theory and of action, of doctrine and of practical initiative. He is surnamed by some Ibrahim. So is Abraham remembered in Arabian legends and the Koran. By the Parsees Zoroaster is known as a priest and itinerant teacher, head of the Magi, a priestly tribe. The Chaldees, or "*Chasdiim*," seem to have been just the same, a tribe devoted to religion and science, and Abraham was one of them. As Zoroaster gave a new impulse to his clan, so did Abraham to his. Zoroaster left Medea, may be, as a persecuted reformer, even as such Abraham left Chaldea (Genesis 12 and Midrashim). There is a well-known Midrash that the tribe of Levi in Egypt was a free and learned class, even under the Pharaohs, hence the intellectual superiority of Moses. Thus the Levites among the Hebrews, the Magi among the Medes, and the Chaldees in Babylon were the priestly clans producing respectively Moses, Zoroaster and Abraham. Abraham is thus a "Chasdi," a Chaldean priest and wandering preacher in Hebrew legend. Zoroaster announced Ahura as the highest Spirit and Creator. Abraham taught the "highest Power, owner of heaven and earth." Zoroaster inculcated the duty of man to fight Angro Mainyu. The peaceful Abraham did not hesitate to surprise and route the aggressive marauders, Kudur-Legomer and his allies (Genesis 14); a practical illustration of combating wrong and evil. Zoroaster taught Ahura as the "*Highest*," *not as the only one.* Abraham taught the highest Power and Creator, allowing room for assistant, subordinate, divine beings (Genesis 18), simultaneously. No doubt Abraham is spoken of in Genesis as a real, substantial, historical person; while Zoroaster is almost a myth with a nucleus of truth. But this difference is not personal to them. It is characteristic of the Arian and the Semitic literatures. The Hebrew scriptures are mostly sifted, sobered out matters of fact, the real nucleus of the traditional story. The Arian one is juvenile, poetical, mythical, given to apotheosis and exaggeration. The Heathen myth has a historical kernel, too. Even the Bacchus Saga may have a true nucleus. But that nucleus is overgrown and stifled by poetry, juvenile tales and laudation. The Hebrew writ contains the kernel cleansed of its halo of lies, poetry and ancestor-worship. The Hebrew heroes claim an honest father and mother and are born in wedlock. The Greek or Roman one's pretend to be demi-gods, descendants from gods and godesses. The first go to "sleep with their fathers; the latter ascend to Olympos after death. Compare Samson and Hercules, David and Augustus, etc. More illustrations we have seen in my Messiah Ideal, Vol I., Parallels.—Dr. Fr. Spiegel, in his "*Eran . . Beitraege*," mentioned before, follows a similar line of parallelism between the Aryan and the Semitic leaders of monotheism. This parallelism, on the whole, coincides with ours. He sums up his argument as follows: A very early intercourse seems to have taken place between Aryan and Semitic tribes; a common belief in One spiritual and eternal God; a striving after purity in thought, word and deed, or practical morality; a paradise at the sources of the Oxus and Yaxartes; Haran as the common dwelling-place of both the reformers. The Biblical Haran is identical with the Avesta Airyana. Semitic and Aryan tribes lived then, as now, in close contact; and from that ancient hearth of civilization they started towards the East and West.—Our remarks on Abraham and Zoroaster do not yet amount to a full hypothesis, less so to a theory, that Abraham and Zoroaster are one and the same person in fact and in deed. But they go fairly to show that the same ethical movement and impulse which the Arian East referred to Zoroaster, the Semitic West did to Abraham. In both cases there is a solid nucleus of historical fact with a halo of poetry. In Zoroaster only is the myth predominating, in Abraham is the historical one preponderant. The inner nucleus of both the constellations is the same, the halo is strongly reduced in the Bible, it is a blaze in the Avesta. Divest it of the mythology and both the movements may be identified, perhaps the persons too, after future maturer studies of the theme. At any rate I believe there is fair ground for presuming that the ethical movement of Irania is a full parallel to that of Haran and Judaea, that the movement of Zarathustra, Abraham and Moses has been continued by Judaean prophetism; and that this impulse has been propagated in the West by Christianity, in the East by the Koran, in modern times by the reformation and in present times by the humanitarianism of Roussean, Mirabean, Lessing, Mendelsohn, etc. The present Parsees of Bombay identify Zoroasterism with Monotheism. So is and has been, from begin, Mohammedanism; and the drift of the

Reformation and present liberal thought points in the some direction. The countless parallels between Mazdaism on one hand and on the other Christology, Talmud, Islam and Qabbala are not necessarily one-sided ; these latter were not always the borrowers, nor the Parsees ever the lenders, as assumed by Shorr and others.   But I agree that there was reciprocal influence.   I feel inclined to assume, judging the past from the present, that in all rationalistic movements, Christians and Jews were the originators ; in all mystic movements, the Parsees gave the impulse. And since Zarathustra or at least the Avesta, started with the hypothesis that from begin the universe was ruled by two sets of spirits, holy and unholy ones, I think with many writers preceeding me on this topic, that a great deal of our present exaggerated supernaturalism, and that nearly all the superstitious practices and notions yet current in our days, are derived from Parsee and Brahmanic spiritualism.

CONSIDERATIONS ON THE AVESTA.

In the preceeding pages, we have seen that the Sacred Books of the Parsees are not yet perfectly accessible to the modern scholar.   Their mode of writing, their idioms, figures of speech, hyperboles, metaphors and technical terms, allow us rather to guess than exactly to know their meaning. For long centuries, they were probably handed down orally, by tradition.   When later they were entrusted to parchment, they were but epitomized as mere helps to memory, intelligible only to the sacerdotal class, but not accessible to laymen ; and a sealed book especially to foreigners. Then they were repeatedly lost and re-written in idioms and a handwriting not yet fully deciphered.   Therefore will it take yet a good while before modern scholarship will be enabled fully and correctly to interpret them.   The estimate one may now be able to make, and even that with great hesitation, would be the following, viz : The Avesta represents that phase of religion just appearing after nature-hero-ancestor-and fetish-worship ; just after man issues from barbarous life.   A small fraction of society having provided for the necessaries of life, find time and leisure for contemplation and observation.   The surroundings inspire them chiefly with wonderment and with fear ; with admiration and gratitude on one hand, with misgivings and deprecation on the other, with the feeling of dependence upon external, superior powers who can do them good or harm. Hence come worship, cult, supplications, deprecations, offerings, sacrifices.   In the first stage of civilization, we fear and venerate natural bodies and fetishes, as mountain, river, sun, star, father, hero, chieftain, etc. We gradually advance to worship forces; storm, fire, lightning; next abstractions, divinity, victory, beauty, goodness; we then personify: These things, bodies and abstractions, become living beings, couscious, free agents. At last we spiritualize and apotheosize them. This is the stage of polytheism. Each object of our love or of our fear, of admiration or horror, becomes a god. Gradually we begin to discriminate, to group these forces, to subordinate and superpose them. So all mythologies had a few superior gods and many subordinate ones. Each object in nature had its prototype, its genius and divine patron. As such a divine type and patron, are yet imagined the messiah in Jewish mysticism and Christology, Buddha in eastern Asia; primordeal man or Adam Qadmon in Talmud and Qabbala, is such an old reminiscence, an old idea with another name. Contemplation went on, pantheism slowly became polytheism, then reduced to a few duties, to three, to triads in Hindostan, Assyria, Egypt, etc., until it arrived at the Dualism of Persia. This is the Mazdean doctrine. The teachers of that philosophy placed themselves upon the simple, human, personal standpoint. As the author of the Mosaic Genesis contemplated creation from his own point of view, the earth, even so the author of the Avestean scheme : Everything in this world bears some influence on man, a good or bad influence, pleasing or displeasing, desirable and useful, or not. Hence he divided all existence into two such antagonistic creations, presided over by two opposing, inimical Powers. And these two are supreme. They have an infinitude of subordinate agents; they alone are supreme. The principle of Good was symbolized by Light; that of Bad by Darkness. That explained all the phenomena of human conditions. Light, goodness, happiness, growth, beauty, all things useful and agreeable to man, belong to the creation of Ahura Mazda, the Spirit of Good. Darkness, pain, death, fraud, lies, crime, toil and misfortune come from Angro Mainyu, the Spirit of Evil. Let us illustrate. The prophet Ezekiel (33. 10) of the early Babylonian exile, upholds the prophetic conception that morality and practical happiness are linked together, as cause and effect: "Son of Adam tell to the house of Israel: Never do I wish the death of the wicked; let him repent of his evil ways, and he shall live. The goodness of the righteous will not save him as soon as he sins ; nor will wickedness harm as soon as it is abandoned."—Now the Magi philosophers were neither so naive, nor so sagacious as the prophets. They believed to find out that the wicked may be happy and the good be unfortunate—hence did they postulate the presence from begin of *two Principles;* and Ahriman accounts for the presence of Evil in the human world.

This division into good and evil spirits is discernable in the Hindoo Vedas too. But there it was not developed. There nature consists of bodies and forces. The Avesta ushered in the new postulate of mind. It made the important step of spiritualizing, of breathing in life, personality, divinity into nature; of dropping polytheism, star, hero, force and fetish worship and ascending to two Supreme Principles, one the Power for Good and one for Evil. The human mind advances but by small steps. These two principles in embryo are in the Vedas. In the Avesta, they but gained prominence; they became the pivot of the system. On the other hand polytheism was far from being entirely abolished. The Avesta retained six Ameshas Spentas, in all some thirty or more divine peers, a large number of venerable *Yazatas,* and a host of other subordinate good spirits. Then came Ahriman's hierarchy. Each and all were invoked, prayed and sacrificed to as deities. Each object in nature had its prototype in .heaven, it was its genius and patron. Each body in the universe was spiritualized and personified. Even abstract qualities, as each force and each phenomenon in the world was personified; it was a thing and a genius, a bodily object and a spiritual person. If useful to man on earth, it was ranged under the creation of Ahura, if hurtful, disagreeable, ugly, it belonged to Ahriman's dominions. This dominion of Evil was in every respect a counterpart of Mazda's creation. So had the Ameshas Spentas, the other peers and entire hierarchy of Mazda their corresponding compeers and magnates in Ahriman's realm of Darkness. The Avesta has also a strong inclination towards pure, Mosaic, prophetic monotheism. Ahura Mazda there is often described with all the attributes of Ihvh, as the only one, omnipotent, omnipresent, omniscient, eternal, all-just, benign holy Creator and sustainer of all. The many other gods are really, merely his attributes or his agents, angels, messengers. Nevertheless is Ahura limited and antagonized by his compeer, Angro Mainyu, who as seen, has his full creation, with his court of grandees and hosts of subordinates. All well weighed and counted, there is yet in the inner scheme of the Avesta, a clear balance of preponderance for monotheism; viz: it teaches: In the end of days, after the nine thousand or twelve thousand years, ([1]) of the simultaneous reign of

---

[1] The original compact was for 12000 years. But Zoroaster arrived 3000 years later.

the Two Principles will be closed, a prophet will appear and engage
in battle with Ahriman. He will route, vanquish and send to hell
him and all his hosts. Then Ahura Mazda will be finally and forever supreme ; then the kingdom of heaven will be inaugurated and
vice and tears abolished among men. Thus is monotheism held up
as the goal of all history. It is monotheism with ethical and social
improvement in combination with the messiah-ideal. So it is in
Judaism and in Christianity. It is the philosophy that monotheism
is yet antagonized by idolatry, that the messiah " at the end of
days," (¹) at the close of this wicked epoch, will come and
make God triumphant and man pure and happy. The Avesta has
little of external cult, pompous temple worship and sacrifices, no
trace of idols, except fire. It emphasizes everywhere spirituality,
purity and good works ; a worthy parallel to prophetism. Yet side
by side with that, it teaches the dominion of Evil, the Devil and his
hosts. Gradually it introduced mithra-worship, the Sun-god with
the "quick horses and chariot," with 10000 eyes and wide fields ;
the six Ameshas Spentas adored with their chief, Ahura, and often
depicted as real sensual personalities. Many more gods are worshipped in idolatrous shape, so are Ardvi-Sura and Tistrya, genii
of water and fructification. They are represented as endowed with
corporeality, just as the Greeks painted or sculptured their full
idolatries. So is Ahura sometimes spoken of as having wives and
children, as Zeus is. His first born son is *fire*, the greatest Yazata.
The emblem of deity was fire. Reading such divine descriptions,
we are puzzled whether they are but metaphors or meant in real
earnest, and this is halfway idolatry. All those gods, genii, fravashis or departed spirits are worshipped ; prayers were addressed to
them as protectors and their help was invoked. Nay, we find sometimes Mazda himself recurring to their help, and offering them sacrifice ; as we shall see later. Thus we find in those fragments of
the Avesta real remnants of worship from all stages and grades,
from fetishism to monotheism, from nature to spiritualism ; from the
cult of fire, haoma, stars, gods, genii, ideals of man and things to
Ahura Mazda, described with all the sublimity of Isaiah's "*Ihvh* Lord
" of the universe." (יהוה צבאות) all powerful, all present, and all knowing.

The Avesta appears therefore to be a complication not only of
books from different periods but of systems and doctrines, that have
been successively reigning during long periods of ages. Their origin

¹ Isaiah II. and Micha IV. ובאחרית חמים

may go back to thousands of years before Socrates, Lycurgus, Moses and Abraham ; indeed as believed by the Classics, they may date from prehistoric times and hoary antiquity; hence the diversity of idioms, theories and standpoints. From many gray parts of the Avesta, we may be justified in fairly assuming that its starting chapters describe a time when Iran had but a rare thin population scattered in the mountains, leading the primitive life of shepards and tillers of the ground, in small groups of families and clans, occupying huts in villages, happy in their honest poverty. The dog was the faithful companion and friend of man ; the ox, cow, sheep and horse his housemates ; living on roots and fruits, without flesh ; water and milk being the only drink, and haoma the only intoxicant ; with a naive world-conception and an Arcadean simplicity ; with love and veneration for deity, horror of crime and evil genii ; their worship was the fire-cult on free heights and bare rocks. Gradually the population increasing, advancing, and spreading westwards, they formed into principalities and conquered their neighbors. A new period began. They refined, altered, developed, speculated, eliminated and fused their own, with their adopted foreign ideas, and gradually brought about that variegated *mosaic*, the doctrines of the Avesta now extant. It embraces the entire religious scale, from the naive fairy-tales about family-gods and tutelary genii ; the fetishes of nectar-haoma and ambrosia-draona ; the fire, brilliant Son of the Supreme ; Mithra with quick horses ; the Fravashis, bright souls of departed heroes and ancestors;—to the sublimest conceptions of Ahura Mazda, the Only One, Supreme Being, Omniscient Intelligence, sole Creator and Providence, who in course of time, in the far future, will eliminate Evil and bring about the kingdom of wisdom and justice on earth, the goal of all human history. Thus in the Avesta as in other sacred books of old, we find the law of development going on. Really we meet yet there pantheistic nature-worship spiritualized. The worshipper invokes all to appear and receive their share of homage, all the parts of existence, bodies and spirits ; all the gods and the genii ; every real and ideal thing is personified and divinized.   It proceeds to polytheism ; it advances to the triads of Ahura, Ahriman and Mithra ; it arrives at dualism, the Two Powers of Good and of Evil ; it nearly approaches the precincts and halo of monotheism, the Ineffable, Eternal One, the all holy *Ahura*, the Essence of 'Being.

As seen, Ahura, Ahu means existence, being ; the same is expressed by Ihvh. And Brahman, too, designates that in Hindoo terminology. That goes to say: That the priests of Semites, Arians and Hindoos really worshipped the same deity, they did so consciously and deliberately. While the masses, catching at words, hated and fought each other, believing to stand in opposite camps. It is not easy to say which of these phases Zoroaster represented. The general opinion is that he conceived the doctrine of mind above body, that behind nature there is God, not simply force. But this is understood differently, again. Some believe that he taught Two Spirits, those of Light and of Darkness; hence is he the actual author of dualism, that the universe, as it is, is governed by two supreme principles, emanating two antagonistic creations. While others opine that the only Avesta fragments derived from him are the *Gathas*,(1) and that these have no trace of dualism, of an independent God of Evil; nor of the entire hierarchy of gods and genii; nor of two creations of light and of darkness. Hence they think that Zoroaster really taught monotheism with purity and useful activity. Should that prove correct, then is Zoroaster the Eastern Iranian type and parallel of the Western biblical Abraham. If such be the case, then would Zoroaster be but one of the many composers of the Persian Bible, he would be its reformator. The construction would then be: that he had been preceded by polytheism, that he had a glimpse of monotheism and was followed by dualism; that was the result of subsequent wars, conquest and crude amalgamation; that Zoroastrian religious fusion compromised upon actual dualism and the vague doctrine of the future saviour, who, at the end of days, was to bring about full monotheism by the annihilation of Evil and the inauguration of the "kingdom of God." It is not altogether impossible that Zoroaster was but the reformator of the Iranian religion, and that he taught not dualism but qualified monotheism; that after him, his doctrine degenerated again into dualism, Mithra-worship and even idolatry. That seems to contend against the theory of evolution, but not against proven historic facts, as shown elsewhere. Long peace, well-being, a few great men, etc., will bring about progress. Wars, famine, wretchedness will cause retrogression. Even so may Zoroaster's epoch have been one of enlightenment and advance, and after him came collapse and deterioration, since he himself died at the hands of Turanian enemies. The Biblical traditions of Genesis narrate a similar fact: that once there was established the worship of Ihvh, and then again idolatry broke in with war and corruption. (Genesis IV. and VI.)

1 Hymns and meditations of the Yasna prayer-book.

But more: There is no doubt that Abraham initiated an ethical and religious reform; "proclaiming the highest God, owning heaven and earth." Nevertheless deterioration came on with the Egyptian, Canaanite, and Assyrian, etc. epochs; and Moses and Ezra had to do over the work of Abraham. Even so may Zoroaster have taught Ahura, without dualism ; Ahura as the Supreme Being, sole Lord of entire creation; as seen above, Zoroaster in the *Gathas* may be but the version of Eastern Asia, of that same monotheistic movement which the soberer Semitic Bible of the West attributes to Abraham and Moses, with the "sacrifice of Moriah" and the "burning bush of Horeb." It may be the same historical era, and the difference be only in name, place and display of sacred poetry.

AVESTA RITES, IDEAS AND MESSIAH IDEAL REVIEWED.

In this and my foregoing treatises we have seen that a great many ideas and ceremonies are common to our Bible and the Parsee Avesta. My book,[1] often quoted in these pages, enumerates a large number of such parallels. In further illustration, I shall mention here but a few. Of course the custom of covering, or rather muffling up, head, face and shoulders at divine service, was most rigidly adhered to among the Parsees. The impurity of the human body was there even a more saliently established doctrine than in the Bible. The ostensible claim there was, that the evil spirits haunt the flesh. The probable cause was the desire to enforce, through superstitious fear and threats, strict cleanliness upon primitive and not over refined peoples. The uncleanness of the dead body of man was, in both Avesta and Bible, equally accentuated. As ancient nations carried filial piety to the excess of idolatry, as they practiced hero and ancestor-worship, and no doubt long retained in their homes decayed corpses, the legislator was compelled, as a salutary reaction against that excessive piety, to declare dead bodies impure and defiling, "belonging to Ahriman and the evil spirits." Hence comes the idea in Avesta, and practically among all ancient peoples, that the dead are haunted by the demons.[2] On the same grounds were, later, "penates, lares, teraphim," and all idols declared impure, haunted by the Evil one, and defiling the living, because they were remnants of hero and ancestor-worship. Wherever I see a religious enactment that at first sight, and to the modern mind, appears nonsense and superstition, I am inclined to

---

1 Thoughts on Religious Rites.

2 "The nasus takes hold upon the dead."   רוח חטמאה

the more charitable view that there must have been a solid, tangible, reasonable and useful cause for enacting such a law, as, for instance, burial, dietary and sexual discriminations. And of that nature is the claim that the dead bodies are defiling the living ones, and must be quickly removed. Such, too, is my view about the causes why all ancient peoples and religions discriminated between clean and unclean animals, as allowable or not allowable for human food, among quadrupeds, birds and fishes. No great lawgiver ever acted from superstition, selfishness or vulgar over-reaching the ignorant. Any real legislator, outliving his century and his district, must have been a superior man, and his motive must have been good and noble ambition. Now the noblest and highest ambition is to be useful to one's people and race. Such discrimination between clean and unclean is therefore not ignorance, nor priest-craft, but the real desire to teach people correct hygienics and good habits; to secure to them sound bodies and by that, sound souls, which condition was termed *holy*, and when corroborated by science, it is holy. The doctrine of the impurity of the dead human body was in Parseeism carried to the last extreme; this, no doubt, by the blind zeal of the followers of Zoroaster. That over zeal carried the original sound notion to a facetious excess; a trait which we often find repeated in the Talmud in its treatment of the enactments of the Bible. In Mazdaism it was equally forbidden to bury the dead from fear of defiling the earth; or to cremate them or bury them in the sea, for these were even more holy elements; or to let them decay for the air, too, was holy to Ahura Mazda. How then dispose of the dead? We have seen it. In an isolated place, far away from town, a high tower was erected called *Dakhma*. By fictions and rites, it was presumed to be so constructed as to be isolated from all the surrounding elements, the earth inclusive! In such a manner it was thought the holy creation of Ahura was screened against pollution. On the top of that tower, on crossing iron bars, the corpses were deposited and left to be devoured by birds of prey. At the advent of the messiah, such bodies would be reclaimed by the triumphant Ahura Mazda.

The Parsees prayed a great deal, several times daily. They pronounced benedictions by the scores, at every act of life, at each meal, at enjoyments and at bereavements, just as in the Synagogue. They insisted upon (levitical or) priestly purity, declaring the common people habitually impure, as we find, too, in the Talmud.(1)

---

1 There the הארץ עם, the commoner, is habitually impure.

They were austere of manners, of puritanic simplicity and habits, in dress and in meals, and of the highest morality. They celebrated the New-moons and the Seventh day, Sabbath. They abstained from wines presumably idolatrous; they discriminated between clean and unclean in sexual intercourse, animals and food. They abhorred all kinds of idols and material representations of the deity. The deity was a pure spirituality, depicted with all the lofty expressions of goodness, greatness and holiness, as the Bible attributes to Ihvh himself. Indeed Ahura Mazda was the Parsee version of Ihvh, with the sole difference, by no means a small one, that Ihvh was and remained One and unique ; while Ahura Mazda had a formidable rival, Angro Mainyu, the biblical Satan, the well-known Anti-Christ of Church dogmatics. The Parsees further had a priestly caste and a supreme pontiff, as the Biblical "Kohanim" and the highpriest. Such has the Christian Hierarchy.([1]) They had also especially holy men, as the later Hebrew Hassidim, the Catholic hermits and saints. They taught the immortality of the human soul and the resurrection of the body, paradise and hell, and the advent of the messiah, when the God of Evil, Angro Mainyv, will be vanquished with all his hosts, by the messiah, and the Only God Ahura Masda, will remain supreme here and hereafter. Just so is in the church the victory of Christ over Satan at his second advent. Even that is the popular version concerning the advent of the Jewish Messiah, while the philosophical meaning is only the reign of political and social justice among mankind at large. As the Rabbinical pietist wears a skull cap, a four-cornered vestment with fringes and mystic knots close to his body, a girdle around his waist and over all his garments, an ample sacred scarf (talith) enveloping him entirely, especially during prayer, from his 13th year onwards ; even so the true Mazdayasnian. From early boyhood he wore the skull-cap, the *Kosti,* or sacred girdle, over his garments, with the four mystic knots, perfectly answering to the *Arba Kanphoth*([2]) of the Hebrew *Hassid.* The Parsee had besides another piece of sacred cloth perfectly corresponding to the Rabbinical sacred scarf. That vestment was called *Soudra,* often mentioned in the Talmud by the same name. It was a large veil, covering mouth, face and shoulders, with most of the body. He constantly wore the sacred girdle around his waist. It was accounted frivolous to put it aside, and of ill omen to lose it. Just so it is with the girdle and the fringes of the Hebrew

---

[1] A pontiff, but no priestly caste, no hereditary priests.   [2] ארבע כנפות

Hassid. That kosti had the four mystic knots of Mazdaism. The one was to remind him of the One only God, Ahura. The second knot should remember the truths of the Parsee-religion ; the third bring to mind that Zarathustra is the only true prophet; the fourth cause the believer to resolve upon keeping God's commandments. Similarly reads, Numbers XV., 38 : "They shall make fringes to the corners of their garments . . . and contemplating them, you shall remember the'commandments of Ihvh . . . and be holy."

Here is a striking instance of the parallelism of religious rites. But this analogy is not only in rites and forms, it is in doctrines and conceptions too. The Pentateuch teaches God as the Supreme Being, the pure spirituality, eternal and omnipresent. In later biblical books we find an additional, subordinated power looming up, viz : Satan, the evil personified. In the New Testament and the Rabbinical literature, this dark power assumes ever grander proportions, to such an extent, as if the original Divine Omnipotence had suffered a split. In ancient Greek mythology, we read of celestial wars and usurpations, Ouranos, Chronos and Zeus' dissentions ; then of the latter one's civil struggle with the Titans in the aethereal realms. Qabbalistic and Aggadic mystics turned these mythic revolutions into philosophic evolutions. They speak of God, the *Ancient of Days*, the unknowable, the infinite—Ain Soph—unfolding into Ten *Sephiroth*, or divine Emanations; the Messiah born before Creation with hosts of angels, to conquer Satan, God's formidable rival, with his myriads of demons defying creation. In Christian later dogmatics, those ideas take even vaster proportions and become the very base of a new creed. That course of thought with demonology and angelology found their place in Mohammedanism too; and even so do we find these same mystical ideas and conceptions in Parseeism, running along in certain parallel lines with Brahmanism. Thus after the streams of the Brahma, Zoroaster, Abraham and Bible-religions have been spreading the vast world over in different channels, we are enabled to retrace their steps to their original source and starting point, not only in their rites and forms, but even in their ideas and doctrines. As the Biblical religions had their phases of monotheism struggling against idolatry, even so did Parseeism, according to the *Ghathas* in Yasna. It originally started with pure, lofty, uncompromising monotheism, God's name is Ahura Mazda, meaning : "Being Supreme, and Intelligence." Later, possibly with the Persian conquest of Parthia and Medea, etc., when brute force and war, the devil, the principle of evil became more potent, it seems as if a deterioration took place; viz: Ahura Mazda, the pure, the just, the holy one is not alone reigning. No, the good is not absolute in this world. Side by side with that, there is also the evil: hate, selfishness, rivalries, the brute forces with which we have to reckon. Ahura Mazda has a counterpart, a formidable rival; it is the principle of Evil, Angro Mainyu. Both are the offspring of the primordeal power, the Homeric fate, necessity, Zrvana Akarana, Eternity of space and of time. As long as the universe was not differentiated and continued under the shape of boundless space and eternity, good and evil were one. But with creation and with man, the two were rent assunder, as light and darkness, life and death, right and wrong, truth and falsehood. Ahura Mazda represents the principles of good; Angro Mainyu, that of evil. The world is divided between them.

Thus some claim Zoroaster as a pure monotheist, and dualism as a later deterioration, he being a pioneer and forerunner of monotheism—as Abraham. This is inferred from the *Gathas*, by one set of Zend-interpreters. Other scholars understand the Ghathas and Zoroaster as teaching at once the two opposing principles, dualism, and nothing but dualism; monotheism and Zrvana-Akarana being later phases. But they say that the Avesta holds out the victory of the good principle as the coming millennium. At the end of 12000 years, agreed to by the two powers, the descendant of Zoroaster will appear and fight Ahriman, who will yield; and Ahura will be victorious; he and Zrvana-Akarana will be one again—at last. Both these ways of constructing Zoroaster and the Gathas may well be reconciled. Monotheism is final, dualism is intermediate; the last evolution is the principle of good. The dualist acknowledges that evil is self destroying; the monotheist confesses that evil is hard to reconcile with an omnipotent, all-wise Ruler. The reconciliation is made by the fact that evil is but temporary and apparent, considered from a human standpoint and in the divine plan, viz: to bring out final good. It is apparently this way of bridging over the difficulty, to which Rabbinical moralists allude by the doctrine of " *Trial*;"[1] Evil overtakes man in order to chasten him and make him better and stronger, that means: evil is the means of good. Such is the Zoroastrian millennium. That is the Parsee Messianic Ideal. It is identical with "the advent of the kingdom of Heaven" of the Christian. It is one with the Biblical hope: " When all nations will stream to the mount of the Lord, when justice will reign su-

---

1 נסה   " God tried Abraham," Genesis 22: 8.   " with ten trials."

preme and war be forever undone; for wisdom will cover the earth as the waters fill the ocean's abyss."—Surveying the vast field of mysticism, from hoary antiquity to our own times, mysticism in ancient, in mediaeval and in present times, from the domain of popular notions, to that of living religions, and of abstract philosophy; mysticism in Talmud, New-Platonism, Christology, Mohammedanism down to Qabbala, Jewish Hassidaism and American Spiritualism, the source of all that mysticism may be clearly retraced to Bramo-Parseeism.   (See "Thoughts on Religious Rites," p. 99.)   The host of ceremonies, rites, litanies, benedictions, charms, perfunctory lip-services, penances, confessions, fasts, monastic self-abnegations, etc., all hail from that quarter.   Nearly everyone and each of our modern mystic observances in church, mosque and synagogue may find their parallels in the fire-temples of the ancient eastern creeds.

PART II

THE VENDIDAD.

CHAPTER VII.

SURVEY OF THE VENDIDAD.

In the foregoing pages we have seen that Avesta, in old Persian: Abasta, means the Law; Lex. nomos, תורה. It is a collection of fragmentary works representing the remnants of the sacred books of the most ancient and venerable creed, doctrines and mythology of the religion of ancient Persia, for many centuries a world-empire, mistress of half of Asia and part of Africa and Europe. That religion is known as Parseeism, Mazdaism, or fire-worship. Popularly it is attributed to Zoroaster. Zertusht or Zarathustra, the East-Asiatic Lawgiver of gray antiquity. The foremost book of that Avesta-collection is called, the *Vendidad*, the subject of these pages. Concerning that, the present Parsee priests assert[1] that there were anciently 21 *nosks*, 21 complete books containing their sacred Law-collection, which books mostly have been lost, or destroyed during and after the conquest of ancient Persia by Iskander the Rumi, or Alexander of Macedonia. They affirm that the Vendidad is the only book that has remained *entire* from that conflagration of Persepolis, and that it has come down intact to our own period; after a lapse of time of more than 2000 years, the ruin of the people, the devastation and loss of the country, and the long migrations of the ancient Persians, down to the present homes of their few descendants, the now Parsees or Guebers in Hindostan. But when we closely examine the Vendidad, we find it hard to accept that book as one integral whole. As the Avesta, so is the Vendidad rather a compilation of diverse fragments of different treatises, compositions and hands, put together with a rough view to general order and continuity. The Vendidad, as now before us, consists of twenty-two chapters or *Fargards*, and treats of the following subject matter and themes: The first and second chapters appear to be remnants of an ancient cosmogony or creation of the then known world, land, heaven and water; of the first man, a version of the biblical Adam, the human race and their fortunes. There are some attempts at a description of innocence in paradise, of a relapse and universal

---

1 See Vendidad by James Darmesteter, p. p. 32 and 83; Ravaets, by Anquetil. Memoires de l'Academie des Inscr. et Belles Lettres 38, 216; Spiegel Zeitschrift d. Deutsch-Morgenlaendishen Geselshaft 9, 174. So, too, Haug and others.

destruction, and a salvation according to the pattern of Noah's deluge, his ark and restoration of the animal kind. Chapter III. shows the dualism in the creation ; the good and the evil world, the action of Ahura Mazda, the Holy Spirit, the Genius of good, the Lord Omniscient God ; and the counter action of Angro Mainyu, the Evil Spirit, the Genius of bad, literally the wicked spirit, the devil ; thus dividing the universe into a pure and an impure realm, two dominions in the same universe, two absolute masters, each in array against his peer. Chapter V. may correspond to the Exodus 21–23 of the Pentateuch. It gives an outline of the Iranian Code of hoary times, the civil and criminal codes, civil transactions, damages for breach of contract ; mutual responsibility and solidarity of relatives ; penalty for outrages, perjury, assaults, wounds, murder, etc. It is a code of justice, human and divine, on earth, in heaven and in hell. Chapters V–XII. teach the Iranian theology : The leading feature of Zoroasterism is dualism ; there are two powers, two masters, two creations and two worlds in this one universe, and it is the paramount duty of every rational believer to further the dominions of the holy Principle, Ormazd, and to destroy that of the wicked one, Ahriman. The major part of the Vendidad treats of the criteria of these two halves of the universe, and of the means how to further the holy half, and to annihilate, or curtail at least the fiendish one ; the laws of cleanliness and holiness in body and in soul ; of defilement and of purification, in *thought*, *word* and *deed*, by lay means and by religious means. Ahura Mazda is the God of life, light and happiness ; and Ahriman is the God of death, darkness and misfortune. Sickness and death are accounted, therefore, the triumph of the latter. Death is fraught with danger for the entire living creation, and for that of healthy, pure matter. Hence all possible precautions are taken for isolating the sick, the defiled, and especially the dead persons, that they should not become a source of contamination, contagion and fresh deaths. So, too, the elements are holy, and must be kept pure from dead matter. These means of purification are again human and divine, hygienic and ceremonious, rules of health and mystic spells, right living, with lustrations, prayers and sacrifices. The conditions of men, and especially of women in their menses and their sickness, claim a large share of legislative and priestly care, hygienic and ceremonious, placed side by side. There we find many and striking parallels with the Laws of Mosaism and of Rabbinism on the defilement by dead matter, especially sexual and dietetic laws.

The Chapter IX. is particularly devoted to the leading Parsee ceremony of Barashnum, viz: Cleansing from contracted defilement by man or woman. There we shall feel struck by its parallelism with the Mosaic lustrations and the *Red-Heifer-rite*, which appear to have been widely pervading the ancient priestly ceremonies in Judaea as in the Hindoo-Iranian countries. The Chapter X. treats of mystic spells, prayers and recitations of mostly salient, sacred Avesta-passages, especially from the *Gathas*, hymns from the Parsee ritual and service, *Yasna* (עבודה). They were used as probate cures and means to chase away the legion of evil spirits, the death impurities, the devil or *Drugh*, and to help restore the health and purity of the "haunted" patient. Parallels to such usages, some recognize in the Rabbinical "phylacteries, the fringes with their knots," the inscriptions on "the door-posts and the city gates," and such other talismans as enlarged upon in the Talmud, but oftener rejected there as idolatrous (דרכי אמורי). The Parsee ritual calls them *Taavid,*([1]) evidently the *Totuphoth* of V. M. VI. 8, a venerable custom first, soon degenerated into a spell. Chapter XII. continues the above subjects on the treatment of the uncleanness of the relatives and of those in contact with the dead; of the forms of mourning, of the condition of the house, where the person died. The idea was, as mentioned, that death, the triumph of evil, is unlucky to all the surroundings, living beings or lifeless, pure matter. All have fallen a prey to Ahriman and are a source of danger to their environments. People were afraid to enter such a house or even into its neighborhood. The house and its inmates were in mourning, isolated from other beings, and in need of a thorough purification before they were released from that ban. J. Darmesteter([2]) remarks, that even nowadays, in Mohammedan Persia, that superstition has not disappeared: "The house where a person has died is looked upon with tremulation. The son deserts the house of his dead father; "the unlucky step, *bad qadim*, is in it." "Every man's house should die with him." The heir lets it go to ruin and builds another one further off. Certain Rabbinical mourning laws, and especially many mourning usages every where, may depart from such gray oriental premises. To my personal recollection, such superstitions, such dim, unconscious misgivings, such secret terrors and fears to be harmed by the dead,

---

1 Much used formulae, exorcising evil spirits and sickness, mystic "spells."

2 Darmesteter Vendidad 145.

are still pervading the Jewish Ghetto, and no doubt other sects, too, among the uneducated. To watch alone with and near a corpse, to be alone in a room where a recent death has occurred, to touch a corpse or his clothing, to be alone in the cemetery especially on a dark night, was something unconsciously horrifying. It made the young ones shiver and shake. It comes from an unavowed fear of the departed ghost, dread of the evil one haunting him who might overtake and harm the living. Among the Parsees, to be alone with the dead was actually a crime. Of course everything in the mourning house was unclean in Parseeism, so, too, in Rabbinism, and must be cleansed if at all possible. The Vendidad is very explicit on that. All fires were to be removed from the house. This may have given rise to the Rabbinical custom : that the mourners partook of a meal tendered by the neighbors ; since fire and cooking was discarded in the house of mourning. While a candle was lit in the Jewish house just in opposition to the Parsee usage of removing all fire. Chapters XIII. and XIV. treat of the *dog*, so important in primitive times in a village and shepherd-community, upon which interesting subject we shall enlarge later. The same theme is continued in a part of Chapter XV. This Chapter XV. treats chiefly of the most heinous misdeeds, according to the Zoroastrian Code, that which constitutes a *Peshotanu*, an unpardonable criminal. Chapters XVI., XVII. and part of XVIII., are a continuation of the laws on purification, completing Chapters V. to VII., concerning the things coming from the dead body, and how to be removed; also in impure men, spirits, lusts, etc. Chapter XIX. treats of the temptations of Zoroaster by Ahriman, finding its parallel in Christology ; of Zoroaster's victory and subsequent revelations by Ahura. The revelations are delivered by Ahura in the shape of replies to Zoroaster, who asks and receives an answer. Chapter XX. deals with the chief rite of Mazdaism, the Haoma, the mystic plant and genius of salvation, corresponding on one hand to the biblical *"tree of life,"* and on the other, to the mythologic *nectar* and *ambrosia.* The *Haoma,* confers eternal youth, heals diseases. 10000 healing herbs are growing around that *plant of life.* Thrita and kindred mythological genii in Avesta and Rig-Veda are its priests, ordained to administer to health and combat sickness. Sickness is there assumed as coming from the poison of the *serpent,* which serpent is killed by the god Thrita, the priest of haoma, hence is he the first healer. There may be here a parallel with the Greek Asklepios and his snake wound around his staff—as also with the

serpent of the Biblical Paradise persuading man to rebellion, in connection with the "tree of knowledge and of life." That serpent and
its poison is but another metaphor for Ahriman and his guile.
Chapter XXI. treats of the holy elements, water and light, of the
holy *bull* and of other personified natural bodies, enlarged upon
later on in these pages. Chapter XXII. completes the themes of
the preceding Chapter XX. *Angro Mainyu*, another name for the
snake mentioned, creates 99,999 diseases, i. e., the ills of man.
Ahura Mazda applies as a healing balm, his own *holy word*, viz :
Airyaman. This is an old Indo-Iranian god, found also, as most
of the Zoroastrian divine abstractions, in the Hindoo-Rig-Veda.
His name, like Mithra, is "the friend ;" a god of light, beneficent
and helpful to man—representing another attribute of Ahura, viz :
the sky. Varuna, Ouranos, שמים is another etymology of the Parsee
Ahura, besides its kinship with Ahu, being, שו, sire and Herr, as
seen above.

Thus the 22 chapters, called *fargards* of the Vendidad exhibit a general outline of the Avestean doctrines. They postulate
two supreme powers in the universe in bitter antagonism to each
other' for the term of 12000 years ; after which time, the *Soshiosh* or
Messiah will appear, fight and overcome the power of evil, and give
absolute dominion to the power of good. These two divine and independent genii or supreme gods, bring forth each their creations,
embodying their own self; the one, a world of light and goodness,
the other a world of darkness and vice, as alluded to. We have
therefore in the first fargard, an outline of cosmogony, as all religious legislations of antiquity begin with. The two supreme gods
are denominated respectively, Ahura Mazda and Angro Mainyu.
Each has brought forth his own world and creation; each his own
court of grandees and peers, each has his own residence, the one in
heaven, the other in hell; each has his subjects, vassals and administering spirits assisting him in the performance of his task.
Yima corresponds there to our biblical Adam; be begins in purity
and in happiness, in a paradise, with the reign of peace and good-
will ; but things get worse, hence we find also something corresponding to our own deluge, destruction of life, Noah's Ark and restoration
of the race. But this position of Yima is contradicted (See Vendidad Darmesteter 75) in other parts of the Avesta. His confrere,
Yama, of the Vidas, is the first man. Yima is rather assumed as
the first founder of civilization, as a social era, *Gayo Maratan* is the
first man. Closely seen, it is the same with Adam ; apparently rep-

resenting the first man, he is really the Mosaic era of the first civilization. After that regeneration of the human kind and its differentiation, we slowly arrive at a sort of an Arian-Abraham, just as
Yima is the Avestean Adam. Yima or Yemshed deteriorated and
fell from his rank as religious teacher. A daeva occupied his
throne, and the exalted office of renovating lawgiver devolved upon
his successor, Zoroaster, Zarathustra, meaning perhaps : *lustrous
star*, the beacon light and spiritual father of Iranian mankind, as
the Semitic initiator is called Abraham, Ab-Ram, the sublime father,
the teacher and "blessing of many nations." Zoroaster is the
bearer of divine revelations, the medium of Mazda's oracles to in-
struct mankind in the divine Avesta, the Iranian, *Thora ;* He receives
the revelations and delivers them to King Vistaspa of Bactria and
the Iranian tribes. He is the Abraham and Moses of the Magian
religion. His late descendant, at the end of the present millennium, is the expected *Soshiosh*, Saviour, who will vanquish Ahriman and restore the world to the undivided sway of Mazda. The
Soshiosh is the pattern of the redeemer, the Jewish *messiah* and the
later Gospel *Christ.* The Vendidad further contains a fair outline
and ideal of purity, virtue, holiness ; and of their reverse in body
and soul, with its full apparatus and grand display of the ways and
methods of attaining at the one, and avoiding or annulling the other.
Those means are real and ceremonial, essential and formal, inwardly
and outwardly. The law aims at purity and goodness in *thought, in
word, and in deed.* Purity of body is urgently necessary to holiness
of soul. As the Pentateuch, so the Avesta urges on : " Holy shall
ye be, for holy is your God,"—as shown below. There is too, an
outline of practical legislation, of rendering justice between man to
man and beast. Most primitive it is, honest and humble, clearly
pointing to its hoary antiquity, its early social state and polity ; a
country of hamlets, villages, small farms, cattle-breeders and owners
of flocks, a humble mode of existence. The flock and the farm are
the only property. The ox, cow, horse, sheep, etc., are almost the
members and the inmates of the family. No arts, no commerce,
and no wealth are discernable. Especially prominent is the dog.
He is the companion of the villager, agriculturer or shepherd; his
faithful friend, his watchman, the guardian of his home, his cradle
and his flock, his unfailing assistant and co-worker; he is the most
prominent domestic figure in that humble society. He accompanies
man and woman in life and in death ; in administering to the flocks
and tilling the ground. He is their fellow-mourner in death, their

companion in heaven or in hell, he meets them at the bridge *Kinvad*, leading to either. The dog's sympathetic last look soothes the dying Parsee and chases away, infallibly, the *drugh*, who stands there, eager to catch up the departing soul and hand it over to eternal torments.

For such a primitive, political organization are the statutes of the Vendidad framed. It is idle to assign such a primitive code to the times of the Sasanidae or even the Achaemenidae, five centuries before, or three after the Christian era. When we examine the Pentateuchal laws, they unmistakably point to gray, archaic times; the times not of Jeremiah, Zedekiah, nor Solomon, but much earlier, viz: just as they claim to be fifteen centuries B. C. To such conditions and environments, point the Mosaic Chapters 21–23, etc. of Exodus in the Pentateuch. But to a much earlier period reach the Vendidad laws on contracts, dealings by word of mouth or handshake, transactions "of the value of an ox, a cow, a sheep, a man, a woman," etc. Its criminal procedure on outrages, assaults, man-slaughter, ceremonial trespasses, theological offences, capital crimes, marriage between near blood relations, etc.—all that points to an incipient and raw society. Its mode of worship, benedictions, prayers, hymns, spells, exorcisms, sacrifices, etc., all that has its "raison d'etre," all that presupposes a primitive, social organization, more naive, archaic and aboriginal than Mosaism is. The Vendidad is not contemporaneous with the Pentateuch, but even much more antique ; indeed it stands at the dawn of civilization in Middle Asia ; it is as old as Abraham, if not much earlier, to all appearance. The greatest space and most elaborate treatment is given to the question of purity and purification. Actually that occupies most of its pages. The sickness of men, the menses of women, the treatment of the dead, their burial, away from the elements that are, too holy and must not be defiled by the sacrilegious contact of dead matter. That occupies the greatest attention of the Vendidad writers. That is not the Arian Pentateuch, but its *Leviticus*, its priestly code par excellence. The ideas of hereafter, of reward and punishment, of heaven, paradise and hell, of angels and devils have their full share in our chapters in discussion. We shall later see that they were the sources from which Jewish, Christian and Mohammedan legend, angelology and demonology largely drew their information. Even the *Houris* of the Alkoran hail from the Avestean heaven, though exaggerated and attired in Arabian colors. Finally the same chapter devotes some space to the treat-

ment of priests and physicians, giving some wholesome hints concerning those learned professions, their pay, their character, etc.
A careful perusal of these 22 fargard's of the Vendidad unmistakably suggests that the book is but a compilation and epitome of a
much larger work on that legislation.   It was not compiled quietly,
leisurely and deliberately, by official priests having complete documents at hand before their eyes, intent on the compilation.   The
careful examination of the book shows that it contains an abrupt
synopsis, a hap-hazard collection of a larger work or works, lost in
the stress and storm of social upheavels and disruptions.   Parts
only of the original material have been rescued from incendiarism
or total loss and oblivion.   Such scraps and remnants from partly
destroyed parchments and papers, or from half effaced memory,
carrying over to posterity but the most practical parts and most
urgently necessary elements of religion, have been saved from loss,
and committed to writing in those 22 fargards of the Vendidad.

THE VENDIDAD ANALYZED.

I follow the text translations of Prof. Darmesteter, edited by
Prof. F. Max Mueller, Oxford, 1886.   Fargard I.   Verse 1.   "Ahura
Mazda (the Supreme God) spake to Spitama,(1) Zarathustra (the
beneficent prophet) saying :   Verse 2.   I have made every land
dear to its dwellers ; even though it had no charms whatever in it ;
had I not made every land dear to its dwellers, even though it had
no charms whatever in it, then the whole living world would have
invaded the Airyana Vaego.(2)   3. The first of the good lands and
countries which I, Ahura Mazda, created, was the Airyana Vaego,
by the good river Daitya.   Thereupon came Angro Mainyu, who is
all death, and he counter-created by his witchcraft, the *serpent* in
the river, and the winter, a work of the daevas.   This serpent appears to be identical with the same individual of Adam's paradise,
a personification of the evil spirit.   The grim, freezing winter is his
fit creation of mischief.   As the biblical serpent corrupted Adam,
etc., so the Avestean one killed Yima, Adam's Iranian colleague.
Yima was king of Airyana Vaego, as Adam was lord of the Garden
of Eden.   The one and the other lost their respective paradise and
were ousted into the rough world of tribulations.—Verse 4.   " There
are ten winter months, two summer months, and those are cold for

---

1 Spitama may be a proper name or mean, "the holy one."
2 Man's first happy dwelling place, corresponding to Adam's Garden
of Eden, the fairly land of the Iranian race.

the waters, cold for the earth, cold for the trees. Winter falls there with the worst of its plagues." This is to show the wickedness of the evil spirit trying to counteract and annihilate the good work of the Supreme God by interposing evil.—Verse 5. " The second of the good lands and countries which I, Ahura Mazda, created was the plains in Sughda," (Sogdiana). Thereupon came Angro Mainyu, who is all death, and he counter-created, by his witchcraft, the fly Skaitya (possibly the cattlefly), which brings death to the cattle."—Verse 6. " The third of the good lands and countries which I, Ahura Mazda, created was the strong, holy Mouru (Mirv)." Thereupon came Angro Mainyu, who is all death, and he counter-created, by his witchcraft, sinful lusts. The chapter goes on enu-merating the good lands Ahura created, sixteen in number, partly still recognizable in middle-Asian countries, lying between Arabia, the Black Sea, the Caspian Sea and India. Partly they are oblit-erated or but mythic fairy-lands. To each good creation, Angro Mainyu opposed his own wicked one of some plague, vice or mischief-bearing region, in order to counterbalance the benevolent intentions of Ahura. Among these wicked creations of the evil one are: the corn-spoiling ants, unbelief, the mosquitoes, evil spirits, pride, unnatural fleshly lusts, burying the dead (the Magian allowed not that), witchcraft, the evil eye, wicked spells, total infidelity, burning the dead (cremation, too, being forbidden by Parseeism), abnormal menstruation, foreign oppression and tyranny, excessive heat, and other works of the devil. Among the creations of Ahura is also the four-cornered Varuna, Ouranos (heaven), and many auspicious deities, as " Thraetaona," a beneficent, subordinate god, who killed the *serpent*, Azis Dahaka, the murderer of Yima, the Avestean Adam. The sixteen regions and dominions enumerated in this chapter are simply the world, earthly and heavenly, known to the writer of that Fargard. This chapter contains simply a cos-mogony, a creation, generally corresponding to the first chapter of Genesis. Vaguely it narrates the creation of heaven and earth, the sixteen lands, angels and devils, inclusive of paradise or Airyana Vaego, the serpent, Azis Dahaka, the first man, Yima, etc. The writer, an earthly inhabitant, mostly pays attention to the lands of the earth, and but as accessories mentions the heavenly regions. The sixteen lands are simply the Iranian countries, alone known to him, he being the teacher of Arian races. The Arian world is to him the universe. The last redactor of that fargard, remembering that there are, besides, other lands and races, adds, *par acquit de conscience*, in the closing verse 21: "There are still other lands and countries, beautiful and rich, desirable, bright and thriving," of course belonging to Ahura's creation, he being the Lord of all good.

This first Fargard outlines the theological and cosmological standpoint of the writer. That standpoint is dualism : Two independent supreme powers are in this universe ; they are involved in eternal antagonism. The world is the embodiment of these opposing gods. There are two worlds within this one universe. This universe is not the work of various single forces, of multiple deities, counting by hundreds or tens of thousands, as many as there are single objects or forces of nature, as previously assumed by the polytheisms of the former Indo-Iranian, Babylonian or Greek mythologies. No; that first standpoint of the infantile thinker is vanquished. The Magian priest made this important progressive step. From childlike polytheism, he advanced to riper dualism. There is in this universe not accidental action and counter-action, not struggle of each object and force against all other objects and powers. No, all things and their driving springs are united and arrayed in two camps, two and no more, dualism, not polytheism. Each of these two halves is a solid unit. The universe has two sides, one consists of light, life, virtue, holiness, happiness ; the other is its counterpart, darkness, death, vice, defilement, misfortune. Each half is presided over by its own genius, god, supreme creator and ruler. Ahura Mazda, the *Lord omniscient*, superintends the creation of light, life and reason. Angro Mainyu, the angry, wicked spirit, is master of the creation of darkness, death, evil passions, etc. To all appearance, the Magian priests thought that monotheism could not account for the presence of evil in the world. An all-powerful, benign and wise Being could not allow evil to exist. Hence must there be a second divine Being creating it, independent of the former ; hence dualism. Another passage in *Yasna*, an important book of the Avesta, in one of its most venerable parts, denominated the *Gathas*, hymns, especially ascribed to Zoroaster, accepted by Zend-scholars as genuine and of a more antique age than the Vendidad—such a passage makes the following utterance concerning our theme, the two principles, dualism of the Mazda religion. According to the translation of Prof. L. H. Mills (Edition of Prof. Max Mueller, Oxford, 1887), it reads thus : (Yasna Gathas 30, page 29). Verse 2. "Hear ye then with your ears ; see ye the bright flames (the holy fire of the Parsees, emblem of deity and reason) with your better mind. It is for a decision as to religion . . . each for himself . . . Awaken to our teachings! (Verse 3.) "Thus are the primeval spirits, who as a pair, yet each independent in his action, have been famed of old. They are a better thing, they two, and a worse one, as to thought, as to word and as to deed. And between these two, let the wisely acting choose aright, not as the evil doers."

The Commentator, Neryosangh, renders it in the following manner: "Thus the two spirits (Ormazd and Ahriman), who uttered first in the world each his own (principle, one of good and the other of evil); these were a pair in thought, word and deed—a highest and a lowest one."—Let me call attention to the striking similarity of this Gatha to the well-known Aggadic version of this dualistic doctrine. Here these two principles are termed *Yezer Hatob* and *Yezer Harang*, the inclination for good and the inclination for bad. In Gatha and Aggada, they are yet *things, conditions*, not yet fully personified—persons they became later. But the Gatha places them in the universe; the Aggada in the human breast. In the first, they are the poles and pivots of the world; in the latter, the hinges and levers of human actions. Hence their supremacy in Avesta, and their subordinate place in Aggada. The earnestness, the pathos of this Gatha, exhibiting Zoroaster as urging upon his hearers the fitness of choosing the inspirations of the spirit of good over that of evil, vividly reminds of similar innumerable passages in our Sacred Writ. I shall only quote V. M. XXX. 15, etc.: "Behold I have put before thee life with good, and death with evil;" bidding thee to love God and walk in His ways; then He will bless thee and give thee a good country . . . or if thou turnest to the idols, then ruin and loss of country will follow." . . . Closing there in verse 17: "I call to witness heaven and earth: Life and death, I have placed before thee, blessing and curse, choose thou life!" The radical difference between these Avesta and Bible passages is theological; though the ethical kernel is identical. Their theories are different, because their standpoint is different. The Avesta teacher resigns himself and surrenders to the desolate idea that there are two powers, both divine, both omnipotent, in eternal struggle against each other. Reasoning from a human standpoint, he finds plenty of ill, wrong, stupidity and misfortune in the world. This cannot be the result of an allwise and omnipotent God. Hence must there be a second God who chooses the wrong, willfully and intentionally, in spite of the benevolence and wisdom of Ahura. There is also the Evil one. He acknowledges Angro Mainyu as hardly inferior to Ahura. Nevertheless, he calls

upon man to choose Ahura and reject Ahriman. Just as the Mosaic
writer enjoins to worship God and reject idols. Now this is the
weak point of Zoroasterism. If Ahriman is supreme, it is idle to
call on man to fight him; for man cannot fight supreme power!
The Hebrew writer has vanquished that phase of Magian thought:
Polytheism, the struggle of all forces in the world against one
another, is not true. These many forces are but aids, or elements
of the one Central Power. These subordinate forces are agents
of one Supreme Intelligence. Whence then comes evil into the
universe? There is no evil in the universe. There is evil in the
human world! It is the product of brute interference, of man's wil-
fullness. Man has brought it on. His ignorance, blind selfishness
and rebellion have produced it, to mar his own world, his own happiness. From man comes the trouble. There is none in God's
universe. Let man do his duty, and his own product, mischief, will
disappear. Man, his evil inclination, personified as Satan, devil,
יצר הרע, his own passions have created it. Part of it, man
imagines. Wishing a larger share of happiness than compatible
with his own human nature, he complains of snow-storm, heat, cold,
fatigue, work, pain, decay and death. He lays claim to immunity
and complains of being wronged! This is the reasoning of the
monotheistic thinker. And this is the standpoint of prophetism
and the Pentateuch. To the question: "Why prospers the path
of the wicked?" (Jerem. 12: 1). They answer: God's world is
perfection, beauty and fitness; man and his ill-guided passions
produce injustice and misfortune. The later Hebrew thinkers,
probably learning from their Magian neighbors, admitted a secondary, inferior principle. Satan tempting to evil who gradually, in the
wake of Persian Ahriman, claimed an independent existence, outside of man, but ever remained subordinate to God. He tempted
man to sedition and abuse of his freedom, but he left him his free
choice. Man could withstand Satan and obey God. He could by
this, increase his moral strength and bring out character. Thus
were tried Abraham, Pharaoh, Hiob, etc. This may have been the
standpoint of the quoted *Gatha*, too. It is not of the Vendidad.
The Vendidad teaches Ahriman on a level with Ormazd, Supreme;
hence it is idle to fight him.

For a perfect understanding of this, our important theme, let
us dwell longer upon it. Hindoo and Greek mythologies were the
result of the first thought of poetic youth; each body and force
around was deemed a person, had its genius, "was a god." These

innumerable genii or forces personified, are struggling against one another. There is in nature war of all against all. The stronger for the time being, succeeds, till overthrown by a still mightier one. War was the salient feature of nature. War was the leading trait of human society. The Parsee philosopher made a further step in thinking. It is not true that there is in the universe war of all against all. Behold day succeeds day alternating with regular night. So alternate, punctually and exactly, summer and winter; the seasons, the years, the astronomical cycles of years, follow one another most regularly. There are laws in nature which, except by divine interference, are never infringed. There is beauty, harmony, order, law, grandeur, sublimity and fitness pervading the universe. Hence it is not true, thought the Magian reasoner, that each body, each force is independent and absolute, obeying but its own caprice. There is unity, one law is prevading all. There is hence, a supreme God, and all the forces of nature are but His agents, the messengers of His will, worshipfully executing His de-·signs. Is there then but One God? wistfully asked again the Magian thinker. But behold, side by side with unity, intelligence, fitness, harmony, beauty and grandeur, I see also there, and here, close by, in my own proximity, the very reverse of all that. I see there also clashing opposition, brute force overwhelming an inferior force; dumb power crushing mental and ethical fitness; an earthquake swallowing up myriads of innocents; the hyena devouring remorselessly a mother and her babe, etc. I see disintegration and stupidity triumphing, ugly incoherence and crying injustice, discord, meanness and hypocracy. Here is wickedness, cunning, lying, overbearing, cruelty and arrogance; there is gross overreaching and taking advantage; here, is innocence weeping, the poor starving, the strong devouring the weak, injustice unrestrained . . . . Is the one Supreme God, owner of all power and wisdom, benignity and fitness, the Holy One who dictates right and fairness and has the omnipotence to enforce them—is He tolerating them? A frown of his eye-brow and they would disappear! A nod, and tears would be dried and death effaced. Why is he silent to wrong? Wills he the wrong? Or is he indifferent? Can he help it or not? Is His wisdom, His goodness or His power to be questioned? Or is perhaps polytheism right. . . . . . But there is order, harmony and intelligence visible everywhere in the vast universe! . . . . But there is disharmony, brutality and stupidity visible in the human world! There is pain and death, strife and

war, murder, envy and passion visible in the sphere close around
man! Meditating, long and deeply about that difficult problem, the
Magian philosopher arrived at the conclusion of dualism :   There
are at least two supreme powers in the universe.   There is a power
of good and another of evil.   Everything useful, bright and noble
is derived from the first.   Pain, lies, fraud, crime, darkness, etc. are
derived from the second power.   Soon feeling the gloom of this
outlook, contemplating his cravings for happiness and goodness, be-
holding the bright, glorious, cheering, inspiring universe, he shrunk
from the despair of dualism and mitigated it by his faith : that evil,
though powerful, is not all-powerful, "at the end of days" it will be
vanquished : The new millennium will come with the Soshiosh-mes-
siah and redeem the world of that unhappy rival power.   Hell and
death, lies and tears will be abolished, and the Spirit of light and
goodness will be supreme and alone guide the destinies of man and the
world.   Man must assist in this work of redemption and hasten the
advent of Zoroaster's son, the Soshiosh.   This is virtue, duty, human
holiness.   It is this mitigated, dualism, we find in the Gatha above
quoted from Yasna XXX. : " The primæval Spirits are a pair ; each
independent in his action ; the two are a better thing and a worse
one, as to thought, as to word and as to deed.   Between these two,
let the wise choose."   Here is the Magian dualism of actuality.

Now came the Shemitic thinker, be he Abraham, Moses, Isaiah,
Esra or Hillel : " The Parsee philosopher was correct in one way
and incorrect in another way.   He was right in finding polytheism
unsubstantiated.   There is no multiplicity of independent gods or
uncontrolled forces.   The universe in its harmony, beauty, happiness and everlastingness saliently reflects one Supreme, all-powerful,
benign Intelligence.   This fitness and harmony prevails everywhere.
Night and day, life and death, summer and winter, etc. are necessary poles, no antagonism.   Any catastrophes in nature are beyond
our ken and comprehension, but they, no doubt, do not break the
universal rule, they belong to the scheme of the world-plan.   Whence
then comes the evil near by ourselves, lies and stupidities, tears,
murder, war, etc. ?   They come from man, man himself is his own
spirit of evil, he is his own Satan and demon.   Endowed with a
small margin of free will, he often from sheer blindness and ignorance, causes his own and his neighbor's harm.   Man creates his own
hell.   There is no evil in God's universe.   Tears and murder, lies
and wrong are the creatures of man.   They spring up in man's
artificial world, not in God's.   Hence there is neither polytheism,

nor dualism, nor Ahriman, none but the one Supreme Intelligence, the essence of Being, *Ihvh!* Wilt thou, man, vanquish the Evil one in thine own breast, the יצר חרע? Then: "behold here are before thee life with goodness and death with wickedness, choose well and happiness will be thine." (V. M. 30, 15–17) It must be acknowledged, here too is a strong parallel between Judaism and Parseeism. This pure, unqualified, cheering monotheism is often obscured, if not tampered with in the Aggada and Jewish mystics. Especially bitter, unrelenting misfortune and persecution brought many teachers to the threshold of Parsee mitigated dualism. They never declared Ahriman, the equal of God; but half way they reasoned that Satan is a power, and only the Messiah in the coming millennium would restore the rule of the one God. This explains the unspeakable gloom of such Aggadas : *There is evil in the world!* That is pessimism. (See Hagiga 14, etc. on Acher.)

Now it has been hinted at by many Zend scholars, that the entire doctrine of dualism in the Vendidad, is but a deterioration, a misunderstanding of the original teachings of Zoroaster; that he himself meant by Ahriman, but the evil propensities of unbridled passion, but the biblical "wicked heart," ([1]) the rabbinical "evil inclination," or instinct; that he himself never taught Angro Mainyu, the personal devil, that Ahriman was but a popular fiction, a metaphor for the ill in the world or in the human constitution. If it is so, then was Zoroaster a perfect Monotheist, a follower or predecessor of Abraham. It is claimed that the *Gathas*, that come nearest to the ideas of Zoroaster, have hardly anything of a real personal evil spirit. Our above quoted text from Yasna 30, 3, may well be construed that way. "There is a good and a bad thing, choose the good " in thy own breast. Just so in the Talmudical literature as also in the homiletic Aggada, we find these two poles of Mazdean theology or mythology, often mentioned as the two instincts of man, but personified to two beings, struggling for mastery in the human breast; two spiritual forces or agents, the one inclining man towards good and the other towards evil; termed the *Yezer ha-tob* and *Yezer ha-ra* ([2]) Sometimes, they seem to be living beings, genii, an angel and a devil. But with the more rational rabbinical thinkers, they are impersonal, ethical instincts, emblems of virtue and of vice, inborn inclinations, directions for good and evil. With the vulgar and the superstitious, they are supernatural agents;

---

[1] יצר לב האדם רע Genesis viii. 20. יצר הרע

[2] יצר הטוב, יצר הרע

with the thinkers, they are reason and passion. Even so it is in the Parsee literature. In the *Gathas*, they may be the two inclinations, the poles of human aspirations. In the Vendidad they are the two supreme powers, the world's practical rulers, corresponding to our church conception of God and devil. A fact it is that the present *Desturs*, at least the educated Parsee priests assume that the gloomy Angro Mainyu of the Avesta-writings, is not a real, personal being, that he is but a personification, a metaphor of the instinct of evil in the human heart, and has no other existence but there ; thus fully corresponding to the rabbinical " Evil inclination," the personified "instinct of evil." The Talmudists knew well the Parsee doctrine of the two independent, divine powers in the universe. They termed that theory : שתי רשיות, two autonomies, and deprecated it as anti-Jewish and gross heresy. One teacher, the well-known *Elisha ben Abujah*, predecessor of the Mishna compiler, Rabbi Meyer,[1] is reported to have yielded to that doctrine, hence he was termed אחר, Ahriman.[2] A popular legend is told there that when dead and buried, smoke came out from his grave, until his said pious pupil prayed for him and his ghost had rest. Thus the Talmudists were well acquainted with this two-sidedness of Parsee theology, first the two supreme rulers, Ormazd and Ahriman ; next their inner sense, divested of all personality, as names for the inborn human instincts of good and evil. The sad and subdued mysterious tone of the story (of the four teachers daring to approach Zoroaster's doctrine) in that remarkable Talmud passage, proves how much they dreaded it, as both Anti-Judaic and pessimistic, to which despondent people fell a prey.

AHURA MAZDA AND ANGRO MAINYU.

The very last chapter of the Vendidad [3] introduces these two powers of Parseeism in the following way: XXII. I. Vendidad. " Ahura Mazda spake unto Spitama Zarathustra saying : I, Ahura Mazda, the maker of all good things, when I made this mansion, (the Garotman, Ahura's residence, Garo Demana or nemana,) the beautiful, the shining seen afar . . . Verse 2.—Then the ruffian Angro Mainyu, the deadly, looked at me and wrought by his witch-

1 In mentioned Babli. Hagiga 14.

2 The famous rabbinical name and person אחר appears to me to be but the abbreviated Parsee Ahriman ; the real spelling is Akhriman, abbreviated, Akhar—אחר. The Vendidad (of Darmesteter) XXII. 21, counts Aghra and *Ughra* among the most formidable she-devils of Parsee demonology—Aghra is no doubt the feminine of Aghar—אהור.

3 J. Darmesteter's Tran slation.

craft 99,999 diseases. So mayest thou heal me, O Manthra Spenta, (holy word, the Avesta) thou most glorious one. Verse 3.—Unto thee will I give in return a thousand fleet, swift running steeds, etc., etc. Offer them up as a sacrifice unto the good Saoka, made by Mazda and holy . . . And I shall bless thee with the fair holy blessing spell . . . that makes the empty swell to fullness and the full to overflowing, that comes to help the sickening . . . Manthra Spenta declares, unable to perform the task. Verse 7.—Ahura Mazda calls for another divine messenger, Nairyo-Sangha, the herald, an impersonation of the sacrificial fire and sends him on the same errand. In obedience to Ahura, Nairyo-Sangha went to Airyaman, another Indo-Iranian god, beneficent and helpful to man, an impersonation of the healing power, and brought him Ormazd's order to heal (the world?) of Ahriman's 99,999 diseases, offering him the same consideration, thousands of steeds, camels, oxen and small cattle. Quickly came the much desired Airyaman to the mount of revelation and performed the solemn rites of purification; the Barashnum, through which all evils, moral and natural, wicked passions and death will be removed.(1) He pronounced the solemn spell: "I drive away [Ishire, Aghuire, Aghra, etc., sickness, death, pain and fever . . . I drive away . . . rottenness, infection, etc. which Angro Mainyu created against mortal bodies." (Verse 22.) The Chapter concludes, Verse 23, with the prayer: May the much-desired Airyaman come here, for the men and women of Zarathustra to rejoice . . . with the desirable reward won by means of the law, and with the boon for holiness vouchsafed by Ahura . . Verse 24. May he smite all diseases and deaths, all the wizards and witches . . . . Verse 25. *Yatha ahu Vairyo.* The will of the Lord is the law of holiness. Riches are given to him who works for Mazda . . . and relieves the poor . . . Reveal to me the rules of thy law . . . Teach me clearly thy rules for this world and for the next, (invoking many Iranian gods.) Keep us from our hater, (the devil) O Mazda! Perish fiendish drugh. O brood of the fiend! never more to give unto death the living world of the holy Spirit." . . . That tone strikingly reminds of that in the Hebrew funeral-ritual and dirges: "Let death be forever annihilated."(2)

Closely seen that chapter 22 means plainly to say: When Ahura Mazda created his beautiful residence, the universe, Angro

---

1 Wilson, 'The Parsee Religion,' p. 341.

2 The Sepher ha-chaim (funeral-ritual) seems to re-echo Parsee spells and exorcisms. Qabbala and Zohar are brimful of that.

Mainyu, envious of that sojourn of happiness, and in order to spoil it, created in addition the innumerable ills thereof, 99,999 diseases. Then Ahura sent for Zarathustra to bring down as a corrective, as a healing balm, the Manthra Spenta, the holy law, the Avesta, the holy fire-worship, etc. They came, and the ills of the world were healed. The conclusive verse 21 points to that: "Ahriman created 99,999 ills *against the bodies of mortals.*" That shows that the world, not Ahura, suffered of Ahriman's diseases. Darmesteter, and more so Geldner, following literally the words of the text, have missed its real sense, I apprehend. That is the point of the entire chapter, viz: The universe sickened by Ahriman's device. It would otherwise be quite derogatory to the dignity of the Supreme God. Ahriman corrupts the world, not Ahura himself. The chapter may be ambiguous as rendered by Geldner. But the closing verses settle it clearly and expressly. It reads: I drive away the diseases, rottenness and infection, etc., which Angro Mainyu created by his witchcraft " *against the bodies of mortals.*" The Fargard I. and XXII., the first and the last, indeed the entire Vendidad, shows clearly the position of Ormazd and Ahriman towards each other— an apparent parity with an inherent superiority of the principle of good. This superiority is more prominent in the *Gathas;* less so in the Vendidad. It becomes subordinate in the biblical and rabbinical literatures. There the serpent (Genesis III.) is the con- temptible genius of mischief and lies, the Parsee *drugh.* Later it is Satan the tempter, offering man the opportunity for sin, and leaving him the choice of virtue. He is an educational means, a pedagogue; the touchstone of hypocrisy and genuine goodness; one of the divine agents to bring out man's character by offering temptation. The Aggada to Genesis XXII., "trial of Abraham and Isaac," has a fine opportunity to bring out the respective relation of the biblical Satan, trial, the patriarchal family and the Supreme One.—"God tried Abraham? What for did He, since the Omniscient undoubtedly knew the result of the trial? Why did he subject Abraham to it? Answer: In order to bring out his character. Abraham had the latent capacity. God caused Satan to try him in order to call forth that inborn potentiality into real actuality.([1]) . . . Satan appeared to Abraham in the shape of an

---

1 Rabboth and Yalkut: ‏כרי שיוציא מח שכבוה אל הפועל.‏

old neighbor: "Will such a man as yourself offer his son as a sacrifice?" . . . . " The holy One knows best," Abraham replied. Satan repaired to Sarah, assuming the shape of a gossip: " You

let your son go to Mt. Moriah, . . . you will never see him again!"
. . . "God's will be done," Sarah answered. Satan went to Isaac:
"Abraham is preparing thyself as a sacrifice !" and Isaac submitted :
"God's will be done." Here is the role of the rabbinical Satan
exhibited in his relation to God and man.

As mentioned, literally taken, that 22d chapter Vendidad is
much more mythologic than my rendition of it is. Let me show
the reader this mythological side of the Avesta, too. I shall follow
now the rendition of Prof. Karl Geldner. He introduces the chapter thus :([1]) "Ahura Mazda has built himself a new mansion.
About to transfer his residence there, he is bewitched with sickness
by the Evil one. At first he intends to have himself cured by
Manthra Spenta for rich reward, but he declares to be inferior to the
task. Now Ahura sends Nairyo Sangha (as Manthra Spenta; another
personification of the holy word) to Airyaman, with the same
request. Ready for the service, the latter one appears with gifts
for Ahura on the divine mount (the Zoroastrian Olymp and Sinai),
and begins his preparations for exorcising the malady. "Ahúra
Mazda spake to Spitama Zarathustra : I, the creator Ahura Mazda,
the giver of all good. When I had built yonder beautiful, shining,
magnificent castle, I was on the point to move therein, when, descry-
ing me, the wicked, withering, evil Spirit wrought on me 99,999
diseases. Now thou shalt heal me, thou the holy, heavenly Word.
For that I shall give thee at once 1000 horses, 1000 camels, 1000
sheep, etc. And I will bless thee with a fine, powerful blessing, . .
that makes perfect the deficient and abounding the full, that sickens
the healthy and heals the sick. . . . The holy Word replies : How
can I cure and drive away the 99,999 diseases ? Ahura spake to
Nairyo Sangha : Rise and go to Airyaman unto his house and bring
him my behest . . . (as before) . . . And soon, not long thereafter that
took place . . . the good Airyaman arriving on the mount Spenta-
Frasna (the Iranian Olymp), a gift of nine stallions he brought,
a gift of nine camels, nine bulls, etc. Nine rods he brought, nine
trenches he dug." . . . That is poetry, nonsense, hocus pocus,
much more fit to hide the sense than to express it. That is just
the way of mythology. Theology expressed by metaphor and
poetry creates—idolatry. Darmesteter comes nearer the true sense.

I believe to have unriddleed the real meaning of the allegory.
The first and the last chapter of the Vendidad correctly

[1] Zeitschrift Vergleichende Sprachforschung, Avesta Translations,
p. 551. Berlin, 1879.

state the Avesta position of Ormazd to Ahriman as the two supreme
principles superintending the world.   The beneficent spirit and the
withering, raving fiend and *drvant*.([1])   Prof. James Darmesteter
says : (Vendidad, p. 62) " Whereas in India, the fiends were daily
driven farther and farther into the background, and by the prevalence of the metaphysical spirit, gods and fiends came to be nothing
more than changing and fleeting creatures of the everlasting, indifferent, (viz : neutral) Being, Persia took her demons in real earnest.
She feared them, she hated them, and the vague and unconscious
dualism that lay at the bottom of the Indo-Iranian religion, has its
unsteady outlines sharply defined and became the very form and
frame of Mazdaism.   The conflict was no longer seen and heard in
the passing storm only, but it raged through all the avenues of
space and time.   The evil became a power by itself, engaged in an
open and never ceasing warfare with the good.   The good was
centered in the Supreme God, in Ahura Mazda, the bright God
of heaven,([2]) the all-knowing lord, the maker, who, as the author
of every good thing, was the good spirit, " Spenta Mainyu."   In
front of him, and opposed to him, slowly rose the evil spirit, "Angro
Mainyu."   J. Darmesteter shows there how the original, Indo-
Iranian dualism, incipient and shadowy as yet, was developed and
crystallized in Mazdaism.   The universal war of nature was deemed
as but intensified in the storm.   In the Vedas, that silent or intensified universal struggle was imagined as a " battle fought by *Indra*,
armed with thunder and lightning against the serpent *Ahi*, who had
carried off the dawns or the rivers described as divine milk-cows,
and who keeps them captive in the clouds."   The poetical allegory
of the Veda mythology, was taken literally and turned to pic-
turesque theology in Mazdaism.   Athar, the fire-god, the formidable
weapon of Zeus in Greek mythology, became the son of Ahura
in Magian mythology.   The serpent, Azi-Dahaka, was the most
redoubtable offspring of Ahriman, as Athar was the most noble one
of Ormazd.   Azi-Dahaka wanted to rob the light of the *hvarena*
(heaven); Athar fights and vanquishes him, freeing the light of day,
covered by the clouds.   There was here a naturalistic myth and a
theological dogma.   The storm driving the clouds and robbing
heaven of its light, was the naturalistic myth, symbolizing the war
in nature.   Evil trying to oppose good, Ahriman opposed to Ormazd,

---

1 (Isaiah 66 : 22), " The *drvant* of all the flesh,'' וחין ורֿאין לכל בשר
creating disease for all mortals.   Vend. 22 : 21.

2 Varuna-Ouranos—אלהי השמים—מקום, שמים ' topos.

was the meaning of the battle of Athar against Azi. Athar and
Azi simply represented their parents, the two Avestean, supreme
Gods.

This hoary tale, denuded of its grotesque and rude
mythology, of its crude naturalistic sense, viz : war in nature; and
of its dualistic misconception, as depicting the antagonism of the
evil principle against the holy one—this is also remembered in
Genesis III., in the allegory of the first human couple abetted to
rebellion by the *serpent*. In the Vedic myth Ahi desires to carry
away the dawns, the daylight or the rain, the milk-cows. In the
Avesta myth, Azi undertakes to rob the light of hvarena, ouranos.
There the battle takes place in mid-air, and here in *Vouru-Kasha*,
the sea above the clouds. There *Ahi* is vanquished by *Indra*,
armed with the lightning ; and here *Azi* is conquered by Athar the
son of Ahura. In the Mosaic allegory is Ahriman not the peer
of God, but a vile and cunning creature, eager to corrupt man and
tempting him to the premature enjoyment of the *Tree of Knowledge*.
In the Vedas, the Avesta and the biblical allegory is the *serpent* the
representative of the evil genius himself and his dearest offspring.
Azi-Dahaka is depicted as three-mouthed, three-headed and six-
eyed, the most dreadful *drugh* of Angro Mainyu (Yasna IX. 8).
Even so is *Kerberos*, of Greek mythology, depicted by Virgil,
Homer and Hesiod, etc., as a three-headed monster guarding hell.
The scene of the Avestean fight between *Azi* and Athar is in the
four-cornered *Varuna*, Ouranos, heaven. The battle of Ahi in the
Vedas against Indra, is in the clouds. The biblical allegory places
the scene in an earthly park, Eden; it degrades Ahriman to a reptile,
and declares "eternal war between him and the offspring of woman."
It is most interesting to observe how here the Mosaic writer took
up into his allegory every little kernel of truth, every grain of fact
and morals, clothing it, too, in a fine poetical garb, a beautiful
tale for children and a theme of deep meditation for the sage; but
denuded of all the Avestean, Vedic or Greek myth rendering it
incapable of any idolatrous construction. God is supreme, Ahriman is a beguiling snake; man is free, capable of crushing temptation on the head, while the snake can only bite and lie. Thus
Ahriman was ever faring from bad to worse. In the Vedas he is
akin to the gods, son of the Everlasting ; in Greek mythology he is
yet the colleague of Zeus;([1]) in Mazdaism he is the all-powerful fiend ;
he sinks in the biblical allegory to a wretched underling and sneak-

1 Elsewhere I showed *Here* to occupy that place.

ing snake, creeping on his belly, eating dust, the most despicable among the animals, shorn of his dragon's wings, biting man's heels, and crushed by him on the head. That is the sad story of proud Here, fierce Ahi, formidable Azi Dahaka, Aeshma, Drvant, raving fiend Ahriman, cunning, sneaking, dust-eating serpent. At last to be totally killed by the Avestean Saoshyant, by the Aggadic Messiah and the gentile Christ. Poor devil indeed.

Intelligent reader! Do not misconstrue my comparisons of ethical themes in mythology and in Sacred Writ, as indifferentism or disrespect. Reviewing such conceptions from their incipiency to their present development, in their diverse stages from naturalistic mythology to Brahmanism, Parseeism, Hesiod, Rabbinism, and the Bible, that is not belittling religion but glorifying it; that shows it in its full import, in its growth, its ramifications, its universality; from the vague conceptions in poetry, in the infancy of our race, to its full manhood; passing from naive exhuberant imagination to a mythological stage and to popular notions; rising to the dignity of a philosophical hypothesis and idea, as in the transparent veil of Vedas, Avesta and Edda; at last finding its highest expression in Bible and truth. Comparative religion is the study of growing truth. It shows such ethical conceptions to be deeply imbedded in human nature, with their roots in the eternal rock of divine truth. That is comparative religion. We shall continue such studies in the Vendidad and the Avesta. That curious sphinx is even a more wondrous riddle than her elder sister of Egypt. No doubt we shall find there a good deal of nonsense, childlike myths and even cunning priestcraft. But searching farther, looking deeper, between lines, unravelling the real meaning of those uncouth, strange figures, metaphors and hyperboles, as yet but half deciphered, we shall find there a great fund of real, genuine piety, the head of the Nile of many ethical conceptions; above all, a deal of true piety and real religiousness. Next we shall find their genius striving for truth, attempting to lift the impenetrable veil of hidden deity and contemplate the *Schechina* face to face. The Gathas, when well deciphered, may contain many a pearl of wisdom and truth. While the naivity and primitiveness of the Avesta apparently testify to its genuineness and hoary *antiquity*,perhaps prior to all history. Of course our affirmations concerning that literature are yet uncertain. Carl Geldner in his Avesta rendition, (Berlin 1879, page 542) says: " A translation of the entire Avesta must miscarry even to-day.—Our lexicalic and grammatical resources are yet too incomplete. Innumerable,

disfiguring misrepresentations and interpolations there, must be cor-
rected. Only in single chapters, we are able safely to follow the
general drift of ideas and recognize the full sense of the text."—I
believe, too, that we may find in the Talmud and later rabbinical
literature an unexpected help to reconstruct Zoroasterism and unveil
its real sense. We find there innumerable passages bearing on
Parsee doctrine and customs. These had among the Jews imitators
and antagonists, parallels and contrasts, which both will help to
elucidate Mazdaism ; and may be, Rabbinism too.

CHAPTER VIII

PARADISE, YIMA, YAMA, ADAM, TREE OF LIFE.

In the Vedas, *Yama* is the first man and the first priest on the earth. *Yima* is his Indo-Iranian brother. He too participates in the same qualifications. But in later Mazdaism, Zoroaster alone assumed the honor of law-giver and first prophet. The dignity of Yima was therefore circumscribed to that of first civilizing leader. Yima corresponds to *Adam* of Genesis as much about, as the Vendidad corresponds to the Pentateuch. The mythology of the Avesta is remarkably sobered out, purified of its fables, its dross, its crude ethical conceptions ; and in the shape of charming allegories and moral teachings, the nucleus and marrow of the Magian books are to be found in a renovated garb and purified essence in our own sacred books of the West, furnishing a striking illustration of the identity of the essence of religion.

VENDIDAD, FARGARD II. DARMESTETER'S TRANSLATION.

Chapter II. 1. Zarathustra asked Ahura Mazda : "O Ahura, most beneficent Spirit, creator of the material world, holy One ! (¹) Who was the first mortal before myself, with whom thou didst hold converse and teach the law ?—2. Ahura answered : The fair Yima, the great shepherd, O holy Zarathustra ! he was the first mortal before thee with whom I conversed and whom I taught the law.—3. Unto him I spake, fair Yima, be thou the preacher and bearer of my law. Yima replied : I was not born and taught for that.—4. Then Ahura said : Since thou desirest not to be the preacher and bearer of my law, then make thou my world increase; nourish, rule and watch over my world.—5. Yima accepted that mission . . . . . . I will nourish, rule and watch over thy world. While I am king, there shall be neither cold nor hot wind, disease nor death.—7. Then I, Ahura, brought him a golden ring and a poniard inlaid with gold, (as the symbols of sovereignty.)—8. Thus under the sway of Yima, 300 winters passed away and the earth was replenished with flocks and herds, with men, dogs, birds and blazing fires and there was no room for more . . . . 11. Yima made the earth grow larger by one-third than it was before, and there increased herds and men, etc., as many as he wished . . . . " According to the Shah-Namah, is Yima the founder of civilization, social order, arts and

¹ The identical rabbinical expression. קדוש ברוך הוא. רבונו של עולם

sciences and the first builder.—12. "Thus under the sway of Yima, six hundred winters passed away and the earth was replenished with flocks and herds, dogs, birds and blazing fires, and no room left for more . . . . Twice more Yima enlarged it by his prayer to *Spenta Armaiti*, (the genius of the earth). The earth with men, flocks, etc., increased three-fourths over its original size. Twice did the earth grow too scant for its inhabitants, and as often did Yima meet the sun and address Spenta Armaiti, and at his wish the earth enlarged and its inhabitants increased. Nine hundred winters passed away under that happy reign in the *Airyana Vaego* of Yima." This apparently corresponds to Adam and Eve's Garden of Eden, " with all the trees good to eat and pleasant to see and the trees of life and of knowledge among them." (Genesis II., 1–3).—The oriental exaggerations and poetical embellishments are mostly discarded in the Semitic allegory, yet enough poetry is left to enhance the ethical kernel of man's original purity and innocent happiness. Concerning the Parsee paradise, we read in Vendidad V. 19, (by Darmesteter) some more parallels : " The waters run back from the Sea, *Puitkia*, to the Sea, *Vouru-Kasha*, towards the well-watered tree whereon grow the seeds of my plants of every kind."

The Sea, Vouru-Kasha is assumed to be on the top of the Mazdean Olymp, from which the waters come down to the earth, lakes and rivers, and to which they rise again, thus allegorizing clouds and rainfall, and corresponding to the biblical " the waters beneath the firmament, and the waters above the firmament." (Genesis I., 7.)—The " well-watered tree with all seeds," corresponds to the " tree of life,"[1] of Genesis II. In other passages of the Avesta that tree is alluded to as the " *White Haoma*," the "source of life," around which all " healing plants are growing," and with whose juice, Ormazd will restore the dead to life and resurrection. That identifies it with the " tree of life," of Genesis II., 9.

The myth moves on. The scenery changes : Farg. II. 21. "A meeting was called in the Airyana-Vaego. Ahura, Yima and the celestial gods appeared. And Ahura spake : 22. Upon the material world, the fatal winters are going to fall, with fierce, foul frost. . . And the three kinds of beasts shall perish (cattle, fowl, fish)."[2]

עץ החיים

[2] The commentary has here *malkosan*, akin to the Hebrew גשם מלקוש. viz : winter-rain and winter itself. Mark the affinity of the both. According to Sanhidin 108 a., the fish perished not there. דגים שבים לא מתו

According to the commentary, not really winter but cold *rains* would cause that destruction. That apparently identifies the Yima catastrophe with *Noah's Deluge*. Ahura continues: 25. "Therefore make thee a *Vara* (an enclosure, again a version of Noah's Ark) long as a riding-ground, and thither bring the seeds of trees, sheep, oxen, men, dogs, birds and blazing fires . . . seeds of every kind, of cattle, of the greatest, best and finest. All those seeds shalt thou bring, two of every kind,[1] to be kept there inexhaustible." 29. "There shall be no hump-backed, nor bulged forward; no impotent, no lunatic, no poverty, no lying, no meanness, no jealousy, no leprous, nor any brand wherewith Angro Mainyu stamps the bodies of mortals." Mosaism teaching no devil to plague men, and accounting natural events from a moral and monotheistic standpoint, motives the deluge in Genesis VI. by the corruption of men and the anger of God. The Avesta presupposing the opposition of Ahriman to Ahura and the former's 99,999 ills as settled facts, needs not these biblical arguments of man's sin. Winter and deluge come there over man full of moral and bodily decreptitudes, not for his sinfulness, but because of the doings of Angro Mainyu. Verse 30. "In the largest part of the place (Vara) thou shalt make nine streets, viz: six and three streets,[2] and thereto bring the seed. . . . That Vara thou shalt seal up with the golden ring; and thou shalt make a door and a window self-shining within." That corresponds to the Hebrew version: A Zohar, צהר, self-shining window, thou shalt make to the ark and a door at its side (Genesis VI. 16).[3] 31. At the advice of Ahura, Yima kneaded the earth with his hands, as the potter does his clay, made thereof a Vara and brought thereto the seeds of sheep, oxen, man, birds, etc., into different compartments; each seed of the finest kind . . . of tree and fruit—none of the brands wherewith Angro Mainyu stamps the mortal bodies. Chapter II. 38. "The Vara or park he sealed up with his ring, made a door and a self-shining window within." The closing verses of that chapter are not in harmony with the rest. Apparently there is a break in the narrative, the conclusion is lost

---

1 Just so Genesis VI. 20. Two of each shall come to thee for propagation. שנים מכל יבואו לחחיות.

2 I surmise this is an incorrect rendition. There must be here something corresponding to Genesis VI. 16: "a first, second and third story."

3 Zohar means: a light, a lustre, something self-shining. Window is *halon* חלון. The Hebrew zohar and the Avesta "self-shining window" may prove that both have drawn from the same source of tradition.

and other kindred matter added. Let us also remark that while in verse 25, Ahura bids Yima: "All those seeds, shalt thou bring, *two of every kind*," we find in verses 30 and 38 that Yima brought 1000 seeds of men, and further 600 and 300 seeds. . . . The Zend-scholars presume that our fargard fuses several kindred myths into one. One myth required the world to end in a frightful winter, when some people would be saved in a Vara, a sort of celestial park and hothouse. Then spring would come, and the world be re-peopled by those saved in the Vara. Another myth claimed that the serpent, Azi Dahaka, would swallow up sun, light and warmth; grim cold would ensue and entrance the earth. *Keresaspa*, the personified sun, or his son, or the late descendant of Zoroaster, the Soshiosh (messiah), would appear and kill Azi, liberate nature and light, and restore vegetation. This symbolized spring returning, or the world redeemed. Others spoke of an eternal spring to follow after the world's destruction by winter, with eternal earthly life. Such is the messianic redemption of the rejuvenated world. In Mazdaism the world is to last 12,000 years, to end by fire. These several myths are fused into one in Fargard II. The leading one follows up the idea of the deluge, Noah's ark and the restoration of the world from the seed of the Vara or ark. Mark the parallels of the Vendidad myths and the sacred narrations and allegories of Genesis. They show evidence that both drew their information from hoary traditions common to the entire human race, and that some nucleus of historical fact is their common parent. The Semitic version strips that legend of its mythologic exhuberance. The Arian narrative envelopes it in the garb of poetry and infantine exaggeration. Future, closer renditions of the Zend-text will increase, no doubt, their affinities. Mark the striking parallels now palpable in the narrative: Farg. II. 2, describes Yima as first man and prophet. So does the Hebrew Saga and Midrashim, their own Adam. Vend. II. 4. Ahura bids Yima: "Undertake thou to nourish, to rule and to watch over the world." Genesis I. 28. "God blesses Adam and Eve: multiply and fill the earth. I gave you all upon it; rule over it." Hebrew tradition associates Eve in that earthly dominion. Not so the Avesta of the Arian races, where woman was not the equal of man, but his inferior, as Pandora of Greek fable. Mark "*Keresaspa*, the Sun-god;" compare that with *Heres*, חרס, in Judges v. 13 ibidem xiv. 18; Job ix. 7, etc., and with *Hristos* of the Church; further parallels are:

Farg. II. 3, "Airyana Vaego, is the most delicious of all the (16) lands Ormazd has created." So is the garden of Eden,([1]) where God caused to sprout every tree pleasant and good to eat and to look at (Genesis II. 9). So Yima's land grows threefourths larger and increases wonderfully, according to his wishes (Farg. II. 19).— "God blessed Adam (and Eve). They increased and multiplied and filled the earth and domineered over all," (Genesis II. 28).—Ahura bade Yima: "Be thou preacher and bearer of the law,' (II. 3). Yima refused. So counts the Hebrew Aggada Adam among the patriarchs and worthies. Later on he sinned and descended from his high position, he loses Eden, is accursed; he, his wife and the earth, and delivered to toil and death (Genesis III. 18, etc.) So is Yima, too: he loses his prophecy, throne and kingdom, and is devoured by Azi, the dragon, as Adam is undone by the serpent. A Talmudic legend narrates: "Adam first filled the space between earth and heaven. When he sinned, God made him small."([2])

YIMA'S VARA AND NOAH'S DELUGE.

The second half of the myth compares, too, with the deluge. Yima is allowed there a high moral character and a royal position. So is after Adam, also Noah, "who was a righteous and perfect man in his generation (Genesis VI. 8 and VII. 1).—(Fargard II. 21, 22). Ahura said: "Fair Yima, good shepherd, of high renown in Airyana Vaego: upon the bodily world the fatal winters are going to fall, and all the living creatures shall perish."—So (Genesis VI. 13): "And Elohim said to Noah: The end of all flesh has come . . . for they have deteriorated and I shall destroy them." This shows the biblical standpoint: religious and moral wrong is punished by natural catastrophes. (Farg. II. 25): "Therefore make thee a *vara*, long as a riding-ground,([3]) and thither bring the seeds of men, oxen and sheep, dogs, birds and fire . . . Make thee a vara to be an abode for man, a fold for flocks, etc. Bring there all seeds, two of every kind."—(Genesis VI. 14): "Make thee an ark, in several compartments make it . . . for thee, thy wife and thy children and for all the living creatures—a pair of each kind for propagation, thou shalt bring unto the ark, from fowl, cattle and creeping things . . . . a male and female of each species."— Vend. II. 30, prescribes the division of the vara, each for one kind of animals. It ordains a door and a self-shining window to be made therein. Genesis VI. 15, etc., describes the dimensions,

---

1 גן בעדן means a park of delight, a paradise. 2 Hagiga 12a.
3 Two hathra, two English miles, square; quite a celestial city.

divisions and stories of the ark, and recommends a light or lustre, a *zohar*, self-shining from above, and a door at its side.—(Vend. II. 36): "Yima brought thereto the seeds, two of every kind, to be kept inexhaustible there." While we read in II. 38: "He brought a thousand seeds of men . . . 600 seeds and 300 seeds . . . (according to the importance of the kind)." And this wonderful discrepancy we find also in Holy Writ: (Genesis VII. 7 and 15): "Two by two, they (the animals) came to the ark; a male and a female, as bid by *Elohim*." Even so Genesis VI. 19: "Of every kind, thou shalt bring in by twos." But in Genesis VII. 2, it reads: "Of every clean beast, thou shalt take seven by seven·pair, male and female; and from every unclean beast a pair, male and female," (to provide for sacrifices, say the commentators).—(Vend. II. 38: To the streets of the largest part, he brought a thousand seeds; . . to the middle part six hundred seeds; . . . to the smallest part 300."—In Genesis VI. 14, the ark is made into three compartments, and into a lowest, second and third story (verse 16). That proves sufficiently that both these narratives had a common sacred tradition as their source, which each writer used according to his own and his nation's genius; the one from a monotheistic, ethical and common-sense standpoint; the other dualistic, with a strong admixture of polytheistic myth and imagery. It is, therefore, apparent that the myth of Yima is an identification of the narratives of both Adam and Noah. Yima's Airyana Vaego is Adam's paradise; and Yima's vara is the ark of the deluge of Noah, narrated from the standpoint of dualism, where all misfortune is attributed to fate or Ahriman. I do not hesitate to express my humble opinion that, when the study of the Zend-books will be more advanced and fully understood, more striking parallels and identifying points will be found in the above Fargard II. I respectfully refrain from uttering any opinion concerning the priority of these documents. But what we can see now in the different renditions extant, the preponderate aspect of the Yima legend, with his royalty and activity, runs through the same phases as Adam and Eve's in the garden of Eden. Ahriman with his "99,999 diseases for the bodies of mortals," the "ruffian who is all death," "the creator of the serpent in the river of winter," etc., represents the phase of the "cunning *snake* who beguiles the first couple and causes their loss of paradise and of immortality, and confines them to an existence of toil, pain and child-rearing. Yima, the pious and fair, experiencing a withering winter, and saving the remnants of man,

beast and tree into a *vara*, from whence the world is again repeo-
pled—that is the Iranian version of the Semitic tradition of "Noah,
the just one of his generation," in whose time man deteriorated,
a deluge came and swept away all living creation, and he saved
into an ark or safety-boat, the seeds of all living beings, which
after the deluge repopulated the earth.

Breaking off here, for some reason, Vend. II. 39 and 40 asks:
"What lights are there in the *Vara* of Yima ?" and Ahura answers:
"There are created lights and uncreated lights." The Talmud
also mentions such lights of a two-fold nature, but both created.
So we read in Aggada 14: "By the light that God created on
the first day, Adam could see the world from end to end. But as
soon as God reflected on the human wickedness, he hid that light,
reserving it for the future world. . . . Adam occupied the world
from end to end. Since he sinned, God made him small."—Vend.
II. 41: "Every fortieth year to every couple two are born, a male
and a female. So for man and for cattle, too. The men in the
vara live the happiest life." The vara tallies, also, with the original
Airyana Vaego, with Garden of Eden, with Paradise and the Hereafter in heaven, open for the departed just ones, under the sway
of Yima, king of the dead. In one point we find a characteristic
discrepancy between the two versions   Yima acts alone; no female
partner the Avesta mentions at his side ; for his female partner was
not considered his equal. Whilst Adam ever appears with his Eve,
as his companion and help meet ; she shares the his dominion and his
tribulations. Here is the view and the superiority of the West over
the East, of the Bible over the Avesta ; that is interesting, it marks
an advance, ethical and sociological.

AIRYANA—VAEGO. EDEN.

The Airyana Vaego, Yima's "Garden of Eden," is thus
described by the *Mainyo-i-Khard* (according to West's translation): "Ormazd created *Eravez* better than the remaining places
and districts of the world, and its goodness was that man's
life lasted 300 years, and that of cattle and sheep 150 years.
There pain and sickness are little known. There is among
them no falsehood, no lamentation and weeping, and no
avarice. Ten men are satisfied with one loaf. Every forty years, a
couple bears one child. Their law is goodness; their religion is
primeval; and when they die, they are blessed. Their ruler is
Srosh (the beneficent god)." Mark: A human couple had one
child every forty years ! Thus child-bearing often was deemed a

curse! Mohammed, too, in the Koran, designates it as such. Mazdaism declares frequent menses as the work of Ahriman, and to be shunned by men. So Genesis III. 16, reckons frequent child-bearing as one form of punishment imposed upon Eve for her disobedience to Elohim.

After having sketched the above, I find that Prof. Karl Geldner,([1]) as also Dr. A. Kohut, incline toward the opinion that Fargard II. 21–38, is a version of the tradition of the deluge and the ark of Noah. A. Kohut's treatise I have not at hand. But Geldner's translation offers even more than Darmesteter's, points and sentences in striking parallel with the biblical Noah traditon: Vend. II. 21: "Ahura and the celestial gods held an assembly in the land of the Arians. To this council came the noble prince Yima with his best men.—22. Ahura spake: "Excellent Yima, the wicked human kind shall be destroyed by winter. A hard freezing frost shall come and destroy degenerated humanity, with deep snow upon the highest mountain tops and the dales of the Ardvi.—23. Quickly shall the cattle retire from there, from the mountain hights; from the threatened places, from the valleys of the deep lands and the enclosed stables.—24. Before that winter, that land bore rich pastures. That will now be submerged in vast water-waves when the snow has melted down, and a sea will appear there, where are now pastures for cattle and sheep."

The biblical narrator, writing in Palestine, Arabia, etc., could not speak of snow and freezing winter and killing icy frost, since such do not exist there. He spoke of continued rains, floods that chill and drown the animal creation. The Persian or East-Asiatic writers know of winter, snow and frost, and they depict the deluge as caused by excessive snowfalls melting, and submerging the lower lands. I have no doubt that further elucidations of the text will corroborate this view of Fargard II.

ZARATHUSTRA. TEMPTATION. REVELATION.

Farg. XIX. (Darmesteter). 1. "From the region of the North, forth rushed Angro Mainyu, the deadly one, and thus he spake, the guileful daeva: Drugh! rush down upon him! Destroy the holy Zarathustra! The drugh came rushing along, the unseen death, the hell-born.—2. "Zarathustra chanted aloud the Ahuna Vairya.([2]) "The will of the Lord is the law of holiness. The riches of *Vohu-*

---

1 Zeitschrift für Sprachforschung. Berlin, 1881.

2 The Honover, a prayer of great efficacy, (as the credo with Jew, Christian, Mussulman), older than creation. Yasna XIX.

Manu (Ahura's first peer) shall be given unto him who works for
Mazda . . . and relieves the poor . . . Profess the law of the worshippers of Mazda."—The drugh, dismayed, rushed away. . . .
6. "Again to him said the guileful Angro Mainyu: Renounce the
good law of Mazda, and thou shalt gain such a boon, as did the
murderous ruler of the nations." (Azi Dahaka, Ahriman's son,
ruled 1000 years, according to myth, he killed Yima). 7. "Zarathustra answered: No, never will I renounce the good law of Mazda!" , . 8. "Angro Mainyu rejoined: By whose word wilt thou
repell my creation?" 9. "Zarathustra replied: The sacred mortar, the cup, the haoma, the Word taught by Mazda; these
are my weapons." 10. Zarathustra chanted the Ahuna Vairya:
"Teach me the truth, O Lord!" The chapter closes with: "They
rush, they run away, the wicked, evil-doing daevas, Angro and Indra and Aeshma . . . into the depths of hell. . . (v. 43–47)." The
thoughtful reader will remember the temptation of Jesus in the
Gospel.

AHURA'S REVELATION TO ZARATHUSTRA.

Fargard XIX. 11. "Zarathustra, sitting on the mountain by the
Darega River, praying to the Amesha Spentas (Ahura's peers),
asked: O Ahura, most beneficent Spirit, Creator of the bodily
world, holy One. 12. How shall I make the world free from that
drugh, the evil doer, Angro Mainyu? How drive away defilement
. . . the Nasu? (impurity of the dead). How cleanse the faithful?
Verse 13. Ahura replied: Invoke the good law of Mazda. Invoke
the Ameshas Spentas, who rule over the seven *Karshvares* of the
earth."—The Indo-Iranians, as the Semites, conceived the world to
be sevenfold; hence were the earth's genii seven. Hence, too, comes
the holiness of that number among all antique peoples. In Hebrew
is seven שבעה a solemn oath. Sanscrit, Indo-German, Slav and
Semitic languages, all have a like term for seven. Most of
things holy were seven in number. The Parsee gods were seven,
of whom Ahura was the chief. Later, that number was raised to
ten, then to twelve; corresponding to the successive phases of the
Zodiac. Soon they were simply the attributes of the one supreme
deity, all the personified attributes residing in him; he thus being
the father of all the gods or Ameshas Spentas. The interesting
passage in Talmud, Hagiga, 12a., "With ten words the world was
created," the ten emanations of Neo-Platonism and of Gnosticism,
and finally the ten Sephiroth of the Qabbala, all have the same
origin; vague astronomical conceptions, philosophems, theosophic

mysteries, and mystic formulas ; hence their invocation and efficacy.—
XIX. 13. "Invoke, O Zarathustra, the law of Mazda, the Ameshas
Spentas, the sovereign Heaven, the boundless Time and Vayu (light-
conqueror), the powerful Wind and Spenta Armaiti—(earth).—
14. Invoke my fravashi (the divine Essence), whose soul is the
holy Word. Invoke this creation of mine.—15. Zarathustra made
these invocations;" viz : as a means of coming in contact with deity
by plunging into His attributes, realizing His full essence, and by
that absorption partake of revelation.

DIVINE SERVICE AND CEREMONIES.

Vend. XIX. 17. "Zarathustra asked: Creator of the good
world, Ahura! With what manner of sacrifice shall I worship and
forward Ahura's creation ? 18. "Ahura answered : Go toward that
tree (whereof the Baresma is taken), that is beautiful, high-growing
and mighty ;([1]) among the high-growing trees and say : hail to thee
O holy tree, made by Mazda . . . 19. "Let the faithful man cut off
a twig of *baresma*, long as a ploughshare, thick as a barley-corn (?)
The faithful one holding it in his left hand, shall not leave off keeping his eyes upon it, whilst he is offering up the sacrifice to Ahura
Mazda, the Ameshas Spentas, etc." The baresma or barsomon is
the emblem of Zoroasterism. It symbolizes the struggle of the
Mazda-worshipper against Ahriman, his devotion to purity and his
opposition to defilement. The entire creation was divided into two
dominions; one belonging to Ahura, and the other to Ahriman.
The latter was to be put down by all means at the disposal of the
pious, and the baresma in the priest's hand, killing flies and toads and
driving away the devil, was the symbol of that activity. The ceremony of cutting off that twig usually from a palm-tree, was a solemn
one. Hence the close description above. This rite and ceremony
appears to have been known to other creeds and peoples too. The
Druids and the Germanic priests practiced it likewise. The ceremony
of cutting the *mistle-toe* or a log of wood in mid-winter from the tallest
tree in the forest, ([2]) bears a strong parallel with the baresma-
cutting of this verse.

BARESMA. LULAB.

The Persian palm tree, being no plant of the North, the mistle-
toe, growing upon the highest tree, or the oak-log was substituted
there instead. But we find even in the Bible and Rabbinism a striking
parallel to it. Levit. XXIII. 40, prescribes for the feast of Booths and

---

[1] פרי עץ הדר. כפות תמרים   Levit. 23. 40 is its parallel.
[2] See my ' Messiah Ideal,' Vol. I., p. 36.

the fruit-harvest: "And ye shall take of the fruit of the magnificent tree,([1]) twigs of the Palm or date-tree, etc., and rejoice before your God."—Jewish tradition has justly identified that twig with the date- and palm-tree ; but it separated that clause from the preceding one : " Fruit of the perennial, beautiful tree, and branches of date-tree . ." The Vend. XIX. 18, identifies the baresma twig with the "beautiful high-growing tree," *as one and the same, not two*. In the Pentateuch, the rite is rationalized and made an appropriate ceremony, symbol- izing the flora of the field, representative of the harvest celebrated in Judaea on the feast of Booth. The Magian Baresma was trans- formed into a naturalistic harvest-festival. Look to this fact; it is an instance of the natural evolution of rites. The gray rite of *baresma*, meaning originally, perhaps, nature worship, and later opposition to Ahriman, is found again in Germany as cutting off the log from the noblest oak ; in Gaul and Britain as culling the mistle- toe from the highest tree ; and in Judaea, as the palm-tree branch with fruit and flower-bouquet, representing the flora thankfully re- ceived from the Giver of all. Should an old-time Parsee examine that biblical passage, (III. M. 23–40), he would say : The Rabbis have altered the text in opposition to Zoroaster. But criticism would say : Mistaken ! That is the result of the natural evolution of rites. The rites continue, their ideas change. Judaea no longer believed in Ahriman, but she felt grateful for the flowers and fruit ; *hence palm-branch* and no baresma. Even so later ; the oak-log and the mistle-toe became obsolete, and the Church substituted the Christmas Evergreen.

Observe here the Talmud tradition, which often is but an echo and a remembrance of ancient popular customs, hailing from pre- Sinaitic, or even from contra-Sinaitic phases. That ceremony as- sumed again its old ghostly significance, There it is again assumed as a weapon against the evil one, just as in Persia. The palm- branch (לולב) plays quite a role in rabbinical mysticism. It was used with great pomp during the entire eight days of the feast of Booth, at home, in the street and at the synagogue, by all the males. A solemn benediction was pronounced over it ; mystic motions and shakings were performed with it ; pointing to the four corners of the universe, towards heaven and earth, above and below. Of course Jewish commentators assume that symbolizes the omnipres- ence of the deity ; yet many passages in Talmudical and mystic Aggadas naivily betray the secret in declaring these Lulab motions to mean : " To drive away the evil ghosts." This is downright and

---

[1] פרי עץ הדר The rabbis translate : Perennial-tree. Treatise Suckoth IV.

genuine Parseeism! Here is the Persian baresma fully restored!
Here is the doctrine of the prevalence and the warding off of
Drughs and of Ahriman, foisted or re-enacted upon a biblical
beautiful ceremony. The *baresma*, palm-branch, it thus appears, is
a universal ceremony, dating back to pre-historic antiquity, having
its vestiges and rudimentary ramifications everywhere. There it is the
oak-log, and there, the mistle-toe, solemnly cut with a golden knife
from the tallest tree in Gaul and Britain, or in Germany. There it
is the palm-branch, symbol of victory and dominion, of imperial
conquerors all over the world. There it is the symbol of the harvest, of peace and honest labor, as in ancient Judaea and Arabia.
Mysticism here, as often elsewhere, did but catch a Tartar. From
over-piety, it fell into Pagan vanquished notions. It brushed off
and renovated gray Parseeism with lame discredited Ahriman and
his ilk. It took from his shoulders his worn-out Persian garb and
had him don a new coat, the skin of the "old serpent." It had the
Lulab (baresma) shake and move in all directions. It pompously
instituted its *Hoshanoth*,—the exact imitation of the Parsee bar-
soman bundle. And on the last day of Booth, the "*Great hosan-
na*,"([1]) it had them beat and smite in such a fearful manner as to
smash them and shake off all the leaves, drive and chase away and
thrust all the devils to hell; just as the Persian Magi did to show
their zeal for Ahura battling against Ahriman. Further on in our
Avesta Studies, we shall have occasion to surmise some further
Parsee, mythic re-echoes in the extra *Hoshana*-prayers on the
Hoshana-Rabba, an extra rabbinic festival It reads: "We Pray,
O God Hoshano! and save us, we pray, thou art our father! ([2])
Here is another instance, parallel with the well-known Mithra and
Metatron, cordially received in Aggadic mysticism as a divine peer.
One of the worthies of the Magean pantheon, bears a name much
akin to *Hoshana*, as we shall see in another place.—Let us add, that
bringing in juxtaposition these several forms and religious rites, we
must not be induced to scoffing and railing, but to recognize the
great fact of the universality of the religous sentiment and its
adequate expressions.

BARASHNUM-PURIFICATION.

Vend. XIX. 20.   "Zarathustra asked: O thou Omniscient One!
Vohu Manu gets directly defiled and undirectly defiled . . . from
dead bodies. How shall Vohu-Manu be purified?" Vohu Manu
means here man, a faithful person, a Mazdayasnian believer).—21.

אנא אל נא. תושענא. והושיע נא. אבינו אתה ²   הושענא רכה ¹

" Ahura answered: Thou shalt take some Gomez from a bull un-
gelded and such as the law requires it. Thou shalt take the man,
who is to be cleansed, to the field, made by Ahura, (a place destined for that rite) and the man that is to cleanse him shall draw
the furrows. . . (A most complicated rite. See Farg. 9, 10.)—22.
"He shall recite a hundred *Ashem Vohu*. Holiness is the best of
all goods . . . happy is man who is holy . . . . He shall chant two
hundred Ahuna-Vairya . . The will of the Lord is the law of holiness. The riches of Vohu Manu shall be given to him who works in
this world for Mazda . . and relieves the poor . . He shall wash
Vohu Manu four times with Gomez (urine) from an ox, and twice
with water made by Mazda." (another passage requires six gomez
and three water washings.)—23rd verse is claimed to prescribe that
the clothes of the unclean "shall be laid down under the bright
heavens for nine nights."—24. "When these have passed, thou
shalt bring libations into the fire, hard wood and incense, and thou
shalt perfume Vohu Manu (the cleansed man) therewith.—25.
"Thus shall Vohu Manu (the cleansed one) become clean . . . who
shall say aloud: Glory be to Ahura and all the holy beings . . "
This is the most solemn and complicated rite of the *barashnum*, for
cleansing persons in contact with dead matter; so emphatically
treated in an important part of Leviticus too. A large space, out
of the way, is selected; diverse holes are dug at prescribed dis-
tances; furrows are drawn; the unclean stands within; prayers are
recited; spells against the daevas muttered; with a spoon and a stick
dipped in Gomez is the unclean sprinkled; limb by limb he is
washed and sprinkled; at each, the drugh, Nasu, retires, until at
last he is totally expelled and in shape of a raging fly, he flies to
the North. . . . Nine nights and days more go on; the unclean
must yet stay in the "*place of infirmity;*" outside of the community.
More washings with gomez and then with water are performed;
more spells are pronounced and prayers are recited: "Keep us
from our hater, O Mazda . . . . Perish, O fiendish drugh! Rush
away, never more to give unto death the living world of the holy
Spirit." The Nassu (death-impurity) gradually retires, fighting its
way from limb to limb of the unclean (deemed as possessed by the
evil one; so too in sickness). Fifteen times he is rubbed with holy
dust from the ground, then washed with water, then perfumed . . .
when he is allowed to go home, but remains there *isolated*, and for
many days yet performing the same ablutions, when at last he is
deemed clean and restored to the community. (Vend. IX).—That
ceremony or rather ordeal was inflicted on every Mazdayasnian who

came in contact with the dead body. But it appears this was believed a radical way of curing each and all impurities, sickness and devil's influence. It was therefor deemed a sacred duty for every faithful one, at least once in his life, to perform this barashnum-rite. It was a kind of Parsee baptism, renouncing Ahriman and devoting to Ahura. Now, however extravagant that appears to a stranger, still we must not forget that all religious lustrations and sprinkling originally meant the same. The Pentateuch prescribed such with ashes from the *Red-heifer*.(1) It may be surmised too, that the Gomez spoken of, was, simply, water, not cow urine. The Parsee Mythology fabled of a *bull*, genius of production. That meant probably the clouds and rain fructifying the earth, and Gomez may have been pure rain-water.

THE KINVAD BRIDGE AND THE HEREAFTER.

Vend. XIX. 26. " Zarathustra asked Ahura : O thou all-knowing one, shall I urge upon the godly man and woman, as also upon the wicked, that they have once to leave behind them the earth and all its wealth ? . . . . Ahura answered : Thou shalt. 27. Zarathustra asked : Creator of the world ! where are the rewards given ? Where does the rewarding take place ? Where do men come to take the reward they have earned in the material world for their souls ?—28. Ahura replied : When the man is dead, then the hellish daevas assail him ; and when the third night is gone, the morning appears and the sun rises upon the mountains . . . . 29. Then the fiend, *Vizaresha*, carries off in bonds the soul of the wicked. The soul enters the way of time, the way both of the wicked and of the righteous. At the head of the *Kinvad* Bridge, made by Mazda (extending over hell and leading to paradise, miles wide for the righteous, and narrow as a thread for the sinners who fall into hell), they ask for their souls the reward for the worldly goods which they gave away below."—This bridge is popularly known all over the world in nearly all creeds. I heard of it in my childhood on the shores of the lower Danube ; it is known everywhere. It is known to Christian, Mussulman, mythologist and Jew. It is the fright of many a poor sinner and stimulates many an honest conscience. Mohammed took it up into his Koran : the " Sira-bridge." The current expression, " To fall into hell," is borrowed from that idea of hell beneath a narrow bridge. The rabbinical legendary has the same term (נופל לגהינם:).

1 IV. M. 19, 2.

KINVAD EVERYWHERE ELSE.

In Yorkshire, England, they sing of "the bridge o' dread, na brader than a thread." (Thom's Anecdotes 89). The French peasant sings of a board:

"Pas pu longue, pas pu large
Qu un ch 'veu de la Sainte Viarge . . ."

It is put by Saint Jean, the Archangel, to connect paradise with this world. The song continues:

"Ceux qui sauront l'oraison,
Par dessus passeront.
Ceux que la sauront pas
Au bout mourront."—(*Melusine, p. 70. Darmesteter, p. 213*).

XIX. 30. "Then comes the well-shapen, tall-formed maiden, with the dogs at her side, who can distinguish, who is virtuous and wise. . . She makes the righteous soul go up above the Hara-Berezaiti (the Mazdean Olymp); above the Kinvad bridge; she places it in the presence of the gods themselves. This "well-shapen, tall-formed maiden" is the clean conscience of the righteous. The maid is of fiendish ugliness if she represents the conscience of the wicked. For she is the reflex of one's own doings. She leads the dead ones to heaven or to hell, according to their own deserts. This well-shapen and tall-formed maid, gave to Mohammed the type of his maiden, or *houri*, in paradise. He gave her an even more sensuous outfit, to answer the amorous propensities of his countrymen. The dogs that accompany her belong to the Iranian paraphernalia. The dog was the habitual watch and companion of the Persian mountaineer; of the creation of Mazda; man's best friend, highly esteemed there; having a purifying effect upon the dying soul; watching at the Kinvad bridge. Mythology, too, has *Kerberos* watching at the gates of Hades.—31. "Up rises Vohu-Manu from his golden seat, and exclaimed: How hast thou come to us, thou holy one, from the decaying world?" . . . . Vohu-Manu is the first attribute of Ahura, the genius of mankind; he is the door-keeper of paradise, as Abraham, Peter and Mohammed are such in their respective sectarian hereafter.—32. Gladly pass the souls of the righteous to *Garo-nmanem* (Garothman), the abode of Ahura, the Ameshas Spentas and all the holy beings. . . . . 35. "Zarathustra took those words from Ahura and invoked all the gods, all the bodies of the good creation . . . and all its personified moral and mental virtues and forces, offering them the customary sacrifices.—47. "They run to and fro in dismay and trepidation from the holy Zarathustra. the evil ones, frightened and dismayed; they rush away into the depth of hell. . . ."

CHAPTER IX.

PRACTICAL VIRTUE AND HAPPINESS.

Vendidad. Fargard III. 1 (Darmesteter's Translation): "Creator of the material world, holy one, which is the first place where the earth feels most happy? Ahura answered: The place whereon one of the faithful steps forward with the holy Wood in his hand (for the fire-altar), the baresma,[1] the meat (of sacrifice), and the holy mortar (to crush the haoma, ready for the divine service of Mazdaism). 2-3. Which is the second place where the earth feels most happy? Ahura answered: The place whereon one of the faithful erects a house with a priest within, with cattle, with a wife, with children and with good herds; wherein cattle is thriving, holiness is thriving, the dog, wife, child, fodder, fire and every blessing are thriving," (fire and dog, the primitive tokens of civilization in the humble village.) 4. Which is the third place where the earth is most happy? Answered Ahura: The place where one of the faithful cultivates most of corn, grass and fruit; where he waters the ground that is dry, or dries the ground that is wet. 5. Which is the fourth place where the earth is most happy? . . . . The place where there is most increase of flocks and herds. 6. Which is the fifth place of earthly happiness? . . . . Where flocks and herds yield most dung. . . . . 7. Maker of the material world, which is the first place where the earth feels sorest grief? . . . . Ahura answers: It is the top of Mount Arezura (at the gate of hell), whereon the fiends rush. (Arezura was first the name of a noted fiend, perhaps identical with the Semitic Azazel;[2] then it meant the mountain he haunted.) 8. Which is the second place where the earth feels sorest grief? . . . . Where most of corpses are buried. . . . 9. Which is the third place where the earth feels most grieved? Answer: There where stand most *Dakhmas*, where corpses are deposited. (That place will never be clean again. So, too, in the Pentateuch, could a priest never come to a burial place). 10. Which is the fourth sorest place? Wherein are most burrows of (obnoxious) creatures of Angro Mainyu. 11. Which is the fifth place of earthly grief? It is the place where the wife and children

---

(1) Bundle of sacred twigs of the pomegranate, date, or tamarind-tree, held by the priest while praying. (Strabo XV. 3, 4): Tas de epodas poiountai polyn hronon rabdon myrikinon lepton desmen katehontes.

2 עזאזל III. M. 16, 8.

of one of the faithful are driven into captivity, raising a voice of wailing. 12. Who is the first to rejoice the earth with the greatest joy ? He who digs out most of corpses (cleanses and restores the soil to agriculture). 13. Who is next to give joy ? He who pulls down most of *Dakhmas* (for the same purpose)."

These verses contain much excellent common sense, vitiated in part by current superstitions or by priestcraft, the Magian legislation being essentially a priestly one.

VIRTUE, PURITY, HOLINESS.

Vendidad IV. 43. (Darmesteter's Translation). "And they shall thenceforth in their doings walk after the ways of holiness, after the word of holiness, after the ordinance of holiness." Holiness is claimed to be the final aim of Mazdaism. Holiness there seems to mean : purity of body and of mind, a virtuous tenor of life, and healthy, clean, daily habits and manners. That strongly reminds one of the Mosaic ideal of a worshipper of Ihvh, very often repeated and emphatically impressed in the Pentateuch : " Ye shall not defile your persons . . . . and not render yourselves contaminated, for I, Ihvh, am your God. Ye shall sanctify yourselves and be holy, for I am holy, I who brought you out of Egypt to be your God. Be ye holy." (Levit. XI. 43). Similar verses run along the leading chapters of the Pentateuch, motiving the injunctions about personal cleanliness. Vend. X. 19. " Make thyself pure, O righteous man. Any one in the world here below can win purity when he cleanses himself with good thoughts, words and deeds." This is a closing remark to the complicated ceremony of the Barashnum purification. It evidently means to say that this ceremonious cleansing symbolizes an ethical one, and that this latter one alone is real and essential. Here are the two versions and two hands of the Avesta, the ethical teacher and the ceremonious Athravan or Magian priest. So in the sacred books of all peoples and creeds, we find such two categories of teachings, one moral and real, the other ceremonious and formal, the garb and necessary expression of the inward contents. Even so we find the " prophetic " teachings and the " priestly " rites and observances in Gentile, in Parsee and in Sacred Writ of Judaea, as soul and body, or as the body and its shadow.

PENTATETCH AND VENDIDAD ON THAT.

Cleanliness of body and purity of soul, appears to have been the objects of Mosaism. Bodily and ethical purity the Pentateuch terms holiness. For that purpose the Sacred Writ discriminated in

diet, worship, marital connections and sexual intercourse; prescribing rules for each, according to the ideas and the standpoint
of those times, with the conscious object in view to induce a solid
hygiene in matter and in mind; to rear up a nation of solid bodies,
with solid souls. It is highly gratifying that Zoroasterism runs
parallel with Mosaism in that highly important respect. Only a
better knowledge of the Zend-books will enable one to judge about
priority. Mazdaism exaggerated much; as its starting point, was
dualism, an all-powerful God of good, and an all-powerful God of
evil, the two all-powers in the one universe, could not but collide;
hence came vice, war and disharmony, and man had to choose
between the two. This gave rise to demonology and angelology,
to that profuse mass of notions, conceptions and ceremonies, partly
ideas and symbols, and partly empty sounds which now appear to
us rank superstition, but were mostly believed in, in those remote
times, older than Moses and Abraham. As everything in the world
had its genius above, and every idea its heavenly prototype, so had
sickness not simply a bodily cause, but also a spiritual author.
Hence the universal belief in evil spirits to be the cause of sin and
of sickness. While Mosaism kept clearly in mind the idea of a
solid diet to insure solid bodies and souls, Mazdaism forgot that
often, and aimed at pursuing the evil ones as real entities, out of
man's heart, and thus lost itself in this chase in the realms of the
imagination, the will-o'-the-wisp of the Orient, arriving often at the
shallow banks of superstition, of the ridiculous and the chimerical.
The same was often the fate of mystic Rabbinism. Indeed it was
the same mysticism and exaggerated spiritualism in both the camps.
Both parties lost their original way to a wise and natural hygiene,
and became entangled in the labyrinth of vulgar ghost-and-hell
belief. Both, then, overshot their mark in their infinite rules of diet,
cleanliness and ceremonialism, spells and overstrained devotions.
Mazdaism went off the farthest, on account of its radically false
doctrine of the evil one and its hosts. Whilst Mosaism ever found
its way again at the beacon-light of rational monotheism, which
was its safe Ariadne-thread, to [bring it back to the path of reason
and truth.

SOUND VIEWS ON LIFE, PURITY, CLEANLINESS.

Vend. IV. 47. "Verily I say unto thee, Oh Zarathustra, the
man who has a wife is far above him who begets no sons; he who
keeps a house is far above him who has none; he who has children,
is far above the childless man; he who has riches, is far above him

who has none." Comment: "In Persia, the king gave prizes to those having most of children (Herod. I. 136). He who has no children, paradise is closed to him. The first question which the angels ask the dead is, whether they have left a substitute behind themselves. If not, they are not allowed to enter paradise (Saddar 18, Hyde 19). It is a Brahmanical doctrine that a childless man goes to hell because there is nobody to pay him the family-worship." This is the original sense of the mass, the requiem and the *Kaddish*, in cathedral, church and synagogue. IV. 48. "Of two men, he who fills himself with meat, is filled with the good spirit, much more than he who does not do so," . . . 49. "It is this man that can strive against the onsets of *Asto Vidhotu* (death spirit); that can strive against the winter fiend with thin garments on." This is plain talk. The spiritual and the material are simply one thing from different standpoints. It is interesting what good, prac- tical sense original Zoroasterism exhibits, yet it soon deteriorated into artificial spiritualism. The legislator aimed, as the Pentateuch did, at healthy bodies and souls, and he ordained as the means to that purpose, cleanliness for the body and purity for the soul, insuring thus holiness. As an inducement, he used the popular belief in ghosts. Misunderstanding him, his inapt expounders insisted upon the ghosts and neglected his hygiene. They chewed the straw and eschewed the grain. They forgot the object for the means. Closely looking at all religious legislations, they often suffered of that same fate, viz: priestly misunderstanding. To insure good, healthy habits, they gave as their motives but the current popular inducement,[1] viz: superstitious fears. Soon the apish expounders laid stress merely upon those superstitions and lost sight of the real important objects. That is evolution backwards.— Vend. V. 21. "Ahura: This (purification) is the best of all things. . . . Purity is for man, next to life, the greatest good. That purity is procured by the law of Mazda to him who cleanses his own self with good thoughts, words and deeds." What a healthy rational- ism without' the particle of mysticism! All is solid sense, truth, matter of fact. Gibbon and Rousseau could not be more outspoken. All the jargon of the Magian priest is gone, and he introduces us into the very sanctum of ethics. He cannot be identical with the composer of the rite of purification. There must have been several Lawgivers. Evidently there were many hands busy in the com- position of Mazdean doctrine. Such paragraphs and whole groups

רבחה תורה כלשׁין בני אדם 1

of paragraphs are of the purist rationalism ; the ghostly element is a later interpolation, or at the utmost, but the vehicle and out-ward form, whilst the essence is of the most concentrated and exquisite uncommon sense, without the least alloy of mythol-ogy. Such refreshing passages are striking and salient proofs that the Avesta had several authors, epochs and redactions : " Purity is for man next to life, the greatest good," is one strata of thought. " That purity is procured by the law of Mazda," is another strata, by a Magian priest. " To him who cleanses his own self with good thoughts, words and deeds "—not the tedious Barashnum with Gomez—that is a third layer, from the same quarry as the first. Or the middle sentence is an interpolation to neutralize the rational-ism. Afraid of that rationalism, a later hand superadded the middle clause: " Procured by the law of Mazda." *Next to life is purity the greatest good,*" is the oldest version of that new current proverb, " cleanliness is next to godliness." The Talmud too has a version of this saying. It appears to be originally Zoroastrian. It is a feature of his own unadulterated doctrine, purity being its chief object.—Vend. VII. 73. " Zarathustra asks Ahura: Can house-hold vessels be made clean that have been touched by the carcass of a dog, or the corpse of a man ? 74. " Ahura: They can. If they be of gold, wash them once with Gomez, (ox-urine) rub them with earth, then wash them with water, then they are clean. If of silver, do so twice as much. If of brass, thrice as much. If of steel, do so four times as much ; if of stone, six times. If of earth, they are unclean forever."

The rabbinical law too, declares defiled earthen vessels incurable. The whole is a striking parallel to Talmud casuistry on kindred topics: same method, same accuracy, same over-anxiety and hair-splitting. Hillel came from Babylonia! Of a solid calibre are the fine passages of Vend. Farg. III. 1–7. " Which are the most happy places on earth ? Answer: Where the faithful erects a house with cattle, with wife and children ; where all is thriv-ing ; where most of corn, grass and fruit are cultivated ; where the dry grounds are irrigated and the swampy ones drained ; where flocks and herds increase and yield much dung for agriculture," etc. What excellent and sound common sense ! Whether that passage is not written expressly to contradict asceticism, monachism, the lazy, contemplative propensities of some Oriental visionaries, is hard to tell, since we do not know at what time that passage has been written. It is well-known that the monasteries had their predeces-

sors in Egypt and in the East long before Christianity arose. Side
by side with this phase of reasoning, comes another one, a different
hand amends it; a new train of thought, more mystic and more
spiritual, or more priestly is superadded: "The happiest place on
earth is, where there is a priest with holy wood and Baresma, with
holy meat and mortar, invoking Mithra and Hoastra (sun and production). The worst place is the Arezura mount, whereto the
drughs rush from hell; where corpses are buried, etc."

ZOROASTER, PAUL AND RABBIS ON THAT.

Vend. VIII. 26, treats of involuntary self-pollution which is
punished with 800 stripes.—Voluntary one cannot be atoned at all.
Later it received some mitigation. The first is exhorbitantly rigorous. As to voluntary pollution, the Rabbis too deemed it so. [1]
VIII. 29. "The law of Mazda takes away the bonds of sin from
him who confesses it. It takes away the sin of breach of trust, murder, burying a corpse, etc. There are ideas strongly reminding of
Paul's doctrine, of atonement by faith and grace. The Talmudic
halacha teaches the very opposite: "The day of Atonement, atones
only for sins against God. As to sins against man, there is no
atonement unless the wrong is practically righted, pardon asked for,
and forgiveness obtained from the offended party. [2] . . . . The
rabbinical views contrast nobly with Parseeism, etc.concerning repentance and confession. Here is their norm, according to Maimonides
Yad Mada Tshuba I. viii. "All the Pentateuchal commandments
when transgressed, must be confessed to God—(not to the priest)
and sincerely repented: "I repent, feel ashamed . . . and shall
never commit again . . . . " Sacrifices do not atone; nor even the
secular punishment of crime; nor restitution will. Sincere repentance and confession are, besides, absolutely necessary for atonement.
. . . Above all, is non-repetition of the crime necessary . . . Nor will
the natural consequences of sin, as poverty, pain, sickness, etc., be
spared the sinner. They are the necessary conditions of pardon.
. . . To confess a sin and not abandon it is hypocrisy . . [3] When
our neighbor is wronged, we must, besides, right the wrong by
practical restitution, by public acknowledgement of the wrong committed and by asking and obtaining pardon. Such a confession
must be public and frank, or it is hypocrisy and unavailable."—That
is salient, good, common sense, holding good for all times and
creeds." The merits and sins of man are weighed and computed.

---

1 Maimonides Mada Tshuba III. 6. .המושך ערלתו איז לו חלק לעיתב

2 Ibidem II. 9. וירצתו לו חייב שהוא מה שישלם   8 בידו ושריץ מבל

The preponderance of either, renders man respectively just or wicked ; the even balance suspends judgment. This seems to be Parsee and rather popular . . . . All Israelites have a share in future life. So too have the righteous among the Gentiles. Excepted of future life are: Atheists, polytheists, idolators, epicurians, apostates, public seducers, self-seekers, informers, political tyrants, " bosses "—in all 24 classes. . . . Nevertheless, if sincere repentance, restitution, confession, etc., have taken place, life eternal will be the share of any repentant sinner, for nothing stands against repentance. . . Man is absolutely free in his self determination ; he can be good or bad, therefor is he responsible for his conduct. Neither the omniscience, nor the will of God, nor the surrounding world offer man any excuse for his private determination. Hence is he fully responsible."

PURITY.   PRIEST'S AND PHYSICIAN'S FEES.

We have seen Vend. IX. treating of the complicated rite of the *Nine night's purification*, (Barashnum nu shaba). It is the most laborious ceremony for cleansing those polluted by contact with the dead. Later it was recommended to every good Parsee, at least once in his lifetime, especially to the young ones just initiated, the " confirmants." It is the Magian baptism, to wash away the natural sin contracted in the mother's womb, the original genuine sense of the " original sin, contracted by the fall of Adam and Eve." The train of ideas reminds one of the circumcision of the Synagogue, and of the baptism from original sin of the Church. We saw above, Zoroaster teaching : " Purity is procured to him who cleanses himself with good thoughts, words and deeds. (Vend. V. 21.)—For that laborious, complicated, ecclesiastical work, the Vend. IX. 37–41, prescribes a precise fee for the priest, according to the rank and condition of the cleansed one. It emphasizes that the fee should be conscienciously paid, in order that the priest may leave the cleansed house well pleased and free from anger. . . . If he leaves displeased, then the drugh, Nassu, re-enters (the patient) by the nose, the eyes, even the end of the nails and he is unclean forever. . . . . It grieves the sun, moon and stars to shine upon a man defiled by the dead." That is Magian indeed !

THE UNWORTHY PRIEST.

Vend. XVIII. 1. " There is many a one who wears a Paitidana (a priestly cover of the mouth) but who has not girded his loins with the law. When such a man says : I am an Athravan, (priest) he lies . . . . 2. " He holds a Khraftraghna (an instrument to kill insects and snakes) in his hands, but he is not girded with the law. When he says I am an Athravan, he lies. 3. " He holds a twig, the baresma, in his hand, but he is not girded with the law. When he says I am an Athravan, he lies. 5. " He who soundly sleeps the entire night, does not pray, learn nor teach, he lies when he says: I am an Athravan. 6. " Him shalt thou call an Athravan who throughout the night sits up and demands of the holy Wisdom (studying the Law), is free from anxiety, with dilated heart and cheerful (about the future) at the Kinvad bridge. . . . Demand of· me (teachings) Zarathustra! that thou mayest be the better and happier (true priest)."—Even better expressed, more to the point and without verbosity, is the XXII Psalm: " To Ihvh be-longs the earth, the universe and all in it . . . Who shall ascend his holy mount ? Who shall stand in his holy place ? He of clean hands and pure heart, whose soul aspires to no frivolous things, and who swears not for deceit. He will carry a blessing from Ihvh and benevolence from the God of his Salvation.

PHYSICIANS.

VII. 36. " Zarathustra asks Ahura : If a worshipper of Mazda wants to practice the art of healing, on whom shall he first prove his skill, on worshippers of Mazda or of the daevas ? VII. 37 and 38. " Ahura answeres: On worshippers of the daevas shall he first prove himself. If he treats with knife three times, and each time the daeva-worshipper die, the physician is unfit to practice for ever and ever . . . . and if he does, that is wilful murder. VII. 39 and 40. " If he treats three times the daeva-worshipper and he recovers, then he is fit to practice the art of healing, upon the Mazda-Wor-shippers too." VII. 4-43, also prescribes the fees for physicians which is according to the rank of the patient. VII. 44. " If several healers offer, (their services), one healing with the knife, one with herbs and one with the holy word, (spells) the last one will best drive away sickness . . . . . . Let him have the preference."—That is sterling good sense. The commentator humorously adds: It may be that spells will not relieve, but they will not harm !" Pin-daros (Pyth. III. 51,) mentions too, that threefold classification: " Asclepios relieved the sick now with caressing spells, now with soothing drink and balm, and now with the knife." Pity that faith-cure is out of fashion. Zoroaster appears to have been the forerun-ner of that and of homeopathy, giving the preference to spells *that do no harm.* Vend. XX. 1-3. " Zarathustra inquiring about healers and remedies, was answered: " Thrita it was who first drove back sickness, fever, the poniard and death. He obtained the remedies for that from *Khshathra Vairya*, (the genius of metal, with a knife and herbs in hand) to withstand the disease created by Angro Mainyu against mortal bodies." XX. 4, " I, Ahura, brought down the healing plants that by myriads grow up all around the one Gaokerena, the white haoma."—It is the tree of "Eternal life" rising in the midst of the sea of paradise. The same Thrita is known to the Rig-veda, under a similar name and attributes. He appears to have been the first priest of haoma, and he is hence the first healer. According to Hamza, he was the inventor of medicine (See Ed. Gottwaldt, p. 23). The *Taavids* or exorcising cameas were inscribed with his name. As mentioned, disease was thought to come from the doings of Ahriman ; or the poison of the *serpent*, a theory quite as rational as the bacilla of our own time ; whilst the remedies were not quite so dangerous as those of Pasteur and Koch. Ahura continues : XX. 5. "All this health, do we call down by our blessing spells, prayers and praises upon the bodies of mortals." V. 7, 8, " To thee, O sickness, I say avaunt ! To thee, death, pain, fever, disease, I say avaunt ! By their might, we smite down the drugh ! Perish, world of the fiend ! . . . Verse 11. "May the much desired Airyaman come here with the men and women of Zarathustra to rejoice with the desirable reward won by means of the law."

From a great many Avesta passages, we may fairly infer that the priestly doctrine of Mazdaism is that the gods need sacrifices, as food and drink to sustain their powers. We see even Ahura accepting and offering such sacrifices. While the later ethical view is more refined. Something akin, we may detect in the Pentateuch. So we read in Yast. VIII. 23. Tistrya, worsted by Apaosha, cries to Ahura : Men do not worship me with sacrifice and praise. If they should, they would bring me strength . . . Ahura offers him a sacrifice and brings him the asked for strength. Tistrya then vanquishes Apaosha after renewed battle.

PURITY AND MOURNING.

Vendidad (Sadah) XII. treats of the uncleanness and the isolation, corresponding to the modern mourning, of the relations of the dead and of their needed purification by an abridged Barashnum. Such matters are also treated largely in the Pentateuch. Prof. Darmesteter thinks that chapter alludes especially to the uncleanness caused by the simple fact of relationship to the dead, besides those coming in actual bodily contact with him. I do not believe that simple kinship, without contact, constituted uncleanness in Parseeism. The chapter treats of relatives living in the same house with the dead, and who were thus defiled by breathing the same air. That constitutes uncleanness in the Pentateuch and in hygiene, too. It is a pity that this is so often overlooked in modern practical life. The home-funeral ceremonies, often in crowded, sickly rooms, harm the crowd of attendant friends and relatives more than it does good to the dead.—Etiquette required that the near relatives should be longer in mourning than distant ones. At first those days of isolation for the mourners were a measure of hygiene and cleanliness. Soon they became conventional signs of mourning, hence a social duty toward the dead. As such near relations had to be longer isolated, independent of their bodily contact with the deceased, betokening their higher regrets. Vend. XII. prescribes how long the relatives shall be isolated, viz: for the sake of decorum, this was according to their degree of kinship, corresponding to our mourning days, which differs, if for a parent, a husband, brother, child, etc. The purification ranged according to the same criterion. The house, the person, the clothes, utensils, etc., must be cleansed, and for a time isolated. Originally that was all simple hygiene, under the form of religious ceremonies. Only after such cleansing, fire, water, men and the gods could enter the house. XII. 21 purports: "If a stranger dies, who does not profess the true faith, does he, too, defile? Answer: No more than a frog does, whose venom is dried up and that has been dead more than a year ago. Whilst alive that wicked ruffian defiles . . . for he does harm to the faithful; not so when dead." That is plain language, an exponent of the times. The principle is: The defiling power of the *Nasu* is greater or lesser, according to the dignity of the dead. The rabbis, too, follow the same principle and the ritualistic result is the same.

HAIR, NAILS AND PURITY.

Vend. XVII. 1. "Which is the most deadly deed whereby a man increases the strength of the daevas? Answer: It is when a man combing his hair or paring off his nails, drops them. . . From that, unclean creatures are produced . . . which spoil the corn, the clothes, etc." A good deal of humor has been spent on that as puerile and superstitious. All over the world such ghostly stories are told concerning unsavory manners and throwing about of hair and nails. They are to be found among the humbler strata of all creeds and peoples. Yet look closely to these verses, bidding to bury nails, etc., anxiously away in a hole, with a prayer—that is simply good habits and hygiene, taught to ignorant people, careless of health and cleanliness, inculcated with the rod of superstition. The living body is for good, and belongs to the creation of Ahura. The dead body has surrendered to that of Ahriman and hence is *possessed*. Even so is of Ahriman, everything that once belonged to the human body, and now separated from it, as the shaved off hair or pared nails. It partakes of the impurity and nature of dead matter, and must be treated alike. Just so considers Parseeism all human eliminations, even the warm breath coming from the mouth. Leaving the living body, it is dead matter, and is impure. Therefore wore the Magian priest whenever praying, a *Paitidana* or *Penom*.([1]) It consisted of two pieces of white cloth hanging loosely down from the bridge of the nose to beneath the mouth and chin, in order to intercept the breath, lest it should, through the air, soil and defile the sacred fire and place. It was an exaggeration of the use of our modern handkerchief.

PURITY; LUST ACCURSED.

Vend. XVIII. 61.   "Zarathustra asked: Ahura! who is it that grieves thee with the sorest grief?   Answer: 62. It is the Gahi([2]) (courtesan), who goes a whoring after the faithful and unfaithful, after the wicked and the righteous. (Commentary). When such a one yields her body to three men, she is guilty of death. 63. Her look dries up the mighty mountain floods and withers the golden-hued plants ; her touch withers the faithful's thoughts, his strength and his holiness. The Saddar 67, Hyde 74, comments: At her look, running waters fall, trees are stunted, and man's intelligence is withered." This horror of unchastity is here no doubt most energetically expressed, and yields to no moralist, Hebrew, Greek, Roman or modern.

WOMAN AND PURITY.

Vend. V. Farg. —. Darmesteter's Rendition.   V. 45. "Creator of the bodily world : If, in the house of a Mazdayasnian, a woman brings forth a still-born child, what are thy prescriptions? Ahura answers : 46. In the place of that house, farthest from man, fire, flocks, baresma, etc., an enclosure shall be erected, and there she shall be established with food and clothing. First, she shall drink gomez, mixed with ashes([3]) from the holy fire, to cleanse her womb.

([1]) Haug. Essays, p. 273, II. Edition Anquital II. 530.

([2]) Gahi is both the demon and the woman of lust.

([3]) So. IV. M. 19. The suspected woman drank such ashes with water.

Afterwards she may drink and eat everything she likes except water, (that is holy). After three nights, she shall wash herself during nine nights more with gomez and water, (Bareshnum,) then she is clean." Among modern Parsees, she remains isolated under the above regimen, during forty days. The Pentateuch and Rabbis' prescribe an isolation of from forty to eighty days, which time was later variously changed. Her clothes, too, must be washed and exposed for six months to sun and moonlight. But even then they can be used only by *Dashtan* women (women in their menses). Unclean persons have their hands continually wrapped in old linen, lest they should touch and defile things around. Even so in Leviticus 13: 45, "And the leprous one with the plague shall have his clothes torn, his head uncovered, and his mouth veiled (the Parsee Penom). Unclean! unclean! he shall call." We smile and wonder at such minute and rigorous prescriptions. But no doubt in those rude and primitive times of cutaneous, leprous and venerian diseases, such precautions were necessary for public hygiene. It is a fact that many diseases of the most contagious and virulent character have been since stamped out, just by such rigorous rules of cleanliness. We smile at such methods and think them hard, vain, superstitious and spectral, because we forget that modern society is free from such ulcers. Remember the Pentateuch is very anxious about the same matters, without entertaining the ghost scare. We moderns laugh at the means, having attained the object. I emphasize that the Pentateuch does not postulate Ahriman and daevas; nevertheless it insists so much upon such rules of disinfection, as isolating the sick, the woman in the menses, the dead, etc., often so strikingly parallel to Zoroasterian methods. That proves that the ghost-theory was secondary in Parseeism, and that private and public health-considerations were the real scope there as in Mosaism.— Vend. XV. 7. " It is a deadly sin (Peshotanu) to have intercourse with a woman in her menses."—The same it is in the Pentateuch: *Kareth* penalty. No doubt hygienic reasons are at the bottom of such injunctions. The Avesta gave its spectral theory as the cause, the Pentateuch, the will of God and nature's instincts.— XV. 8. " It is a deadly sin to have intercourse with a woman (even one's wife) when quick with child " (in an advanced stage of pregnancy, mother and child being endangered by such). The Talmud, too, was much inclined to such a rigorism. But the final decision (Halacha) looked away from it. One teacher wittily quoted the

Ps., God is the guardian of the fools.(1)—XV. 9. "If a man comes near a damsel and she conceives, she shall not willfully procure her menses, . . . and from dread of the people, she shall not destroy the fruit of her womb, . . . or there is the guilt of murder on both the parents." The commentary adds: "The father must acknowledge his paternity and become the woman's husband." XV. 15. "The father must support her until the child is born, . . if not, and mischief comes on, there is wilful murder. . . ."

PURITY AND SICKNESS.

XVI. 1–7. "A woman in her menses must stay away in an isolated building, higher than the surroundings (lest she may touch and defile the earth). She must not look upon the fire; she shall stay away from the water, the baresma and the faithful. . . . . Her food is reached out to her; in the commonest vessels; no flesh-meat for three days; the food must be of the plainest kind and the smallest quantity." The ghost-theory is advanced as the cause. But hygiene is really the reason: no meat, small quantity, plain quality. XVI. 11. "If her menses last over nine days, that is the work of the daevas (devils). 12. They shall wash the woman for her purification with gomez and water (according to the rite of Bareshnum). 13–18. Any sexual intercourse with her, or even simple blandishments, are most rigorously prohibited." All that is essentially, hygienic rules of personal and public health; but exceedingly severe from the reason that in those primitive times of coarse habits and brutal licentiousness, the lawgiver had to recur to severe punishments, really only threats of punishments to insure obedience. The next reason is that such hygienic transgressions were then more disastrous to the health of generations than in our modern times, when venereal diseases have been much reduced, as remarked. The Pentateuch enjoined generally that same line of hygiene as a divine commandment, having as its object, "Ye shall not defile yourself . . . . but be holy, for I, your God, am holy. . . . " Parseeism motived such injunctions by its theory of the principle of Evil to be reduced in its baleful efforts to harm. As shown above: death was its triumph; hence everything leaving the body, as the breath, perspiration, blood issue, secreted matter and pus, amputated limbs, any issue from sickness, above all the menstruation of woman belonged to the daevas; therefor a wizard too, could use them and do harm to the owner, as tokens of Ahriman's triumph. Thus the sick and the dead were considered as overpowered by him;

---

[1] Ps. 116 : 6.   שומר פתאים יהוה

spells, conjurations, invocations of the gods, sacrifices, purification, some painful and revolting, were used to break and expel the power of Angro and restore the patient or even the dead, to the author of life and light, Ahura Mazda.

Purity is the reason why woman during her natural sickness, is removed from the contact of the pure world; that she is forbidden to look on fire, to drink water, to touch the earth and all the holy elements; that her clothes, even after being washed, are unfit for "priests, warriors and agriculturists," fit only for unclean persons; that the husband should not even touch her nor eat with her; that the food is handed her with a long leaden spoon; that it is of the plainest kind and scant of quantity; that she is painfully and tediously purified after a long period of exclusion and isolation, with gomez, etc., for she, as all sick persons, was deemed specially possessed by the evil one. Yet, no doubt can be entertained, that behind this screen of the ghost theory, the real causes were preventive hygiene, health and cleanliness, aiming at sound bodies and souls; sound offspring: holiness! Hence their great, striking analogy with the Pentateuchal rules on such matters. Leviticus hardly knows Ahriman, nevertheless the same anxiety is exhibited concerning the same objects. That proves that the real reason thereof is not Ahriman, but something deeper, more realistic; and this is rational hygiene and psychology, healthy souls in healthy bodies. Holiness it is termed in both legislations.

DAHKMA. BURIAL.

Purity too, is the reason why the dead were not allowed to be buried in the earth, nor to be cremated by fire, nor to be buried in the sea; for the dead are impure; earth, fire and water are holy. They were exposed on high, isolated towers, out of town, called *Dakhma*, there to be devoured by dogs and birds. Their bones after having been washed and cleansed by the falling rains, were buried beneath in a pit, there to await resurrection. The Dakhma was constructed with symbolic metallic wires, isolating it from its surroundings, a casuistic fiction by which it was deemed to be isolated from the earth, to stand in the air, and not to contaminate. That fiction is also known to rabbinic casuistry as (עירוב) *Eirub*, viz: different houses and streets are by a ritual-wire isolated from their surroundings and connected as a single integral whole. When Zoroaster asked Ahura why the rain comes down upon the clean and the unclean, Ahura answered with a mythological fiction: "The waters from the earth return by way of the clouds and are cleansed by boiling in the heavenly sea *Puitika*. From there they flow pure and restored to the sea, *Vouri-Kasha*, the great, heavenly water-reservoir feeding the earth." Without myth and metaphor, that means that man distinguishes from *his own standpoint* between clean and defiled, pure and impure. As to the universe, there is a constant flux and reflux, composition and decomposition, birth, growth and decay; everything comes again into its pristine right place; the bad is neutralized; the good alone remains. Hence there is impurity with man, not with God and his creation.

NASU AND THE DEAD.

Our foregoing remarks will explain the following verses concerning the *drugh* Nasu, the treatment of the dead, clean habits, etc. Vend. VII. (Darmesteter). VII. 2. " Directly after death, as soon as the soul has left the body, the drugh, *Nasu* (ghostly impersonation of death) comes and rushes upon him from the regions of the North (¹) in the shape of a raging fly. . . . 3. On him she stays until the dog has seen the corpse (²) or the birds have consumed it. 25. Can he be clean, O Ahura, who has brought a corpse into the waters or the fire? 26. Answer: He can not. Such has turned to *Nasu* . . that increases winter, cattle-pest, etc. Vend. XVIII. 30. " With uplifted club, the holy Sraosha asked the drugh: Doest thou alone in the material world bear offspring without any male coming unto thee? She answered: Not so. There are four males who are mine : he is my male who, being entreated by a faithful poor, does not give him anything of his wealth treasured up. 36. What can counteract that? 37. " Answer : When a man unasked, kindly and piously gives to a faithful one, be it ever so little, of his wealth." 38. " Thereby he destroys the fruit of my womb." 39. " Who is the second of the males of thine?" 40. " Answer : He of unclean, natural habits."(³) 43. " That is counteracted by scrupulous cleanliness and frequent prayers." 45. " With uplifted club, Sraosha asked again: Who is thy third male?" 46–47. Answered the drugh : " He that during his sleep emits seed.(⁴) The recitations

---

¹ The same idea as in Jerem. I. 14, and IV. 6, etc. : מצפון תפתח הרע.

²'The glance of the dog was deemed purifying.

³ Nec stando mingens . . facile visetur Persa. (Amm. Marcellus XXXIII. 6). Mainyo-i-Khard II. 39—Saddar 56, Hyde 60—Polack, Persians I. 61, narrates : A Persian living in Paris was proven to be an apostate from his own law by eating pork and making water standing.

⁴ The Rabbinical legendary reports exactly the same; akin also it is concerning natural functions.

of certain prayers will counteract that . . . . . 53. " Who is thy fourth male? Answer: 54, " He who over fifteen years old walks without the sacred girdle and the sacred garment."

HOLY VESTMENTS.

These are the Parsee *Kosti* and the *Sadara*. (Mainyo-i-Khard II. 35—Arda Viraf XXV. 6). They correspond to the hassidaic girdle, and the Mosaic upper garment with four corners and fringes, usually termed Talith and Arba Kanphoth.([1]) The Kosti symbolizes the bond of the Parsee with Ormazd. It is the badge of the faithful. He who wears it not is an outcast. (Saddar 10 and 46). The Kosti consists of 72 filaments and goes three times around the waist. It is worn by males and females. There is a combination of numbers in its make up, corresponding to the chapters of the Sacred Books. Such are the knots and the threads of the Kosti. All is symbolical, allegorical. Its four knots shall remember the Parsee of Mazda, his worship, his law and Zoroaster. The Kosti knots symbolize about the same as the Pentateuchal four-cornered garment with the (rabbinical) fringes *mystically-made up ;* their threads and knots too, are qabbalistically interpreted. They too mean the allegiance of the Israelite to the laws and to Ihvh.([2]) In Brahmanism also, the faithful are metaphorically bound to God by a sacred girdle, *Mekhala*. The Sadara (the rabbinical סודר) is a sort of sacred shirt, with short, broad sleeves, reaching only to the hips, with a small pocket above in front It may correspond to the hassidaic טלית קטן, and may perhaps be the Parsee version of the upper-garment with the sacred lot of the high-priest of the Tabernacle.([3]) The phylacteries, with the sacred inscriptions, as those on the 'door posts' were also well-known to the Mazdayasnians. It is unwise to sublimize such practices as of supernatural import, or to ridicule them as mean superstitions and priestly hocus-pocus. We must take them for what they are really intended, as means and symbols of edification, reminding men of their duties: " And ye shall see them and remember my commandments." At a remote epoch when education was the privilege of the few rich and high-born, and books the privilege of the priests and the princes, allegorical vestments, colors and shapes, with select verses on parchment, could do good service and were appropriate educational means. Then the real law-giver instituted them as effective helps and

1 טלית קטן   ארבע רגפות טלית
2 וראיתם אותו וזכרתם See my 'Religious Rites,' on that.
3 אפור אורים ותמים

supports for gradually ennobling the masses. The priestly vulgarian or fraud, used them for imposing upon the ignorant, for driving away the ghosts and conjuring up the protecting genii. Nay even the honest priest and wise pedagogue may well be excused when he inculcated good habits, cleanliness and orderliness by such extra-natural means. Who would take it ill when such an educator forbade the "scattering of cut-off hair and nails, because that breeds devils and vermin, spoils the crops and ruins the clothes! (XVII. 3)." No doubt that is exaggerated, but it is filthy enough to be deprecated. Even so the baleful result of carelessness in regard to the menses, the sick, the dead, etc., justify the law-giver in having insisted upon quarantines, precautions and preventives, on pain of the evil spirit on the alert to do harm.—XVII. 55. "At the fourth step (of a man going without the sacred girdle and holy garment), the daevas wither him to the tongue and marrow. . . . There is no means of counteracting that crime."—The rabbinical law does not allow to walk four ells without the fringed garment.—XIX. 11. "Zarathustra asks: Ahura! how shall I free the world from the drugh ; from the evil-doer, Angro Mainyu, how drive the Nasu from the houses of the faithful, how purify them ?" He is bid to invoke the law of Mazda, invoke the *Ameshas Spentas*, the pure creation, the embodiment of all the gods, the forces of nature; pantheism being at the bottom of Indo-Iranianism.

FURTHER TREATMENT OF THE DEAD.

Above we have read about the disposal of the dead on Dakhmas or symbolical towers, deemed isolated from the elements and exposed to the birds of prey. Vend. V. 10. "During winter what shall be done with the dead? Answer : In every borough they shall raise houses for the dead. 12. And they shall let the lifeless body lie there till spring . . . 13. Then they shall lay down the dead, his eyes towards the sun. If not done so within a year, that is a trespass as grave as murder. There the corpse shall lie until it is eaten by the birds. 40. Out of that house they shall remove the baresma, the cups, the haoma, and the mortar (utensils of worship, to avoid their defilement). 42. After nine nights in winter and a month in summer, they may bring back the fire, etc., into that house (of mourning). 61. Whosoever throws any clothing on a dead body shall have no place in the happy realm (of paradise)." The dead was exposed face upwards on the *Dakhma*, naked, tied to its bars. Modern Parsees allow him old shrouds, clean but worn. Yet on the fourth day after death, rich garments were offered him (for heaven—Sadder 87, Hyde 64). The Greeks gave him rich garments. So the Jews, too; until Rabban Gamaliel set the example of being buried in simple, linen shrouds, used by orthodox Jews to this day. VI. 1. "A year long shall the ground lie fallow whereon dogs or men have died."—The dog is the holy animal of Mazdaism.—10. "If a man shall throw on the ground a bone of a dead dog or man, not yet dried up, that is punished with from thirty to a thousand stripes," (according to its size, for defiling the earth). According to rabbinical law, to throw on the ground bones of man is defilement, too, and that soil was unfit for tillage. Volumes of casuistry are spent on that matter. We have mentioned that it was considered a heinous crime in Persia to bring the dead in contact with fire, water, trees, earth, all of which the corpse defiled.— VI. 44. "Where shall we bring the dead for definite burial? 45. On the highest mountain summits, where there are always corpse-eating dogs and birds. 46. There they shall fasten the corpse, lest parts of it should not be carried away (and bring defilement). VII. 10–22. Clothing and bedding in contact with the dead are, according to the degree of uncleanness, destroyed or washed with gomez and exposed to the air; then it can be used by sick, unclean persons." This is, we remarked, a hygienic measure, dictated by prudence and inculcated by superstitious, popular reasons, the only inducement at hand of the lawgiver, then. VII. 50. "Urge every one to pull down Dakhmas. His sins in thought, word and deed are atoned for (by that act restoring the earth to agriculture). XIX. 29. When a man dies, hellish daevas assail him, fiends and gods struggle for the possession of his soul, to take it to hell or to paradise (Mainyo-i-Khard 2). The struggle lasts for three days, during which prayers should be offered for the soul to secure to it the divine protection. . ." Here may be the source of the "Seven or three day's divine services" in the mourning house. VII. 52. "When the righteous dead enters the blissful world, the stars, moon and sun rejoice at him, and Ahura says: Hail, O man, thou who hast past from the decaying world into the immortal one." Similar tales abound in all legendaries, Christian, Mussulman and Jewish. VIII. 11. "The corpse-bearers shall wash their hair and bodies with gomez (Comment.), besides the full purification afterwards." Here is the parallel of "hand-washing" after funerals. VIII. 23–25. "Throwing clothes upon the dead entails punishment of from 400 to 1000 stripes." It is hard to guess the full meaning of this strange prohibition. It may have been a reaction against the reigning custom, of throwing rich clothes, jewels, arms, etc., upon the corpse and into the funeral pile. We find such in Homer, and even in Virgil, etc., (See Aeneis, etc.), when burning the bodies of the great ones. It was a manner to show one's love towards the departed. That amiable folly was prevalent everywhere, in Judaea too. We mentioned that Raban Gamaliel ordained to bury his body in plain shrouds, in order to discredit that custom. The Zoroasterian enactment may have aimed at the same abrogation of a childish custom. The modern Parsees, probably actuated by modern thoughts of decency, cover the dead with cleanly washed, but worn-out shrouds. There were probably in primitive times economic reason at the bottom : not to be wasteful with good clothes, a waste upon the dead and useful to the living in a poor community. But something more was claimed by it : to give the dead the benefit of the sunlight. It was a kind of prolongation of life, the protection of Mithra against the drugh. In the Hebrew funeral legendary, too, it is not allowed to close the eyes of the moribund as long as complete death had not taken place. VIII. 33, 34. "A dried-up corpse, dead more than a year ago, does not defile. XII. Shows the house where a person died, to be unclean, too, needing purification. It defiles the relatives and inmates breathing its air, and this for different periods of time, according to their degree of contact and relationship. For dead sinners, it lasts longer than for righteous dead. . ." Christian and Jewish funeral pomp, our modern mourning days, staying at home, closing the store, interruption of business relations, wearing old clothes, funeral services, etc., are the evolution of those old Parsee customs, enacted from various reasons and notions. There were, no doubt, there combination of reasons of disinfection and preventive hygiene ; of decorum, tenderness and pious mourning ; of the ghost-theory and priestcraft, too. Remnants may be detected in the to-day's funeral customs of all nations. The ghost-story is not yet entirely discarded ; the hygiene is neglected ; tenderness, decorum, and pomp are most conspicuous nowadays.

CHAPTER X

HOLY ANIMALS. THE DOG.

We have alluded above at the great importance of the dog in Indo-Iranian mythology and the practical life of Persia. The dog was the privileged, the holy animal of the Iranian world. He played a part in the Mazdean religion, on a par with man. He was the constant companion and co-laborer of the warrior and the farmer, the guardian of his house and children, the keeper of his flocks, his intimate friend, his fellow, a member of his household. His glance re-assured the sick and soothed the dying. He chased away the Nasu-drugh from him when dead, purified his soul and devoured his body on the *Dakhma;* he prepared him for and accompanied him to eternal life. He was standing at the Kinvad bridge, pleading for him and admitting him to paradise, or howling him down to hell. He had essentially the same rights and privileges as man. To kill a man was punished with 90 stripes; to kill the water-dog was punished with 10,000 stripes! Egypt, the country of agriculture, worshipped Apis, the sacred bull, its symbol and great help. The Iranian, a semi-monotheist, could not worship the dog. He cherished him and gave him the place of honor at his fire-side. The dog was watching with him, fighting his battles against wolf and bear, thief and robber, he accompanied him on his lonesome mountain escapades and forrest ramblings; his trusty follower through life to heaven or hell. Most frequently is the dog mentioned in the Avesta. The Vendidad treats of that animal very considerately and benevolently. Ormazd has a dog, so has Ahriman. Paradise and hell have each one. There are two creations, of crimes and of virtues, benevolence and wickedness : light and darkness, and each has its dog. He is entitled to food, housing and care when he is sick. To kill him is worse than murdering a man. Let us quote a few verses. Vend. XIII. 2. "The dog . . . is the good creature . . . Among those of the Good Spirit, that from mid-night till sun-rise, kill the creatures of the evil Spirit." 3. "And whosoever shall kill the dog . . . kills his own soul for nine generations ; nor shall he find his way to the Kinvad bridge, unless he has atoned for it . . . " 30. "A mad-dog, or one biting without barking is responsible for his deeds and punished just like a man for each offense." 37. "A mad-dog shall be tied to a post and cured—If neglected, that is a deadly sin." (Peshotanu, 200 stripes). XIII. 39. " I, Ahura, have made the dog watchful, wakeful, sharptoothed, born to take his food with man and to watch over his goods. I made him strong of body against the evil-doers." 49. " The shepherd's dog and a house-dog passing by the house of a faithful, let them never be kept away from it." XV. 1-8. " There are five deadly sins (Peshotanu) viz: To teach another religion (apostatize); to give too hard bones or too hot food to a dog; to smite a bitch with young or even to frighten her; to have intercourse with a woman in her menses or quick with child . . . . . 21. " A bitch with young, lying on the road, he whose house stands nearest by, must support her until the whelps are born. If he does not, that incurs the penalty of·wilful murder."

PENTATEUCH. AVESTA. MYSTICISM. TALMUD.

The import of the dog in Iranian life and creed, is one of the salient proofs that Mazdaism is of hoary antiquity, beginning at the cradle of mankind, older than the Pentateuch; older than Abraham; as old as the Greek classics generally assume it to be. It proves that the Sasanidae and Achaemenidae were but its late followers, that the redactors and legislators of Mosaism saw it already as an established system and legislated expressly in view of it, in parallelism or in opposition to it; favoring or antagonizing its doctrines and modifying many others, to suit their own standpoint, their own objects to be reached. Of such a grand antiquity is the Avesta. Tychsen says: (Gottingen, Nov. Comment. Sec. Reg. 1791), " There is nothing in it but what befits remote ages and man philosophising in the very infancy of the world."—The well-known credo of Judaism: (V. M. 6, 4), "Hear, O Israel, Ihvh is our God, Ihvh (being) is One," yea, the very "Creation" in Genesis, both are there expressly for the purpose of stating the Mosaic standpoint with regard to monotheism, as opposed to dualism; with regard to one creative Power and one Essence, contrasting with the two Powers, the seven Ameshas Spentas and the many more assisting genii of Zoroasterism. Both teach that there is but one divine Essence, not two of good and evil, light and darkness. monotheism in opposition to polytheism, Hindoo and Iranian dualism, Greek and Assyrian mythology. The II. Isaiah continually alludes to Mazdaism, approving or opposing it. Isaiah 44-46 calls ' Cyrus,' God's shepherd who will fulfill his desires and build his sanctuary." " Thus speaks the lord to Cyrus, his anointed one (messiah) whom I hold by the hand, I the eternal who calls thee by name. Let them know from East to West that there is no God but *Ihvh*. He created the light and he created the darkness. He makes peace and calls forth evil. I, Ihvh, am the maker of all that is . . . I am the first and the last, there is no saviour besides me." This plainly means: There is no Ahriman, no Mithra and no Ameshas Spentas; no divine dynasties, no emanations, genii or assisting arch-angels—the later memra, ten words, ten Sephiroth and heavenly Sanhedrin,(1) as claimed by rabbinical mystics of later developments. Carefully studying Zoroasterism, it seems to be a version of the one eternal, natural Ihvh-religion to which Genesis IV. 2, alludes as pre-Abra-hamic: "Then they began calling on Ihvh." That hoary religious phase was crushed out and gave way to idolatry " when the sons of the gods came to the daughters of men, and the land became cor-rupted in the eyes of Deity." (Genesis VI. 1 and 11). Mazdaism was a re-action against that corrupt idolatry. It was an improve-ment. It was a form of that more ancient Ihvh-worship anteceding that corruption; but it was an imperfect type of Jahvism; it was the necessary step after gross polytheism; it was the logical link be-tween that and its sequel, as everything goes by slow development. It rejected polytheism, but stopped at dualism; a power for evil at the side of the supreme power for good. Mosaism proceeded to Ihvism, to pure monotheism, rejecting not only polytheism with star, ancestor and idol-worship, but also Zoroasterism with its dual-ism, Ahriman combating and the genii assisting Ahura. That step Mosaism made. But nothing daunted, Talmudical mysticism kept up the old mythology. The late Qabbala is its restoration.(2)

THE COCK.

The cock is the next holy animal of the Avesta. XVIII. 15, etc. " The bird named Parodars (who foresees), . . lifts up his voice toward the mighty dawn: Arise, O men, recite the *Ashem yad vahistem* (a prayer), that smites down the daevas. . . . For three excellent things be never slack, viz: good thought, good words, good deeds. . . Rise up, here is the cock calling thee up; which ever first gets up, shall first enter paradise . . . with well-washed hands . . . saying his prayers . . . then will herds of oxen and increase of sons be his; and whosoever shall give to my Parodars-bird his fill of meat, shall directly go to paradise."

It is well known that Greek and Roman mythologies had their sacred birds. So was the eagle the bird of Jupiter, and the pea-cock with the Argus-eyes was devoted to Juno; the dove to Venus, etc. The Geese were sacred and cherished at Rome on account

—————————

1 ממרא. אדם קדמן ממליא של מעלה
2 See on that ' Philosophy and Qabbala,' by the author.

of their vigilance during the war against the Gauls. But none had the honors of the cock in the Avesta. Because none is so useful as he is in primitive times. He is the first time-piece of the villager. The cock is another witness to the great antiquity of Zoroastrianism. The prophetic period had a sun-dial. The dog is yet a privileged animal in the entire Oriental world now. The tenderness for him is, no doubt, an inheritance from old Mazdean times. The Jew alone thinks him unclean, and has no predilection for him, either from sheer opposition, or because his former Arian Lord used to abet his dog on him. But the cock is a favorite animal in Jewish legendary lore, too. The cock chases away the demons, sends home the ghosts of the dead and frightens off the wizards. At his voice all sorts of unwelcome guests quickly take to flight. Such are the legends in old Parseeism and in modern popular tales of all creeds, epochs and peoples. I heard such in the Ghetto.

THE HOLY BULL—HARA BEREZAITI.

That was another holy animal, mythological, not domestic, type and patron of nature's wealth and productiveness, the bull often invoked by the Zoroastrian. The primeval bull was created by Mazda and killed by Ahriman. He is not alone in Mazdaism. We find his "confrere" in sacred and profane history. It is well known that the Egyptians, too, had their sacred ox, Apis or Hapi. He was the living image of Osiris, the Sun-god, the leading deity of ancient Mizraim, and, as usual in idolatry, identified with Osiris by the people. As may be presumed by his name, he was also identified with the Nile, Hapi and really represented, in conjunction with the sun or Osiris and the majestic Nile River, the agriculture of the country, its leading trait. Apis was considered as the moon-bull, and his colleague, Mneuis, as the sun-bull. Apis was all black, just as the Mosaic "Red-heifer" was all red, in express opposition. Now the Apis mythology was surely not identical with that of the Parsee sacred bull, yet it may be its predecessor and mother to the Magian myth, which also meant fructification and production. The modern Mardi-Gras may be its late echo. So, too, its earlier colleague, the Druid December Ox. In express contrast to Parsee and Egyptian myths, the Pentateuch has its Red-heifer-rite, Numbers 19, which is not to be worshipped as a god, but burnt to ashes as the image of sinfulness and perishableness—a striking contrast. The Pentateuch and the entire Sacred Writ have much to narrate, and the prophets ring with denunciations, about the idolatrous 'Sacred Bull," that made such inroads into the Ihvh-worship,

beginning from the very Exodus to the destruction of the Kingdom
of Israel and of Judah. (Exod. 32). "The people, seeing Moses
tarrying to come down from the Mount, called on Aaron, Rise and
make us a God to lead us on, Moses being gone." That is just the
idea of the Egyptian Apis. Apis was not Osiris; and the Golden
Calf was not *Ihvh*. But the people wanted a symbol, a bodily
representative of the Deity. That was Moses; he not coming back,
they reverted to the Egyptian idol. Later, King Jeroboam wishing to wean off Israel from the rival-people and worship at Jerusalem, instituted at Bath-el and Dan the Apis-Calfs (I. Kings 12: 28),
which lasted to the end of that kingdom, and found imitation in
Judaea, too. A witty midrash, remembered too] in the Koran,
claims that golden calf was made of the gold which the Hebrews
had borrowed at their Exodus (12: 35). There is a fair presump-
tion that the "Red-heifer" rite meant to discredit the calf-worship:
Apis-Osiris vanquished by *Ihvh*.—The Aggadah has a legend
nearer to the Avestian bull; there it is surnamed the Wild Ox
(Shorhabar שור חבר), and reserved for the righteous in Messianic
times. So it has, too, about the cock chanting "praises to the
Eternal." The Hebrew morning prayer contains a benediction:
"Praised be Thou, O King Eternal, who gavest understanding to
the cock to distinguish between day and·night." There is no benediction, but pithy tales about the *wild ox*, served up to the pious on
the advent of the Messiah; God himself being the host. The
primeval bull was in many myths the type of the animal kingdom,
the emblem of productiveness, of the heavenly clouds, of cows emitting rain and fructifying the earth. It was in Mazdaism the image
and the genius of cattle yielding food to man.—Vend. XXI. 1, 2.
"Hail, holy bull, beneficent bull! who makest increase . . . who
bestowest thy gifts upon the faithful. . . . Come on, O clouds, to
destroy sickness. . . . Shower down new waters, new trees, new
health." . . . This sacred bull seems to be the brother of the
Egyptian Apis. Whosoever carefully reads this entire Farg. 21
will surmise there the identical myth, differing exactly as much as
Mazdaism does from Egyptian mythology. The latter is more
veiled and more favorable to idolatry. The Avesta, discarding
image-worship, could entertain no Apis in a temple. It translated
him into the sky, and by poetising the same myth, showed its real
meaning to be rain, clouds, production. Egypt condensed the
poetry of nature to image-worship. Persia rarified it to a poetic
myth with a transparent nucleus: the productiveness of the clouds

rising to the skies by evaporation and coming down as rain and food. Both the myths have but one nucleus. In Hindoo pantheism, the deity permeates the universe. Every object is spiritualized and personified. So were the clouds imagined as a bull or a cow, emitting rain and fructifying the earth. Each realm had its chief or genius, and the bull was such of the animal kingdom. XXI. 4, 5. " The sea *Vouru-Kazha* is the gathering place for the waters. It is in the center, on the top of the Hara-Berezaiti. The sun produces light for the world, from that same place down comes the sun. From that sea flow down the rains, and thereto they return. . . ." The *Hara Berezaiti*, Mount Alborz or Albord, is the seat of the Avestean gods, the Greek Olympos. It is also the seat of revelation to Zoroaster, as Sinai is to the Jews. Light and water are derived from there (Bund. XX.), and return thereto. The clouds connect the ocean below and that above. Genesis I. 6, etc., seems yet to reflect that idea of a heavenly ocean.

ARBOR-WORSHIP AND CONTINUITY OF RITES.

We have seen the import of the dog and the cock in the Persian family, and that of the holy Bull in Avestean mythology. Such domestic affections and poetic cult of Persia have been universally traced. We shall now give another instance of that continuity of ideas, conceptions and rites concerning the cult of trees in old Mazdean Persia and in modern Mohammedan Persia, as well as in Western Europe and America to this day. James Darmesteter justly calls attention to the remnants of Avestean worship of trees and plants in present Mohammedan Persia[1]. Alluding to his dictum that there is nothing in worship but what existed before in mythology,[2] he quotes Jules Patenotre (in " Les Persans chez eux," Revue des Deux Mondes, 1875, tome VIII. p. 162), who says: "At a crossing mid-way in Persia, a solitary thorn-bush rises with a thousand thorny branches, reaching out on all sides. Heaps of little pebbles are piously piled up around it. Small pieces of cloth hang down the branches as offerings and witness of the veneration of the inhabitants (for a forgotten deity, of the long extinguished Mazdean cult; viz: the Amshaspand of trees and plants, Ameritat). Our mule drivers do not neglect to fulfill this religious duty. . . . When we ask them what is the meaning of that ceremony, we receive the naive answer: " Such is the custom." People know no more about it. The usage has

---

1 In his Haurvatat et Ameritat, p. 51. Paris, 1875.
2 In his Vendidad Translation, p. 37. Oxford.

scrupulously been preserved from age to age ; every one conforms to it without any further inquiry." This ceremony we find there in a comparatively barren region. But two centuries ago Chardin found the same cult of trees and plants in the very paradise of Persia, in Chiraz. He narrates :(1) " The most beautiful things at Chiraz are the public gardens, about twenty in number; the trees there are among the largest of their kind to be seen anywhere. They are of an exceeding height, and three mens' arms could not embrace them. The inhabitants believe such trees to be many centuries old and offer them their devotions. They hang upon the branches chaplets, amulets and pieces torn from their own garments. Invalids offer them incense, and light candles on their branches, hoping to regain thereby their health. Persia has everywhere such venerable trees superstitiously worshipped by the people. They call them *Dracte Fazel*, viz: auspicious trees (belonging to the good creation). They are full of nails holding up pieces of cloth as pious offerings." Barbaro, who travelled in Persia in the 15th century, met everywhere these *good trees*. As the cause of the adoration rendered them, he assigns the popular belief that these trees ward off fever and all other kinds and symptoms of maladies.(2)

There is no doubt that we are here, in presence of genuine Avesta conceptions. Here is a remnant of the worship of the plant-goddess, Ameritat. It is an echo of ideas, feelings and adorations belonging to the mythology of ancient Zoroasterism, inoculated upon a later religious stem and growth, Mohammedanism. The Koran has chased away the gods and genii of the Avesta. But it did not the natural feelings of gratitude and veneration for light, shade, food and water, yielding trees and plants. Though Haurvatat and Ameritat have been exiled to the wilderness, as poor devils as the biblical Azazel, though their names have been forgotten, their being and their worship live yet and will continue, as long as juvenile poetry and worship will live. Nay, we shall see that such naive, mythic conceptions live yet with Christian and Jew of to-day, too, in Europe and America. And if they are no longer rites of the established church, they exist as eternal religious feelings holding their place in the human heart. It saliently substantiates our theory

1 Chardin, Voyage II., 200 Ed. Amsterdam,

2 Incide interdum in spinarum arbustum cui ingentem segminum et scrutorum adhaerere copiam vidi ; per quae hoc illi intelligi volunt : quasi febrim et morborum alia symptomata arceant.

that leading religious ideas and rites are universal.([1])   Barbaro and
Chardin assign, as the popular reasons for that cult: "The trees
are believed to ward off sickness, death and fever. Just so says
Ahura to Zoroaster :([2]) "Thrita asked for a remedy against sickness,
death and fever which Angro Mainyu created for mortal bodies.
Then I, Ahura, brought out the healthy plants by hundreds and
thousands([3]) . . . in order to ward off malady, death, fever and
suffering."—We need not go to Persia to find the ancient Avestean
cult of plants and trees. We meet it to-day in our own midst.
Our Anglo-American Arbor-day, our decoration-day, the Christmas-
tree with lit candles and branches full of presents, etc., are no
doubt, the development of the cult of plants.   Its parent, the
Druidic forestrian mistle-toe and the Teutonic "mid-winter log" from
the tallest oak, are varieties and evolutions from the same rite.
A refinement upon that is the Pentateuchal bouquet of the feast of
booths.([4]) It is the same original material with an additional national development, ethically interpreted. The ancient and the later
Persians decorated the humble bramble-bush or the majestic Chiraz-
tree to screen themselves from sickness. The Teuton strews the mistletoe on his fields to induce fructification. The Pentateuch ordained
it as a token of God's blessing on the field. The Talmud naively
superadded the shaking of the palm-tree branch and the paradise
apple([5]) "to drive away the evil spirits," innocently reverting to
vanquished Parsee conceptions of plant worship. Thus we recognize the universality of religious rites and ideas. So we see that
the Pentateuch ordains to put on the *Taavids* with certain religious
inscriptions, on forehead and arm ; to fix such inscriptions on door-
posts and city-gates; to make fringes on the four-cornered garment,
and show symbolic colors on the upper garment, etc. The Koran
ordains the same, and with just the same motive as the Pentateuch:
"That you should see and remember all the commandments of
Ihvh and conform to them . . . and be sanctified to your God."([6])
Such usages were recommended, too, in the Vendidad. Indeed,
the word Taavids (Hebrew טוטפת) is originally a Zend-Avesta
designation. The Christian Church is not wanting either in such
amulets and sacred inscriptions and on the same score. That proves

---

[1] See Fluegel "Thoughts on Religious Rites," on that.

Vend. XX. 1.

According to the Bundahesh, Chap. IX., these plants are 10,000 in
number.   [4] Levit. XXIII. 40.   [5] אתרוג ולולב

[6] See V. M. 6 and 11, and IV. M. 15.   וחיו למים פות בין עיניכם

the tenacity of such practices.—Chardin(1) says: "Devout people in Persia take pleasure in praying and in meditating rather under these sacred trees than in the Mohammedan mosques, since so many holy men, too, came there to pray. These venerable trees make thus serious competition to their neighboring mosques. Some devout dervishes pass even the nights under the shade of such trees, where they do not fail to see apparitions of the good souls who made their devotions in former centuries. . . . Sick persons devote themselves to these departed spirits and find often their cure."—J. Darmesteter remarks :(2) "Thus the cult of trees eminently Mazdean, has survived Mazdaism: the tree chases away sickness, now under the *Moula* as under the *Mobed*. The peasant of the nineteenth century hangs on those trees some rags of his mantle and worships the same god as the Persian Emperor Xerxes did, who suspended his gold chain to the tree on his route. The sole difference is, the present peasant knows not the name of that god, whilst the Persian king of kings did know. But this is a small difference in the eyes of comparative theology, which cares rather for the spirit of beliefs than their names. That spirit of belief is one and the same with the pious Mussulman and the worshipper of the Ameshaspand, Ameritat. That belief goes back to the past beyond Herodotus and beyond Xerxes. Xerxes received it from his ancestors. It is as old as the religion of the Achaemenides, who have engraven its catechism in the rocks of Persepolis ; as old as the language of the cuneiforms which was dead already twenty centuries ago."—The excellent J. Darmesteter thus recognized the great continuity of religious rites and ideas to the farthest past. The same reasoning will show its continuity from the past to the present and to the future, ever evolving higher and nobler types. These rites and ideas change their shape and name, they develop and refine, but their inner spirit remains the same.

AVESTA CIVIL, PENAL AND MARRIAGE LAWS.

Vendidad IV. 1. (Darmesteter): "He that does not restore a thing lent, when it is asked for back, again, steals the thing, robs the man. So he does every day as long as he keeps it." Herodotus I. 183, narrates: The basest things with Persians are, to lie and to be in debt.—2. There are six contracts: I. The word-contract, (by word of mouth). Denying it is the worst of sins, (Gr. Ravaet 94). II. Hand-contract, (striking a bargain by closing hands). In Roman law: Stipulatio; in Rabbinic law: תקיעת כף. III. Contract

---

1 Chardin II. 44 and 201.   2 Hourvatat and Ameritat, p. 66.

to the amount of a sheep, viz: 3 istirs, or 12 dirhems, about $7. IV.
Contract amounting to the value of an ox, viz: 12 istirs, $28. V.
Contract to the amount of a man, 500 istirs. VI. Contract to the
amount of a good land . . . Each contract broken, is redeemed by
the one above it, viz: IV. 3, 4. " The word-contract broken shall
be redeemed by the hand-contract ; that shall be by the sheep-con-
tract, etc., etc."—5. " If a man break his contract, all his family are
responsible for it (to the ninth degree)." This was Persian and
generally ancient law too. So reports Am. Marcellinus XXIII.
6.([1]) The ancient Hellenic Law adjudicated the property, the person and the family of the insolvent debtor and contractor to the
creditor. According to Caesar, etc., this was the case also among
the Gauls and the Germans. The well known *Twelve Tables* recognized the same principle in the Roman empire. It was only the
Justinian code which mitigated in part that harshness. The Law of
Athens and of Sparta upheld it. That led to disastrous political
and social results. Solon's great legislative innovation was its abol-
ishment. Only the property of the debtor and contractor was to
be security to the creditor. His person, his labor and his children
could not be alienated and enslaved. Solon, further, nullified the
past mortgages on land. He lowered the currency value by about
twenty-seven per cent., to help the poor debtors disburden themselves of their obligations with a degreciated currency. All that
was unjust, but it saved the State from economic and social ruin.—
The Mosaic Legislation also grappled with that problem. By the
original equal distribution of the soil, and by the prohibition of
alienating one's patrimony, of taking interest on money and making
profits on goods, etc., and lastly by the solemn principle that a
fellow-citizen can never be enslaved, neither he, nor his children,
nor his family-plot, by the declaration, that man and soil are
ever free and can never be alienated—by all that, the Mosaic
law repudiated that iniquitous polity. The Deuteronomist
XXIV. 16, expressly states : " The parents shall not suffer for their
children, nor the children for their parents." But in practice it was
not carried out. So (II. Kings IV. 1) " the widow complains that
. her children were carried away into slavery for the debts of the dead
father."—11 : 17. " The breaking of a contract was punished with 300
to 1000 stripes. " Thus an attack upon property was more severely
punished than upon human life. The Mosaic law punished purse for

---

1 Leges apud eos impendio formidatae, et abominandae aliae per
quas ob noxam unius omnis propinquitas perit.

purse and person for person, not otherwise. This is more conform to human dignity and equality. The Mosaic view substantiates thus democracy, the Gentile one underlies aristocracy.([1])—IV. 17–55, treats of outrages : They are classified into menaces, assaults, blows, wounds, bloody wounds, broken bones, manslaughter, repeated crimes with manslaughter, perjury. The first six misdemeanors are punished with stripes, varying from 5 to 90. Ninety stripes was the punishment for manslaughter. Repeated crimes without previous atonement for the preceeding crime, multiplied the punishment.

Vendidad XVII. 13–18 : "Intercourse with women in their menses is one of the most heinous crimes and was most severely punished."—Be it for its real or its imagined danger to health, as it was believed that veneria and leprosy originate their; or on account of Ahriman theory.—Marriage, and woman too, was an object of contract. She was sold by her father or guardian, from the cradle, often. Betrothals took place sometimes at the age of three years.([2]) Marriage in tender age is yet customary in the Orient and was more so in antiquity. Selling of women as servants or into marriage was customary among all ancient nations. Exodus XXI. 7, alludes to it, but limits it apparently for marriage purposes, securing to her and her children all the rights of an honorable wife. Indeed inferring from the Koran, buying a wife was the practice in the Orient and became the norm for the lawgiver. Girls of good families had to go through the forms of the slave-merchant to pass into the house of the husband.([3]) The Talmud curtailed the right of the father to sell his daughter, even into marriage, and abolished it practically. At last the rabbinical *halacha* required the free consent of the woman to be married, just as that of the man to marry.—The Mishna has yet the expression : "A woman is *bought* for money, contract and cohabitation,—"([4]) as a remnant of olden times, but it was really mean ngless. Woman could not be married without her free consent. The moral law and common sense gradually vanquished the barbarous privilege of the stronger.

CAPITAL PUNISHMENT.

Vend. VIII. 74. "Ahura says : Surely they shall kill the man who cooks or burns a corpse."—The Commentator adds : four men can be put to death by anyone, without an order from the Dastur : He who burns a dead person (Nasu) ; the highwayman, the Sodomite and

1 Fluegel's ' Spirit of Bibl. Legislation,' p. 32, etc.
2 D. Franjee. Parsees, p. 77.   3 M. Fluegel, Koran, p. 187, etc.
4 Kidushin I. 1.

the criminal caught in the act."—IX. 47–49. "He who does not
know the rite of cleansing and undertakes it nevertheless . . . they
shall tie his hands, flay him alive, cut of his head and give his body
over to the ravens . . " So is killed he who alone carries a dead
body (III 14). Besides, the punishment inflicted upon the *Peshotanu*,
viz: him "worthy of death," punished with 200 stripes with the
horse-whip, or upwards of 200, that is tantamount to capital punishment, if not by far worse.—" A *Peshotanu* is worthy of death.([1])
Such is inflicted upon him who serves bad food to his dog ;([2]) "who
tills a land wherein a corpse was buried during that same year ;([3])
"A woman delivered of child that drinks water ;([4]) " who holds intercourse with a woman in her menses ;([5]) " who performs a sacrifice
in a house defiled by a recent dead ;([6]) " who neglects fastening the
corpse to the bars of the Dakhma ;([7]) "who throws the bone of a
corpse or dog receives 200 to 1000 stripes with the horse-whip ;([8])
" four hundred for him who touches water or trees when in a state
of uncleanness ;([9]) "400 to 800 stripes for covering a dead person ;([10]) " 500 to 10000 stripes for killing a dog."([11])—For killing a
man only 90 stripes are inflicted. Happily the severity of such laws
never was carried out. According to Chardin, the number of
stripes there really never exceeded 300, in the old German law 200,
and in the Pentateuch law, never over 39 stripes. The Pahlavi
Commentary distinguishes three sorts of atonements : by money, by
the horse-whip and by confession and repentance, the Patet." This
latter one presupposed yet previous restitution and reconciliation
with the offended human party. Then came religion. The practical wrong was first to be righted. Even such is the rabbinical view,
quoted above : " The Day of Atonement reconciles only sins of man
towards God. Sins of man against man that day atones not, except
when practically righted and the offended party reconciled.([12]) Full
restitution to the offended party, with asking and receiving of pardon, were the first requisites. Then pardon from God on the Atonement-Day was possible. Thus Parsees and Rabbis did not favor
the "trade of absolution."

J. Darmesteter further shows (Vend. Introd. 23) that certain
sins termed *anaperetha*, inexpiable, were meant to be punished with

1 Farg. IV. 20–V. 44. 2 Farg. IV. 40. 3 Farg. IV. 5. 4 Farg. VII.
70. 5 Farg. XVI. 13. 6 Farg. V. 39. 7 Farg. VI. 47. 8 Farg. VI.
10. 9 Farg. VIII. 104. 10 Farg. VIII. 23. 11 Farg. XIII. 8 and Farg.
XIV. 1.

12 עבירות שבין אדם למקום יוכ מבפר.   שבין אדם לחברו אין מכפר עד שישלם לו וירצתו 12
Maimonides-Mada-Tshuba.

death here below and torments hereafter. We have mentioned the crime of burning the dead. Such punishment was further inflicted for burying the dead (I. 13); for eating of dead matter, (VII. 23); for unnatural sin, (I. 12); and for self-pollution, (VIII. 27.) From Greek accounts and from Parsee tradition; it seems that punishment of such crimes was death by blows.

ESTIMATE OF THAT CIVIL LAW, ETC.

In the above paragraph, we find a meagre outline of the Vendidad's civil and criminal legislation. It knows the full value of contracts. The contracting parties were bound to their stipulations by divine and human coersion. Even a verbal agreement. was solemnly binding and the anger of Ahura threatened the liar. The whole family was, to the ninth degree, answerable for its fulfilment. Bodily assaults were judiciously graded from simple threatening to manslaughter. Repeated assaults aggravated the misdemeanor ; and if not atoned, the punishment was multiplied in its severity. Prof. Darmesteter finds that simple menace, "agerepta,"[1] seven times repeated amounted to manslaughter. Every crime makes the perpetrator guilty here and hereafter, except when he confessed his guilt.[2] Penalties were inflicted by stripes with a horse-whip, rising gradually from 5 to 90. Threatening with the fist (agerepta) had five stripes. whilst manslaughter was punished with 90. A second manslaughter had the Peshotanu-penalty, 200 stripes. The Peshotanu-penalties rose from 200 to 10000 blows. But were probably but a menace. Wrong and crime have no absolute value. They are conditional, social, relative; hence are they differently estimated and diversely punishable. When one bethinks himself concerning said laws, that a simple menace was punished with five stripes, manslaughter with ninety stripes, covering a dead person, by several hundred stripes and killing a water-dog with 10000 stripes, we feel bewildered and exclaim, Nonsense, priestcraft, superstition and barbarism ! But should we on the other hand remember, justly remarks Darmesteter, that each nation and law have their own peculiarities, which are denominated barbarism by those standing outside of its precincts, then we might be more indulgent to the crudities of the Persian law. So the Greeks acted similarly for defiling the sacred ground

---

1 Agerepta is identical with אגרפ. Exed. xxi. 18, and Is. lviii. 4; menace with fist.

2 So is the rabbinical law too. S. Maimonides, Mada Tshubah and so the Parsee confession called the *Patet*. Here is the first mentioning of confession, so important in Catholicism and Judaism.

Delos (Diodor XII. 58). So the Athenians put to death their victorious generals for neglecting to bury their dead soldiers in the stress of battle. So they gave to Socrates the cup of hemlock for not believing in the gods. So the church exterminated the Albigenses, the Hugenots, etc., for not believing in the saints. So Europe was during a century and a half, brutally converted into a slaughter-house for thinking diversely about certain doubtful religious formulae. So Calvin put Servetus to death for being too forward, and Luther outlawed the Jews, the peasants and the Anabaptists for desiring their share of emancipation. So Huss and Giordano Bruno, Galileo, etc., were persecuted in Italy on theological grounds. So were Quakers and Unitarians banished in America on the same plea. So Jewish populations are decimated, pillaged and expatriated in Russia, even now, because they believe otherwise than others claim to. Bethinking ourselves of this sad chain of our argument, from the Persian criminal law to that of our own times, we shall see that that Persian law may have been no more absurd, than that of other times, nations and their prejudices.

Zend-scholars have suggested that the excessive rigors of the Vendidad laws might be explained by the assumption that these stripes were converted into fines. Indeed the enormous riches of the fire-temples may have originated there. . . . The Pahlavi translation (to Farg. XIV. 2) alludes to, and Parsee tradition confirms, that the bodily punishment was actually converted into pecuniary fines. In the Ravaets 200 stripes are estimated at 300 isters—$700. In Parseeism every sin has its value in money. So has every merit. "Both can thus be accurately weighed in the scales of Rashnu" at the Kinvad-bridge, and thus determine, to the ounce, whether the dead candidate should be admitted to paradise or go to hell. Other Zend-scholars again suggested that these horsewhip stripes, so liberally administered by the hundreds and thousand, might perhaps have fallen, not upon the culprit, but upon the backs of the drughs and daevas, or upon the insects and creeping things, the creation of Ahriman. The Mazdean priests indeed were ever armed with such a bundle of twigs, smiting fearfully Ahriman's followers and relieving themselves of their own sins. We find such exercises frequently recommended to the faithful as a partial expiation of sins. [1] . . .

PARSEE AND RABBINICAL JUSTICE.

I shall now be allowed to add the following new suggestion, and this from analogy. Whosoever studies the Talmudical crimin-

See Darmesteter, Introduction Vend. V

al Jurisprudence, will no less be bewildered at its apparent severity. Reading the treatises of Sabbath, Sanhedrin Makkoth, etc., one will find there hundreds of deeds, trifling in themselves, declared as worthy of stripes, of extermination, of death, by stoning, burning, beheading and strangling. [1] The frequency of such punishments and the pettiness of the offence—in the opinion of the outsider, the layman, not understanding the technicality of legalism, makes the reader shiver and think those rabbinical law-givers were blood-thirsty cannibals, Baal's-priests Torquemada's, inquisitorial ministers of the "holy hermandad." Carrying, on the Sabbath, your stick outdoors ; or your handkerchief in your pocket ; or grinding a pow-der for medicine ; or lighting a match in grim winter . . . . on the Sabbath, are punished with death. Such cruelly punished trifles one will find by the myriads. But when one examines such cases thoroughly, one will find they are but innocent scare-crows, means to enforce absolute Sabbath rest by frightening the uninitiated. Often they are even less ; the dry outcome of the logical deductions from certain far-fetched premises. When one admits that any trifling work on the Sabbath is punishable· even with death, and when one admits that a walk beyond the limits [2] is work, then of course, a stroll into the country on the Sabbath is a deadly crime. But practice from theory is at a great distance. To punish such a deed was necessary : witnesses, a warning at the committal of the deed ; announcement of the penalty ; the perpetrator's declara-tion of acceptance ; his being in earnest and in his good senses: a most intricate trial, full of so many technicalities, that it became il-lusory, impossible, utopian. Having educated the faithful under such ethical restraints, the rabbinical moralist was satisfied. As to actual punishment, the judge nullified such Draconic laws by a host of clauses, fictions and legal technicalities. Walking over 2000 yards on the Sabbath, or carrying outdoors one's own handkerchief, incurs the death punishment—on a hundred conditions, all nearly impossible to obtain ; to such an extent that conviction will hardly ever take place. [3] What good then did such a law do? It was an educational means. It reared the Jewish people under self-control. It stimulated the ethics of law-abiding. It produced the 'kingdom of priests and holy nation' the noblest feature of histor-ical Israel. It freighted them with superstition, but it stimulated re-spect for law. It rarely punished criminally. It rarely inflicted death. It was the most humane of ancient times. It could conscienciously say : "A court that pronounces the death-penalty once in 70 years is a murderous court." Such was the effect of the apparent severity of the rabbinical code, and such its real humanity. I know of no legislation, ancient or modern that is so careful, mild and humane, so much afraid of ever being unjust toward the innocent, as the rabbinical jurisprudence. Its clauses and restraints were so multiple that actual criminal punishment was almost impossible, and the entire law became but educational and preventive.

Now I think, it may have been the same with the said severities of the Mazdean legislation. It was no more puerile than any other law. It seems so to outsiders, just as ours may seem to strangers. And as to its apparent rigors, these were but theoretical, but on paper, never carried into practice ; preventive of crime, not hasty to punish. They looked the more severe, the less they were intended for practice. Their aim was to frighten into obedience, never to blast and to kill. They threatened with hell and with torture, the more to avoid both. Their law was their educational means, as with the Jews ; their school-master, not their hang-man. Mind the hoary time of its original enactment, a scattered, lonely, rough and harsh population, little tutored to restraint, recognizing no other than their own caprice, the law had to be severe in form, in order to be mild in essence. Rough children need a strait-jacket. I am even inclined to assume that the Talmudical method alluded to, that of infinitely multiplying transgressions and commandments, sins, misdemeanors and crimes, stripes and exterminations, burnings and stonings, etc., and yet reducing such punishments to mere educational means, that method of theoretical severity and practical mildness,—the Rabbis have learned from the Persians. Their opponents, the Sadducees who were inclined to be more earnest with the legal severities of the Pentateuch, nicknamed them Pharisees, viz : Parsees, Persians, which name later became an honorable distinction, designating their levitical purity, extended from the priest to the entire people, just as the Magi had done in Persia.

CHAPTER XI

RABBIS AND MAGI. A KINGDOM OF PRIESTS.

This remark may need some more elucidation. It has justly been surmised by keen-eyed Zend-scholars([1]) that Zoroastrianism was at first but the doctrine of the Magians, one of the six tribes of Media ; that gradually they spread beyond that country, and by spiritual arms gained over whole nations and countries, as Bactria, Iran, Persia, Parthia, etc., the dynasties of the Achaemenians, the Arsacians, and at last the Sassanians ; that even during the Achae-menian reign, the Magian rules were not yet generally practiced by the bulk of the people, that the universal mode of burying the dead in the earth, was yet the practice among the Persian people too,([2]) and that even burning a corpse was occasionally attempted. Grad-ually and much later, during the Sassanian rule, the Magian religion became identified with the Persian practice, was fully endorsed by the rulers and the people, and became the state-religion. Indeed it requires an extraordinary effort on the part of the masses to follow out the minute regulations and precepts of the Magi. Their rules of purification alone absorbed all the attention and time of ordinary men. Such rules are made only for a priesthood, a retired, contemplative caste, given to leisure and holiness. It must have taken long centuries until the Persian people consented to become " a kingdom of priests and a holy nation." The Magian tribe of Media, one of its principalities, was the prototype of that "*King-dom of priests and holy nation*," with hundreds of commandments and prohibitions, and a host of prayers and religious observances. It took centuries of indoctrination until that ideal was realized and extended from the Magian tribe to the entire Persian people. Now just this was the course in the polity of Mosaism and Judaism. Originally Mosaism had a tribe of *Kohanim*, and Levites, spiritual nobles, with an exalted theology, ethics and laws. For long that tribe of " Levites and priests" strove to gain over the people to their rigid discipline in theory and practice. The Pharisees were the teachers who succeeded in that difficult task of extending the Levitical or priestly voluminous and minute rules, as embodied in Thora and Talmud, to the mass of the people ; of making of them all a " kingdom of priests and a holy nation." No doubt can be entertained, that the Kohanim, the children of Aaron, were consid-

---

[1] J. Darmesteter, p. 44.   [2] Herodot. I. 140.

ered as a distinct people, the nucleus of Israel. So they are termed
" children of Aaron, thy holy people."([1]) in the atonement ritual and
the services in the Moriah temple. The Pharisees extended the ranks.
All Israel is that priestly people. The priestly diet, the Levitical
purity, sobriety, religious sanctity, all expanded and became obligatory to Israel. The Kohanim, the Hebrew Magi, lost their superiority, their exceptional position. That was an immense innovation. Hence were the authors of that denominated, Pharisees,
פרשים, from Parsees, as also from the new rules of purity imposed gen-
generally upon the laity. No doubt can be entertained that the Pharisees greatly modified their own theology after the model of Persia.
Rigidly adhering to monotheism, they yet found room for Ahriman.
There he obtained the second rank, yet constantly and overtly in
antagonism with God. The angelology and demonology, the
wicked world, its limited duration and the new millennium, Ahriman to be defeated by the Messiah, the hereafter, resurrection and
the renovated world, all that is Parsic.

This immense reform was carried out by the Babylonian initiator, Hillel, the head of Tradition, of the Talmud. By his pliable
Hermeneutic rules, he engrafted upon the Pentateuch all those
priestly rules denominated tradition, as coming down from Moses
and Sinai and implied in the Pentateuch. These were later extended
infinitely to the maze of present rabbinic Judaism. The Talmud may
thus stand in the same relation to original Mosaism, as the Avesta
is to original Zoroasterianism, if Haug's view be correct. Rabbinism
is the Zend-Avesta, viz : Law with traditional expounding, of the
Thora. But it must be emphasized that, though largely adopting
from and initiating the Parsee theology, the Talmud teachers, the
Rabbis, nevertheless, knew well not to trespass certain bounds; not
to put forward too prominently the Ahriman and drugh theory;
they declared not the elements holy ; they interdicted not burial
and cremation ; no washing with Gomez, nor wearing a *Panom* at
prayer. True, later even some such notions were borrowed, as hiding
away the nails, shaking the lulab, the bundle of twigs, and the hierarchy of good and bad spirits . . . yet monotheism saved the
Jews from falling into the pool of Persian superstition and ridicule.

Whatever the reader may think of this parallel phenomenon,
between the Magians and the Rabbis, it is a clear and uncontestable,
historical fact that the Avestean rules of purity were for long but
the distinctive sign and norm of the Magians, and gradually they

---

בני אהרן עם קדשך 1

were extended to, and accepted by, the people at large, thus setting the example of a " Kingdom of priests and holy nation." The same is the fact with the Pharisees in Judaism. They created, as the Mobeds in Persia, the "people of priests and holy nation," by causing the commoner to accept those Levitical rules of purity, diet, sobriety, devotions, habits of spirituality, etc., originally intended but for the priests. Gradually, and after centuries of rabbinical discipline and indoctrination, those priestly privileges were extended to the bulk of the nation and accepted by it, not as a burden, but as the privilege of the "kingdom of priests and holy nation," instituted by God, fiom the very start of its existence.

EASTERN RELIGIONS AND THE TALMUD ON LOVE OF STUDY.

We have studied in these pages the growth and development of the leading ethical ideas and views of the East; how by the eternal laws of mind, by the innate force of their own fitness, they propagated from one system to another, and gradually became the mental and moral property of all nations and climes, vested often in similar symbolical rites. We have seen that among the Brahmans, the cultivation of the Vedas and of science in general, among the Magi that of the Zend-Avesta, and with the Buddhists that of their own sacred writings, the Sutras, etc., with the other sciences as auxiliaries, was accounted as the very first duty, as the proper natural task of the priest, the Brahman, Atravan, Mobed or Bikshu. The culture began with their sacred books, around which nucleus clustered all sort of knowledge, secular, mechanical, scientific and purely experimental. All knowledge was considered auxiliary to the sacred books and accounted as a proper domain of a true and genuine priest. Learning, study, was the greatest glory, and secured honors on earth and in heaven. Learning was the holiest virtue, the noblest accomplishment. It earned the brightest diadem, it forwarded a man into the very presence of, and identified him with, the deity. This was so among Brahmans, Buddhists, and Magians. We shall show here that this idea was, and is, also predominant in Judaism. Even Israel of recent times is pervaded by this native respect for learning. The highest accomplishment, the greatest glory was that of learning, of knowledge, *Thora;* first Bible, Talmud and Commentaries; but next every kind of knowledge, reasoned and experimental, even good manners was *Thora.* " It is Thora and I must learn it,"(1) is a known rabbinical axiom. *Thora*

1 תורה היא ולימר אני צריך

actually means learning, knowledge, science. This is the original sense of the word, from the root רוי, to teach. Even so is the meaning of the word *Veda*, akin to the Greek oida, I know. The meaning of "sacred writings" is but secondary to each of these terms. We shall render here verbatim some passages from the well-known treatise Abboth, that will show the propagation of this view, the enthusiasm for study, the self-sacrifice for the acquisition of knowledge, science, as the highest object of man. This ideal taste was entailed by the East upon the West—from Benares on the Ganges, to the Ghetto in Prague and the university of Leipsic and Halle: (Abboth III.) R. Hanania says: Two persons talking together about matters appertaining to Thora, the Shekhina is with them: For it is written (Maleachi III.): Then discussed they who fear God, and He listened and received it graciously, and it was inscribed in the book of memorial in His presenee."—But if their theme of conversation be not about holy matters, it is a meeting of scoffers. Yea, even a single person occupying with the Thora is sure of reward.—R. Simeon says: Three persons taking their meal at one place and discussing matters of the Thora, are considered, as if eating at God's own table. But if they talk of common things, they are accounted as partaking of a funeral feast (heathen).—R. Nehunia says: Whosoever accepts the yoke of the Thora is relieved of the yoke of government and the world—the care of livelihood and of obligation to the state.—R. Halafta says: Ten persons meeting in a discussion about the Thora, God is in their midst. So it is when three, two or even one occupy with the law, for it is written: " Where my name is mentioned, there I shall come and bless thee." (Exodus II.) Other Rabbis say :(1) Whosoever journeys through cultivated fields, meditating upon the Thora and interrupts himself with the remark: How beautiful is that tree or acre, he endangers his life.—Who forgets or neglects his study, forfeits his life.—Precious is man born in the image of God.—Precious is Israel, for it is written : " Children ye are of your God." (Deuter. 14). Especially chosen is Israel, as written : " Good teachings I gave you, my Thora, forsake it not." (Prov. 4). Ben Soma says: Who is wise? He who learns from every one.— Who is a hero? Who conquers his temper.—Who is rich? Who is satisfied with his lot.—Who is honored? Who respects others.— Despise no person and no thing, for every one and each thing have their opportune hour.—Be very, very humble, for the future

---

1 Abboth III.

of man is—worms."—That is of Buddhistic sound and color, it savors decidedly of the East. We have seen such among the Buddhist proverbs. It has the ring of *Nirvana*.

The reader will remember the Brahmanic and generally the eastern doctrine of the wanderings of the soul to expiate the sins of former existences. She assumes a nobler or meaner shape and body according to her merits in her past career. She is thus rising or falling, in the scale of her earthly existences, by inhabiting the body of a god, a Brahman, a Tchandala, an elephant, a wolf, a snake, a plant, etc. The rabbis did not go to that length, but transmigration was well known to them. Especially they connected phenomena of nature and of history with the moral conditions of man. So we read in the same treatise, Abboth V.: "Seven modes of misfortune befall the world on account of seven chief transgressions: When some pay tithes and some not, drought is the punishment. When all refuse tithes, drought and lawlessness cause famine. . . Crimes not punished, induce pestilence. War comes upon the world for refusing justice to the innocent. Perjury is followed by beasts of prey; exile is visited upon the idol-worshippers, the incestuous, the murderers, etc. The minute casuistry of the Brahmans, their hair-splitting distinctions and miscroscopic argucies, their endless litanies, myriads of prayers, abstinences, penances, fastings and self-mortifications; their tenet that the body is but the prison of the soul and the source of evil; their charms, incantations and talismans against the evil spirits; their often overstrained humility and suicidal ascetism, side by side with selfishness, exhorbitant arrogance and self-deification—such views and claims have not died out, without leaving their distinct traces. These theories and practices have found their immediate echoes in Zoroasterism and Buddhism. They have their analogy and parallels in all the creeds and sects of the West, in Asia, Europe and America, of modern times. This propagation of ideas and opinions proves incontestably, how nothing remains isolated, how the beliefs, thoughts and practices of the East influenced the West. In a modified and mitigated form, they traveled from Brahmanism to Iran, Ceylon, Thibet, and found there echoes in the to-day's western religions: for good and for bad, we are the heirs of the past and the nephews of the Easterners.

Let us quote a few specimens more from the Rabbis on the import of study, learning, Thora, in parallel with Hindoo and Iranian dicta: "The Sages taught in the spirit of the Mishna: Praised be God who selected Israel and his learning. Whosoever busies himself with the Thora unselfishly, merits many good things—yea, the world exists on his behalf.   He is called a companion and friend of God, he is a partner of God in his creation."([1])   This is de- cidedly a Brahmanic and Zoroasterian view: "A man doing good and fighting evil, assists the God of good."   Now follows a mag- nificent description of such a man and saint, with all the enthusi- asm, the naivety, the exaggeration of the East.   The proudest names are spent upon him, the highest epithets, almost divine honors.   Monotheistic sobriety yields the place to Eastern, almost mythic idolization, " He gives joy to God and men—His robe is humility and piety; he is capable of becoming a righteous and holy one ([2])—the *Dvidsha* and Ascetic of Brahmanism, and the *Yazata* of Parseeism—"He is sinless and nearest to over-merit, *Sechuth*, dispensing council, salvation, wisdom and strength.—To him are given royalty, dominion and the dispensation of justice.   The mys- teries of the law are revealed to him,—he is a never failing stream of holy emanations; he is pious, long-suffering, forgiving injuries, superior to and sublime over all creatures."—Here is the exalted position of the Hindoo Ascetic and hermit; of the Parsee sage and Yazata, who stand higher than the gods, assisting the Supreme in His creation, patrons of men and of the world.   The *Zaddik* and *Hassid* of this Rabbinical passage is absolutely and identically de- scribed as the Brahman Dvidsha or Ascetic, as the Magian Yazata, as Buddha: mendicant and angel; in rags and with a crown.   This rabbinical *Hassid* and *Zaddik* is decidedly identical with the Sage of Kapila and Plato.   As to *Yama*, as to *Manu*, so to him are given dominion, royalty and dispensation of justice.([3])   Such is the *Hassid* of old Abboth, of mediaeval Qabbala and of to-day's mysticism ! " Every day a Bath-Qol, a holy echo issues from Horeb proclaim- ing: Woe to the people who neglect the Thora . . . A free man is he only who industriously studies the Thora . . . . Whosoever learns of his neighbor even a verse, even a letter, owes him respect forever . . . For honor is but in the Thora.—Good is but the law. . . . Such are the methods of Thora and learning: Eat bread with salt, drink water moderately; sleep on the bare ground, live poorly and scantily, but busy thyself with learning.   Then hail to thee in this and in the next world. . . . Ask for no greatness, desire no honors beyond thy learning.   Work, and long not for the table of kings. For thy table is nobler than theirs and thy crown is more lustrous

---

[1] כל העולם כרי הוא לו—נעשה שותף לחקבה כמעשה כראשית   Abboth end.

[3] צדיק וחסיד   נותנת לו מלבות וממשלה וחיקזר דין

than theirs . . . . Great indeed is the Thora, superior to the priesthood and higher than royalty. Royalty is acquired with thirty
degrees; priesthood is with twenty-four; but learning is gained
with forty-eight degrees." . . .

These forty-eight degrees to the acquisition of science, sacred
and lay—for this is really the sense of Thora—comprises all the
noblest and most exalted of ethics, virtue and intellectuality, coupled
with humility, asceticism and self-sacrifice; just as the requirements
of a Magian or Buddhist teacher, a Brahmanic *Dvidsha*, Plato's
and Maimonide's Sage. Indeed it is the identical doctrine of the
high worth of mentality and virtue, reduced to sober possibilities in
these passages of treatise *Abboth.* " Great is the Law, it dispenses
life here and hereafter."—So R. Jossi narrates : Once upon a time
I was on a journey, when a man met me and greeted me, asking:
Where are you from ? I answered: from yonder great city full of
learned and wise men. He said: Rabbi, will you come and live in
my place, and I shall give you myriads of gold, pearls and precious
stones ? I replied: Should you offer me all the gold, pearls and
gems in the world, I would live but in a place of learning.—It concludes: when man dies none of his silver, gold or precious things
accompany him—nothing except his learning and his good deeds."

This enthusiasm and self-sacrifice for high mentality and virtue—the Rabbis inherited it from the East; and they entailed it
upon the West. Have we Occidental's cause to call the Orientals
barbarians and put them under the heel? Should not the West now,
pay its old debt of gratitude, and help rekindle there the torch of
civilization, lit at their sacred fires thousands of years ago? Would
that not be a nobler triumph than that of compelling them to buy
our manufactures and submit to our rule?

TALMUD AND AVESTA ON ANGELS AND DEMONS.

Zipser in the *Orient,* 1850, in the wake probably of Nork (the
Brahmans and the Rabbis, 1836, p. 100), called attention to the fact
that the mysterious Metatron of the Aggadah is identical with the
Parsee Mithra, the well-known mediator and intercessor, between
Ahura and man. He is often invoked in the *Yasna,* in that capacity. The Rabbis too, imagined Metatron as such a mediating angel,
interceding and bringing up the prayers into the presence of the
Schechina. (1) So, according to the Hindoos, the souls of the pious
perform that office, bringing the prayers of the faithful before heav-

---

1 באיו על נפל ונפל משטרון בא Midrash *Tanchuma* to Va-eschanon, V. M.
iii. 23.

en.   The same do, according to the Parsees, the Fravashis; and according to the Rabbis, the souls of the pious, Hassidim, especially
the patriarchs.   A well-known prayer to that effect is in the Hebrew
prayer-book. (¹)   Of Mithra is claimed that he teaches the law in
Heaven.   (Yast. 64).   So too the Rabbis: (²)   Metatron teaches
Thora to the children in school.   They appear sometimes to think
Metatron and Elias as one and the same person; of the latter one they
said "that once in the day, he is allowed to plead mercy for Israel."
(Hagiga 15.—Sometimes Metatron is called the "Great Chancel-
lor (³) of Israel."   Just so they said of Elias: "In past times a man
did good and the prophet wrote it down; now it is Elias and King
Messiah who do so."   (Waikra Rabba, 34).   So too in Kidushin
70: Elias writes and God seals. (⁴)   Mithra knows all secrets and
he has messengers announcing to him, all that happens, (Yasna 45,
46).—So in the book of *Henoch:* "Every member" of my council (⁵) knows and discloses to him all the secrets."—According to
the Parsees, Mithra, Serosh and Rashnu, are the three judges meeting the dead at the bridge of Kinvad.   Even so the Rabbis:
"When a man dies, three angels meet him,"—Treatise Kalla, etc.—
Elsewhere we have alluded to that formidable bridge over hell leading to paradise, to be found in Jewish, Christian, Mohammedan,
Parsee and Babylonian legendary.   It is universally known that the
Avesta teaches as subordinate to Ahura Mazda, his six peers, the
Ameshas Spentas.   Ahriman too has his court of six wicked grandees, corresponding to Ahura's six good genii, each of the first set
has one of the other set, as his particular opponent.   This we find in
the Talmud too.   The six angels of good are termed angels of the
(divine) Presence or of the service. (⁶)   The opposite six, are the
angels of wrath. (⁷)   Yet there is the following radical difference in
the two conceptions.   To the Parsees, the one set are divine genii,
of light, assistants and peers of Ahura, the others are of Ahriman,
genii of evil, drughs residing in hell.   In the Talmud either of these
categories are messengers of God, one for good and its reward, the
other in punishment, for bad; both are angels and both perform
divine behests.   The following will make plain that radical differ-

---

אליהו בורא וחקבה חוחם 4   סופר חגרול 3   עבורה ורח 2   מבניסי רחמים 1

5 ממליא של מעלח   For these parallels, etc., we follow often O. H. Shorr
in Hechaluz, 1860–1869, though we do not always coincide with his
conclusions which are often extreme and unwarranted.

מלאכי זעם 7   חשורח or מלאכי הפנים 6

ence between Aggada and Avesta: In the Midrash, (¹) we read:
"When Moses was ripe for death, God bade his angel Gabriel to take
away his soul. The angel declined it. Thereupon order was given
to the angel Michael to perform that task and he declined too—he
and his colleague being angels for good.—Then God repeated
the command to Sameal—a messenger for bad and he declared
ready. Then Moses anxiously prayed: "God deliver me not
into the hands of the death angel! God replied: Be reassured,
Moses! I myself will take care of thee." Hence we read, (V. M.
34, 6) Moses died by the mouth of God, (viz: with a divine kiss),
and He, (God), buried him in the valley," (²) etc.—This pretty
legend best illustrates the angels, good and bad, of the Talmud, as
radically differing from those of Zoroasterism, of which they are,
with all that, but a nobler development. This delicate, but most
important differecce, between the angelology and demonology of
the Rabbis and the Parsees, is the dividing line between me and the
great scholar and inquirer, O. H. Schorr. The neucleus is
identical, the evolution is a nobler one.

As Mithra assumes a special importance in the mythology of
later Parseeism, even so Metatron, in the Talmud: That non-Jew
said to R. Idis: It is written: And to Moses He, God, said, Come
up to Ihvh. Come up to me, should be there? The Rabbi,
answered: That is Metatron who speaks, and whose name is identical with that of his Master. (³) Shorr surmises that the ideas of the
East-Asiatic peoples, the Chaldeans and Babylonians greatly influenced all, Mosaism, Talmud and Zoroasterism, though he knows
not clearly in what way that was done, either that there existed some
ancient connection, long before Moses, between the Babylonians and
Canaanites, as believed by *Chevolson ;* or by the intermediation of
Media; or that the last redaction of Holy Writ took place later, as
according to Bohlen, Dozy and even some Jewish sages. (⁴) He
identifies too, Abraham's origin, education, and birth-place, Ur of
the Chaldees, with the Babylonian science and priesthood ;—and his
later sojourn in *Haran,* with the Zoroasterian *Airyana Vaegho* of
the Avesta. Thus he hints at the possibility that Babylonian ideas
found their way to Palestine and vice-versa ;—showing strong parallel lines between Mosaism and Parseeism, not only in single laws,

---

1 Debarim Rabba XI. and Ptirath Moshe to V. M. 34, in Midrash Me-
ucher—Also in Babl. Sanhedrin 21—Sabbath 104—Jerusalem Aboda
Sara I. 5, etc.   ויקבור אותו בגאי ²

3 Sanhedrin 39, b.   עלה אל י״ת עלה אלי מזכעי ליה זהו מטטרן ששמו בשם רבו

4 Hechaluz, Vol. VII., p. 12—Vol. I., p. 109—Vol. III., p. 99.

but in the method and the spirit of those legislations. Such is for instance: The order of the Creation, the fall of Adam by the temptation of the serpent (following here, Rosenmiller, Bohlen Spiegel and Windischman). Such are the traditions about the Garden of Eden, its four Rivers, the Trees of knowledge and of life, the deluge, clean and unclean animals, etc. These biblical traditions go parallel with those of Chaldee, Hindoo and Avesta.—Following Rhode,([1]) Shorr surmises that both, Parsees and Hindoos, drew from the same sources, viz: Babylonia and Chaldea, whence Abraham hailed and which views he carried over to Haran and Hebron in his immigration thereto ([2]) having fled from the persecution of Nimrod, conqueror of his native country.—These historic traditions concerning the Chaldean science and religious influence are frequently alluded to in the Talmud. Abraham's countrymen are so, as נפתי Nabateeans, inhabiting a part of Babylonia and whose civilization was older than that of the Hindoos and the Hebrews. Their idiom was a Semitic one, akin to the Aramean. The Talmud mentions that. In Jerus, Sabbath chapter 16, they are termed נפתי, Nabateeans, and in Nedarim 9, they are called Khutheans, כותי, their chief dwelling-place being Khutha. An interesting tradition about Abraham is in the Talmud. (Baba, Bathra 91): Rab said: Ten years was Abram incarcerated: three in Khuthi and seven years in Qardia. R. Chisda says, *Ebra the Little*, of *Khutha*, that is the biblical *Ur of the Chaldees*, the birthplace of the Hebrew patriarch. From remnants of Nabateean literature, Chivolson has shown that long before Moses, Babylon's sages inveighed against idolatry, etc. Of these ideas, Abraham may have been the monotheistic link between Chaldea and Kanaan, connecting Ur, Haran and Hebron.

CONTINUATION: TISTRYA, ELIAS, AP-BRI AND OBRIMUS. ([3])

Spiegel shows that according to the Vendidad, rain is in the power of Ormazd, but later on it was placed under Tistrya. Similarly the Rabbis: (Tanith 2): Three keys are in the hands of God and that of rain is one.—While in Sanhedrin 113, they say the key of rain was delivered to Elias. ([4]) The Commentators add: Sometimes such keys are temporarily given to God's messengers, as it was to Elias on Karmel.—Another such genuis of rain is called *Ap-bri;* such is in Midrash Tilem 78, about whom there is a poem in the holiday *Poetans.* Shorr thinks Ap-bri identical with Aware and Abhra and Vara, meaning: cloud and rain. I have my own

---

1 Beitraege, I., 55.   2 Hechaluz, Vol. VII., p. 10 and 12.
3 Shorr, Hechaluz VIII. 6, etc.   4 אתיהב אקלידא דמטר לאליהו

opinion on that, viz : In these pages I have called attention to the Greek Obrimos, the All-Powerful, a Homeric epithet of the leading gods of the Hellens, showing its relation to the Hindoo *Brahman*, of the root bri and brim.   Now I venture the suggestion that Ap-bri אפ-ברי, the genius or god of rain, refers to the same *obrimos*, it means " Abri, brim," the Almighty.   One of the frequent epithets of Zeus is: " The cloud-gatherer or rain-maker, "Nephel Egereta ;" so too in Latin authors: *nubes cogens.*   Etymologically and logically, this seems to me the best derivation.   Spiegel, Yasna I., quotes *Berejya* as the patron genius of mature fruit.   In Sanhedrin 95, Gabriel is detailed to that office.

PARSEES AND JEWS. MORE PARALLELS. (1)

Spiegel counts *Aparim napat* as another genius of water. (Khorda Avesta Introduction 19).   Shorr remembers the Rabbis quoting *Ierakim,* as patron of hail-storm (2) to which the legend : When Nebuchadnossor threw Hanania, Mishael and Asaria into the firy furnace, arose *Yerakim,* Lord of hail and said : Holy One, shall I go down and quench that burning furnace ?   God answered : That is not my office ; thou art master of hail ; all know that water quenches fire."—The Parsees know and pray to the *Menthra Spenta,* the holy Word of Mazda, his revelation.   Treatise Kalla, of R. Meir, has such a genius too, called : patron of the Thora. (3)   In Daniel X., we read : I, Daniel, alone saw the vision, but the men with me did not, yet a great trembling seized upon them, and they ran away. Who ran away ?   Haggai, Sacharia and Maleachi !   What for did they run away, since they saw not the vision ?   Because their *Luck,* מזל, saw the danger.   Rashi comments : Their patron saw it, since every man has his patron in heaven.—This, says Shorr, alludes to the Parsee *Phervar.*   Another Talmudical saying is : Israel has no such a מזל, patron-*Phervar.*   The idea that every man has his lucky angel is found among the Hindoos, Parsees and the Jews, too.

Innumerable are the Talmud passages quoting the discussions between Parsees and Jews.   I shall mention here but a few. Babli. Sanhedrin especially contains a myriad of such.   " That renegate told to R. Gamaliel, he who made the mounts, did not make the winds," (each having its own genius).   Told that Magian to Ameimer, " from thy midst upwards, thou art of Ormazd's crea-tion ; downwards of Ahriman's."—Of course the spelling there is in-correct.   So is there Rashi who naively interprets : " Ahriman, God

---

1 Ibidem Shorr.   2 ירקמי שר הברד.   Midrash Tilem, 137.   3 שר תורה.

is so called." (¹)—A Magian (not Sadducee) said to R. Abahu : God
who is a priest, how could he bury Moses ? (that being defilement) :
He cleansed himself with fire !" was the answer. Many fine points
are there but hinted at.

Let us give one instance in full. In Babli. Hagiga, 13, etc.,
we read the following, concerning a leading Rabbi, who turned to
the doctrine of the Magi : " Four men entered paradise (mystic
doctrine) viz : Ben Asai, Ben Soma, Acher and Akiba. B. Asai
looked and died. (²) Ben Soma looked and was punished. Acher
lopped off the branches. (³) Alone, Akiba left in peace . . . R.
Yohsha b. Hanania was standing on the height of the Temple-
mount and B. Soma seeing him, did not rise before him.—"Soma
whence and whereto, he asked ? Soma answered : I was looking at
the waters above and the waters below, and there is no more than
three fingers breadth between both," alluding to 'water' as the original
matter of the world, (according to Thales), or to the two creations of
Parseeism.—R. Jehosheiah declared him as standing outside of the
faith.(⁴) . . . As to Acher, he lopped off the branches (of Judaism).
What did he see ? Metatron having permission to note Israel's
merits (⁵) . . . Are not there two Powers ? (⁶) . . . A divine voice
called : Return ye wayward childern . . . except Acher !" This
Acher is Elisha ben Abujah, the teacher of R. Meyer, so famous in
the Mishna. He is reported as given to sensuality and holding the
following discussion with that pupil : " Is it not written : (Ecclesiastes 7) : "Even this, opposite to that, God created ? (The two
spirits of good and evil and the two creations.) He is answered :
Both the contraries are made by the same Creator. Acher continues
tempting his pupil, but is· ever pointedly met with a repartee. R.
Meyer intimates that Acher may yet become a penitent. But
Acher replies : " Long ago I have understood, it is too late for me."
Once upon a time Acher was riding on horse back, on the Sabbath,
and R. Meyer walked behind him, learning Thora from his
mouth, (⁷), when he, Acher, called : " Stop here and return !"—For
the Sabbath allowed the latter one no further to proceed.(⁸) When R.
Meyer replied : Stop thou too,—viz : from thy heresy !—" Too late !
he exclaimed—R. Meyer insisted and Acher followed him into 13
schoolhouses where, in each, he ominously heard holy verses deprecating and repudiating apostasy. The verses are sharp, and cutting,

---

1 Sanhedrin, 39, a :   קרי הכי   אחרימין חקבת   ² חציץ ונגע   3 קיצץ בנטיעות

חוא ממטרון דאתיהבא   מיה רשוחא ליתב ולמבתב זכוחח וישראל   5   6 מבחוץ

6 The sense of that passage is intentionally obscure,   ב רשיות

7 מפו תורח   ללמוד   8 תחום שבת

the last being especially pointed. (Ps. III. 16.) "To the wicked God said: What for dost thou speak of my law! (Acher yet occupying with it); but Acher understood the child saying: "To Elisha," instead of *Rasha*, "'o the wicked" as in the text. ([1])—When he died it was said, (in heaven) "We shall not condemn him, since he occupied with the Thora, but he shall have no future life, since he apostatized."—To which R. Meyer objected: Let him be punished, but not forfeit eternity. His opinion was acted upon; a smoke arose from Acher's grave, ([2]) R. John regretted this hell-fire in Acher's grave and promised to release him when in the hereafter. So it was; when R. John was dead, the smoke from Acher's tomb stopped([3]) . . . Acher's daughter came to Rabbi: "Support me Rabbi!" "Who art thou?" "Acher's daughter!" "Has the wicked one reared children?" and she replied: "Rabbi, remember his learning, not his deeds." "At once a fire came down and began burning his footstool!" (in punishment of his unkind words)—That passage is often intentionally obscure, the subject being delicate. The name Acher is whimsically explained there. I think it is simply Ahriman—Acherman—Agherman. Ughur and Ughra being fierce devils in Avesta mythology. *Acher* means simply the "evil one," devil. Shorr's explanation of the name is far-fetched. ([4]) He believes him to be the founder of a sect, the *Mendaites*, whose name was Elchsai and who taught a doctrine compounded of Judaism, Christianism and Magism, that he especially accepted full dualism and part of other Parsee tenets. I quoted here that entire long passage from Hagigah, to show the relation of Parsee doctrines and views to Rabbinical theology and mysticism; especially the surprising instance of several leading Rabbis, occupying with foreign teachings and philosophy; some even passing over to them and yet not breaking off their intercourse with former Jewish friends and pupils, and their former mental occupations. Later rabbinical generations really wondered at that toleration (Ibidem 15, b). "That R. Meyer learned of Acher." They quoted different verses all going to say: that "he ate the fruit and threw away its stones."([5])

DAEVAS IN PARSEEISM AND TALMUD.

The same identity of Persian and of Rabbinic demonology is shown in Babylonian Berachoth 51. a: "R. Ismael, son Elisha said: Three things told me Suriel, the lord of the divine Presence([6]):

---

1 זלרשע instead ולאלישט   2 סליק קוטרא מקבריה דאחר   3 פסק קוטרא מקבריה דאחר

4 Hechaluz VIII. p. 9.   5 אכל תחלא ושרא שותלא לברא   6 שר חמגים

Take not thy shirt from the hands of thy unwashed servant when dressing; nor shalt thou take thy water (for hand-washing) from him whose hands are not washed; nor must thou return the cup of thy morning drink(¹) but to him who handed it to thee, for the evil spirits are waylaying man for such opportunities to harm him."(₂) The same Rabbi is elsewhere claimed to have risen to heaven by means of a sacred talisman. Another legend claims to have the same information, not from Suriel, but from the death-angel, with the addition of this: "Do not stand before women when they return from a dead person, because I, the death-angel, am dancing before them, with my sword drawn and having permission to smite." He to whom this happens must get out of the way, reciting the verse of Sacharia III., "God forbid, thee, Satan," etc., until he has passed.—We see that the Talmud as the Magi, connected the ideas of uncleanness and sickness, death and mischief, with the evil spirits, spectres, devils and daevas. Physical impurity, moral depravity, and mental untruthfulness, error, lies, fraud, etc., were all but one and the same thing, looked at from different standpoints, all leading to destruction, the work of Ahriman, the Genius of death. Shorr (Hechaluz VIII. 8) shows further that the Talmudical ideas about the habits of the evil spirits, are like those of Parseeism. They eat and drink in preference, things unclean and of evil odor. They sojourn in graveyards and pair there. They know all that will happen as the angels do. They like dirty places and take pleasure in ugly things. Similar notions we find the Rabbis holding of the devils: (Berachoth 3). One shall not enter a ruin from fear of the evil spirits. They are usually termed the mischievous, hurtful ones.(₃) (Jerushalmi Jebamoth 15). The devils are to be found in pits.—No man shall drink in the night from the river or pond (Psachim 112). Since they frequent the graveyards, it is the custom in the South to wash after a burial. (Jerush. Berachoth II.)—They are masters during the night, etc.

SICKNESS AND TALISMANS.

Both, the Hindoos and the Parsees, assumed that maladies are mischievous, evil spirits. Against every sickness, they had a spell, to chase it away. The Hindoos sometimes flattered the devils, hypocritically. While the Parsees ever spoke to and of them

---

1 כוס אספרגוס

2 אימתי . . . מפני שתכספות, ואמרו לח איסתלגנוס של מלאכי חבלה מצפין לו לאדם

יבוא וילכד
Takhaspis is no doubt the Persean Khraphastras viz: soiled things, infected with the Evil one.   3 מזיקין

spitefully and harshly: "Accursed be thou, fever! Avaunt! flee!
Here I expel the daevas, the accursed ones." . . . . Even so the
Rabbis thought maladies and distempers as dangerous evil spirits.
(Psachim 114—Sabbath 67, etc.)—Their spells, too, were, conform
to the Parsee pattern, spiteful and contemptuous: "An Arrow in
the eyes of Satan "(¹), (Qidushin 81).—The Avesta and the Talmud
used sacred verses as approved weapons against the devils.   Layard
found such Jewish cameos, or written spells and talismans, of Babylonian Jews of the seventh century, with names of Persian angels
and daevas, which make it undoubtful that such came from Magism, correctly argues Shorr.   He points to their likeness among
Rabbis, Babylonians and Buddhists, as proof that they were not
confined to the Parsees, and may be older than the Avesta.   Even
the Arabians before Mohammed, used such spells and talismans to
guard the children against the evil ones, hanging over their necks,
teeth of the fox or the cat.   The Mishna, too, remembers the fox-
tooth.(²)   So did the Parsees use their holy Writ, verses from the
Avesta, to drive away the devils and heal diseases.   (Vend. and
Khorda-Avesta).   Even so did R. John allow to heal with passages
from holy Writ (Sabbath 67).—Other teachers forbade it.   Shorr
thinks that especially the knots in the phylacteries and the fringes
were believed to guard against the evil one.   The Parsees used
also to that end the Baresma twig.   So did the Rabbis use the
Lulab and the *Shophar* (cornet).   (See Sukka 31).   Parsees and
Talmudists were also afraid of the *evil eye* (Babli Baba Bathra 118;
Berachoth 95).   Rab and R. Chijah both say: Ninety-nine persons
die of "an evil eye " and one by divine decree."   (Shorr Ibid).

AGGADA AND AVESTA.(³)

In the following instances, Shorr allows the priority to Parseeism.
But in many cases that may be contested.   It may be claimed, either
that such sayings and teachings are so common sense like, that they
spring up everywhere from the native soil; or that they are wandering
proverbs, from East to West sometimes, and at other times, from West
to East.   Shorr is over-modest in assuming the Magi ever original
and the Rabbis always copyists.   Priority can only then be safely
vindicated, when the adage is the necessary outcome of the peculiarities of a people or a doctrine.   So the Bible teaches God without Ahriman nor Daevas.   Hence when later appear Spirits, Satan, etc., that
is of Persian derivation.   Spiegel says that the Zoroasterian right-

¹ גירא בעיני רשמנא   ² Sabbath 86 and 66—שן של שועל
³ Following Shorr Hechaluz VIII. p. 17.

eous, dwelling in paradise or *vara*, are shining as lights, and the
Fravashis are lustrous stars.([1]) Similarly is found in Sanhedrin 19
and Midrash Tilim 75: "As the sun and moon shine in the world,
even so do "the just ones."—It is written: "Praise Him, ye stars of
light," these are the just."—That may well be originally Midrashic.—
In Sanhedrin 102, we read that Achab, son Omri, had half of his
sins forgiven, because he used to assist scholars with his wealth."
This idea, Shorr thinks, is not Jewish, but rather from the Vendidad,([2]) where it is said that confession of sins, to the priest, earns the
pardon of a third part of them." Here, Shorr, in his disinterestedness
is over-scrupulous and far-fetched. That: "Charity saves from
death," etc., is grown upon genuine Bible soil.([3]) Indeed such
ideas are current everywhere, and their aphorisms are universal,
expressed in all literatures, going back to the dawn of civilization,
and there is no telling to whom belongs the priority. That Vendidad passage has another interest; it shows whence hails the idea
of confession and the power of the priest to pardon sin. On the
Atonement-Day, the Mosaic highpriest confessed to God, not to
man; he prayed for divine forgiveness, but he did not grant it. The
Talmud expressly states that neither the priest, nor the Atonement-
day "wipe off the sin committed against a fellow-man,([4]) except
when practically righted and fully made good."—According to
Vend. III. 119: Whosoever neglects the study of the Avesta, the
drughs will fetch him to hell. So the Rabbis: Who neglects the
study of the Thora, he will not stand the day of misfortune; he
will fall unto hell (Berachoth 18, Horayoth 13th, etc.)—"A Parsee
should not destroy goods of even the smallest value given him by
Ahura (Spiegel Comment. V. 168). Similar (in Berachoth 62):
Whosoever wastes useful clothing will at last lose their benefit." That
adage is universal, too.—The Parsees thought that lascivious, un-
chaste persons contaminate by their looks water and trees (Vend.
XVIII. 125, Spiegel's amended translation). So the Rabbis: The
sin of unchastity detains the rain. (Tanith 81).—That, too, is
biblical. Vend. 19. 4 and 5, according to Shlottman, conveys the
idea that a female drugh is ever about the holy man to seduce him;
but deep study protects him against her temptations. Even such
anecdotes are in Babli Moid Qatan 18, with the same moral: "temptations of R. Chiya, R. Chisda, etc."—Even so Vend. 19. 89.

---

1 Comment. Vend. II. 131.   2 Comment. Vend. III. 142.

3 Ps. 106, 3; Prov. 11. 18, 19; 12. 28; 13. 6; 10. 2.

4 עבירות שבין אדם לחבירו אין יו״כ מכפר   Maimonider Helchoth Tshuba
Mada.

According to Spiegel and Rhode: "Who busies himself with good deeds, the evil spirit will let him unmolested."—Indeed the Avesta is the only protection against Ahriman.—So the Rabbis: I created the evil spirit (evil inclination) and its remedy, the Thora. If you occupy with the Thora, you are free of that. (Sephri Ekeb; Qidushin 30; B. Bathra 21). Hail to Israel, as long as they busy themselves with the law, they discard the evil one. The evil one in the Aggada is actually termed " evil inclination"([1]); but it seems it was soon personified as in Persia, no longer meaning the bad passions or instincts, but the personal mischievous spirit of the followers of Satan, as in Persia of *Ahriman*. Such figures of speech often change their real meaning ; in one generation they may be understood literally, and in another figuratively. With Parsee and Jew, they may first have expressed inclination and passion, and next the personal devil. But there is no telling who is initiator and who is imitator. Persian dualism first taught Spento-mayniu and Angro-mayniu, holy spirit and wicked spirit. Ahura-mazda is a later designation. In Mosaism is monotheism alone pervading. Satan appears much later ; hence is Satan of Persian origin.—The Persians believe that the old Bactrian, the idiom of the Avesta, is the language of Ahura ; it is probate to chase away the daevas, even when said without understanding (Spiegel Comment. Vend. 1. 84). The same claim the Hindoos as to the Vedas (Laws of Manu. VI. 84).—The Rabbis say : The Hebrew is the language of the Only One. (Jerush Megila 14). It is meritorious to read it even without understanding it (Seder Eliahu Zuta 2.—Babli Megila 31).—*Amour propre* is universal !—The Parsees believe there is a treasure in heaven of the supernumerary merits and good deeds of the right-eous, to spend therefrom in behalf of persons of doubtful goodness, with whom neither good nor bad predominates. (Spiegel Vend. 19). Such is the belief of the Hindoos too. Similar we find in Hebrew poetic litanies and in the Midrash: "And I shall be merciful on him whom I shall love;" that means : God showed Moses all the treasures of the rewards held ready for the just . . . for those performing the commandments, for those supporting orphans . . . and for those without merits, I shall freely spend to them . . . David spake: God, am I to enjoy of the world hereafter ? To whom God replied : All will enjoy of the surplus, the over-merit, of thy prayers."—So we saw above, R. Meyer promised to redeem Acher from hell with a surplus of his own merits. Again we read :

---

[1] יצר הרע

"A sage who pardons his wrong-doers, will gain for himself the
surplus of the life deducted from the sinner . . . (Shemoth Rabba
45; Midr. Esther 3; Jerush. Hagiga 2; Aboda Sara 18; Hagiga
4 etc.)—(Windischman Mithra 126) "Mithra dressed in white robes,
leads on the righteous to paradise. Even so is the legend of Simon
the Just: " Every year an old man in white habiliments conducted
me into paradise," (Jerus. Yoma III. 11).—The angels are dressed
in white (Qidushin 72).—According to Vend. 19, by Spiegel: " The
just reside in heaven, beneath the throne of Ahura and the Ameshas-
Spentas."—So says R. Elieser (Sabbath 122): " The souls of the
righteous are hid beneath the throne of glory." So Hagigah 12:
" There are the Ophanim, the Seraphim and the souls of the just."—
(Pesikta Rabati): " When the just one dies, three sets of angels
are busy with him, saying: Let him come in peace . . . Let him
rest on his couch, etc. When the wicked dies, three sets of angry
angels meet him, shouting: No peace to him . . in trouble he shall
remain . . . down with the hardened sinners.[1] Just so in Yasna
48, 11: The daevas meet the wicked dead and receive them with
laughter and scoffing, and compel them to eat disgusting food.—
Further in Khorda-Avesta 35: When the just one dies, zephyrs
from the South fan him, impregnated with the odor of all spices.
. . . Ormazd lets him have of the finest dishes, sweet and fat."—
Each saying characterizes its own origin.—Midrash Bamidbar Raba
13: " God will spread a banquet to the righteous in paradise, and
zephyric winds will blow and waft the best odors from Eden. . . .
The noblest spices will burn and scatter their perfumes . . . amidst
groves of cedars and myrtles, cheered by the angels."—This is
Parsic, lacking but the Arabian *Houris*, plentifully supplied elsewhere.

Hundreds of proverbs and tales, moral sayings and fables are
literally cited by Shorr to be found in Persian, Hindoo and Babylonian literatures, which have made their way into the Talmudical
and Midrashic tomes, usually, though not always, accurately
mentioning their sources. But these do not show with sufficient
evidence, who is the borrower and who the lender. According to
him, not only the Persian sacred books, but also the Hindoo,
Buddhistic and Chaldaic literatures were translated and accessible
to the Jews of Babylon and Palestine. Let us quote the following:
Ardeshir, the Sasanian king, used to say: " Happy is the prince
possessed of an honest friend, who in prosperous and joyous times

[1] עֲרֵלִם

would remind him of reverses to come, in order to quell his pride."(1)
Similar to that we read in Berachoth 31.—Another Persian king
said: "Liberality is the best of revenues. True wealth is, to know
to be satisfied with one's own lot." The rabbinical version is identical: Who is rich? He who is satisfied with his lot.—Persian,
Hindoo and Rabbinical proverbs are: "If you have wisdom,
what do you miss?" "If you have acquired knowledge, what need
you more?" "The timid will not learn, nor can the angry one
teach." "Let your tongue learn to say: I know not; tell no
lies, that you may not be detected." "A needle's breadth is
enough for two friends; not the world's width for two enemies."
"By three things one may recognize the wasteful heir: He dresses
magnificently, drinks from costly, brittle glassware, and does not
watch over his laborers." "The salt of riches is charity; if you do
not salt with it your wealth, it will corrupt."—Its rabbinical parallel
is more pithy and pointed: "The Salt of money is mercy."(2) Here
is the occasion for it: A Rabbi asked the poor daughter
of the wealthy Naqdimon, son Gurion: Where is gone the wealth
of thy father? She answered: Rabbi, it is not justly that the
proverb says: "Salt thy wealth with charity,"—for her father,
Naqdimon, was notoriously both, wealthy and charitable.—"Three
characters hate one another: dogs, whores and scholars of Babylonia."—"Poverty goes after the poor."—"Three things prolong
life: Good clothes, a good house and a good wife."—"Who teaches
not his son some craft, is, as if teaching him brigandage."—"A well
wherefrom you drank water, throw no stone into it."—"Where a
man is needed, try and be thou the man."—"A deed of virtue produces another virtue, and one of vice another vice."—"The wicked,
even alive are as dead; the just, even dead are deemed alive."—
"Know whence you came from (earth), and whereto you go
(earth)."—Shorr thinks, without always giving proof, that what the
Rabbis found of good sayings in foreign literatures, they gave it
out as if coming from their own teachers. Here, for instance, is a
pretty epicurean sentence: (Eirubin 54): "My son, if thou hast
(wealth), enjoy it; for in the grave there is no pleasure, and there is
no tarrying in death."—This saying Diodor. II. 23 and Strabo 671
attribute to Sardanapulus, who engraved upon his tombstone:
'Well knowing that thou art mortal, enjoy and be merry, for there
is no pleasure for the dead.'" Samuel in Eirubin, says: "Quickly
eat and drink, for this world is like a wedding."—That also some

---

1 Mirkond in Gutshmid.   2 מלח ממון חסר Kethuboth.

attribute to Sardanapulus, whom it befits better than the Rabbis.—
The following proverbs, of a nobler ring, Shorr finds, too, among
Hindoos and Buddhists—they are well-known ethical sayings of the
Rabbis: "Who is a hero? He who restrains his passions."—
"What is hateful to thyself, do not unto others." "Adorn thyself
first, then adorn others."—"A man finds out all defects, except his
own."—"Man's good deeds meet him after death, and joyfully
welcome him in the hereafter." . . . . Here are a few doctrines of
the Parsees and the Rabbis of parallel value: According to Yasna
47. 9 is "true life but in the hereafter ; the world here is full of anxiety and disappointment."—Even so Waikra Rabba III., we read:
" Better is a handful of satisfaction," that means the hereafter, " than
two handfuls of tribulation," that is this world.—The Parsees say: The
Avesta is among those things first created.([1]) The same affirm the
Rabbis of the Thora, (Nedarim 39); and so say the Hindoos of the
Vedas (Manu I).

LEGENDS AND MYTHS COMPARED.

Of a strikingly Avestean physiognomy are : ([2]) "The relatives
of the dead spend charities to the poor for the benefit of the
deceased." (Spiegel Introd. Vispered 38). Such is the rabbinical
teaching too: " The dead are atoned for by the money of the living.
(Old Responses. Constantine 276). R. Sherira Gaon there opines
that to pay the debts of the dead, or to spend charity in their
name, does them good."—The *haoma* juice is mentioned in the Talmud as Hama, ([3]) (Abodo Sara 25 and Psachim 116, etc.). According to Spiegel, Vispered 73, will Ormazd awaken with that, the
dead and restore them to life. Other passages say the " *Malkosh*"-
rain will bring the resurrection. Such is in Sabbath 88: "A loving
rain God will pour down to enliven the dead."—It is claimed that
the just, as Yima, the Persian Adam and others, lived up to the
Avesta. long before Zoroaster, (Spiegel I. 47, Yasna). Even so the
Aggada: Adam, Noah, Abraham, etc., followed practically the
Thora (Yoma 28). All what the Parsees said of Yima, the Rabbis
claimed of Adam. Yima was born for eternal life, and when he
sinned, he had to die (Spiegel Khorda Av. 59). Even so in Sabbath 25 and Eirubin 18. etc.: Since Adam sinned, he was punished
with mortality. Had he obeyed God's commands, he would never
have died (Yalkut Kthubim 906).—After Yima had sinned, a daeva
usurped his throne (Spiegel Introd. Khorda Av. 59). Even so

1 Khorda Avesta Spiegel, p. 35.
2 Followidg Shorr, Hechaluz VIII. p. 28.   3 אמה

(Gitin 68):   Since King Solomon sinned, *Ashmedai*, the devil, set upon his throne and he begged his bread.—The Parsees said of Zoroaster that he smote Ahriman and his followers by his *Honover* (Khorda Av. 33).   So the Aggada of Moses: When he ascended the Mount, he recited a hymn [1] and the evil spirits took to flight. The same, Christian legend claims of Jesus, and Islam legend of Mohammed.   The *Bahman Yasht* enumerates what hardships will happen in the Messianic Age at the end of days (Spiegel Tradit, Literatur, 136, etc.).   Similar is Sanhedrin 96–99 about the Messiah, his age, tribulations, advent, wars, calamities, etc.

UNIVERSAL MESSIAH IDEAL COMPARED.

Let us elucidate this theme, one of the leading subjects of this series.   The following we read in Babli. Sanhedrin 96–99, concerning the Messiah : " R. Nahman said to R. Isaac: Do you have any tradition when " *Bar Nephele* " will come ?—R. Isaac : Who is Bar Nephele ?   A. : The Messiah !—Q. : Why do you call him Bar Nephele ? (son of the fallen, in Hebrew).   A. : Because he will raise the *fallen* Kingdom of David.—R. Johanan said :   In the generation when the son of David is to come, the sages will be but few, the people will pass their lives in sorrow and anxiety ; tribulations and oppressive government will daily become worse . . . The Seven-years-week, when the son of David is to arrive, will exhibit the following phenomena : partial, then total drought and famine, men, women and children starving ; even the Hassidai (pious) perishing from hunger, and learning disappearing.   Then will come better days, fulness and plenty, joy and study.   Then again ominous rumors ; at last wars ; when Son-David's will appear.—R. Jehuda thinks :   Then unchastity will abound, society will be unhinged, the sages disgraced, impudence rampant, truth disappearing and honest men laughed at.—R. Nehorai says: Then will the young men scoff at their seniors, the seniles be in awe of the youths, the daughter rise against her mother, impudence be the general rule . . . the government become heterodox—all moralizing will stop as useless . . . denunciations will multiply, scholarship decrease, no money in the purse and all hope given up.—R. Katina says: Six thousand years the world will stand and for one thousand years be destroyed.—Abaya says : For two thousand years . . . As the fields in Release-year remain fallow every seventh year, even so the world will, every seven thousand years . . . —Eliahu said : The world must stand at least eighty-five Jubilees (4250 years); during the last Jubilee

---

[1] שיר של פגעים Aicha Babbati and Midrash Tilim,

Son-David's will appear . . . —R. Hanan states: In the Persian archives, I have found a scroll and there was written: "After 4291 years of the world's creation, will the world come to an end, the monsters will rise in mutual destruction, the wars of *Gog* and *Magog* will take place; thereupon the Messianic age will open. For God renovates the universe, but after seven thousand years . . . . —R. Aha opines: After five thousand years . . . —R. Nathan argues from the verse in Habaquq II., 3: "There is yet a vision for the pre-destined term; the end is dawning; it will not fail; if it tarries, hope for it, it will come; it will not tarry . . . Not as our teachers reasoned. (From Daniel vii. 25): "They will be delivered unto his hand *for a time and times and a half a time;*" not as R. Simlai who argued (from Psalms 80: 6): Ye will eat the bread of tears and drink tears in a triple measure;" . . not as R. Aqiba who ex-pounded (Haggai II. 6): "Yet a little while, and I shall shake heaven and earth, sea and land!"—But this: The first dominion will last seventy years; the second dominion, fifty-two years, and the dominion of Bar-kosiba, two and a half years (120 P. C., he fought against and succumbed to emperor Hadrian) . . . . —R. Samuel says: A curse upon those speculators about the "end of days" (Messianic age); for such may prove fallacious . . . But thou remain ever hoping for him . . . —Rab says: All such specu-lations are idle, the Messianic advent depends upon Israel's repent-ance and good deeds . . . —R. Elieser says: If Israel improves, he will be redeemed; if not, not.—R. Josua holds: God will raise rulers like Haman. Their cruel government will induce Israel to improve . . . R. Ulla thinks: Jerusalem will be redeemed only through justice and mercy . . R. Hillel boldly opines: Israel has no Messiah. For long ago they have devoured him in the days of Hesekiah—(Was that not an allusion to the Nazareth epoch, etc. In the beginning of the third century the Nazarenes were but a Jewish sect, Jews believing that the Messiah had come.)—R. Joseph deprecates any such ideas . . . Diverse Rabbis assume the messianic age as lasting: 40, 70, 400, 365, even 7000 years, all proven by sacred verses.—Samuel says: All the difference between now and the Messi-anic age, is but "Israel's enslavement" or political liberation.—R. Pappa says: That age will dawn when the haughty ones will disap-pear, the *Magians*, those judges with the "Knout."[1]—R. Jose says: That will be, between yonder city-gate being destroyed and rebuilt . .

---

[1] That alludes, sarcastically to the Parsee punishments with the horse-whip, up to 10,000 stripes!

He recommends to his followers to bury his coffin very deeply in the ground, for there is in Babel no tree to which a Persian horse would not be tied ; nor a coffin in Judea where a Parsee horse is not to take his food, (the dug-up coffins used as mangers).—R. Johanan says : When thou seest a generation ever decreasing and full of tribulations, look out for Messiah. Son-David's will come during a generation, either entirely good or entirely bad.—R. Josua, son Levy found Elias at the door of the cave of R. Simon, son Jochai. Of him he inquired about the advent of Messiah. Elias said : Go and ask the Lord himself, there. Where is he ? There he is, at the city-gate ! among the poor and the suffering . . administering to their ills, one by one . . —R. Josua said to Messiah : When will thy Lordship come ?—" *To-day !*"—To-day, indeed ? Elias interpreted reverentially : "*To-day*, when you listen unto His voice," (Ps. 35). Messiah will appear as soon—as the people will listen to the voice of God.

The above is but an epitome of that long and remarkable Talmud passage. There we have a succinct discription and outline of the rabbinical messiah-ideal. Now, that rabbinical messiah-photograph is identical with that we find everywhere. The Brahmanic, the Parsee and Buddhistic ideals are all alike ; the same kernel and nearly the same drapery ; the like halo and the same nucleus. That nucleus is : Man is vicious and unwise ; hence he is unhappy. He will morally and intellectually improve, from sheer compulsion. He will learn to trace his misfortunes straight to his own folly and viciousness. He will become happier, only by becoming wiser. Of course, that is a long way, but the only sure one. That messianic hope of the Talmud and East-Asia, is also the Christian messianic ideal in essence and parapharnalia. Jesus of Nazareth is found at the city-gate among the poor, the sick, the persecuted, the outcasts. And such, historically, was Buddha. He renounced his crown, court and kingdom, and associated with the lowly and the beggars. And such was Mohammed; from the hut, the date-meal, the patched clothes, he rose to the throne of Asia, a beggar and a king. He himself declined the messiah-doctrine. But practically he assumed its part and privileges, and history vindicates to him both, the position and the insignia. He sat for that photograph. Thus the realistic nucleus of that ideal, and its habiliment are everywhere pretty much the same. According to prophet Sacharia IX., he is: " A poor man riding on an ass," exhalted beyond the angels, restoring poor humanity to pristine goodness. Such is the prophetic Messiah, the Gospel Christ, the Hindoo Manu, the Persian Soshiosh, the Chinese Buddha, the Mohammedan Prophet; the same kernel, but other names. The messiah is a man, he is an angel, he is divine. According to Daniel VII., 13 "he is coming from the clouds of heaven." — Or "from behind the throne of the Almighty," according to the mystic books of Henoh, Targums, etc. It is for that, Aggada and Talmud call him *Anany* and *Bar Nephele*, etc.([1]) That means "a man from the clouds:" *Nephele* is, I think, not of Hebrew derivation, as Sanhedrin 96 b, suggests; but rather of Greek terminology: *nephele*, cloud; and *Bar Nephele* means *Son of the clouds.*" It is identical with: "*Anany* and *Bar Kokhba;*" all are messianic epithets used in the Talmud. Even so designate Homer, Hesiod, etc., their Zeus as "*Nephel Egereta*, the cloud gatherer."—Thus we believe to have retraced the vestiges of the Messiah-Ideal among the Jews, Greeks, Christians and Moham-medans in the West; Brahmans, Parsees and Buddhists in the East; and everywhere we have found it identical in spirit, akin in drapery, and differing only in name.

PARSEE LAWS AND CUSTOMS COMPARED.

Shorr in Hechaluz adduces a large number of rabbinical laws, *halachoth*, that either run parallel to, or expressly contrast with the Avesta. We shall mention but a few in illustration of their spirit: "Persons carrying the dead are unclean." The same are they ac-cording to Talmud.—"A verbal promise is a contract." (Vend. VI. 86). Yet some discriminate between believers and unbelievers. Now this discussion is also to be found among the Rabbis (Baba Mezia 49). The Parsees are exceedingly scrupulous concerning an oath: "Yea shall be yea, and nay shall be nay, (Spiegel Vispered 56). So in Midrash, Ruth 87: With the righteous is yes, yes, and no, no. Even so Jesus and Paul repeat the same saying.—The Par-sees thought that the relatives of a perjurer are implicated in the crime and punished with him (Vend. 24–35). Later this rigorism was mitigated.—The rabbinical view is that perjury is morally avenged upon the perjurer and his family. (Jer. Shabuoth 6). While Moses teaches: "Every one shall die for his own sin"—no family vendetta. The Parsees distinguished when beating a fellow-man, "whether blood flowed from the wound or a simple bruise was made," (Vend. VI. 90). Now this is exactly the sense of Exod. 21–25, dis-tinguishing between wound and stripe. ([2])—Even so the Parsees determined the punishment of him who broke a bone of his fellow-man, (Vend. IV. 99); Just so in the rabbinical law, (Baba Kama

---

פצע־חבורה [2]   בר כוכבי. בר גפלי. ענני. ענני שמיא. בבר אנש [1]

91).—"It is forbidden to till during a year the ground whereon a person died. But the place around that is allowed, (Vend. VI. 81). According to Talmudical law: who tills a grave makes it a "*Baith happras*," unclean ground and it is unlawful to be utilized for tillage, (Ohloth 17). The Parsee should not go three steps without the Kosti, (holy girdle). The Jew shall not walk four ells without phylacteries (Sabbath 118), nor without the fringed garment.—"The Barsemon-Branch to be fit for that purpose, must not be mutilated. So the willow-branch of the Jews is unfit when mutilated, (Sukkah 3, 3). The Khorda-Avesta 41:3, makes it a "duty to every Parsee to offer a sacrifice on the holidays, (Gahanbar) each, according to his capacity." So too in Talmud (Menachoth Sephra Vaikra): "Be it much or little, but let it be with a godly purpose."—Yast, (Mithra 122, Windischman Translation): "No priest shall eat of the sacrifices who does not understand the prayers."—So Sanhedrin 90: An ignorant priest shall not get the priestly *heave* (trumah).—The same holds good among the Brahmans.—"It is the duty of the Parsee to make four knots in the *Kosti*, (Sadder) to remind him of his diverse religious duties, etc." The Jews make five knots for the same purpose expressly done.—"A non-Parsee dead does no defile," (Vend. 12, Spiegel).—Even so Yebamoth 61: A dead Israelite defiles all in the room. Not so, an idolator. Nor do so idolatrous graveyards. Later on there arose many controversies concerning that.—"Whosoever says the *Ahuna-Vairya* prayer, even without attention, does a good work," (Yast 19, Spiegel 88). Even so (Berachoth 42) it is with the recitation of *Shema*, the Hebrew Credo.— "Who recites that prayer intently, will have paradise," (Yasna 89)· According to Talmud Berachoth 17: "who earnestly reads the *Shema* inherits this world and the hereafter."—" The Parsic husband has the right to divorce his wife," (Spiegel Vispered 31). The same according to Talmud (Psachim 112).—"A Parsee son, three times disobedient to his parents, deserves death punishment," (Spiegel Visp. 32). Such was the Talmudical law, too, originally, but later mitigated.—The Parsees had certain holidays " when the girls had the privelege of selecting their husbands. (Richardson Gebraeuche 234). Similar in Babli. Tanith 26: "There were no more rejoicing holidays, than the 15th of Ab and the Atonement-day, when Jewish girls were wooing their future husbands" . . —"Who looks impudently to a woman, is a sinner." So in Khorda-Avesta 45, 19— and so Berachoth 61.—Chardin V. 177: " Gamblers cannot be appointed as judges, nor as witnesses, since gambling is not for the public good." Even so Sanhedrin 25: The gambler is unfit to witness, for he does not occupy himself with anything useful. (1) Similar striking analogies are to be found in the sexual regulations, those of slaughtering animals, etc., among Jews and Parsees, all which proves the mutual influence of these sects.

---

1 משחק בקוביא פסיל לעדות

CHAPTER XII

MAX MUELLER AND NAOROYI ON MODERN PARSEEISM.

Having studied the theory and practice of Magism of old, in its sacred books and its past history, the reader will feel, I am sure, a deep interest to know its aspects, now, its latest evolutions and present condition in West-India, where it is yet alive. We shall follow here a distinguished professor of that faith, in London, in his own public utterances, on his people and creed, accompanied by the terse and pointed remarks of Prof. F. Max Mueller, the well-known scientist and Sanscrit expounder of Oxford. I shall follow both in their own words, (¹) without any comment of mine. The reader is well aware of the importance of the testimony of Max Mueller, well-known as a great philologist, and no less great as a rational religion-ist. He is among the foremost who are "striving after a universal religion," who recognized the deep strata of "a common substance in all religions;" that deeper and sublimer than in the sacred books, whispers "the still voice of God in the human heart;" that "all creeds have a common source as their origin, their truly divine ideal and prototype;" that "they are all but varying patterns of the one original truth;" that all teach the rule of God, man's dependence, the immor-tality of the human substance, virtue and wisdom as the essence of worship; that "the law of evolution, of natural and gradual growth pervades the domain of religion, as everything else in the universe;" that no creed is wholly without some truth;" that none is alone the road to salvation; that "none is wholly new, and all are but com-binations of the same radical elements in ever richer growth;" that "the unbiased study of all creeds contributes to the better ap-preciation of each;" that "from the oldest faiths of China and Hin-dostan, to the newest religious phases in Church, Mosque, Syna-gogue and Temple, there is but one great chain of ethical develop-ments and religious revelations, manifesting the deity in the human conscience and reason;" that "science and religion are not antagon-istic to, but rather completing and perfecting each other;" that what the latter divines, the former must verify and prove, and that both are the wheels of the divine "Mirkaba" (chariot) of human civilization, etc., etc.

1 See Max Mueller's: 'Chips from German Workshop,' Modern Par-sees, p. 163.

Let us now see Prof. Max Mueller's opinion on modern Parsees in his own words, in his "*Chips from a German Workshop*," On modern Parsees, page 163, etc.: "While the scholars of Europe are thus engaged in disinterring the ancient records of the religion of Zoroaster, it is of interest to learn what has become of that religion in those few settlements where it is still professed by small communities . . . . " "We believe that to many of our readers the two pamphlets, lately published by a distinguished member of the Par- · see community, Mr. Dadabhai Naoroyi, Professor of Guzerati, at University College, London, will open many problems of a more than passing interest. One is a paper read before the Liverpool Philomathic Society, "On the Manners and Customs of the Parsees;" the other is a Lecture delivered before the Liverpool Literary and Philosophical Society, "On the Parsee Religion."

"In the first of these pamphlets, we are told that the small community of Parsees in Western India is, at the present moment, divided into two parties, the Conservatives and the Liberals. Both are equally attached to the faith of their accestors, but they differ from each other in their modes of life : the Conservatives clinging to all that is established and customary, however absurd and mischievous; the Liberals desiring to throw off the abuses of former ages and to avail themselves, as much as is consistent with their religion and their Oriental character, of the advantages of European civilization. If I say, writes our informant, that the Parsees use tables, knives and forks, etc., for taking their dinners, it would be true with regard to one portion, and entirely untrue with regard to another. In one house you see in the dining-room the dinner-table, furnished with all the English apparatus for its agreeable purposes ; next door, perhaps, you see the gentlemen perfectly satisfied with his primitive good old mode of squatting on a piece of mat, with a large brass or copper plate (round and of the size of an ordinary tray) before him, containing all the dishes of his dinner, spread on it in small heaps, and placed upon a stool about two or three inches high, with a small tinned copper cup at his side for his drinks, and his fingers for his knives and forks. He does this, not because he cannot offord to have a table, etc., but because he would not have them in preference to his ancestral mode of life, or perhaps, the thought has not occurred to him that he need have anything of the kind." . . . . "The *Nirang* is the urine of the cow, ox or she-goat, and the rubbing of it over the face and hands, is the second thing a Parsee does after getting out of bed. Either before applying the Nirang to the face and hands, or while it remains on the hands after being applied, he should not touch anything directly with his hands; but, in order to wash off the Nirang, he either asks somebody else to pour water on his hands, or resorts to the device of taking hold of the pot, through the intervention of a piece of cloth, such as a handkerchief or his Sudra, i. e., his blouse. He first pours water on one hand, then takes the pot in that hand and washes his other hand, face and feet." . . .

" The Liberal party has completely surrendered this objectionable custom, but the old school still keeps it up, though their faith, as Dadabhai Naoroyi says, in the efficacy of Nirang to drive away Satan, may be shaken.([1]) " The Reformers" our author writes, "maintain that there is no authority whatever in the original books of Zurthosht for the observance of this dirty practice, but that it is altogether a later introduction. The old ones adduce the authority of the works of some of the priests of former days, and say the practice ought to be observed. They quote one passage from the Zend-Avesta corroborative of their opinion, which their opponents deny as at all bearing upon the point."— Here, whatever our own feelings may be about the Nirang, truth obliges us to side with the old school, and if our author had consulted the ninth Fargard of the Vendidad (page 120, line 21, in Brockhaus' edition), he would have seen that both, the drinking and the rubbing in with the so-called Gaomaezo—i. e., Nirang—are clearly enjoined by Zoroaster in certain purificatory rites.—"A pious Parsee has to say his prayers sixteen times at least every day—first on getting out of bed, then during the Nirang operation, again when he takes his bath, again when he cleanses his teeth, and when he has finished his morning ablutions. The same prayers are repeated whenever during the day, a Parsee has to wash his hands. Every meal—such there are three—begins and ends with prayer, besides the " grace " and before going to bed; the work of the day is closed by a prayer. The most extraordinary thing is, that none of the Parsees—not even their priests—understand the ancient language in which these prayers are composed. We must quote the words of our author, who is himself of the priestly caste and who says: " All prayers, on every occasion, are said, or rather recited, in the old original Zend-language, neither the reciter nor the people around intended to be edified, un-

1 Our ladies apply a salve to their faces against flies, etc. May that not have been the real object of the Parsee nirang? They imagined the evil spirits as ugly flies and mosquitoes. . . .

derstanding a word of it. There is no pulpit among the Parsees. On several occasions, as on the occasion of the Ghumbars, the bimestral holidays, the third day's ceremonies for the dead, and other religious or special holidays, there are assemblages in the temple; prayers are repeated, in which more or less join, but there is no discourse in the vernacular of the people. Ordinarily, every one goes to the fire-temple, whenever he likes, or, if it is convenient to him, recites his prayers himself, and as long as he likes, and gives, if so inclined, something to the priests to pray for him." . . . In another passage our author says : " Far from being the teachers of the true doctrine and duties of their religion, the priests are generally the most bigoted and superstitious, and exercise much injurious influence over the women, especially, who, until lately, received no education at all. The priests have, however, now begun to feel their degraded position. Many of them, if they can do so, bring up their sons in any other profession but their own. There are, perhaps, a dozen among the whole body of professional priests who lay claim to a knowledge of the Zend-Avesta : but the only respect in which they are superior to their brethren is, that they have learnt the meanings of the words of the books as they are taught, without knowing the language, either philosophically or grammatically." . . . " The Parsees are monogamists. They do not eat anything cooked by a person of another religion; they object to beef, pork or ham. Their priesthood is hereditary. None but the son of a priest can be a priest, but it is not obligatory for the son of a priest to take orders. The high-priest is called Dustoor, the others are called Mobed." . . .

" The principal points for which the Liberals among the Parsees are at the present moment contending, are the abolition of the filthy purifications by means of Nirang ; the reduction of the large number of obligatory prayers ; the prohibition of early betrothals and marriage ; the suppression of extravagance at weddings and funerals ; the education of women, and their admission into general society. A society has been formed, called " The Rahanumaee Mazdiashna ;" i. e., the Guide of the Worshippers of God. Meetings are held, speeches made, tracts distributed. A counter society, too, has been started, called " The True Guides ;" and we readily believe what Mr. Dadabhai Naoroji tells us—that, as in Enrope, so in India, the Reformers have found themselves strengthened by the intolerant bigotry and the weakness of the arguments of their opponents." . . .

PARSEE LIBERALS' CATECHISM.

"A few questions and answers to acquaint the children of the holy Zarthosti Community with the subject of the Mazdiashna Religion, i. e. the Worship of God: Question. Whom do we, of the Zarthosti Community, believe in? Answer. We believe in only one God, and do not believe in any besides him.—Q. Who is that one God? A. The God who created the heavens, the earth, the angels, the stars, the sun, the moon, the fire, the water, or all the four elements, and all things of the two worlds; that God we believe in, Him we worship, Him we invoke, Him we adore.—Q. Do we not believe in any other God? A. Whoever believes in any other God but this, is an infidel and shall suffer the punishment of hell.—Q. What is the form of our God? A. Our God has neither face nor form, color nor shape, nor fixed place. There is no other like Him. He is Himself and singly, such a glory that we cannot praise or describe Him, nor can our mind comprehend Him."

"So far, no one could object to this catechism, and it must be clear that the dualism, which is generally mentioned as the distinguishing feature of the Persian religion—the belief in two Gods, Ormazd the principle of good, and Ahriman the principle of evil—is not countenanced by the modern Parsees.—The catechism continues: Q. What is our religion? A. Our religion is 'Worship of God.'—Q. Whence did we receive our religion? A. God's true prophet—the true Zurthost (Zoroaster) Asphantaman Anoshirwan—brought the religion to us from God.—Q. What religion has our prophet brought us from God? A. The disciples of our prophet have recorded in several books that religion."

Many of these books were destroyed during Alexander's conquest; the remainder of the books were preserved with great care and respect by the Sassanian kings. Of these again, the greater portion were destroyed at the Mohammedan conquest by Khalif Omar, so that we have now very few books remaining. . . .

"We consider these books as heavenly books, because God sent the tidings of these books to us through the holy Zurthost.

"Q. What commands has God sent us through his prophet, the exalted Zurthost? A. To know God as One; to know the prophet, the exalted Zurthost, as the true prophet; to believe the religion and the Avesta brought by him, as true, beyond all manner of doubt; to believe in the goodness of God; not to disobey any of the commands of the Mazdiashna religion; to avoid evil deeds; to exert for good deeds; to pray five times in the day; to believe in the reckoning and justice on the fourth morning after death; to hope for heaven and to fear hell; to consider doubtless the day of general destruction and resurrection; to remember always that God has done what he willed, and shall do what he wills; to face some luminous object while worshipping God.—Some deceivers (the catechism continues), with the view of acquiring exaltation in this world, have set themselves up as prophets, and, going among the laboring and ignorant people, have persuaded them, that, 'if you commit sin, I shall intercede for you, I shall plead for you, I shall save you,' and thus deceive them; but the wise among the people know the deceit."—This clearly refers to Christian missionaries.—" If any one commit sin, the Parsees say, under the belief that he shall be saved by somebody, both, the deceiver as well as the deceived shall be damned on the day of Rasta Khez. . . . There is no saviour. In the other world you shall receive the return according to your actions. . . . Your saviour—are your deeds and God Himself. He is the pardoner and the giver. If you repent your sins and reform, and if the Great Judge consider you worthy of pardon, or would be merciful to you, He alone can and will save you." . . .

" Thus the religious belief of the present Parsee communities is reduced to two or three fundamental doctrines; and these, though professedly resting on the teaching of Zoroaster, receive their real sanction from a much higher authority. A Parsee believes in one God, to whom he addresses his prayers. His morality is comprised in these words: Pure thoughts, pure words, pure deeds. Believing in the punishment of vice and the reward of virtue, he trusts for pardon to the mercy of God. There is a charm, no doubt, in so short a creed; and if the whole of Zoroaster's teachings were confined to this, there would be some truth in what his followers say of their religion—namely, that "it is for all, and not for any particular nation.'" . . . (Max Mueller Chips from German Workshop, 1867, p. 177).

RECAPITULATION OF THE VOLUME.

In this volume is thus offered to the reader a treatise on the eastern religions, particularly on Zoroasterism, the *Zend-Avesta*, the Sacred Books of the Parsees, and the Vendidad in special, the leading code of that collection. The Zend-Avesta may be termed the bible of the West-Asian Iranians or Medo-Persians; and the Vendidad fairly corresponds to the Pentateuch, the Law, Thora, of that once powerful group of nations, now reduced to the East-India Parsees. In the course of our studies of that eastern code, we have been agreeably surprised to learn how often these two

Bibles, of the East and of the West, run parallel to each other. We feel thrilled at the thought that such analogies evidently prove that for long centuries they must have lived side by side with each other, influencing, coinciding with, or antagonizing each other, and that both have often harmoniously combined to oppose, reduce and combat the crude mythologies of the Hindoos and of the Greeks. Generally it should seem that Zoroasterism was a reformation upon eastern Hindooism ; that the Mosaico-prophetic doctrine was a further and more radical reformation of the combined mythologies of the East and West, of Medo-Persia, Greece, Asia-Minor, Egypt and Europe, and that both these reformations have yet earlier joined hands in Chaldea, finding their central point and common focus in the epoch and the activity of the Biblical, patriarchal religion. Thus, Ur of the Chaldees, Haran, Hebron, Bamah, Jerusalem, etc., may have been the links joining together the many rings in the chain of purified metaphysical and ethical thought, between the extreme East and the extreme West of the civilized world of antiquity. The frequent polemics of Deuter., Elias, Isaiah II., etc., point unmistakably to that double character of the Mosaic reformation. Both these reactions against former mythology, began in prehistoric times ; the eastern one commenced with Zoroaster of the Avesta ; the western one with Abraham of the Pentateuch. Each of these two ethical currents had a rationalistic phase and a mystical one. The Zend-Avesta contains both these aspects, the rational and the abstruse one, the logical, reasoning one and the supernatural one. The Pentateuch harbors preponderately the rationalistic one ; but its developments, the Talmud on the one hand and the New Testament on the other, exhibit both, the rationalistic and the supernatural phases. These latter elements, the mystic ones, based on faith and intuition, yet infinitely accumulating in the course of centuries, found their full expression and embodiment, in the later Qabbala and its own bible, the *Zohar.*

In the volumes preceeding this, we have treated of these diverse codes, their legislations and doctrines, their sociological aspects and aspirations, their "Messiah-Ideals." We have discussed the spirit of the legislations of Sinai, of Olivet, of Tarsus and of Mecca. We have now examined into the Zend-Avesta and the Vendidad in special, their leading religious, ethical, legal and social doctrines. While the volume to follow this present one, will occupy itself with the rational and mystical phases of both, the Arian Sacred Books and the Shemitic Bibles, as combined in the system of the Qabbala and its central exposition, the Zohar. Thus having treated in this series of the leading legislations, doctrines and bibles of the world, of the Old Testament, the New Testament and the Koran, these pages have analysed the Zend-Avesta, and partly *Manu* and *Sutras*, to conclude later both these bible groups with our study of religious philosophy, the Qabbala and the Zohar, the mediaeval bible of mysticism and metaphysics. Everywhere we have looked rather to the spirit than to the letter, and given their parallels and contrasts in the other ethical systems. In that manner we have compared the tenets and have tried to elucidate the drift and scope of the several leading schemes, to get an abstract of their religious philosophy and to arrive at their respective ideas and aspirations historically, ethically, politically ; thus to find out the " Messiah-Ideal " of each religion, each nation and each civilization, the final object of this series of treatises on the world's legislations.

This present volume is thus an independent treatise on the Arian religions, laws and socio-political tenets. At the same time it is a necessary link in our series on the leading bibles, codes and religious philosophies of the historical nations. We have spoken of the Mosaic and Rabbinical codes, of those of Nazareth, of Tarsus and of Medina ; this one now, of India-Persia is thus the fifth legislation discussed in our series. It is the third volume on the sociological and ethical aspects, or the "Messiah-Ideal," of each of these civilizations. It is the second study of our considerations on mysticism and its potent influence upon the present living religions. It is perhaps the first attempt at collating and comparing these systems and bringing out their inner kernel, without any invidious sectarian bias; an attempt opportune in a country and at an epoch, where all creeds and races strive to live peaceably side by side. It offers the picture of Arian mysticism, after we have contemplated in the preceeding volumes that of Semitic mysticism united to Arian supernaturalism. The closing treatise on philosophy, Qabbala and Zohar is to complete that *tableau* of Shemitic mysticism, whose elements are gathered there from everywhere, East and West, Persian, Hindoo, Greek and Hebrew, and later giving birth to Spinoza's *Ethics*.

This present treatise has shown that the religious thought, the philosophical thought, the historical thought and the mystical thought in these several religious systems are running in parallels with each other; that they are really but rays of one light, partial contributions to one stream of humane aspirations. This volume is thus a new ring in our chain of reasonings on the identity of what is truly divine, at the basis of the great systems of the world.   It is a further plea for the noble postulatum held up by the great historical legislators : the unity of race, of mind and of man's leading interests.   It is hence a further plea for broad and humane mutual toleration.   It shows religion, ethics and the leading sociological doctrines as lying deeply imbedded in the rock of man's intellectual and moral nature, and that all flows from one and the same divine source of spirituality.   It shows the indissoluble uniou of true science and religion, of rationalism and mysticism, since we learn the known from the unknown, and meditation reveals what was formerly shrouded in mystery.   So we see nature and we divine supranature; we grasp matter and we fairly presume mind; we are in contact with the universe, and we descry the Divine, the soul of the universe.   The Zend-Avesta and the Qabbala unite both these elements.   For in our moral and intellectual nature we cannot disentangle the rational from the mystic, just as we know part and guess another part of the universe, until the revelation of to-day becomes the reasoned conviction of to-morrow, science.   The Zend-Avesta may be termed especially Arian mysticism and the Qabbala Shemitic mysticism; the first hailing from the Orient; the latter apparently from the Occident; the one coming down from gray antiquity; the other seemingly belonging to comparatively modern times.   Yet closely examined, Arian and Semite, Asia and Europe, ancient and modern times are pretty much identical in the tendency of their teachings.   "They pass the same orbits, but in ever broader and higher circles,"—to use Goethe's well-known metaphor.—In our next volume, we shall see Qabbala, as but a further development of the Hindoo-Iranian doctrines, taking up all the elements of rational and mystic thought from Manu, Zoroaster, Abraham, Plato, Philo and Plotin, down to Mose de Leon and Corduero, and effectually closing, not with the Zohar, but with Spinoza's Ethics.   That we shall see in our next volume, completing the series on the Messiah-Ideal.   The last rationalistic word of the Qabbala and the Zohar is the *Ethics* of Spinoza.

CONCLUSION.

The religious element contemplated from that elevated standpoint, becomes thus the highest and noblest factor in man's education, the greatest potency in his civilization; while effete creeds and political selfishness are the greatest obstacles to human advance. State-craft and priest-craft are the very opposites of religion.   Our

study here has shown the religious substance everywhere to be
identical, eternal and divine, permeating the human heart wherever it
throbs, feels and meditates.   While the pride of creed, caste and race
have their source in selfishness and brutality, aiming at usurpation.
The logical result of our researches in this series of treatises, as in
this and in the subsequent volumes, all pointing to the identical
basis of the great religions, to the one doctrine unfolding, since the
dawn of humanity to this day, elaborated by the different sections
of the race,—will contribute to raise the standard of all beliefs and
their churches.   The aspect of sectarian contentions and denomina-
tional antagonisms can but belittle and depreciate them all.   The
spectacle of their harmony, of their congruence, must improve and
raise their estimation.   The moral conviction gained by our comparative method: that deep at the bottom of all the creeds flows
the stream of the one eternal revelation, *the one religion*, the "word
of God" to the mind of man, that can but restore the prestige and
efficacy of virtue, morals and religion ; it must raise even the status of
the churches themselves; it will contribute its mite to invigorate the
relaxed springs of ethics, and give a healthful impulse to civilized
society, to education, to freedom and to intellectuality.

This assumption of the identity of the religious basis and essence is the very opposite to religious indifference.   Indeed the
argument that the religious element is the sublimest and most
potent factor of civilization, should not be misunderstood as religious
indifferentism.   Nor even could it be nnderstood as neutrality and
coldness towards religious symbols and forms.   Our argument goes
to induce religious toleration, not to create indifferentism.   That argument is: that religion, as truth, is one and divine, and that the
religious forms are the products of history and environments.   As
such, the ceremonies are endeared to the denominations and
legitimate.   But they ought not to bias any one to intolerance and
sectarian arrogance ; much less should they palliate violence and
privilege.   Let the Parsee bear his *Taavids*, the Jew his philacteries, the Christian his cross, and the Moslem his crescent.   But let
them all remember that these are forms and emblems, while the
practical essence is: "Thou shalt love thy neighbor as thyself," equally
emphasized and accentuated by Manu, Zoroaster, Buddha, Abraham,
Moses, Socrates, Hillel, Jesus, Paul, Mohammed.   These pages and
series of treatises aim thus not at depreciating creed and symbol,
but at calling the attention of the thoughtful, that they are but the
historical formula ; that our neighbors have their formula, that each

is legitimate, if it answers the purpose of awakening ethical fervor; that everywhere the religious essence and substance tend to the same level and standard; that our neighbor may have other cere- monies and holidays, but he cannot have another religious essence, as long as he is sincere in his creed, be that Mazdaism, Judaism, Christianity, Islamism, etc. Let every believer assume that his own church comes nearest to that ideal religion and cling to it. But let him be fair and consider, that since other denominations have sub- stantially the same essence, and that their forms and churches are the historical products of their own environments, they have de- cidedly the same right to exist side by side with his own.

Thus does the theory of these pages and this entire series of works point out the exact boundary line between tolerance and in- differentism, viz: To be loyal to one's own faith, and be tolerant to- ward one's neighbor's creed, in essence and in form; thoroughly convinced that every great Church may lead to salvation; because the essence, aim and object of each are pretty nearly the same: " Holy shall ye be, for holy is your Lord "—" What asks God of thee? But to reverence him, walk in his ways, love him and serve him."—And what is the practical substance of the love and service of God: " Thou shalt love thy neighbor as thyself " (1) Hypocricy alone must be excluded as the many-colored mask of Ahriman. Thus while assuming our own way to be the nearest to salvation, let us be convinced that there is no hell for any other honest way. That is the exact tenor of our argument. No indifferentism; but broad toleration for every sincere conviction : that loyalty we claim for our belief, we must concede to others for theirs. Let, therefore, the last word of this argument and of this volume be : Loyalty, not indifferentism. nor narrow-mindedness.

1 Levit. 19 : 2.—Deuter. 10 : 12.—Levit. 12 : 18.

END

MISPRINTS CORRECTED.

Page.	Read.	Instead of.
7—Below :	Ernst Curtius	Ernest Curtis
30—Middle :	Theos Aletheias	Oeos Alydeias
44—Below :	*is* Izesne Khane	Izesne Khane
47— "	several . . . systems	modern..systems
49—Above :	a long train	long crowd
114—Middle :	messengers of the Highest.	messengers the highest..
117—Middle :	Babel	Bable
123—Below :	deities	duties
153—Above :	..world, the beneficent.	world. The beneficent..
155—Below :	find there genius ...	find their genius
160—Below :	So do the Hebrew and	So does the
161—Above :	he *lost Eden*, was accursed	he loses, is accursed...
163—Middle :	in his dominion	the his dominion
175—Below :	a particle	the particle
180—Middle :	prayers	pravers
189— "	should be carried	should not be
189—Below :	who has passed	has past
190—Above ;	economic reasons	economic reason
200—Middle :	depreciated currency	degreciated
239—Above :	Ramah	Bamah

"Mosaic Diet and Hygiene."

Professor H. GRAETZ, Breslau: "It pleases me very much and I request you to let me keep the copy . . . . Your *'Shylock and Prejudice'* is beautiful." — He offered to superintend the publication of *"Religious Rites."*

Similar approving utterances by Chief Rabbi H. ADLER, London; ISIDOR LOEB, Paris; L. PHILIPPSON, Allgemeine Zeitung des Judenthums; Archives Israelités, Paris; RAHMER'S Literatur-Blatt, etc.

"Spirit of the Biblical Legislation."

CARDINAL GIBBONS sent an autograph letter with a liberal subscription. Then, verbally, he said: "Your book contains new ideas; . . . and I shall continue my subscription to your continued work."

Right Hon. W. E. GLADSTONE sent a letter with his greetings.

Professor MAX MUELLER sent the same with his portrait.

Librarian A. NEUBAUER commented in the London Quarterly Review: "We have no doubt that this present study will be as favorably received as his *"Thoughts on Religious Rites."* It is an original attempt at comparative legislation and the influence of religion on law."

Mr. HERBERT SPENCER: "Your work contains much interesting matter which I should like to read when my health permits."

Dr. A. SCHWARZ, Rector of Vienna Theological Seminary, finds the book profound and has it reviewed in the "Ungar. Israelit," Buda-Pesth. It says:

"The erudite and sympathetic author of this work has already by other publications earned the warmest acknowledgment and approbation of leading scholars in Europe and America. — The reader of the present work finds there both instruction and enthusiasm.—The author has been very successful in bringing out therein the spirit and the principles of the Mosaic Institutions."

Rev. Dr. A. KOHUT, New York: "It is the product of a systematically trained mind that has well mastered the philosophy of Jewish Legislation."

Bishops Drs. PARET, KEPHARDT and WILSON, Drs. B. FELSENTHAL and MORAIS, etc., write encouragingly.

Professor W. T. HARRIS of the Educational Bureau, Washington: "It aught to have a wide reading among students of religion, sociology and politics . . . . . It is doing much good towards clearing up grave economic misgivings. I hope the author will further bring out his studies."

The Press, political, religious and scientific, here and abroad, has most kindly reviewed the above writings and frequently given them its cordial encouragement.

"The Messiah-Ideal, Vol. II, treating of Paul and the Gospel, Mohammed and the *Koran,"* is just out. On its advanced sheets the Press has most favorably commented.

The address of the author and publisher is:

M. FLUEGEL, 521 Robert St., Baltimore, Md.

COMMENTS ON MAURICE FLUEGEL'S LITERARY WORK.

"The Messiah-Ideal."—Vol. I. Jesus of Nazareth.

The first impulse to that work came from Professor FRANZ DELITZSCH of the Leipsic University, who gave the author a friendly challenge to write on that subject. See Vol. I, p. 296.

Dean GEORGE E. DAY of Yale University wrote next:

"Seeing your style of writing, I have strongly felt what a contribution it would be if you would undertake to show the teachings of the most distinguished of the Jewish nation . . . . . Such a presentation, I am sure, would be welcomed by all thinking men."

Professor MAX MUELLER, England, to whom an outline was sent, wrote: "Your new book bids fair to bring out much interesting matter . . . The Talmud is a rich mine, by far not yet exhausted."

After having received the published volume, he expresses himself thus: "It seems to contain a great deal that is not only new and interesting, but much that is valuable and will be permanently useful."

Dean FARRAR, Canterbury, England: "I read your book with the greatest interest. The Jewish writings, as I have long found, are invaluable, as furnishing many illustrations of the Gospel narrative, etc."

Rector A. SCHWARZ, of the Vienna Theological Seminary: "By the kind transmission of your latest work you have not only given me great pleasure, but shown again how fruitful your pen is. That is indeed a gigantic labor, to which I congratulate you most heartily."

Friendly letters came from Rector ERNST CURTIUS, Berlin University; HERBERT SPENCER, London; Librarian A. NEUBAUER, Oxford; ED. COHEN, Artist, Frankfort a./M.; Dean G. E. DAY, Yale University; Rev. Dr. M. JASTROW, Philadelphia; Dr. B. FELSENTHAL, Chicago, and many more American Ministers, Scholars and University Professors.

"Thoughts on Religious Rites."

To this President W. H. GREEN of Princeton Seminary writes: "This book seems to embody in an interesting way the results of extensive reading, study and careful reflection."

Professor FRANZ DELITZSCH, of Leipsic University: "It is likely to prove a real enrichment to science . . . It is rich in contents, offering much material for reflection."

Professor W. WUNDT, of same University: "Your historical researches are calculated to vividly interest me. I shall utilize your remarks in my studies on Spinoza."

The Right Hon. W. E. GLADSTONE, London: "It appears to be a treatise of great interest. Being about examining into the character of the Mosaic System, *it is very welcome to me.*"

Professor MAX MUELLER: "It is full of interesting information and I hope you will continue."

Grand Rabbi ZADOK KAHN, Paris: "I have read your charming book with pleasure and profit."

COMMENTS ON MAURICE FLUEGEL'S LITERARY WORK.

"The Messiah-Ideal."—Vol. I. Jesus of Nazareth.

The first impulse to that work came from Professor FRANZ DELITZSCH of the Leipsic University, who gave the author a friendly challenge to write on that subject. See Vol. I, p. 296.

Dean GEORGE E. DAY of Yale University wrote next:

"Seeing your style of writing, I have strongly felt what a contribution it would be if you would undertake to show the teachings of the most distinguished of the Jewish nation . . . . . Such a presentation, I am sure, would be welcomed by all thinking men."

Professor MAX MUELLER, England, to whom an outline was sent, wrote: "Your new book bids fair to bring out much interesting matter . . . The Talmud is a rich mine, by far not yet exhausted."

After having received the published volume, he expresses himself thus: "It seems to contain a great deal that is not only new and interesting, but much that is valuable and will be permanently useful."

Dean FARRAR, Canterbury, England: "I read your book with the greatest interest. The Jewish writings, as I have long found, are invaluable, as furnishing many illustrations of the Gospel narrative, etc."

Rector A. SCHWARZ, of the Vienna Theological Seminary: "By the kind transmission of your latest work you have not only given me great pleasure, but shown again how fruitful your pen is. That is indeed a gigantic labor, to which I congratulate you most heartily."

Friendly letters came from Rector ERNST CURTIUS, Berlin University; HERBERT SPENCER, London; Librarian A. NEUBAUER, Oxford; ED. COHEN, Artist, Frankfurt a./M.; Dean G. E. DAY, Yale University; Rev. Dr. M. JASTROW, Philadelphia; Dr. B. FELSENTHAL, Chicago, and many more American Ministers, Scholars and University Professors.

"Thoughts on Religious Rites."

To this President W. H. GREEN of Princeton Seminary writes: "This book seems to embody in an interesting way the results of extensive reading, study and careful reflection."

Professor FRANZ DELITZSCH, of Leipsic University: "It is likely to prove a real enrichment to science . . . It is rich in contents, offering much material for reflection."

Professor W. WUNDT, of same University: "Your historical researches are calculated to vividly interest me. I shall utilize your remarks in my studies on Spinoza."

The Right Hon. W. E. GLADSTONE, London: "It appears to be a treatise of great interest. Being about examining into the character of the Mosaic System, *it is very welcome to me.*"

Professor MAX MUELLER: "It is full of interesting information and I hope you will continue."

Grand Rabbi ZADOK KAHN, Paris: "I have read your charming book with pleasure and profit."

Comments on "Messiah-Ideal," Vol.II.

Paul and the New Testament.—Mohammed and the Koran. Author Maurice Fluegel.

Hon. ANDREW D. WHITE, of the Cornell University, writes: "I will gladly read your works. They show to be of decided value."

BARONESS DE HIRSCH-Gereuth of Paris: "I tender you my thanks for your having dedicated your interesting work to the memory of my late husband."

THE CHIEF OF THE CABINET OF THE KHEDIVE OF EGYPT: "His Highness, the Khedive, has perused with great interest your work, and has ordered it to be placed in his private library."

DR. ADOLPH SCHWARZ, Rector of the Rabbinical Seminary at Vienna, informs that *Messiah-Ideal, Vols. I and II*, have been heartily and approvingly reviewed in the press there

Professor AD. NEUBAUER, of Oxford University, discusses Vols. I and II critically, and at length, in the *London Quarterly Review*, of October, closing: "The second volume is even more original. . . . The Analysis of the Gospels may be considered as the best part. The chapters on the *Messiah Ideal* are full of information. . . . Those on Mohammed and Koran are well arranged. . . .

THE NEW YORK TRIBUNE, of Nov. 24: "Maurice Fluegel needs no introduction. . . . Few men in this country are superior authorities in his line. His *Messiah-Ideal* is written with rare insight. . . . His Mohammed and Koran, too, will be most useful to students. His work is sure to gain the appreciation of the thoughtful. . . .

THE NEW YORK SUN, of Aug. 30 and Jan. 24, devoted three columns to the author's Biblical Legislation and as much space to his "Jesus of Nazareth," closing: "We are not surprised that such men as W. E. Gladstone, Franz Delitzsch, Max Mueller, etc., have united in finding his works most valuable." . . .

THE NEW YORK PRESS, of Nov. 15: "*Messiah-Ideal* combines eloquence with grace of style, scientific spirit and depths of learning." . . .

CHICAGO TRIBUNE, of March 13: "'The book evidences an independent mind, wide sympathies, full of ardor in the pursuit of truth, rising above all bigotry and prejudice." . . .

CHICAGO DAILY NEWS, of Jan. 23: "Among students of the best class the *Messiah-Ideal* will meet with approval. Concentration of purpose and immense research are evidenced."

The Baltimore Sun, American, News, and many more Dailies and Weeklies of other cities reviewed in the same approving and kindly spirit.

Rev. DR. K. KOHLER, New York: "No one can read your 'Biblical Legislation without interest and profit.' . . . Your views, characterization and tracing its influence upon modern legislations are correct. I sincerely trust that your series of works, so brimful of thought and rich in suggestion, will find their way to Jewish and Christian homes, enlightening the people and showing what religion is and works for."

This series on the world's religions, doctrines and legislations, will be continued and gradually published; viz:

I. Zend-Avesta, or the Persian Religious Legislation.

II. Philosophy, Religion and Qabbala, from Zoroaster to Spinoza.

III. Israel, the Biblical people, his past and future.

IV. Spirit of the Biblical Legislation, continued; each in their historical connection, influencing our own times. 300 pages about each volume, cloth bound, large octavo.

SUBSCRIPTIONS ARE SOLICITED.

BALTIMORE, April, 1897.

Spirit of the Biblical Legislation.

COMMENTS ON THE AUTHOR'S PUBLICATIONS.

The Baltimore *Sun* in last June, brought out the prospectus of this work. So did other papers in the East and West. Among the first encouraging letters with subscriptions were those from his Eminence, Cardinal Gibbons, Honorables Attorney-General J. P. Poe, Charles J. Bonaparte, L. N. Hopkins, Baltimore; Attorney-General S. N. Rosedale, Jacob H. Shiff, New York; leading ministers and laymen, booksellers, congregations followed.

Advanced sheets have been submitted to leading scholars, and their opinions were unanimous that: "The book is highly interesting and important, fully deserving public attention." Such are the replies, among many others, by the Rev. Drs. EDWARD A. LAWRENCE, Eutaw Congregational Church; J. T. WIGHTMAN, McCulloh Methodist Episcopal Church; H. M. WHARTON, Brantly Baptist Church; C. A. FULTON, North Avenue Immanuel Baptist Church; R. H. PULLMAN, Guilford Avenue Universalist Church; Dr. CLAMPETT, Druid Hill Avenue Episcopal Church, and Dr. A. FRIEDENWALD, Physician, North Eutaw street.

The Cincinnati *American Is.* published in 1888, two lectures by the author on that theme, delivered at the H. Union College, with *Resolutions of thanks* voted him. The Book will prove interesting and useful to the general reader, as well as to professionals.

The Author's "*Thoughts on Religious Rites and Views*" received the cordial acknowledgment of many scientists, writers, divines and leading Universities in America and Europe. So writes:

President W. H. GREEN, of Princeton. "The book seems to embody, in an interesting way, the results of extensive reading, study and careful reflection."

President ANDREW D. WHITE, of Cornell: "It interests me very much in my hurried examination of it."

President DAY, of Yale, had a continued correspondence on it, desiring the author to write on kindred themes.

FRIEDRICH VON BODENSTEDT, German poet: "I have read your thoughtful tract with lively interest, and marked many passages to talk over with you. I find in it so much instruction and suggestion."

The author and proprietor's address is :

REV. MAURICE FLUEGEL,
2041 DIVISION STREET,
Baltimore, Md.

www.ingramcontent.com/pod-product-compliance
Lightning Source LLC
Chambersburg PA
CBHW030801020726
47499CB00006B/1722